The
Last Princess

Marissa Craig

Copyright 2015 Marissa Craig

THE LAST PRINCESS

Chapter 1: Setsuna

My whole life has been more about what I will be and not who I am today. My whole life I've been conditioned to be a man's wife. I don't know him but I can't fail him. At least that's what father says. Sometimes I feel like he only loves me because of the title he's given me....princess of his nation, the small kingdom of Morinaga.

I'm only twelve but I've heard of girls getting married at this age. My future husband and I will finally get to meet next week. I'm curious to see him but I can't drop the act that I want nothing to do with him.

Secretly I've sent him letters since I was five and could write. He's never written back but I kept writing. I can see why he wouldn't want to be bothered with me. He's about twenty now. I just wonder what kind of man he is. I hope he's nice to me.

"Setsuna-sama! Again!"

I'm supposed to be practicing my walk. Hard to concentrate. I have so many teachers handling me. It's all increased since the Niwa royal family will be arriving soon.

"Setsuna-sama, again."

I turn around and start walking towards her. The dress is supposed to flow a special kind way; I have no control over that. I stop in front of her and she holds her forehead.

"It's not good enough."

It's all so demanding. I hope my future husband will accept me for who I am and not mold me into what he wants. That's all I ever wanted. I'm so miserable here. My last letter to him wasn't too long ago. I always tell him how miserable I am. I wonder if that's what prompted this sudden meeting.

"I need a break," she says.

What exactly has she been doing to get so tired? She stomps off and slams the door behind her. I settle near the window and look out. Because I am so important to bridge our nation with the Niwa's nation, I've been secluded inside the palace walls. If I die, so does the hope of our kingdom.

THE LAST PRINCESS

I don't care but there are people counting on us. I've never met the citizens of our nation but I hear them on t.v. and they love it here. Our nation can't fail them. But deep down, I wish I could be one of them instead.

The door slams open and the court ladies rush in.

"I can't decide on the dress," one says.

"Do the white one to show her purity."

"No, it might be mistaken for a wedding dress."

It's as if I'm not even conscious. They string me up touching me how they like. I do want to look pretty. It's gonna be hard to get Kyoya-sama's attention when he's so much older. I just want to meet him; I don't want a production out of him.

"She'll wear the royal robes," mother steps in. "Same as always."

The court ladies part and she approaches me.

"The same ones I wore when I was introduced to my husband."

"Mother, I-"

"You're not improving. They'll be here in a week and you're not improving. Do you think that's acceptable? It's not just Kyoya-sama you have to impress. He has two brothers and parents. Did you research them?"

"His older brother is Kantarou-sama, a commander in charge of palace security and his younger brother is Kira-sama."

"And Kira-sama is the same age as you and already declared a genius. If you can't be up to his standards how can you hope to impress your husband."

The yelling never ends. I'm never good enough. She stares at me with cold eyes. I think she was nicer before we learned about the engagement. I turn my head away and she yanks it back.

"Ruin this and you'll have no place in this family."

She lets go and walks away. The court ladies follow. I get up and wander around the halls. I can't take this. I'm so afraid of letting someone down. I'm the only offspring and mother is barren and father is sterile from an accident.

After I marry Kyoya-sama I'll be pressured to have kids to carry on our legacy. My mother won't even tell me how to do it. The whole thing is vague.

THE LAST PRINCESS

"Setsuna-chan," I hear.

"Yumi-chan, are you done with school?"

She's my cousin. She kind of understands my position but she's allowed to go outside the palace walls. She only has to wear her royal robes for special events. Mine never leave my body.

"I can only stay a minute. I'm going out with my friends."

"Oh?"

"There's this new movie out and I gotta find a cute outfit."

I follow her down the hall. She's the most glamorous girl I know. She has long hair like me put she's allowed to wear it down and wear nontraditional makeup.

"Can I see what a cute outfit looks like?"

"Of course. I guess I should be passing some advice to you."

"I have a class for that."

"That whole courtship from our ancestors. No. If you wanna keep your man, you have to do things my way."

"My man? You mean Kyoya-sama?"

She starts to chuckle.

"What?"

"Let's get inside first."

I go to her room and she walks straight to her closet.

"I know you're not allowed to see him or have contact with him but you should know he's a very popular guy."

"Tell me about him."

"I can't. Truthfully I've never met him. But let's just say you're gonna have a lot of jealous girls at your feet."

Yumi-chan is closer to his age. She's seventeen. She might be able to understand things more.

THE LAST PRINCESS

"I hear he's a very caring man," I say to her. "Quiet and reserved."

I can't believe I'm talking about him as if I know him. I've never had any contact with him but I figure since he never rejected my letters he must be caring.

"What are you even gonna do with him?"

Her hair whips around. I stand awkwardly in the middle of her room. It's refreshing to be around her. I feel like she's the only one that doesn't shelter me. She's very outspoken.

"I don't know but...what do you think he will expect."

"I think...it will be awkward for you. He's an adult and should be having sex with you but he won't cause that would just be gross."

"Could you explain that to me?"

She comes from the closet defeated. She takes my hand and leads me to the bed.

"Did no one clue you in?" she asks me.

"I've been practicing."

"Practicing what?"

"How to walk and improve my table manners. And I've been studying history and language. I know their language very well."

"It's a dead language so what's it matter. I mean...aside from being a princess do you realize your other duties to him."

"Our marriage is to bridge our nations. That's why I can't mess up."

"Yes, you'll be a great symbol but also...you'll be his fiancée, his girlfriend."

"His girlfriend?"

"And so you take care of his needs."

"I've been studying cooking too-"

"As his girlfriend you have to make him happy. Make him not want any other woman."

She looks at me and I'm afraid to let her know I'm confused.

"I can't blow your mind just yet. With your age difference I know he's not thinking about it."

"Yumi-chan....there are some things I can't practice and that makes me scared."

"But that's the best part. You're going to have your first experience falling in love."

I'm going to fall in love with him? She skips back to her closet and rummages through her clothes. For us to fall in love it means we must really like each other...and accept each other.

"I want him to like the real me," I say to myself.

This training is useless. I want to meet him in clothes I want to wear and talk about things that interest me. They'll be here in a week. I still have time to send him another letter.

"Can you take a letter out for me?" I ask her.

"How long do I have to be your personal messenger?"

"Please, I just wanna say my thoughts to him just in case I can't communicate around my parents."

"Fine, but make it quick."

Chapter 2: Kyoya

"I can't wait to meet you. Since you announced your visit, I've been drilled harder and it makes me want to run away. But my cousin reminded me that aside from being a symbol for our nations, I'll also be your girlfriend. That made me nervous. I mean, I'm not old enough to get married so I'll be your girlfriend for many years. And soon enough we'll fall in love. I don't know how to prepare myself to be accepted by you. I would just hope you would accept me how I am. I will be restrained at our meeting because of my parents but I truly hope we can get along."

She writes like an adult. I know she's smart; she does nothing but study. But all that studying can't teach her social skills. I never really thought of that either. She will be my girlfriend.

THE LAST PRINCESS

This will be her last letter. I'm kind of curious as to what she looks like and sounds like. No one knows what she looks like since she's never allowed to be photographed or leave the palace. She's such a delicate princess. It's a shame to entrust her to me.

"What a pain," Kan-nii comes in.

"What's wrong?"

I hide the letter in my drawer.

"I was pulled off duty to see your wife."

This little girl, my wife. I lean back in my chair. No one knows about the letters. It's labeled as fan mail. It always comes in a peach envelope.

"Aren't you curious? Or are you jealous cause as first born, you're still single."

"Hmph, you wish you had my status. Good luck getting a woman once your engagement goes public."

"And why can't I?"

"You cheat on that little girl and everything is over."

He can't be serious. I won't be able to fool around with her till she's like sixteen or so. Am I to remain celibate until then? I never even thought of that.

Perhaps it's a sacrifice. When I marry Setsuna-san, I'll own everything she owns; she's the only heiress to the nation. Everything will be mine. And with it, I can easily bypass my brother and take the throne. Finally I can go down my own path.

But the sacrifice is too great. I need sex.

"Have you thought of it?" he asks me.

"Thought of what?"

"Her."

"Not in that way. She's just a sheltered child. If we have to visit more often she'll just be more like a sister."

"We'll find out tomorrow."

THE LAST PRINCESS

Yeah, tomorrow. When he leaves I pull out the letter again. She sounds better. Her other letters were sad. She hates not being able to leave. She hates how her parents won't hug her. It's like she has no one that loves her. I smile thinking about it. I never respond but she keeps writing as if we're having a conversation. This is the first time she spoke about falling in love. I wouldn't count on it. But little girls all have thoughts like this. She doesn't know that this marriage is only for show. But to spare her feelings, I hope we can get along too.

With one night left I wander to the court ladies dormitory. I peek my head in while they busy themselves. She catches my eye and I start walking back to my room. I can hear her footsteps behind me.

"This might be our last night," I say out loud.

"You're gonna replace me with a twelve year old."

I stop at my room and she waltzes in. She's gotten spoiled. Regardless of the engagement becoming public, I don't like to look at the same woman for so long.

"Just take off your clothes."

"I bet she-"

"Shut up."

I don't want to hear anyone talk bad about the princess. She's not moving fast enough.

By morning we're on a jet awaiting landing. No one looks happy to be here.

"Morinaga is such a backwards nation," Kira says.

"What they lack in technology they make up for in resources," Kan-nii corrects him. "So much untapped reserves."

"I still think they're all hicks," Kira continues. "Especially the princess."

"I'm sure she's as smart as you," I tell him.

"Don't make me laugh. I bet she's a moron."

No one could touch his level of genius; at least that what he keeps telling himself. I have a plan. No matter what stupid things my brothers say, I feel as though Setsuna-san is already on my side. She put a dependence on me. That's why the letters increased over time.

THE LAST PRINCESS

"Enough, all of you," father cuts in.

Mother nuzzles at his chest. I wish they would tone it down a bit. I turn away from them.

"Darling, leave them be. They know to behave when it's time."

He goes back to nuzzling her and we all look disgusted. How can parents still act like that; they're old. There's nowhere to go. We took the small jet cause the Morinaga palace has such a small runway.

I'm more nervous than I thought I would be. She may be nothing but a kid now but in a few years she'll be a woman and I'll have to marry her. So many sacrifices.

I've always been kind of detached when it comes to women but it can't be like that with Setsuna-san. I can't treat her poorly either or she'll break it off with me.

And I can't let her know I don't have the best intentions.

"We're arriving," father says. "You better win her favor."

Chapter 3: Setsuna

Today is the day. Everyone is running around preparing. I'm trembling. Yumi-chan sits next to me having her make up done.

"I-I'm really scared."

"He'll accept you, don't worry."

"I-I'm kind of excited too."

I want to see him and hear his voice. I bet he's nice; he has to be.

"Hold still, girl," they say to me.

In an instant it's silent. I'm stuck in a room by myself. It's a sitting room that faces the pond in the courtyard. I guess they'll come get me when it's time. Mother never gave me any motherly advice; she only gave me orders. Father hasn't spoken to me this whole time. He only glares and frowns lately. I look over at the door. It may be a while.

THE LAST PRINCESS

I get up and walk to the edge of the room. The pond has the cutest fish in it. It's just what I need to see right now. I'm distracted looking at it. I turn around to check on the door again and see a man standing there.

I'm afraid to acknowledge it but I know this is him. His wears a black suit with slicked back hair like I imagined. He's so tall. I feel uneasy.

"Kyoya-sama?" I say aloud.

He nods.

"Setsuna-san?"

"Yes."

So this is him. I instinctively take a step forward then stumble over my robe. I stop myself but he lunges forward grabbing my shoulders. My heart is beating so fast; I'm nervous.

I look up at him. He really is an adult. I move away from him and we stand inches from each other.

"You seemed distracted. What were you looking at?"

"Our pond. I found it calming."

"Perhaps I should have a look."

He walks to the edge of the room and steps onto the walkway. He sits down right above the pond.

"Sit, Setsuna-san."

I walk cautiously to him. Tripping earlier was embarrassing. Sitting next to him is exciting. I keep peeking up at him but his face is straight.

"D-did you ever get my letters?" I ask him.

"Yes."

I can't help but smile in relief. So it hasn't been for nothing.

"You're sneaky to figure out a way to contact me."

"I know. Please don't tell my parents. They would be very-"

"It's fine. It's okay to keep secrets between us."

THE LAST PRINCESS

I can't stop smiling. This is exactly what I wanted.

"Do you have any more secrets?" he asks me.

"Uh...I uh-"

"In time. You don't have to rush things."

"Do you...I mean...I'm sure you have a lot going on. Is this engagement what you want? My parents won't like it but I can always say no."

"That's sweet of you but you've known about me since you were five and I've known about you since I was thirteen. I plan on marrying you."

To hear it come from his mouth is too much.

"I should ask you....after meeting me, do you really want to fall in love with me?"

"Definitely!"

I spoke without thinking. But I do. He's a great man. I put my hand over my mouth. I'm not supposed to be so outspoken.

"I look forward to it," he says to me.

I can't stop smiling. His face is so calm; it's cause he's mature.

"Setsuna-san."

"Yes."

"We probably won't get much time alone so I want to say as much as I can."

He takes a card from his pocket and hands it to me without looking.

"It's my personal number. Don't show it to anyone else."

"Yes, of course."

This is going so well. I think we like each other.

"You can call me if you want to talk but be sure not to get caught."

I'm so happy right now. This is perfect. I look over at him but he still won't look at me. He's not smiling either. Maybe I'm the only one that's happy. Being here is his duty too. Perhaps he's just being nice so his parents won't yell at him.

THE LAST PRINCESS

"You look miserable. I'm sorry."

I get up and walk back to the door. It's so hard to move in this robe. Before I can slide the door he grabs my hand. I try to hold back tears. No man like him would willingly want to be my friend. He's big and strong and probably has prettier women waiting for him that he had to give up on. I'll never be as mature as him; I'll be nothing but a burden.

"Why are you crying?" he asks me.

"I can't believe you're genuine."

"Why?"

"You won't even look at me."

He lets go of me and still keeping his head away. He thinks I'm ugly. Even all this make up couldn't hide it.

"It's hard to look at you. I am sorry. You should tidy yourself before they come in."

He hands a handkerchief to me with his back turned. I feel like an idiot for being so happy. I try to muffle myself and wipe my tears away. Mother is gonna be so upset at me if she sees my ruined makeup.

I open the door and run out. I can't wait for them to come and get me. I run back to my room and stare at my mirror.

"Setsuna-chan."

Yumi-chan stands above me. She's the only person I can hug.

"He hates me," I say into her stomach.

"What?"

"He can't even stomach looking at me."

She kneels down to me.

"Then deny him. Say you don't want to marry him. This deal benefits the Niwa family more than us."

He was everything I expected but I wasn't what he wanted. She spends time fixing my makeup. Fine, I'll deny him. Seems like something he would want.

THE LAST PRINCESS

"You're growing up all in one day," she says to me. "It would have been nice if it worked out. He's very handsome. Oh and when you see his older brother, Kantarou-sama-"

"I was set on Kyoya-sama."

"You still have to go through with the meeting. I bet they're all looking for you. I'll try to deflect the attention."

"I have to give him my answer."

We head to the main meeting room. She said they were all gathered there waiting for Kyoya-sama and I to arrive. The private meeting was supposed to give us a positive impression of each other.

She opens the door for me and the whole room turns to us. He's here too. I avoid him but he avoids me first just like before.

"Setsuna," mother stands up.

"She just felt a little nervous so I calmed her down," Yumi-chan says to me.

I'm still nervous. That man in the military uniform must be Kantarou-sama. This is my first time meeting another royal family. I remember from training that I'm not supposed to speak. Yumi-chan and I take our seats. Unfortunately my seat is at the head of the table next to Kyoya-sama. His family sits on one side and my family sits on the other.

His parents could be mistaken for one person; they're so close. My parents would never be so affectionate. Father is still frowning. A server places tea in front of me. I keep my head down during the exchange.

"She's just a child. Nervousness is expected," his mother says. "She's such a cute girl. Isn't she, darling."

"She is a work in progress but thank you for the compliment, Tomoko-sama," mother says.

"You're niece is very cute as well. Have you married her off yet?"

"She's not exactly a royal. Her mother is disgraced."

"What a great introduction," Yumi-chan whispers to me.

"But she's allowed to stay here because Setsuna likes her."

THE LAST PRINCESS

I've been squeezing my hands this whole time. I look down and see his number crumpled. The numbers are fading because of my sweat. Would he really have talked to me. His words were sweet but I can't believe them.

"Setsuna-sama, how do you feel about Kyoya?" his mother asks me.

I'm not supposed to talk. But now is as good a time as any to reject him. I look up at him one more time and he turns his head away.

"I...I don't accept him. I refuse to marry him. I'm sorry to waste all of your time."

They all look so shocked. Father stands up and walks over to me. He wouldn't hit me in front of them.

"Come with me a moment."

I naturally obey. I follow him out. It's my decision; I refuse to marry him. I'm doing it for Kyoya-sama's sake.

"Father, I-"

"What the hell has gotten into you!"

I think that's the first time he's talked to me in weeks. We're not far enough away; they can still hear.

"I'm doing this for him. He doesn't want-"

"You don't have a choice and neither does he. How dare you embarrass me in front of them! They rule a nation five times the size of ours. You need him if our nation is to survive."

"I'll run our nation. I'm the princess-"

"You'll run it into the ground. You're an idiot. You would never get a man like that if not for my negotiations. Get on your knees and apologize."

"Father-"

"I'm sorry to interrupt, sir."

Father turns around sharply then lowers his anger. I peek pass him and see Kyoya-sama standing in our hallway.

"Kyoya-sama, there was no need for you to come here. Setsuna was about to come back in and apologize."

"There is no need for that. I understand why she would reject me."

"No, you don't have to be so polite."

"I wanted to ask for your permission to have some more alone time with Setsuna-san."

More alone time with me. That sounds like an awful idea. Father approaches him and they exchange words. Then father walks back.

I don't want any more time with him.

Chapter 4: Kyoya

She's gonna be a challenge. Like I thought, she's smart. She keeps looking over at me and it makes me look away. She wasn't what I expected. Maybe it's the clothes and the makeup. She looks just like a woman and even talks like one.

I thought twelve year old girls were stupid and annoying. Her mannerisms are just like a woman's too. It's only because that's how she was trained.

"Can you do me a favor and rinse all that off," I say to her.

"I'll look even worse if I do that. I already know you think I'm ugly."

"It's not that I think you're ugly. I can't look at you cause you're too beautiful. It's overwhelming."

"Too beautiful?"

"Just wash it off please."

I'm losing the upper hand so long as she has that face on. She walks away with tiny steps. Father's look said it all. I can't allow her to reject me. I need to win her over today.

I'm seeing her title, maybe that's it. I'm certain a sheltered princess just wants to be treated like a normal girl. If I can be the one to break down these walls for her, she'll depend on me.

THE LAST PRINCESS

I wait against the wall. This palace will be mine one day. Setsuna-san will be older and with child. I think I'll get sick thinking about it. That little girl is gonna be my wife. I'll have to…I can't think about it. I'm partly thinking about it and I feel like such a pervert.

That's why I couldn't look at her in that makeup. I'm much cooler with women than this. After some time she walks back to me. She looks completely different. She's youthful, childish, and cute.

When I stare at her she feels insecure and puts her hands over her mouth.

"How about you show me around," I say to her.

"Do you want to see my room?"

Her attitude is different too. She starts walking and I follow. I was intimidated when she looked like an adult but now I feel at ease when she looks like a child. This is what I expected.

"Setsuna-san, have you ever had a boyfriend?" I ask her.

"Of course not. I was trained to be Kyoya-sama's wife."

"Trained? Did they tell you what I like?"

"No."

"That's something you'll have to find out."

"I would like to. If you let me."

"Does that mean you won't reject me?"

"I rejected you for your sake. Don't you feel as though you'd be wasting your time waiting for me to catch up to you?"

She stops in the hall and turns around waiting for my answer. There's a tease somewhere inside her. She's getting so hard to figure out. Is she oblivious or is she playing a game with me. I feel like she's the one in control.

"This one is my room."

I couldn't even answer her. She opens up and I see it's plain. It looks like a guest room.

"It doesn't seem to reflect you."

THE LAST PRINCESS

"I have to hide the things I'm interested in."

She gets to her knees and reaches under the bed. I step in and close the door behind me. She seems to be warming up to me.

I walk to her bookshelf. These are all history books. Nothing here reflects a little girl.

"Ah! Don't touch that."

She runs back to me. She's so concerned about this book.

"You're learning Hangese?" I guess.

I look over at her and she's blushing. Her mouth twitches unable to say "yes." These are pretty advanced books.

"So how good are you?" I say to her.

Her eye brows shoot up like she's surprised she understands.

"Speak to me."

"I've never spoken it out loud."

She sounds cute.

"You know I speak your language, why did you bother learning Hangese?"

"I…I thought it would be nice to speak behind my parent's back."

I start to laugh. She grew up knowing she would eventually meet me. To her, she lived for this moment.

"Have you thought about me a lot?" I ask her.

"All the time. I mean, at times I hated you. I hated that my life had to revolve around you. I wanted to leave and do things like Yumi-chan. I could only live through her stories and watch her be so happy being free."

It wasn't like that for me at all.

"But she told me that the day I meet you would be the day I become free. She said, even if I hate my family, Kyoya-sama would be the one to take me away. So she encouraged me to write to you. She delivered all my letters to you."

I look over at her and she's hugging her book to her chest.

THE LAST PRINCESS

"Over time, I made you my hero even though I knew nothing about you. So when I met you, I was my happiest but when you refused to see me, I felt as though I made you into something you never wanted to be. I was so concerned with you making me free but you're the one that probably feels trapped."

I had my own intentions but I don't mind being her hero if she needs me. I reach out and bring her closer to me. I hold her at my chest and she drops the book in surprise. I hate when she talks so grown up. I want to give her lighter feelings.

"If you accept me, I promise to be your hero," I say to her.

"But what about you?"

"You're the one I want."

I can't let go of her. I know she'll have hardship later on and I don't know if she can handle it. I feel guilty already.

I walk her back to the meeting area. Our parents seem to be getting along.

"Setsuna, what did you do to your face?"

"I apologize. I asked her wash it off. I found it distracting."

We both take our seats. Kan-nii eyes me suspiciously. Normally we can only get women to comply by romancing them. That wasn't the case.

"Don't you have something you want to say to the Niwa family," her mother urges her.

"Yes."

She gets up and walks over to my parents. All eyes are on her. My father is hard to impress. I doubt he's swayed by her. Due to her family hanging on to tradition we're already sitting on the floor. She sits down next him.

"I love Kyoya-sama. Please accept me into your family."

She bows down to him with her head on the ground. That might be a bit much.

"I must admit, it's nice to see what you really look like. She really is cute," mother says.

My brothers have yet to say anything. Mother touches her head and Setsuna-san rises.

THE LAST PRINCESS

"Since Setsuna-sama seems taken with our Kyoya, we should make an announcement to the world," mother says.

"Yes, I would like that," Setsuna-san says.

Mother seems taken with her. I look at father and see him smirk. That's strange.

"I would be honored to be a part of your family," she says.

They all look surprised. Father clears his throat but I see he can't stop smiling. Setsuna-san looks over at me with a smile. I feel bad for her. She doesn't realize that joining our family means she'll never get to see hers again. She won't be able to see Yumiko-san either. I don't know if she can handle that.

After lunch we're showed to our rooms. We'll be leaving tomorrow morning. In a room by myself I sigh but the pounding on the door makes me sigh harder.

"So, you got her."

Kan-nii stands at my door. Kira walks in pacing frantically.

"I guess I should ask what you think."

"I hate her. Pick someone else," he says.

"Has she mastered Hangese?" Kan-nii asks. "That's impressive."

"She's mastered a few languages. I just found out today that one was Hangese."

Kira scoffs. He doesn't want her to be smarter than him.

"I would have never guessed," Kan-nii says.

"I need you to do me a favor. Invite Yumiko-san for a visit."

"A cultural exchange? Why? Are you trying to hook me up with her?"

I just want to get her away from here.

"I think Setsuna-san would be happy about it. Arrange it so she can come with us in the morning."

"Since when do I take orders from you."

THE LAST PRINCESS

"Trust me," I tell him.

Kan-nii leaves out. Kira settles down near me.

"Is she really that smart? She didn't seem smart."

"I don't think she likes being smart. She just wants to be normal. Isn't your brother's girlfriend pretty?"

He pouts and turns away.

"I don't like her."

Chapter 5: Kantarou

This place is a disaster. It's like a civilian house. Where's the security? No cameras, no one patrolling the halls. A man could just stroll up the princess' room without anyone knowing.

"So now you love him. Are you serious?"

"I think so. I mean, he hugged me and I liked it."

"I'm happy for you but I just hope he's not playing games with you."

"Kyoya-sama isn't like that."

I lean closer to the door. It's cracked but I can see them getting undressed. They have so many layers. I should interrupt before I see something I'll regret.

"Princess," I say knocking.

"Who's that?"

The door opens and the little princess stands looking up at me.

"Uh, Kantarou-sama."

"Sorry to interrupt. I was hoping to have a word with Yumiko-san."

"Yumi-chan?"

20

THE LAST PRINCESS

I suppose it is surprising. No disgraced royal would expect to have words with me. This is her only chance. She puts her robe back on and pulls her hair back. I hear these traditional women aren't allowed to be seen with their hair down.

"Step out a minute," she tells the little princess.

I don't know what Kyoya has planned but we need this marriage to work. She's working hard to make herself presentable. Even a disgraced royal knows how to act in front of the first prince.

"You are close with the princess, right?"

"Yes, sir."

"I am a Han commander in charge of palace security. If you wish to be close to the princess you need to know how to protect her. I suggest you take a lesson from me."

"Uh, really?"

"You'll be coming back with us tomorrow morning. You have no parents so I don't really know who you'd ask for permission."

"I'm not fit to be a bodyguard to her."

"So you Morinaga women are used to talking back. All the more reason for you to have a lesson in our culture."

"What are you planning?" she asks me.

"I'm trying to give your life a purpose. When you're found to be useless you will be purged from the palace. I'm trying to give you some usefulness."

"I would never step foot in your country that breeds men like you."

"Suit yourself."

Kyoya wanted her out of the palace for a reason. If she refuses, we'll see what fate awaits her.

"I know you're planning something. You better not harm Setsuna-chan."

"Are you threatening me? You really must not know who I am."

I better leave before I have to show her.

Chapter 6: Kira

    I know these people are idiots. Look at their library, it's outdated. Their technology too.

    "Kira-kun," I hear.

    I turn to the entrance. It's the princess.

    "No one really comes in here except me. I didn't know you like books."

    She walks up to me with that stupid smile on her face. I can't believe she's marrying Kyo-nii.

    "What grade have you finished?" I ask her.

    "Um…not sure."

    Figures.

    "I'm working on my degree in history."

    "What?"

    "It's father's choice."

    Is she really that smart? She can't be. She eyes the books while I eye her.

    "I'm hoping I can give up on all that stuff when Kyoya-sama takes me. I hate studying. I mean, we have our entire lives to gain knowledge. Shouldn't we be gaining experiences now."

    "Knowledge puts you ahead of everyone else," I tell her.

    "Not me. My role is predetermined and so is yours."

    "I'm not an heir; I have a choice."

    "That's so nice. But won't you regret a few things once you achieve your success. I hear you're already a genius, now should be the time to have fun."

    "That's not what I want."

"Don't you only study cause your father tells you to."

If I don't study I can't compete. My brothers are older and successful. I'll get left behind. I have to keep up in some way. I don't like this girl. I don't like her analyzing me.

"I was hoping we could have fun experiences together. We're the same age you know."

"I'm aware."

"Since I'm your brother's girlfriend it'll be like you're my brother too, Kira-kun."

"I can't stand you."

I leave out and I feel her behind me.

"What! I said I can't stand you."

"I was hoping you would escort me to Kyoya-sama so I could say goodnight."

"Leave me out of it."

I walk faster and outpace her. Why am I so agitated? I know she's right. She should be able to understand me. I just hate hearing it from her.

Chapter 7: Setsuna

I know it's getting late but I have a right to say goodnight to him. So much has happened today and I think we ended up in a good place. I just wanted to make sure. This should be his room.

I knock and wait. The door opens swiftly and I take a step back. He surprised me and...he's shirtless.

"I'm sorry, I didn't mean-"

"No, I'm sorry. I thought you were my brother."

THE LAST PRINCESS

He goes back inside and puts on a robe. That's one of our family's robes; use to be grandfather's robe. It looks good on him. Should I tell him that?

"Come in," he tells me.

I step in cautiously. He reaches behind me and closes the door.

"I didn't mean to interrupt. I just wanted to say "goodnight" to you."

"I was hoping to see you to do the same."

"Uh…so you're leaving tomorrow?"

"Yes."

"Will you visit me again?"

He sits down on his bed and signals me over. I walk over to him. The last time we were alone in a room he hugged me. I want another one.

"Of course I will. I'll probably have a lot of press once the announcement is made but I'll see you, don't worry."

He touches my head. His hand lingers and touches my ribbon.

"No, don't."

"What's wrong?"

"I thought you might undo it. It's against the rules."

"What rules?"

"A man cannot see a royal lady outside of her robe or with her hair down."

"So the moment you wake up you put your hair up and put on your royal robes."

"Yes."

He keeps his hand there. It's a tradition I've had my whole life. Only married men may see a woman with her hair down.

"Remember when I said there's allowed to be secrets between us."

"Yeah."

THE LAST PRINCESS

He pulls my ribbon and my hair falls down. He's not supposed to see. I reach for my ribbon and he pushes my hands away. He's able to grab both my wrists in one hand.

He pushes me back to the bed and I close my eyes. If I can't see him then it's like it never happened. I peek and see him sitting with a strand in his hand.

"Your hair is so long."

He looks so much bigger than me. He looks back at me and I close my eyes again. I feel his hand touch my face.

"I always wondered if you were doing okay," he says to me. "You were so sad in your letters. Do you still feel trapped here?"

"Today has been the best day of my life. I've never smiled this much."

I'm starting to cry.

"Thank you."

I reach up and hug him. I don't care about traditions. I just want to hug him. He wraps his arms around me and puts his fingers through my hair. I feel so free in his arms.

"The day will come when you'll have to leave your family behind. You may never see them again."

"Okay."

"Including Yumiko-san."

"Yumi-chan? But I-"

"I'm just trying to prepare you."

"But can't Yumi-chan come?"

"If I let you save anyone, you would want it to be her?"

"Yes."

"Fine. You can have Yumiko-san."

I can't imagine not seeing her again. I dry my tears on my sleeve.

"I may not see you for a long time," I say to him. "I'm afraid to let you go."

"You're too young to be saying things like that."

"But it's true."

"You can stay here with me tonight if you want."

"I'll stay."

"Hmph, you didn't even hesitate."

"What reason is there to hesitate?"

"I see none. I was about to take a shower. Just rest here."

He releases me and walks away. This has been the best day. I was nervous he wouldn't accept me but I think he likes me. He really is a nice boyfriend. I crawl underneath the blanket. I didn't sleep the night before; I'm ready to go to sleep. I want to wait until he comes back but I don't think I'll make it.

Chapter 8: Kyoya

She really is something. I wasn't gone too long and she's stretched across the bed like it's ours. She didn't even hesitate to stay. Then again she was raised to be with me; she has to be obedient.

I reach down and touch a hair strand again. That was surprising. With makeup she looked like a woman. When she took it off she looked like a child. As soon as I saw her with her hair down, she looked like a woman again. I had to study her country's culture. I know what she means about not putting her hair down. Perhaps seeing it pushed me into something more intimate.

I sit on the balcony to light a cigarette. She seems to like me but I doubt we'll meet for some time. Seems unfair to make her rely on me and then abandon her.

"Kyoya-sama?"

I'm too distracted. I didn't even hear her come behind me. I quickly put the cigarette away.

"Did I wake you?"

"I wanted to wake up. I have so much to ask you."

THE LAST PRINCESS

"It's been a long day," I tell her.

I keep my back to her and look to the sky instead.

"You're tired," she guesses. "I'm sorry for being inconsiderate."

She's far too polite. I look back and see her walk away; her robe dragging behind her.

"What did you want to ask?"

I come back inside and guide her to the bed. I feel as though I can't get too close to her. I don't want to be inappropriate with a child. She sits squeezing her knees to her chest among the pillows. She's like a doll. I reach forth and touch a strand of hair. I follow up to her face and see her redden.

"What did you want to ask me?"

"Um…I wanted to know what it's like to grow up with brothers?"

"You're an only child aren't you?"

Very rare for a royal family.

"Yes. I met Kira-kun in the library earlier. Does he like books?"

"Yes."

"I wanted to talk to him more but he ran away from me. He said he hates me. After hearing about him, I thought I would be able to understand him."

"You think you two are alike?"

"I thought so but he said we're not."

"He'll come around. Like you, he's been sheltered. He's never met a girl that could be on his level. I think it intimidates him."

He normally just preys on the servants. They're considered idiots in his eyes. Setsuna-san is just as smart as him. Even I'm surprised.

"And Kantarou-sama? What's he like?"

"Stern. He lacks sensitivity. You shouldn't talk to him much."

"But he's a nice man, right?"

27

THE LAST PRINCESS

"I suppose."

"Are you proud of your brothers?" she asks me.

She's beaming. I can only smile. I never thought of it before. Kan-nii is a commander and Kira is one of the smartest kids in our country.

"I'm proud of them."

"Are they...are they proud of you?"

"I can't say so. I don't have many accomplishments-"

"But you do! You...you're gonna be king of Morinaga."

That's nothing to be proud of just yet. Morinaga hasn't accomplishment anything worthy of me. She thinks the world of her country of course. I nod to her.

"I want your family to accept me," she says.

Her eyes are starting to close. She's tired herself out.

"Just rest now, princess."

"I want...Kyoya-sama to stay with me....I want you to help me....be free."

I put the blanket over her and go back to the balcony. She really is a sweet girl. In just a day, she's already become special to me.

Chapter 9: Setsuna

I get up frantically. The other half of the bed is untouched. His clothes are gone. I go to the balcony and see multiple cigarettes pressed inside a glass.

"He's gone."

What was the last word I said to him; I don't remember. Maybe he's at breakfast. Before I open the door I close my robe and tie my sash. I braid my hair and put it up. There's no trace of him through the halls.

"Setsuna-sama, you're late for class."

THE LAST PRINCESS

I run into one of my teachers. I don't have time for class.

"Um, where's Kyoya-sama?"

"The Niwa family left early this morning."

"So he's gone?"

"Princess, it's time to start class."

I run pass her and go up to my room. His number should still be there. I want to speak to him again. I open my door and mother is waiting for me.

"Where were you last night?" she asks me.

I'm stricken but move to the bookshelf. I know I left it here.

"Answer me, Setsuna!"

I kneel down to the book I dropped. It's not here. No, I dropped it on the vanity when he asked me to take off my makeup. I walk to the vanity.

"There it is!"

Mother's hand reaches for it first.

"What is this, huh?"

No, he told me to keep it secret. She tosses it back to me and I stumble to catch it. The numbers are gone. It rubbed off. Why didn't I memorize such an important number?

"I was in Kyoya-sama's room. I wanted to talk to him more."

"You were in his room after dark-"

"I just wanted to talk to him."

"What if someone saw you? Do you want to be labeled a loose woman? You have no reason to be in the prince's room. You're not married. All you are is a burden to him."

"No, he says he likes me-"

"He's being polite. There's nothing you can offer him besides a title."

THE LAST PRINCESS

I thought that was the case but I think he likes me. He hugged me and listened to me. He took the ribbon from my hair. I nod to her. There's allowed to be secrets between me and him; this will be one.

"You're right mother; I was foolish."

"Clean yourself up and get to your classes."

I want desperately to talk to him again.

"Did you really spend the night with him?" I hear.

I turn around and Yumi-chan steps in. She's about to go out it seems.

"We like each other," I say to her. "He's amazing."

"I'm happy for you," she says smiling.

"What did Kantarou-sama talk to you about?"

She sighs and walks to the vanity. She checks over her hair.

"Oh my gosh! Did he propose to you?"

"No, unless he has a weird way of doing it. He wanted me to come to his country for a cultural exchange."

"That's great!"

"I told him "no." It was because of how he asked."

"Kyoya-sama said his brother doesn't have much sensitivity. Perhaps he didn't know how to ask. But it's such a great opportunity."

"It is but-"

"And I'm sure you'll be learning from the court ladies and not him especially. You always said you hated the reputation your mother put on you. This is a chance to create your own."

She holds her head down.

"That man just bothers me."

"I think you should do it. I'm so jealous of you. Oh, and you can help me and Kyoya-sama communicate," I say to her.

THE LAST PRINCESS

"He did throw his number at me."

"Let me see it. I'll call!"

She passes her phone to me lazily. I'm so close to talking to him.

"They should be off the jet by now," she says to me.

I sit down at the floor of the vanity. Each ring makes me more anxious.

"Only for you, Setsuna-chan," she says to me with her head down.

"Kantarou-sama can give you anything. This is great. You can finally pursue your dreams without being mocked by my mother."

I think he picked up.

"Who is this?"

He has such a deep voice.

"Hello, this is Setsuna Asahina, princess of Morinaga, I would like to speak to Kantarou Niwa-sama please."

"Princess?"

"I'm calling on behalf of my cousin, Yumiko Yamamoto-chan. I have persuaded her to take your generous offer of a cultural exchange."

I feel my training kicking it. I'll persuade him to make her dreams come true.

"To think you have more persuasion over me."

"I find it very believable. I will relinquish her to your care only, and if something happens to her I will hold you responsible. Do you understand Kantarou Niwa-sama?"

"Who do you think you're talking to-"

"You expressed an interest in her, did you not? All the more reason for you to assume responsibility. I assume you're a great man, being a Han commander. This should be easy for you to handle."

I hear him laughing deeply.

"Fine," he finally says.

THE LAST PRINCESS

"I look forward to your return. I will only relinquish her to you. Now....would you be so kind as to put Kyoya-sama on the phone."

"I'm afraid he's unavailable."

"W-what is he doing?"

"He's a busy man. He doesn't really have time. Do you have a message, princess?"

"Um...not really. Kantarou-sama, do you think he'll come back soon?"

"Not likely."

I feel depressed now. I just sent Yumi-chan to Han and that means I'll be here all by myself. I don't even have his visit to look forward to.

"Do you...do you think he likes me?"

"I can't say. I really don't have time to be your messenger."

He hung up on me. Yumi-chan looks down at me from the vanity.

"Very impressive. You sure know how to talk to him."

"Negotiation class."

So he won't be back. I want to speak to him so badly. I pass the phone back to her. It was somewhat comforting to hear Kantarou-sama's voice. I'm getting closer to him.

"Don't be so down."

"But now that I know him-"

"I get it. But he's working hard so that the two of you can be together."

He is. He said he had a lot of press to do. As soon as our nations accept it, we can come together. I smile thinking about it.

Chapter 10: Kantarou

She's pretty impressive. Convincing her stubborn cousin to come is actually helping her not me. I head to his office. He still won't tell me his plan; perhaps it's safer not to.

"Kyoya," I say at his door.

We just got back and he's already writing.

"Writing in your diary again?"

"Just notes about Setsuna-san."

"She just called me."

He stops immediately and picks his head up. I take a seat. He's anxious to get it out of me. He looks at his cellphone and puts it down.

"Is she okay?"

"She's quite a negotiator. She convinced her cousin to come but only if I take responsibility for her safety."

"That's great."

What's with the frilly ribbon on his desk. I reach for it and he pulls it away. He's been weird since he met the little brat.

"Don't look at me like that," he says to me.

"She asked me if you like her," I say to him.

"I do."

"Enough to leave the servants alone."

"Maybe."

"Huh?"

"Kan-nii…when I looked at her, I felt something. When she talked to me, I felt something. I feel-"

"Stop it already. She's a cute girl but, you're not in love with her."

"I'm not but in time, I want to be."

He has to be kidding.

"Kyoya," I say trying to snap him out of it. "Are you just trying to play the part-"

"No...I went there with the intention of playing the part but...I just want to be good to her. She trusts me so much. She has the biggest eyes when she looks at me."

My brother, the notorious playboy, is settling down with a twelve year old. But...I think he's serious. And so he feels guilty about it. I get up and slap him on the shoulder. If he likes her then, I'll have to protect her too.

"Consider the princess' safety my top priority."

"Thank you."

"I have to get back on duty."

"Please bring Yumiko-san here as soon as you can."

He starts to write again. His mind is confused. She met his expectations that's all, maybe even exceeded it.

Chapter 11: Yumiko

You better not mess this up. Do you understand me?"

"Yes, aunt."

"I don't know why Kantarou-sama took interest in you but you better keep it. And you better wear those robes every day, not that whore like-"

"She'll be fine," uncle cuts in. "But please wear your royal robes every day. They need to experience our traditions a bit more."

"Yumi-chan, do you think they'll send Kira-kun here to take your place? I'd like to teach him about Morinaga."

"I don't know."

THE LAST PRINCESS

I never had to wear the robes except for social occasions. I never had to feel the pressure Setsuna-chan feels. But for once, I am the sole representative for the Morinaga Royal Family. Aunt looks me over.

Why did I agree to this? I…like their family. They seem accepting. Tomoko Niwa-sama seemed impressed just by looking at me. She wasn't afraid to be affectionate with her husband. Around here, there's no such love.

"Setsuna-chan," I whisper to her. "Will you be okay?"

"I can handle things better now," she says to me. "You're the one starting the adventure. You get to live with my boyfriend."

"And that monster, Kantarou-sama."

He is the crown prince. That's a big deal. Who am I to talk back to him. Oh man, he was right. We're all waiting in the sitting room. I'm told he landed. My little cousin holds my hand. She does it all and she's finally smiling about it. If I was the last princess, I would fold under the pressure.

"I'm gonna make you proud," I whisper to her.

"I want you to make yourself proud. Tell him you want to pursue modeling."

"He'll laugh at it."

"Kantarou Niwa-sama has arrived," a servant steps in.

We all stand to receive him. His heavy boots bang on the floor. His eyes scan all of us then land to me.

"Thank you for your visit, Kantarou-sama. It's nice to meet you again. How is your family?"

"Preparing for the press release. I was told to remind you to watch."

"Of course," aunt says. "I'm sorry our daughter cannot be a part of it."

"How are you, Setsuna-san?" he says to her slyly.

We're not supposed to talk which such a heavy presence. She bows to him.

"Yumiko-san will be in my care. Thank you for trusting her to me."

He bows lightly. We're all surprised.

THE LAST PRINCESS

"I'm gonna miss you," Setsuna-chan says to me.

She breaks away from her mother's side and hugs me.

"I'm gonna miss you too."

"Girls, show some respect-"

"No," Kantarou-sama speaks. "It's quite alright. These girls seem like sisters."

"Say hello to Kyoya-sama for me," she says.

"Yumiko-san, we have to get back," he says to me.

He reaches his hand out to me. I guess it's a formality. I take his hand and feel his strength immediately. I cross the room to his side and my family seems so far away now. Setsuna-chan fights back tears.

"I'll see you soon," I say to her.

"Yumi..."

I walk the hallway in silence with the crown prince. He's still holding my hand. This is a way to start my own reputation but I could easily mess this up. I'd be embarrassing him too so I doubt he'll let that happen.

"I'm glad you came to your senses."

I must remember the training I had when I was younger. I'm not supposed to speak back. We leave the house and walk the runway. I've never been on a private jet. I've never been allowed to leave the country. The wind blows fiercely and I touch my hair to keep it in place.

I follow behind him up the steps to the plane. Out of sight he finally lets go of me and plops down in a seat. I guess I should sit across from him. He's so tall. He crosses his leg and commands the seat he's in.

A servant hands him a drink; it looks like alcohol. He starts ignoring me immediately.

"You have a habit of staring."

"Sorry."

"Sit beside me. You don't deserve to sit across from me."

THE LAST PRINCESS

I move to the window seat beside him. He doesn't even bother to uncross his legs. I have to squeeze to fit in. I guess my first cultural lesson is to stay quiet. Han men seem stuck in another century.

"Where's that fire you showed me before? You're not talking back now."

"If I may speak. I would like to apologize to you. Indeed I didn't realize your position when I spoke back to you. I am honored that the crown prince would take me in his care."

"So you see what a big deal I am."

"Yes, I do."

"I've been meaning to ask you something. Why are you called a disgraced royal?"

He doesn't know. I guess he wouldn't take the energy to inquire on his own. There's no secret.

"My mother and the king are siblings. She married a general from our army. It came out when I was about ten that the general wasn't my father. Mother couldn't say who my real father was. The general divorced her. He wants nothing to do with me. She left the palace out of embarrassment. I haven't seen her for many years."

"So she was labeled a whore cause she didn't know who the father was."

"It's not that she can't remember. She just couldn't say."

"But you've since been labeled the same. So you can't be married off."

"I suppose."

"You'd make a great mistress. You're plenty beautiful."

I look over at him. He's looking over at me. Is he checking me out? Am I even in his league?

"I'll keep you away from Kyoya."

He laughs and continues drinking. I was flattered when he said I was beautiful. I touch my cheek thinking about my makeup. I despised him this morning. That won't change.

"Since you're in my care, I will not allow you to soil your reputation. You will be my assistant from now on."

THE LAST PRINCESS

"Assistant?"

"It will be great exposure for you. I'll be changing your uniform. That dress is too provocative."

There's not even a piece of skin showing. It's hard to move in so I don't mind a change. It goes against what my aunt said but I don't mind.

"You can leave us," he suddenly shouts.

I didn't realize the servant was behind us. A door quietly closes. Looks like we're taking off. I've never been on a plane before. I've been on a roller coaster so I figured it must be the same. It's fast and….I'm scared.

"Looking out the window won't help."

He grabs my head and pulls me into his chest. The engine is so loud. I hear his heartbeat and try to mimic the pattern in my head.

"You women are so backwards. This is your first time on a plane."

I'm gonna ignore him. It gets quiet as we settle in the air. I try to pull away from him but he's set on keeping me at his chest.

"I think I'm okay. I won't look out the window."

I open my eyes and it's dark. He had the servant close all the shades. He pushes me away and goes back to his drink. That was sweet of him to shield me.

"Thank you," I say to him.

He finishes his drink and throws it to the seat across. He turns his eyes to me and takes hold of me again. I'm quiet as he lowers me down and lays on top of me. I'm not naïve, I know what's going on. It's not my first time with a man.

He kisses me and pulls at my belt. It's a hard outfit to get off but he's strong enough to pull me out of it. As good as all this feels, he said I was only good enough to be a mistress.

"No," I say to him. "Please stop."

"Why?"

His voice sounds gentle for once. He has so much longing. His hands are so big; he fits my face so well. I want to stop but….oh it feels so good. I squeal and try to hide my face.

38

THE LAST PRINCESS

I don't want to be the mistress but what else can I be. I'm not good enough to be with the crown prince.

"For now on you call me commander," he whispers to me.

"Yes."

I'm ready to explode just from his kisses. Suddenly he stops. He gets off me and stands up. I lay motionless as he stares as me.

"Fix yourself," he says. "I got carried away."

It's quiet for the rest of the trip. He sits in the seat behind me. What made him want to make out with me and what made him stop. I can't even scan his face for clues.

Chapter 12: Kira

"So Kan-nii gets a girlfriend too."

"Shut it!"

He slaps my head. I'm only saying what it looks like. Seems a bit backwards that he gets the slutty cousin when he's crown prince.

"Yumiko-san is my new assistant. She's taking part in a cultural exchange. Try to respect her, brat."

I fix my hair back. She smiles at me. I know that look.

"Nice to meet you again, Kira-sama."

"You're thinking that I'm cute, aren't you?"

"Yes, how'd you know?"

"That's what everyone thinks."

He starts walking and she follows behind him. Everyone follows him. It's cause he's a leader. He's a leader, Kyo-nii is a strategist, and I'm nothing.

THE LAST PRINCESS

I walk over to father's office. It must be his stupid idea to make the slutty cousin his assistant.

"When I see you, you're always pouting?" he says to me.

"Yumiko-san just arrived. She's Kan-nii's assistant."

"That should be good for her."

"I think it's stupid."

"I think my little Kira is jealous cause he doesn't have a girl to play with," mother comes in.

She pulls me in the office and to the couch. I ignore her as she plays with my clothes. Always tugging and shining buttons.

"You're a handsome boy so don't worry."

"I know I'm handsome but…"

"Are you jealous because Yumiko-san will be playing with Kantarou? She's a bit too old for you-"

"Ugh! You're impossible!"

The real problem is that I'm not important around here. Where's my assistant and my future bride. They give me nothing but books. I…I like girls too.

"How come Kyo-nii and Kan-nii are so good with girls?"

Mother holds her mouth. She should just leave. It's embarrassing to talk around her.

"Tomoko, can you leave us alone."

"Yes, darling."

She leaves out snickering. I wish she would act her age. Father stays at his desk with his paperwork.

"Kantarou is twenty-five and Kyoya is twenty. They have had time to develop their interactions with girls. They weren't always as smooth as you think they are."

"What do you mean?"

THE LAST PRINCESS

"They were nervous the first time they found a girl they liked. No amount of studying can prepare you for that. They just followed their instincts, no matter how awkward it was."

Seems they've always been good with girls. So they make mistakes too.

"To be honest, Kyoya was never crazy about girls. He just let them be around him. Kantarou…"

Father starts laughing.

"What?" I urge him.

"He's really awkward, even today. I know he thinks Yumiko-san is attractive. Just watch their interactions."

"He likes her?"

"I don't know about that but he's attracted to her."

"What's the difference?" I ask him.

"Right now, his mind is fixated on her beauty and her body. He wants to touch her. He hasn't given himself the chance to like her."

"He talked to you about this?"

"No. That first meeting showed a lot. When we met with the Asahina family I could tell everyone's feelings. Kantarou was lusting after Yumiko-san without even knowing it. Kyoya was smitten with Setsuna-san. And you…you were jealous of Kyoya."

"What!"

"Because you and Setsuna-san are the same age, you want to be engaged to her instead. Yes, it makes more sense but I think Kyoya and Setsuna-san are well matched."

Damn that old man's perception skills.

"But what about the age difference?"

"It seems like a lot now because she is a kid and he's an adult but it won't matter when she's older. And you know…I could tell Setsuna-san likes you. She wants you as a friend. Neither of you have any."

THE LAST PRINCESS

"But...when will I get to be with a girl?"

"They're everywhere, just find one you like."

That's his advice to me. It's terrible but he's right. I never thought much about brother's engagement. I never had the feeling of wanting to be with a girl. As the meeting approached, I grew jealous. If Setsuna-san was promised to me, I wouldn't have to struggle to find a girl or have her accept me. She would just be waiting for me. She would have prepared her whole life to meet me. Stupid Kyo-nii.

"Hm? What do you really think of Setsuna-san?" he asks me.

"I think she's an idiot. So is Kyo-nii."

"Kira," father says.

I want to storm out.

"Be patient."

So I should just wait. Wait for a girl to like me. I don't see how that can happen. I'm fairly intimidating.

Chapter 13: Kyoya

"Welcome Prince Kyoya. It's very rare the royal family has an announcement to make concerning you."

I sit on stage among a crowd of reporters, fans and cameras. I convinced father that I can handle this myself. I can but, my exposure to the people is fairly limited. They don't know much about me so now is my chance to have them cheering for me.

"Thank you for having me."

"You're a busy prince. I wonder what you could have to say."

"I'm to be married soon," I say out loud.

The crowds riles up. I bet she's watching too...Setsuna-san. Coming forward with this brings my plan even closer. The guilt strikes my heart again.

"Yes, it all seems to add up. Your trip to Morinaga and the beautiful Yumiko Yamamoto-san coming into the palace. You're a lucky man."

THE LAST PRINCESS

"I'm afraid you're mistaken. But I do admit that Yumiko-san is beautiful."

Setsuna-san will no longer be my secret.

"I'm to marry the beautiful princess Setsuna Asahina."

"The princess? Isn't she a child?"

"She is in age but her intellect is very advanced. And so in time, I will become the King of Morinaga."

Perhaps this was too much to say at once.

"Are you serious, prince."

"Yes. The princess and I are different in a lot of ways. She's a traditional Morinaga woman, with traditional values but she values our culture as well. She speaks perfect Hangese. I hope people can believe in us."

"Prince, how could you make this decision-"

"I'm not surprised by your opposition. I'm sure there are many that are opposed. But know that as a Han man and a prince I have very high expectations. The princess exceeds all of them. I should hope she feels the same about me."

"I don't exactly have opposition. This is just surprising-"

"The union is far off."

"But, prince, you speak like this is a personal union between the two of you. This is clearly Morinaga trying to secure a future king."

"If that was really all it was, I wouldn't speak so highly of her."

The opposition is good. It's better than I thought. Even my interviewer is opposed. Time to end it.

"I hoped congratulations were in order but this is fine with me. I have business to attend to."

I get up and leave the stage. Kan-nii and his assistant wait for me behind the curtain. She hands me a bottle of water.

"Thank you, Yumiko-san. I still think this is a waste of your talent."

THE LAST PRINCESS

"Don't spoil her," he cuts in. "But I must say, I like the arrogance you showed out there."

"Figured you would. I don't really think I was being arrogant."

"I'd say you made the people feel ashamed of their displeasure," she says to me.

"Did I say you could voice your opinion?"

"No, she's right."

It's exactly what I wanted. I want to visit her one more time. I want to make sure she can handle all this.

"I'll be going back to Morinaga to check on her."

"You spoil your woman already," Kan-nii scoffs.

"I think it's sweet," she tells me. "I'm glad you care about her. Would you mind delivering a present for me?"

"Not at all."

"You better leave before the reporters sneak in," he tells me. "I'll have the press directed at father while you're away."

My car is waiting for me. As I approach the side door I stop hearing high heels after me.

"Yes," I say back at her.

"Can I ride back to the palace with you?"

"Certainly."

I feel on edge around her. She's going to suffer too. She rides next to me in the town car. She's changed a bit from being here. It's been a few weeks. She dresses in that tight uniform Kan-nii picked for her and she's become mild spoken.

I feel like I know her from Setsuna-san's letters. She's the only one to treat Setsuna-san like a normal girl. Yumiko-san got to live a normal life after her mother's disgrace. I remember the story. Father warned me that even royal women can be disloyal, not mother of course.

"You," she starts to say. "You care for her a lot."

THE LAST PRINCESS

"She couldn't have survived her captive years without you. She told me so."

"Really?"

"In her letters."

"I misjudged you. I didn't think you would care enough to read her letters."

"But you still encouraged her to write me. Why?"

"Cause it kept her going. Why are you so nice to her? Isn't she a burden to you? Deep down you must want to play with women your own age and live the life of a rich prince."

"I want you especially to understand that....when I met her, I took her seriously. I plan on falling in love with her. Even though she's not here, she's on my mind. I wonder if she's sad or not. I wonder if she's smiling or lonely. I wonder if she has the same thoughts about me."

"You're serious?"

"I am."

She looks over at me. I need Yumiko-san to believe in me too.

"You and your brother are very similar. You're both snakes."

"I would agree to that on all matters except this one. Call me whatever you want."

My intentions are bad. She's right about that. Kan-nii and I only care about power, that's true. But I'm not lying about loving that girl.

We get to the palace and I announce my intentions to travel back to Morinaga. I should bring Setsuna-san something too. I don't know what she likes.

"How could I not know?" I say to myself.

"She always wanted to try Han food. You should bring her some," Yumiko-san says at my office door.

She holds out a little box to me. It's pink with a red ribbon.

"What is this?" I ask her.

"Her gift. It's a bracelet I saw in the market."

45

THE LAST PRINCESS

"I should have bought her jewelry."

"I think it's cute that you're flustered about this. Have you ever had a girlfriend?"

I look up from my desk. I've been with many women but now that I think about it, I don't think I've ever had a girlfriend. Is that why I'm acting this way?

"She'll like anything you give her."

She leaves the box on my desk and walks out. So Setsuna-san is my first girlfriend. Did I do that on purpose?

"Sir, your plane is ready," a guard comes in.

Now I'm thinking about it. My first girlfriend.

Chapter 14: Setsuna

It's the rare t.v I get to watch and I'm watching it over and over.

"He did well, didn't he?" I ask father.

I followed him to his office after the broadcast to watch the replay of Kyoya-sama's interview. Father is on the phone discussing it.

"He's well spoken, don't you think?"

"Not now," he says to me.

It's all political to him. I was hoping he'd be impressed. I'm impressed with him. I get up and leave without him noticing. There's no one for me to talk to since Yumi-chan left. I'm not allowed to speak on the phone and talking to her is no exception. There should be a letter coming soon or something. She couldn't have forgotten me. I wanna hear about Han…and Kyoya-sama.

Even mother is making calls to our leaders. I go to my room and start my homework. I'm happy he would go public with the engagement. He said such nice things about me. No one here seems to notice.

"He thinks I'm beautiful," I keep saying to myself.

It's hard to concentrate. I waste the day dreaming.

46

THE LAST PRINCESS

"Princess, dinner is waiting."

The day is ending already. I go downstairs and see mother and father in the sitting room. Normally they're at the table before me. Probably a late meeting.

"Setsuna, come here. We have a visitor."

They normally don't want to me to meet the political leaders. I step into the sitting room. It must be okay for me to enter without my veil.

"It's nice to see you again, princess."

The man turns around.

"Kyoya-sama!"

"Manners, Setsuna."

I'm stunned to see him. He's really here.

"He came to see you right after his announcement."

"Can we have a moment alone?" he says to them.

"Join us in the dining room, when you're ready," father tells him.

"Actually I have other plans, if you don't mind."

My parents walk out and the door closes with a creak and a bang. Did he really rush here to see me?

"You look well," he says to me.

I step towards him unsure of how to greet him. When I'm within reach he grabs me and pulls me to him. I knew he would know what to do. I'm so happy to be close to him again.

"I thought about you every day," he says to me. "You've been lonely, haven't you?"

"I have. Yumi-chan is gone."

"She's fine. She's having a lot of fun as my brother's assistant."

"Really?"

"She wanted me to give you this."

THE LAST PRINCESS

He takes a box from his pocket. We part and he holds it out to me.

"Go on, open it. You'll feel better."

I open the lid and inside there's a jeweled bracelet. She remembered.

"I can't believe she was listening."

"What do you mean?"

"I told her about this gem native to Han. I told her it was the most beautiful thing I've ever seen."

"It looks plain to me."

"It's a plain rock but it's the story behind the rock. It's about a princess trapped like me. Her uncle was in love with her and she refused to return his feelings. He trapped her in a cave deep in the mountain to punish her. And then she saw a trail of these gems. She followed it and it led her out."

"Who left the path?" he asks me.

"No one knows but she's certain it was the prince that loved her that was trying to save her."

Yumi-chan remembered. I complained to her so much about how I hated being trapped here. My eyes start to get heavy and I cry. It's a plain bracelet; it really is just a rock but it means so much to me.

"She told me…Kyoya-sama would lead me out. Just like these rocks."

I can't hold myself back. I start to cry with the bracelet at my chest. He grabs me again taking me back in his arms.

"There's no need to cry. You'll be out very soon."

"Yumi-chan remembered."

"She's special to you?"

I nod to him.

"You're special to her too. I'll make sure you two are always together."

"You…get along with her?"

"Yes, we get along well."

THE LAST PRINCESS

"I'm glad." I say wiping my tears.

I feel embarrassed crying in front of him.

"It's okay to cry with me," he says. "Soon enough I'll know how to make you stop."

"I'm not sad-"

"I know."

He puts a hand on my head. I'm happy to see him and I'm not even acting like it.

"I want to go somewhere private with you."

"Um...we could go to my room."

"That's fine."

I walk back to my room with him. Mother and father are having dinner by now. I guess I'll eat later. Being with Kyoya-sama is more important. He wants to be alone. I think he's afraid of the servants listening in. I've never been suspicious of them.

We enter my room and he closes the door.

"Will you be staying over?" I ask him.

"Yes, it's pretty late."

"That's wonderful."

He stands nervously. He's been here before.

"I wanted to get you a gift too but I have no idea what you like," he says.

"I don't need a gift from you. You are my gift."

He looks down at me smiling.

"I feel the same about you."

"But if I knew you were coming, I would have given you something. Oh! Let me show you something."

THE LAST PRINCESS

I run to my bed and peek underneath. Through the years I gathered neat things that I wanted to share with him. It's in a box in the corner; I haven't taken it out in a while. I pull it out and feel him bending over me. I throw the box back in surprise and he backs away.

"Sorry, I was just curious."

He sits down on the floor with me. I reach over and gather the contents. Where should I start?

"Oh, this is a Han actor I always wanted to ask you about. One day, I was sneaky and saw a movie with him in it. I wondered if he was famous there."

"He's Jon Ju."

"Jon Ju?"

"He's very famous."

"Have you met him?"

"Actors and royals don't cross the same paths."

"Really? But you know about him?"

"I've seen his movies too."

"You get to watch movies, Kyoya-sama?"

He chuckles with his head down. I only get to watch educational movies on television. I don't want to make myself look uncool. I better move on.

He moves closer to me and I look down to see his legs are around me. I'm sitting between his legs while he's looking at me sort through my junk. His legs are so long.

"What's this one?" he says leaning forward.

"This seems stupid. I was so young when I gathered these things. This is a color I saw and I didn't know the name of it. I wanted to ask if you liked the color too. This is a list of Hangese words that I don't know how to pronounce. It's childish-"

"It isn't. But I want to you think less about gaining knowledge and more about experiencing feelings," he says to me. "I think you're very smart, even smarter than me but I think you haven't experienced life."

THE LAST PRINCESS

"But I-"

"It's not your fault. You've been surrounded by the same people your whole life and the same things. With me this close to you, tell me what you're feeling now."

What am I feeling? I've never been this close to another person before. His face is right at my ear.

"I don't know."

"I'll tell you what I'm feeling first. I feel happy to be this close to you. I feel in charge of protecting you. I feel….like I wanna be closer."

I can't hone in on my feelings. Maybe if I was looking at him I could figure it out. I turn around to look at him. Every time I stare at him I feel so far away; he's an adult.

"I feel so far behind you," I admit to him.

He puts his hand on my head. Then he slides to my face. I hold my breath as he comes closer and kisses my cheek.

"Don't feel that way," he says to me. "Consider yourself beside me."

Chapter 15: Kyoya

What's wrong with me? I'm trying to force her to grow up so I can stop feeling guilty. Having her sitting between my legs looking up at me is too much.

I turn away to avoid her gaze. She lays her head on my chest. I'm tempted to take her hair down again.

"Kyoya-sama has a strong heartbeat."

She looks up at me with such big eyes. In this moment I know what I want to do. I lean down and kiss her as soft as I can. Everything about her is pure; everything has yet to be touched. It's waiting for me.

"Excuse me, princess."

I pull away quickly. Who would dare to interrupt? A servant stands at the door. She hides herself in my chest.

THE LAST PRINCESS

"Leave," I command.

"But the king is calling-"

"Leave!"

The door closes. Her room doesn't have a lock on it but I thought people had the manners to knock. We can't stay here much longer. She pulls me back to kiss her again. My hands hold on to her and kiss her like she's a woman, my woman.

I push her away. She tries to kiss me again but I stop her.

"If we continue, I won't be able to stop myself."

"But I like kissing Kyoya-sama."

"When we're alone again we'll kiss. But let's keep this between us."

I need a smoke. I don't even think I should spend the night here.

It's an awkward trip to the dining room, at least for me. She doesn't seem to realize the seriousness of what I just did. I kissed her. It was agreed that we wouldn't have any physical contact until she was sixteen.

"Kyoya-sama, it's this way."

I can't keep my mind still. Her parents are waiting in the dining room.

"You two have returned. It's nice that you're so considerate of our Setsuna," the king says. "I assure you Setsuna will not be in the public eye so there's no need to prepare her."

"Oh, I forgot to mention that I saw you on television. You were wonderful."

"This is the first time you two have discussed it," the queen says. "Then what were you two talking about?"

I feel oddly nervous. I sit down across from the king.

"I asked him about Yumi-chan."

"I hope she hasn't been a bother," the king says.

"How many times have I told you to watch your mouth," her mother scolds her.

"He never said I couldn't speak to him," she talks back.

THE LAST PRINCESS

"He's just being polite."

"He allows me to talk about a lot of things. He's interested in my ideas and feelings."

"No, he isn't. He's just being polite."

"We're in love and you're just jealous."

Now she sounds like a normal girl. I don't want to interrupt. She better not mention that kiss. I take a sip of wine to calm myself.

"Setsuna, you're disrespecting the prince. Keep your mouth closed."

"You're not in love with him," he says to her calmly sipping. "I think it was premature for her to meet you. We'll need to increase her training."

"Training for what?" I ask him.

"To suppress her wild notions."

I see Setsuna-san lower her head. She's not even eating. She's not talking crazy. It's normal for a girl to act his way; it's just a crush.

"I think it's normal for her to have a crush," I say to them.

"She was brought up better than that. She was brought up to respect you. Her actions are unforgivable. We apologize, Kyoya-sama. We'll work on making her better."

With the face she's making, there's no way I can part from her.

"Can you prepare a room for my pilot? I'm not up to flying tonight."

"Consider it done, prince."

So this is how it is around here. They suppress her feelings. No wonder she's so sad all the time. After dinner a servant escorts me to my room. Before I open the door I see her peeking around the corner.

I step in and leave the door open. I could really use a smoke but I don't want her to see me. She steps in nervously and I close the door behind her.

"I wanted to apologize. I didn't realize I was being disrespectful by talking freely with you."

THE LAST PRINCESS

"There's no need for that. You never have to apologize for being yourself."

"I feel as though I do."

"Don't worry about your parents. Their opinion won't matter much longer."

"Father is disappointed in me. He hates me so much. I really wish I could make him love me."

"He does love you."

"He's never once told me, or hugged me."

She really needs to make peace with her parents before it's too late. I hug her to muffle her tears. I don't want anyone to know she's in here. It's not safe for us to stay in the same room.

"You were born into a difficult position. You're the last of the royal bloodline. They just want you to be the best representation of the country."

"When we're together, will you make me continue my lessons?" she asks.

"Not if you don't want to."

"I...don't want to. So I just have to wait for that day."

Just wait a bit longer. We're alone again and I'm thinking about kissing her.

"You should go back to your room."

"Will you say goodbye this time?" she asks me.

"Yes."

I let her go and she looks up at me. I wish she wouldn't admire me so much. She'll let herself out. I go towards the balcony and she grabs my arm as I reach for the handle.

"Um...I feel as though it's not okay for us to kiss."

I wanted to avoid talking about it. I keep my back to her.

"That's right."

"Why?"

THE LAST PRINCESS

"Well, part of the opposition of our marriage is that we're from two different countries and also, in both our countries...it's illegal for a man my age to be with a girl your age. An engagement is just paper but if people found out we kissed, it would be troublesome."

"I wouldn't want to bring trouble to you."

"You seem grown up in many ways but it's still wrong."

"I see. I'm sorry."

It's not her fault. Her hand falls away. I never wanted her to beat herself up over it.

"I won't tell anyone. I'll keep it a secret," she says to me.

But it should be okay to do it in private. I don't want to confuse her. I need more self-control. It's quiet for a while but then I hear her whimper. I immediately kneel to her.

"I'm such a bad person. Even though you say it's wrong, I still want to kiss you."

I feel the same way. I can't go any further or I'll make a mistake.

"It doesn't make you a bad person. Please, don't cry about this. I want you to go back to your room and get some sleep. I promise I'll say "goodbye" before I leave."

She nods and runs off. I want to be there to help her through her feelings but I'm useless since I'm having the same ones. With her gone I sit and smoke. No matter how many, the worries don't go away.

The next day, despite my promise to say goodbye, she won't see me. I eat breakfast with her parents and she's nowhere to be found.

"This is so rude of her. I apologize," her mother says.

"It's nothing."

"The servants can't seem to find her. So childish."

The time for my departure comes soon after. I wanted to say goodbye. I promised her I would. I go back to my room and see her crying in my pillow.

"Setsuna-san," I call her.

THE LAST PRINCESS

I close the door and approach her.

"I can't make it go away. I like you so much. I know it's wrong, like you said, and I should wait but...I like you so much."

"It's not wrong," I say to her. "It's just not something anyone can accept. I don't want any pain to come to you."

She picks up her head from the pillow. I didn't mean to make her beat herself up. I sit down to try to explain myself.

"I kissed you first. It's what I wanted to do. I don't care about what anyone else thinks. But, it's not right to push those feelings on you so soon. You're not ready. When you're old enough, I'll tell you."

She nods to me. So agreeable.

"I need to get back. I have a lot of business to take care of. Promise me you'll make up with your parents today."

"I-I'll try."

"And...just know that I'm always here for you."

"You're saying "goodbye" now?"

"Yes."

She falls to me. I hug her one last time. This is last time I'll see her this happy. I'm sorry.

"Please see me soon," she says to me.

"I will."

Chapter 16: Kantarou

"You've been staggering around here since you returned."

He's writing in his book again. The day must be coming closer. He better not back down. Whenever it happens I better look busy. I should get back to training.

"I want to do it for a lot more reasons," he says to me. "I want to do it for her but...I know she'll cry."

THE LAST PRINCESS

"It's about power, not the brat."

"At first it was but…"

"She must be a siren. What's with that face."

"It must run in the family. You make the same face when Yumiko-san is around."

"What!"

That woman! I feel nothing for her. She can't even make a cup of coffee. That time on the plane was just…me being overwhelmed. We've never talked about it so it must be okay.

"Kan-nii, what if she finds out? She'll never forgive me."

"You better make sure no one finds out."

"But-"

The door slams open. Father stands before us. We both stand up and he turns on the television. What's going on? Are we at war or something?

On t.v is a news report.

"Prince Kyoya and Princess Setsuna's intimate night. How far did they go?" I read.

"What the hell is this!" father screams at him.

A video plays on screen. It's the two of them sitting on the floor of a bedroom. She's in between his legs and he's nuzzling her neck. There's no sound. I watch calculating each frame.

He kisses her.

I look back at him and he's surprised. He kissed that brat. He has his hands on her like she's a woman.

"What were you doing?" father screams at him. "You're making out with a child. You exposed the princess' face. You disgraced the Asahina royal family and ruined the purity of the princess."

The video keeps repeating. I can't believe he did that. He's speechless. Can't even think of a single excuse.

THE LAST PRINCESS

"Is it that bad that we like each other?" he finally says. "If anything won't it make our union stronger. Won't it make the public believe that this isn't just about becoming King of Morinaga. They already think we're hungry for power, can't we just make them believe I want to marry her cause I love her despite age."

He makes a good point. A royal should be able to get away with it. Father still looks frustrated.

"You're not to speak to the public. I have to speak with the Asahina family."

Father storms out. Kyoya turns off the t.v and slams his head on the desk.

"I care more about what she's going through. Her parents are gonna blame her for this. It was my fault. She had no idea what being that close meant. She was innocent."

"Put the plan in place tonight. It makes more sense with the outrage."

"That's too much for her."

"It has to be tonight to make sense. You know it. We're trying to cover your ass, remember."

What's all this concern for the brat. I'll leave him to handle it. I go back to my office and see the girl wide eyed looking at the same report.

"Turn that off," I say to her.

"I can't believe they really kissed. I wish I could call her."

"I said turn that off!"

I sit down at my desk. I can't stand watching him fall for the princess. There was no strategic reason to kiss her; she was already in our hands.

Yumiko-san stares at me. I'm not the reckless one here.

"Commander, are you okay?"

And with the plan going forward I have to keep an eye on Yumiko-san too. It will be too much for her too. She sits down in front of my desk and starts smiling.

"It was such a passionate kiss. Setsuna-chan probably doesn't even realize. I gotta go home and talk to her."

"No!"

THE LAST PRINCESS

"It will just be a short trip."

"You're not allowed to leave."

"Why not? It's not like I'm a prisoner here. I can leave when I want. You never give me anything to do or teach me anything about your culture."

I don't need her that's why I can't teach her.

"I know you're planning something. You have since the beginning. Why are you trying to keep me here."

She's suspicious. I have to turn her attention elsewhere.

"I keep you here cause I like looking at you."

"Huh?"

"I just don't have the nerve to make a move."

"Commander…"

That should keep her quiet. As if I would have feelings for a secondary woman. I look up again and see her blushing.

"I'm a selfish person," I say to her. "I've never tried to hide it."

"So that time on the plane-"

"I don't want to give you the expectation that you'll be queen. If I show any feelings towards you that's what everyone will think."

"I know you would never consider me for that position. But it's flattering to know you would consider me a person worth keeping close to you."

Kyoya owes me so much for this. But the look she's giving me isn't all that bad. The door is locked.

"Come here," I tell her.

She gets up obediently and I back my chair away. There's no need for words between us. She seems to know her position. I grab her waist and she sits on my lap.

She drops her head to my neck and hugs me.

"I'm so jealous of her. I know I can't handle the pressure like her but I would love to be in her position. To have a prince fall for me-"

THE LAST PRINCESS

"I don't intend to fall for you."

"Kan-nii!" I hear at the door.

Interrupted again. It's probably for the best. She's proven that she can kiss and not tell but I don't know how long that will last.

"Let him in, then go to my father and see if he needs any help smoothing things over with the Asahina family."

My hand lingers around her waist as she gets up. She opens the door and Kira storms right into her. His head rests on her chest and he stays there. First time he's been that close to breasts.

"I apologize, Kira-sama," she says.

"Kira, step away from her."

He steps aside with a reddened face. He keeps his eyes away from her.

"I'll report back soon," she says to me.

When she's gone he finally picks his head up. He no doubt saw the kiss too. It doesn't concern him.

"What is it?" I say to him.

He snaps back and starts to pout like always.

"I need to talk to someone."

"Big brother is always here for you so go ahead."

"I don't think it's fair that Kyo-nii has Setsuna-san."

"You think he should have someone his own age."

"Yes."

"Because it's hard enough for a preteen boy to find a girl."

"Yes, exactly."

"If you want to take her from him then go ahead."

"Really?"

THE LAST PRINCESS

"But only if you truly like her. Not because you're jealous he has a girlfriend."

"Um...it's not that I like her but...I just think it's not fair. It was disgusting watching them kiss."

He's just jealous. He'll get over it. He'll get to spend time with her soon enough. I made my mistakes in love early on. He'll make some too.

I can't wait till he gets through this spoiled phase.

"If you wanna impress the princess you should try getting stronger. Be a man in her eyes like Kyoya is. That's why she likes him."

"Be a man...you mean like you?"

"Yes, I'm the perfect example."

"How did you get Yumiko-san to fall for you?"

Has she? He looks around my office staring at my awards. I hadn't noticed that she'd fallen for me. I assumed it was all play.

"Many women fall for me. It's outside of my control."

Chapter 17: Yumiko

It's so crowded near his office. I've only glanced at this place; it really is a command center. I didn't think the kiss was a big deal. It was so passionate and Setsuna-chan doesn't even know it. I think Kyoya-sama might really like her.

I would want to share a kiss like that with Kantarou-sama. I spent so much time with him and he's growing on me. He's rude but I'm starting to see through it now. I don't think he's a mean person; he just doesn't understand other people's feelings. I like the way he keeps me close to him in his meetings. He always touches my shoulder to keep me near him.

"Oh, Yumiko-san," Tomoko-sama says.

I was thinking too much. I'm spacing out right in front of the king's office.

"Um, I was wondering if Eri-sama needed my help talking to my uncle."

THE LAST PRINCESS

"Did Kantarou send you here?"

"Yes, although I'm not sure what I can do."

She guides me away from the crowd and we walk to a quieter hallway. I feel privileged to be treated so well by the Niwa family. They treat me as if I have the same status as them.

"You seem to have a lot on your mind," she says to me.

"I can't bother you with that."

"Tell me."

It's about her son so I don't know if I can tell her.

"You've been here for some time. I think I know what this is about. You've been spending a lot of time with Kantarou-"

"I can't talk about this with you."

"Why not?"

"You're the queen. My problems are stupid," I tell her.

"You like him but you're convinced you're not good enough."

That's exactly it. I nod.

"You are still a young girl. You are only seventeen. It's normal. He is your superior at the moment and he seems to care about you in his own way. You should know that I had the same feelings before I married Eri-san. I felt as though I wasn't good enough."

"Did he accept you?"

"When he saw me gain confidence and feel as though I was good enough, he knew I could handle the position as queen. And whoever Kantarou chooses will have to be able to take the burden."

"I could never be queen. Not after my mother-"

"That doesn't matter. But I do feel as though he will never choose you as queen. When he tries to keep you away, it means he cares about you. He doesn't want you to face the burden. He actually told me that the woman he marries will purely be for show. That's not going to be you."

THE LAST PRINCESS

"But I'll never be able to be with him if that's the case."

"If you want to be with him then be with him. He'll care about you enough to figure out a way. I feel as though you're good enough to be with him."

She places her hands on my shoulders. I should make the first move. Tomoko-sama is so nice to me. I wish my own mother would speak to me and give me advice. I have no idea where she is.

"I heard you knew my mother," I say to her.

"Ju Mei-san? Yes, I did. We went to a few functions together. She was just like you. She never really fit in. She was rough around the edges. Didn't take to all the training too well. And that's okay."

"I better go find him. I want to tell him my feelings."

I wanna see Kantarou-sama again and prove I'm good enough. I know I was supposed to help the king but I have to talk to Kantarou-sama. I don't want to be a mistress. I want to have my feelings validated.

I knock on his office door.

"Commander," I say to the door.

The room is empty. Where could he be? He might be going out to meet with the captains. I run to his bedroom. I can't hold back anymore.

"Commander?"

I reach for the knob to his bedroom and storm in. He's changing into his uniform. I've watched him dress before; he made me watch but this time I'm extra nervous.

"Is there a problem?" he says calmly.

I close the door. My confidence is gone.

"I didn't get the chance to meet with him. His office was so crowded with people. I don't really know what I could have done."

"You're not assertive enough. You're representing me so you need to be more assertive."

"Right," I agree with him. "I have a lot to learn from you."

THE LAST PRINCESS

He pauses in the middle of dressing. He just took off his undershirt. I put my eyes to the floor as he approaches me.

"You're acting weird. What's wrong?"

Just tell him. I have to just tell him.

"Yumiko-san? Did those men really shake you up? I shouldn't have sent you there on your own. I should have known he'd be surrounded by people. Everyone's going crazy from this crisis."

He holds my reddened face in his hand. I'm remembering the queen's words.

"Do you care about me, commander?"

"Hm?"

"Do you care….about me?"

"…yes."

With him this close I want to kiss him but it's not for play. I have serious feelings. I put my hands on his face and bring him closer. I kiss him and he immediately pulls me to him. I want him to hear my feelings.

I brace my hands against his hard chest and my legs weaken. I still want to tell him my feelings but I can't stop myself.

He pushes me away and goes back to his wardrobe. Why does he keep stopping? He must be ashamed of me.

"With Kyoya's news story we can't be too careful. The palace has yet to be secured. All servants have to be checked."

So that's why.

"If we get caught, you feel it will burden me?"

"Me as well."

"I can handle it."

"Hm? I already told you, I don't want people thinking I'll make you queen."

He continues putting on his uniform. I run to him and put my arms around him. He stops. I need to tell him directly.

"I'm sorry but I like you. I don't want you to see me as a mistress. I want you to see me as good enough to walk beside you and sit across from you. When I kiss you...my feelings are real. I'm so disappointed when you stop."

"I should have known you couldn't handle it."

"Please consider me seriously."

He pushes me away and I stumble back. Please take me seriously. I use to play with guys too but I seriously like Kantarou-sama. I guess I deserve this. I could never be serious about a guy before so why should I be taken seriously.

"Can I go home?" I ask him.

"No."

"But I can't stay here and-"

"That's enough!"

I step backwards and hit his door. I can't be near him anymore. I open the door and run out.

Chapter 18: Setsuna

"Setsuna!"

That sounds like mother. Teacher puts down his paper feeling alarmed too. I've been here the whole time. What could I have done wrong?

The door slams open and mother stands angry. Father steps in and approaches me slowly.

"Setsuna, we know Kyoya-sama kissed you."

"You loose girl!" mother screams.

Father holds his hand up to quiet her. She immediately quiets but looks at me with anger. How could they have known? I didn't tell and Kyoya-sama wouldn't tell.

"Will both of you step out," father says.

He waits until we're alone and then sits next to me. He lowers my book and clicks on the keyboard. I'm scared of what he'll say.

THE LAST PRINCESS

A video plays on the screen. I gasp immediately. The servant was recording us.

"Father-"

He raises his hand again. I don't want to watch it. I turn my head away. That was our special moment and now everyone knows about it.

"What did you and Kyoya-sama talk about to make this happen," he says calmly.

"Please don't blame him-"

"Tell me."

"Um...I was showing him some of my memories. He said I should focus less on knowledge and work on understanding my feelings. He said...he said he felt close to me and I said I felt far from him. He said that I shouldn't feel that way."

"And he kissed you?"

I nod to him. The video doesn't show me kissing him back. Father leans on the desk and I reach for his hand.

"I'm not a loose girl."

"I know. I feel as though he might love you."

"I love him too."

He looks up at me and I'm surprised to see him smile. It's scary.

"I'm not upset about him kissing you. I'm happy you like each other. But...this video is troubling because I can't trust the people that swore to protect you. And now your face is exposed. That servant will be on trial for treason and every other servant is being looked at intensely. I don't like to do these kinds of things."

"Have you heard from Kyoya-sama?"

"I spoke to his father directly. He's just as upset. He's trying to handle most of the press."

"Kyoya-sama said that there is a lot of opposition to our relationship because of our age and countries."

THE LAST PRINCESS

"That is true. Han is very different from our county but I believe the Niwa family will follow our wishes."

He continues to rub his forehead.

"This is also troubling because I have to watch my little girl grow up. I know I forced this relationship on you and I felt guilty but…I am happy that Kyoya-sama can make you happy."

This is the first time father has spoken like this to me.

"I…love you," I say to him. "Do you love me too?"

"Of course I do."

"Sometimes I feel as though you only see me as the princess and not your daughter."

"I understand why you feel that way and I am sorry. Sometimes I need to remind myself that I am not just a king but a man, a husband and a father."

He holds on to my hand and smiles at me. So he does love me. And he's not mad at me. I reach out and hug him; it feels like the first time.

"But mother is upset-"

"I'll handle her."

"When I rule Morinaga, I won't be just a queen."

"That's fine. I know you'll be a great leader."

"Me and Kyoya-sama will make it a wonderful place."

He lets go of me. I finally got to tell him my feelings. I love my father.

I don't get to see father or mother the entire day. He has to make so many excuses for what happened. I bet Kyoya-sama is having a hard time too. He might take all the blame; I bet it's hard for him.

I sit in my room thinking about him. I hate that everyone saw our moment but it's still special to me. I look out the window. It's so dark outside. I hope father gets to sleep soon.

THE LAST PRINCESS

I jump up hearing a scream. That's didn't sound like an accident. I walk towards the door. There are more screams. What's going on? I hear a glass shatter and step back from the door.

Footsteps run right pass my door and the screams are closer. I'm scared. I better hide. I go to the closet and close myself in. I wish I wasn't alone. I think the palace is being attacked.

"Princess! Setsuna-sama!"

I peek out the door. It's one of the guards. He turns to see me and gathers me up quickly.

"What's going on?" I ask.

"We're under attack. You have to survive."

"But mother and father-"

"Keep your voice down."

He picks me up over his shoulder and starts running. He seems scared too. The house is wrecked. I move my hair out of the way and see blood on the walls. We're definitely being attacked. He runs down the stairs and slows down peeking around the corner.

He starts running again and I see a man crossing the hall behind us. I don't think he sees us as he drags his blade against the ground hunting. Please don't let him turn this way. Just as we turn the corner his eyes snap towards us.

Who could he be? He has a mask and long hair. The guard frantically looks for a way out while the masked man closes in.

"Behind you!" I scream.

He turns quickly and I fall from him. I look up and see the blade piercing his body. The masked man withdraws the blade and I back away fumbling over my clothes. The man approaches me and slams the blade down near my head. I scream and he pulls it away for another attempt. I can't let him kill me. I'll never be able to see Kyoya-sama again.

I'm the princess to my country; I have to protect myself. I have a blade on me. It's a spring blade loaded against my forearm. I never had to use it but father insisted I wear it for protection. I reach my hand to his chest and he stops. How do I release it?

68

THE LAST PRINCESS

He reaches down for my hair and yanks out my ribbon. My hair falls down and I struggle to remember. It's a slight movement to make it work.

He slowly slides his blade to my face and I whimper at the incision. I push on his chest more.

"Go away!" I scream.

The blade springs out and slides back in. He groans and backs away. I finally got it to work. I run for the nearest exit. I never had to use them before. I burst out into the night running. I keep running and hit the guard wall. Yumi-chan said there was a door around here. I can't see it at night.

"Somebody help me!" I scream.

Where are the guards? Why is no one here? They can't all be dead.

"Help me!" I scream.

Maybe if I'm quiet the man won't find me. There could be more people lurking around here. I sit down against the wall and try to slow my breathing. My heart is beating so fast.

"There you are."

I look up and scramble to my feet. As I run away he grabs my hair and pulls me to him. I can't see him but he pushes me against the wall as if he can see me well.

"Please stop," I say to him. "Why are you doing this?"

He points his blade at my face again and I start to cry. He lowers the blade and punches me in the stomach. My eyes close and fall into his arms.

Chapter 19: Kyoya

"Kyoya-sama, wake up!"

It must have happened. I haven't been able to sleep. I ruffle my hair and rub my eyes. I have to play the part. I can't believe I went through with it. I orchestrated the massacre of an entire royal house. I hope Setsuna-san is alright. I keep thinking about her tears.

I take a breath before opening the door.

THE LAST PRINCESS

"What is it?"

"The Morinaga royal family is being attacked."

I follow him to the main conference room. The entire family is there while the servants and guards are scrambling to secure our perimeter. Everyone sits in pajamas watching the news report with palace guards running around frantically.

Yumiko-san steps in next and holds her mouth.

"Uh, Kan-nii," I say to him.

He reaches back and braces her just as she screams out.

"This is terrible," mother says. "How could this happen? We just spoke to them."

"Are our own borders secure?" father calls back to Kan-nii.

"Of course."

He struggles to hold up Yumiko-san. I'm sorry. I really want to say sorry to her. No one did anything wrong. It's for power. I keep an eye on her and watch her tears. She's making me feel even guiltier. I walk over and touch her shoulder. Kan-nii looks back at me in anger. He knows what I did too. He knew it would hurt her but...he cares enough about her to hate the person that caused it all the same.

"Maybe you should take her back to her room," I tell him.

"Kyoya-sama," she cries to me.

"We'll catch whoever is responsible. I promise," I say to her.

Kira grabs my sleeve and I look over at him. He's in tears but trying to hold it back.

"D-do you think Setsuna-san is okay?"

"I hope so. I hope they're all okay."

But I know they're not. I hold my head. She's somewhere crying covered in blood.

"Get our people over there now," father says.

THE LAST PRINCESS

Mother walks Kira back to his room and I stay with father. I stand over his shoulder while he watches the newscast for every detail.

"I'm really scared. What if she's not okay?"

"This is unprecedented," he says.

"It's because I kissed her. I brought hate to her family."

"Probably. I never would have thought someone could do this. The King…Hajime-sama, I just spoke to him."

He's stressed over this. I did it for power and I did it so I could be with her. I said I would be her hero and she really needs that now.

"I want you to stay in the palace. You might be a target too."

"But Setsuna-san needs me."

"I'll bring her here….if she's alive."

The thought occurs to me that something could have went wrong. She could be dead. I take another breath. No, that can't be. I said to leave her alive no matter what.

I stagger back to my room. It's making me sick just thinking about it. I have to be tougher than this. I'm so sorry. I'll pay for my sins by being a better leader.

Chapter 20: Kantarou

I knew this day would come. I figured I would pat her on the back and be done with her. Her crying is really bothering me. I took her back to my room instead of hers. She's crying in my pillow.

I sit next to her and try to peel her away by petting her head.

"Um…I don't know what to say to you to make you stop crying."

"Please help my family."

"I will."

I'll have to travel there anyway. She finally sits up with red eyes. I don't want to see her this upset.

THE LAST PRINCESS

"What about Setsuna-chan?" she whines.

I know she's alive. It would all be for nothing if she wasn't. I pet her hair again and she falls into my chest.

"Kantarou-sama, if you didn't take me I'd be there too."

I lean back and it's a night of us lying together with me soaked in her tears. After some time she sleeps. I pull myself away and go back to Kyoya. He's awake in his bedroom smoking on the balcony.

"Is she okay?"

"Not really. Probably will have a case of survivor's guilt."

It's going on four in the morning. I just wanted to see if he was okay.

"You should sleep," I tell him.

"Thank you for letting me confide in you. I don't think I could handle this all by myself."

"That's what brothers are for."

"You've always been a great brother to me."

"And we'll both make great kings. Unlike you, I'm not ready to take the throne. Hmph...you're a king now. You surpassed me."

"I'm a king now? I won't feel it unless I have my queen."

"I'm sure she's fine. Make sure you sleep."

I walk back to my room and pull off my shirt. I have no choice but to sleep with her. I get back in and her arms immediately grab hold of me.

It's fine. But this will just confuse her feelings even more. I lean over and kiss her forehead. She's just a pretty girl to me. I don't mind being around her though. She admires me and her reactions make me laugh.

By morning she's still in my arms. I have to get back to work and investigate the massacre. I pull away from her again.

"Thank you for spending the night with me. I'm sorry if-"

THE LAST PRINCESS

"Don't worry about it," I tell her. "I'm going there to see what happened. If you need company, stay with Kira."

I look back and see her sit up. It's arousing to see her in my bed. She pushes her hair behind her ear and starts to sniffle.

I shouldn't rush off so quickly. I go back and sit next to her.

"I can't believe they could all be dead. Who could have-"

"Calm down."

I reach out and cradle her head. I don't want to see her sad. I want her to smile at me again. I lean down to her and kiss her.

"I like kissing you," I admit to her. "If you're a good girl while I'm gone, I'll kiss you again."

I kiss her lips again and she lingers biting my bottom lip. It's hard to believe she's seventeen. That's another way it'd be troublesome if this got out.

"I wish you would only kiss me if you plan on returning my feelings."

"Are you really in a place where you can be picky? I don't invite women into my bedroom but you're here. Can't you be happy with that?"

I get up and go to the bathroom. In trying to comfort her I'm saying too much. I can't even remember the lies I was supposed to say. It all sounds truthful.

Chapter 21: Setsuna

I'm not dead. It's all I can think about at this time. I sit up leaning on my elbows. I'm somewhere in the woods. There's a small creek beside me. The water floats by calmly.

The man is still here. He's leaning over the side with his hands in the water. I open my mouth to speak but nothing comes out.

"I've temporarily sealed your voice to keep you from screaming," he says with his back to me.

THE LAST PRINCESS

I sit up and grab my forearm. The blade is gone. He's rinsing the blood off my blade. If he wanted to kill me he would have done it already.

I might have to describe him later on. He has long black hair. He's tall but slender. I can't see his face just yet.

I sit up and touch my face. The bleeding hasn't stopped. Mother is going to kill me if I get a scar. Mother! Is she okay? I need to check on her. I get to my feet and struggle to stand.

Which way is the palace? It's my first time being outside the palace and I just want to run back to it.

"Don't move," he says to me.

I have to help them. I take one step and he grabs my arm. He pulls up my sleeve and attaches my blade back.

With him this close I stare at him. Half his face is covered with a mask. I can't tell what he looks like. He seems focused on attaching the blade back. I reach my hand up and grab his mask. I have it in my hand. His cold eyes snap to me and I'm frozen.

"If you see my face, I will have no choice but to kill you."

My teachers warned me about kidnappings. I should always avoid seeing the kidnapper's face. He didn't just kidnap me. He killed people. There's no way he could have killed everyone but with all the blood and screams I have my doubts. I release my hand and he finishes attaching my blade.

What happens now?

He pulls my arm and I stumble forward. I try to balance myself from falling in the creek but he gives me a push and I fall in. It's shallow but I'm weighed down by my heavy robes. Can hardly move.

"Stay here until someone finds you. I'll be watching so don't move."

It's cold. I look back to find him and he's gone. So I'm supposed to wait here; no one is looking for me. I can't even scream for help. Every time I open to speak my throats hurts.

Chapter 22: Kantarou

I get to the palace by noon. Things are moving fast. I check in with the lead investigator. They seem to not be able to keep calm. It would be better if I was running the investigation. I would be able to look at their bloody faces without feeling anything.

"Any survivors?"

"Everyone that would have been in the palace is accounted for and dead except the princess."

That seems about right. She can't be far. She must have run away to protect herself. I grip my forehead.

"If this is too much for you, I can take over. I was put in charge of the princess' wellbeing."

"I'm sorry if I sound rude but by who?"

"By her fiancé. He has jurisdiction over her."

"That's a bit archaic-"

"Well that's how it works. Show me a map of the palace."

I'll figure out where she is. She's never left the palace before so she's probably lost. Maybe Kyoya would know.

"I'll have my men search the woods. If she's injured, she doesn't have much time."

"She wouldn't be there."

"Why not?" I ask him.

"She would have run for the town towards the guards of course."

"Not if she was trying to hide. Look, we don't know who did this but they were obviously deadly. Guards wouldn't be able to protect her. Nor would she be the type of person to lead the killer to more victims. It was late and she probably wanted to hide."

THE LAST PRINCESS

"You're not permitted to search as you want. If anything, my men will search the woods."

"You're wasting my time."

I'm the superior commander. I'll find the princess myself. It'll look great on the news. I get up and go back to my men.

"We need to find her quickly," I say to them.

"Commander, I overheard an examiner saying they found the princess' blood at the scene. She was in a struggle."

They won't share all the information with us so I'll figure it out myself. Kyoya didn't share the entire plan with me. I don't know who he chose to do it. It must be someone he trusts but also someone expendable if things get out of hand. It could even be someone that's here.

I'm tempted to call him. If she was hurt then we don't have much time. I brought three captains with me but some seem to have migrated here on their own to help out.

"We need to check the woods," I say to them.

"I'd like to stay behind and see where the investigation is going. I'll report to you from here," one says to me.

"Fine, the rest of you move out."

I take a minute to gather my thoughts and a captain brushes by me.

"She's at the creek. I'll lead you there."

I turn my head to him slowly. So it was Captain Saki. I should have guessed. Kyoya and him were inseparable in the past. He's one of the youngest captains and the biggest palace freeloader. I trust he'll do this without suspicion.

"I'm an expert at tracking so let me take lead, commander."

"Fine. I'll follow."

Chapter 23: Setsuna

It's getting dark. The water feels colder. I feel so weak sitting here. But he's watching me. Probably wants me to die from a fever.

"Setsuna-sama!" I hear.

Someone is looking for me. I open my mouth but still can't scream out.

"Setsuna-san!"

I look for the voice. It's Kantarou-sama. He came to look for me. Kyoya-sama must be here too. Oh no! What if the killer was trying to lure him here so he can kill them. I can't let that happen. I lay down in the creek with my mouth slightly above the water. Please don't hurt Kyoya-sama or his family.

Soon I'm lifted out of the water and cradled in someone's arms. I open my eyes.

"Are you alright?" Kantarou-sama says to me.

I hug him. I'm so glad to hear a familiar voice. Another man stands behind him looking on. He brought his army to find me. More men run up behind him with the same uniform.

Kantarou-sama begins walking back. He stares at my face.

"It's okay to talk to me. Whoever did this is long gone."

I shake my head to him. I really want to. I want to warn him and tell him everything but even if I could I'm not allowed.

"Speak," he says to me. "Can you talk?"

I shake my head again. He tilts my head back inspecting my throat. I don't know what the man did to keep me from talking.

The palace comes into view and he covers my face with a jacket. Everyone seems happy to see me. I'm happy to be alive too.

"At least there's one survivor," I hear.

I peek from underneath the jacket. They all can't be gone. I pull on Kantarou-sama's collar. Tell me they're not all gone. I need mother and father.

THE LAST PRINCESS

"I'm sorry," he says in a low voice.

It hurts to cry. I want to wail but it hurts. I can't recall what's happening. He sits inside a tent and I'm examined. He tries to leave me but I hold on to his sleeve.

I'm alone now.

"Calm down," he says to me. "You're making yourself sick."

I feel sick. I feel like throwing up and passing out.

Chapter 24: Kyoya

Kira and I sit with Yumiko-san trying to distract her. She's been crying all day. Especially since the news report went out that everyone in the palace was murdered. There were no survivors. I know Setsuna-san is safe. They may be hiding it to protect her.

He's attempting to play chess with her. I look at him to keep him from making a stupid comment.

"Is it okay to move the horsey here?" she asks him.

"Why would you? Are you trying to…I mean, yes."

We're in the library trying to keep her away from any media coverage.

"Has Kantarou-sama called yet? Did he arrive?" she asks me.

"He's investigating."

"Aren't you worried?"

"I'm terrified. I feel as though it's my fault."

"Because you kissed her," Kira says.

"Yes. I incited a terrible group of people. I'm sorry, Yumiko-san."

"No, it's not your fault. You would have kissed her eventually. It's not up to other people to decide if two people can be together," she says to me.

I keep looking at my phone waiting for him to call me. I'm anxious for his report too.

THE LAST PRINCESS

"You're terrible at chess," Kira says to her. "No one here is a challenge."

"Setsuna-chan is good a chess. I bet she could beat you," she says to him.

"I doubt it."

"She is."

"Too bad she's dead."

"Kira!" I say to him.

He's just as insensitive as Kan-nii. Her eyes start to water again. There are guards posted at the door watching us. If not for them I would slap him right now.

"I mean, she's probably dead. Of course the killer would kill the heiress."

"Can you please stop," she says sobbing. "I don't wanna think about that."

She puts her head down throwing the chess pieces to the floor. I go to her side and put my arm around her.

"I'll call my brother and see what's happening."

I'll do a video call. Seeing him might calm her down.

"Talk to him. You'll feel better."

His grumpy figure shows on the screen. He's distracted at first then looks surprised to see her.

"Commander," she cries. "Please tell me they're okay."

"Why are you calling me? Where's Kyoya?"

"I'm here," I say behind her.

"Take the phone away from her. I don't want to see her."

I think she needs to see him. He avoids her face.

"Well..." he trails off. "One survivor."

She starts wailing even louder. Kira looks stricken. He's been sheltered too much. He's never experienced heartache himself or seen anyone else go through it.

THE LAST PRINCESS

He turns the camera around to a figure flattened on a bed. I grab the phone from her and pull it closer. She's okay but she's hurt.

"Setsuna-san," I call out.

"She might not make it. She has a strong fever. I found her in a creek. She was probably there since last night."

"She has a cut on her face."

Yumiko-san peeks to see her.

"It's pretty deep but I don't think it's infected."

I told him not to harm her and he cut her face. She'll always remember it.

"And also she can't talk. She lost her voice somehow."

"Who knows about all this?"

"Press already got word. They'll be constructing a sole survivor story."

"Bring her back immediately."

She still hasn't moved. I know she's in a lot of pain but she's got to make it. Just make it to me and I'll do all the rest.

"I have to get back to work," he says to me.

"Wait, can I see her again?"

"I won't let her die, okay. If I can't be near her then I'll have Captain Saki be my backup."

So he knows. I can tell by his voice. He holds the phone up so I can see Setsuna-san. She looks like she's in a lot of pain. She looks so alone.

"Setsuna-chan," Yumiko-san calls behind me. "Please be okay."

He hangs up. I should have known Kan-nii would be smart enough to figure it out. I spoke about my engagement with Ayato-san, or Captain Saki as he's now known, when we were in school together. I went through the same captain training that he did. Back then I saw my engagement as a pain but he saw it as a perk.

"It doesn't matter who she is. It's about what she is. She's your way of becoming a king. You don't have that here," he said to me.

THE LAST PRINCESS

I never cared about having the throne or being well known in my country. I figured I would live a quiet life in Morinaga with my child wife and several mistresses.

The more I hung out with Ayato-san, the more I saw the world like he did. The world is just something to manipulate. The sooner I do, the sooner I can do things my way. Setsuna-san's letter's encouraged me too. Even before I met her I wanted to save her.

I convinced myself that killing her family would be a good thing despite how bad it seems when I say it. I feel so guilty seeing Yumiko-san crying and seeing Setsuna-san crippled. I know I did the right thing but these images are making me think otherwise.

"I'll be in my office," I tell them.

"I'm gonna go too," Kira says.

"No, you stay with her and don't say anything stupid."

Even if Setsuna-san is alive, she's still lost everyone.

The guards part for me and I go back to my office and settle in at my desk. I keep the lights dim and pull out her letters. I wasn't mistaken. She was in pain. But in this one she speaks about how her father smiled at her and how her mother said she reminded her of one of the earlier queens.

How can I stare at her knowing I caused her and her cousin so much agony? I'm thinking too much of myself to think I can take it away.

There's a knock at the door. A court lady stands there sliding her finger down her neck. I've been abstaining since I met Setsuna-san. I want a distraction but…I don't know if I deserve it. I close the letters inside the drawer.

"Prince Kyoya?"

"You're not good enough anymore. I already have a woman."

The sooner she gets here the sooner I can start making this right. I get up and go to the door but she doesn't move.

"What if the little girl finds out about us?"

I have some loose ends to clean up. Getting rid of a senseless maid is nothing to me. With all the attention coming my way, I can't afford to play around.

"That little girl is amazing and she's half your age."

THE LAST PRINCESS

"Everyone's calling you a pervert, you know."

"She excited me way more than you ever could with just a kiss. If you don't keep your mouth closed, I'll close it for you."

Call me what they want. I'm going to make all of this work my way.

Chapter 25: Setsuna

It's been hard to stay awake. I think the nurse lady likes it that way. They're moving me to Han. I should be excited but…every time I think about it I start crying.

Kantarou-sama puts his hand over mine and I look up at him. I can hardly see him with this veil on. I think my scar makes people uncomfortable. It's my first time on a plane and I can't enjoy it. The sunlight hurts my eyes so I can't look out the window.

"I can't wait till we land so Kyoya can look after you."

He's waiting for me. Somehow I hope he can take all the pain away. Maybe he can bring back my parents, my teachers, the cooks that make my food and the court ladies that put on my clothes. Why did they have to die?

The other men are here too, the captains. They all seem to talk around me as if I'm not here. Without a voice I'm nothing. They talk about palace security and if I'm a target. If that man wanted me dead he could have done it. He wanted me to be found so I don't really get what his motive for all this is.

The only surviving royals are me, Yumi-chan and her mother and father. But then again, they've all been disgraced so it just leaves me. That man wanted to leave just me.

I'm boxed in by all the men. I feel safer like this. Kantarou-sama sits near the aisle and Captain Saki sits by the window. He seems friendly but weird. I look pass him to try to get a glance out the window.

"Don't strain yourself, princess. You still have a high fever," Captain Saki says.

I feel my head instinctively. It is pretty warm.

"We should have waited for transport," another captain says.

THE LAST PRINCESS

"That country is unstable. She's better off in Han," Kantarou-sama says to them.

"If that's the case, we should have stayed."

"Their leaders are stubborn. They won't accept Han presence until they see Kyoya as their king."

"We know how to protect them. Perhaps when the princess gets her voice back she can persuade them," Captain Saki says. "Or Kyoya-sama can speak for her."

I don't know how to lead; it will have to be him. It's too much to ask him to speak for me. Even though I am sad and traumatized, I have to think of the stability of my country. Father didn't like the prime minister making all the decisions and if I don't step up he'll run with my power.

Father said that no matter what, I must keep the Asahina family in power. He entrusted his wishes to me and I can't let him down. I know why mother and father trained me so much.

I open my mouth to test myself but nothing comes out. Captain Saki looks down at me while I practice talking and I see him laugh. I move my veil to see him clearly.

His face looks stricken and he touches my cheek. I push him away.

"Sorry," he says to me. "It looks like you're bleeding through your bandages. You shouldn't move your mouth so much."

Kantarou-sama quickly turns me to him.

"Where's that damn nurse?"

When Captain Saki touched my face I was alarmed. I remembered the killer cutting me. I touch my cheek and feel the blood on my finger.

Kantarou-sama holds my hand and escorts me to the next room. I'm shocked at the first thing I see. It's their guns. Assault weapons, knifes and armor. He pulls me along to the corner cot.

The nurse preps herself. I hold on to Kantarou-sama's sleeve to keep him from leaving. Somehow I feel safe around him. He's Kyoya-sama's brother so I trust him.

"Stop holding on to me so much," he says to me.

THE LAST PRINCESS

He sits down beside me annoyed.

"They were all crying over you. Especially your cousin."

Yumi-chan is probably devastated. I take his arm and hold it close to me. She'd be dead too if it wasn't for him.

"You know she's fallen for me. Can't say I'm surprised."

That can't be right. She told me she can't stand him.

"I kinda like her. Keep that to yourself."

I look up at him at him and he turns his head away from me.

"And Kyoya….he can't stop talking about you."

The nurse comes and peels my bandage off. Kyoya-sama has been thinking of me. I want to ask him more. I pull on his arm to get his attention and put my fingers to my mouth.

"The kiss?" he guesses. "Hmph…he wasn't embarrassed at all. He was like, "so what, I kissed her." No one could shame him."

He wasn't embarrassed by it.

"But he feels guilty now cause that kiss is probably what incited whoever did this."

The killer didn't even speak of his hatred. He was emotionless about it.

"For now on, I will be in charge of your security. If you know something about the one responsible, tell me or Kyoya only."

I nod to him. I wince with pain as she continues to disinfect. He looks on and shakes his head. I haven't looked at it but it feels like he cut me from my eye to the middle of my cheek.

We go back and sit among the captains. I feel weak from moving around. I hold onto Kantarou-sama and rest.

84

Chapter 26: Kyoya

I'm told she's here but I don't want to see her. It's going on ten; she's probably asleep anyway. I've been smoking heavily trying to distract myself. I should have just taken the sex.

The door opens quietly while I'm at my desk.

"Ayato-san."

He steps in still in uniform and sits across from me. I don't want to talk about the plot. I don't want to speak of it anymore.

"She's a sweet girl; I see why you like her so much."

"Why is she cut?"

"Too into it, I guess. And it will get her more sympathy."

"You scared her."

"I didn't really go like I planned. She had a blade on her forearm. She stabbed me in my chest. I had to clear my blood off her."

"So you rinsed her in a stream?"

"Like I said, it didn't go exactly like we planned. Anyway, you can trust me with anything. I just wanted to see how you were holding up. You're pretty sensitive on the inside."

"I've never killed a man so I guess I'm not as hardened as you."

"You'd feel a lot better if you saw her. She's just sleeping in the visitor wing."

I don't know if that's true but I need to force myself. He leaves out and I take one last drink. He has no problem getting back to normal despite what he did.

I leave the office and walk slowly to the visitor wing. It's not hard to figure out which room she's in. The door opens and I back up to around the corner. Yumiko-san is leaving.

"I'll be back tomorrow, okay?" she calls back inside.

THE LAST PRINCESS

So she's still awake. There's a guard at the door. With Yumiko-san gone I step out. The guard takes notice and moves aside.

"You can leave. I'd like some private time."

"Yes, sir."

I have to face her now. I open the door. I can hardly see her among all the pillows on the bed. I step in and close the door behind me. I step closer and she's still.

At her bedside I look over her. She has a bandage on her face. I reach out and touch it. She still remains.

"I'm sorry," I whisper to her.

I move my finger up to her hair and slide a strand through my fingers. Everyone's been forcing her to grow up so fast. Even I'm wishing for it. My hands are shaking. Good thing there's a balcony in here. I open the door and get some air. I'm breathing so fast. I want to be hardened like Ayato-san and Kan-nii but I feel so guilty.

I've never had to do the hard work, I only had to think and strategize. I've helped my brother win battles and brought the country money through trade but this is the first time I've felt so burdened by my own mind.

I pull out a cigarette and finish it quickly then take another. I get so frustrated with my dependence that I squash it against the ground.

I respected her father, and I killed him to take his position; I destroyed his whole world.

I turn around quickly feeling someone touch my shoulder. She stares at me with big eyes. I turn my head away. Can't look at her.

She sits down on the concrete beside me. I cringe when her fingers take hold of my hand. Her hand is so small and cold.

"You should get back inside. You're not well."

She holds my hand tightly and leans on my shoulder. I can't hold back anymore. Despite being ashamed of myself, I still missed her. I hug her and she falls back to the ground. I cradle her head in my hand and hold her tightly.

"I'm so sorry," I say to her. "I don't know how to fix this."

THE LAST PRINCESS

I feel her arms hug me and I realize how much I love her. Her face is warm. I better get her back inside. I sit up and reach my hand out to her. She struggles to get to her feet. When she stands her knees buckle. I scoop her up in my arms.

"I don't want you to worry," I say to her. "I want you to get better. I don't want to lose you."

I wonder what she's thinking. I wish she could talk to me. I sit her back on the bed and kneel against it with my head on her legs. I want her to forgive me but she doesn't even know what I've done.

She holds paper out to me. I look up.

"Be a good husband and a good king. I need you more than ever and so do my people," I read out loud.

I look into her eyes and feel myself finally get the strength. If that's all she wants then I'll do it. I'll be a great king for her people and for her. It's what I planned on.

"I want to marry you soon."

I wait while she writes again. She holds the paper out.

"I'm not ready to marry but I give you permission to lead in my place. Please make Morinaga a place my family can be proud of," she writes.

"Really? You're not ready to marry?"

She shakes her head.

"I thought I won you over. Especially with that kiss."

She starts to blush and I chuckle. I'll be strong for her. I'm not worried anymore. I stand up and she takes my hand.

"Don't worry, I won't leave you."

She starts to write again and hands it back to me.

"I missed you," she writes.

"I missed you too, Setsuna-san," I say to her.

I put my hand on her head.

THE LAST PRINCESS

"I know what happened to your family is terrible but...I'm really happy that you would come to me. I was going crazy wanting to see you. Damn, I'm sorry. I don't want you to misunderstand."

She shakes her head. So she understands. She's still feverish. I lay her down and bring the blanket over her. She still holds on to my shirt.

"I'm gonna sleep beside you, okay," I say to her softly.

She lets go of me and I take my jacket off. With the lights off I get in beside her. I lay flat looking at the ceiling. I'm king now; I have to start acting like it.

I reach my arm over and she cuddles into my chest. I tilt her head up. That bandage annoys me.

"Goodnight."

Chapter 27: Kira

Everyone's making such a big fuss about the princess being here. I'm just curious about what she looks like now. I don't want to be seen visiting her. I look around the corner. There's no guard. It must be too early. I go closer and listen at the door.

Right, she can't talk. There wouldn't be any noise. I open the door and step in. I'm about to call out to her but stop myself.

"Kyoya?"

Just how far is he willing to go with her? They're sleeping together. It's not fair that Kyo-nii gets everything. He's a king now. Being the second born was supposed to be useless and he's surpassed Kan-nii and become king first.

I walk over to the bed. Great...and she's fawning over him. What could she possibly like about him? He should be like a brother to her too.

"Stupid Kyo-nii."

"Why are you here, Kira?"

I jump hearing his voice. So he's awake. He sits up in the bed with her still at his side. I can't stand to watch them.

THE LAST PRINCESS

"It's sweet that you came to visit the princess but we're a little busy."

"How can you lay with her? Don't you feel disgusting?"

"Are you asking to try? Come on."

"Huh?"

"I want you to see how it feels. Get on the other side."

"No, are you stupid."

"I won't give you another chance. Hurry up."

He's just making fun of me. His offer is tempting. I never got to be with a girl in bed.

"You're my brother so I trust you to be kind to my woman. I gotta get going so I want you to watch over her."

"Me to watch over her?"

"Yeah."

He gets out from under the covers and I feel suddenly inadequate. Kyo-nii is so big. Of course girls like guys like him, even little girls. I'll never be as big as him. He puts his jacket on and goes to the door.

"I'll be back later."

The door closes. Was he serious? I stand looking at the bed trying to make a decision. I take off my shoes and get in beside her. She's not facing me. I touch her shoulder but she doesn't move.

I was stupid to think a girl would latch on to me as if I'm Kyo-nii. When I came here I thought she would be crying and I thought I could say something cool to make her stop.

"Eh?"

She just put her arm around me. I look over at her; she's still sleeping. I slow my breathing and look up at the ceiling. This doesn't feel bad.

"I'm sorry about what happened to you," I say to her.

THE LAST PRINCESS

I hesitate to touch her hair. It's silky. Why would she fall for my brother? I bet she would have fallen for me if she met me first. We have much more in common.

"I heard you're good at chess. I'd like to play with you. You know, when you're feeling better. And I wanted to show you the library. I was reading up on the Selia war. I'm sure you studied it since you're…getting a degree in history. I-I'll be starting my degree soon, you know."

I didn't realize I'm stroking her hair. I-it feels nice.

"Um…and I wanted to ask you how you felt about this book. You'll have to read it first. I'll lend it to you."

I look down at her again and her eyes are open. I jump out the bed quickly.

"Kyo-nii said I could lay with you. He told me to watch you while he was gone. I didn't do anything…wrong."

She's laughing at me.

"Who do you think you're laughing at? You should feel lucky to be with me. I'm a great person, you know."

She reaches over and starts writing something. I step closer. I'm curious about what she has to say.

"I'd want to play chess with you," she writes.

I doubt she can walk all the way to the study. I'll have to bring the board here.

"Fine, I'll be back."

I exit out and sigh in relief. If she's willing to play chess with me then we can do all types of things together. If she matches my intellect then it makes more sense for her to hang out with me.

She probably hasn't eaten yet. I should bring her some snacks. I carry the chess set back to her room. She'll have more fun with me than Kyo-nii.

"So he was happy to see you?"

Why is she here? I open the door and see Yumiko-san sitting next to her. This was supposed to be our time. I just got rid of Kyo-nii.

"You can go now," I say to her.

THE LAST PRINCESS

"Oh, morning, Kira-sama."

"I was playing with Setsuna-san first."

"Oh, did I interrupt?"

I'm sure Setsuna-san would have gotten rid of her if she could talk. Yumiko-san talks too much; I doubt she could get a word in.

I start setting up the chess set on the table. I know they're family and given the recent events they want to bond more. I turn back and she's still here.

"All the Niwa brothers seem to like you," she says to her. "What's your secret?"

Enough of her. I walk back and hold my hand out to Setsuna-san. They both stare at me.

"You said you wanted to play and….you have trouble walking, right?"

Yumiko-san starts laughing. There's nothing funny about what I'm doing. Stupid girls. I turn away and she grabs my hand. I keep my head away from her but I think she's getting up. I steady my hand so she can rely on it.

I lead her to the table and she sits down. I sit down across from her and it's hard to concentrate. I played chess plenty of times but this doesn't seem like a chess match. I keep my head down but when I look at her she's smiling or biting her lower lip while she thinks of a move.

She's really pretty. Too bad about that bandage on her face. But even with it she's still pretty. I wish she could talk again. She makes a move and I quickly counter, our fingers touch and I tip over the piece.

"You guys are so cute."

"Shut up!"

Setsuna-san touches my hand and I sit back down.

"Okay, I'll leave you two alone. Be good Kira-sama."

She steps out.

"How dare she talk to me like that. I'm a damn prince."

THE LAST PRINCESS

She starts to laugh at me too. Within a few more moves she wins the match. It's only cause I couldn't concentrate.

"So how far have you gone with my brother?"

Her eyes widen and she quickly turns away.

"I'm serious. Is he pressuring you?"

She shakes her head. So she wanted to sleep with him.

"He's not a good guy, you know. He...he doesn't deserve you. He's a playboy just like Kan-nii."

She shakes her head again.

"You don't believe me? He's doing one of the court ladies. One of the ladies that follows my mother around. Her name is Anki."

I'll show her. I grab her hand and pull her outside the room. Kyo-nii is probably in his office by now so I'll avoid that area. The court ladies stay near the basement. I take her down the stairs. She stays close holding onto my shirt with her other hand.

I look back at her. She's sweating.

"Are you okay?"

I didn't think she was that sick. I sit her down on the bottom stair and kneel down to her.

"Setsuna-san?"

She looks up at me smiling. I should at least wipe the sweat away.

"Kira-sama?"

Oh it's one of the ladies.

"Is Anki here?" I ask her.

"Yes, did your mother need her?"

"I need her. Bring her here."

The woman runs back down the hall. I help Setsuna-san to her feet. Once she sees my brother's mistress, she'll want nothing to do with him. Even though he

92

knew about Setsuna-san he still played around with women. And he has the nerve to cuddle her.

"You need me, Kira-sama?"

"I wanted you to meet Setsuna-san. You'll be attending to her soon, won't you?"

"Y-yes, when she's well. How nice of you to introduce us."

I knew it. Anki is shaken. Not many people get to see the princess' face.

"I just thought you'd like to see the girl my brother is engaged to since you know Kyo-nii so well."

"You're referring to our affair. I suppose it's something to discuss. Yes, I am the woman that took care of his needs. I still do."

Setsuna-san pulls on my arm. I want her to hear everything.

"All royal men have women that satisfy them and women they keep for appearances. It's nice to meet the other half."

I didn't think she'd be so honest. She pulls on my arm again.

"Go back to work," I tell her.

I turn back and help her up the stairs again.

"See, it's like I told you. So you can forget about him."

When we get back to her room she shuts the door on me. She must be exhausted from walking. I'll visit her later.

Chapter 28: Setsuna

It's been a few days since I arrived in Han. It's not as fun as I was hoping. They say I'm slipping away. I can't seem to get over my illness and also, the nurse can't narrow down what the illness is.

I told her I don't want to see anyone. The guards have strict orders. I heard Kyoya-sama at the door one night but they were adamant about not letting him in. It hurt me to hear his voice.

THE LAST PRINCESS

I was foolish to think I was his love. Anki-san, that woman, she's more of a match for him. Kira-kun wanted to stop me from acting stupid. At least he had the nerve to tell me.

The therapist comes to see me. I can't talk to him but he reads my writing with various nods.

"You're sad about what happened to your family but also burdened by your position," he says to me. "Why won't you see anyone?"

I felt myself turning cold since finding out about his affair. Father warned me about this. I need to be a leader first. Father was never concerned with love and he was very successful.

"I'm just here for appearances," I write to him.

"But you're getting along with Prince Kyoya, aren't you?"

I shrug my shoulders. Maybe I don't even know the real him. I couldn't even guess that he had a mistress. I bet every word he said was a lie.

"But he'll be accompanying you to the memorial. He's your support."

I nod to him. I have no choice in that. Thinking about it makes my eyes water. It's the memorial for all the people that died that night. I'll have to see my parent's dead bodies.

He quickly leans over to me and passes me a handkerchief.

"From talking with you, it seems like you feel abandoned by your family and almost afraid to be close to your fiancé."

I nod to him.

"It's so much for someone your age."

He still kneels at my chair as I wipe my eyes.

"If you're to get over your illness we must first make sure your mind and emotions are intact," he says to me.

Perhaps my illness is all linked to my emotions. That would explain why I've gotten worse. I nod at the doctor.

There's a knock at the door.

THE LAST PRINCESS

"Setsuna-san."

It's Kyoya-sama's voice. I shake my head to the doctor.

"It's okay, I'll get rid of him."

He gets up and turns the corner to the door. I don't want to see him, not even a peek of him. I wanna forget about him.

"You're disturbing my patient," the doctor says.

"Get the hell out of the way. She's my girlfriend."

My heart hurts when he says it.

"She doesn't want to see you," the doctor says to him.

"Then I'll hear it from her."

Kyoya-sama storms in and I turn away from him. I don't want to see his face.

"Why are you avoiding me?"

I look over at him and he's panting. She was getting riled up banging on the door.

"Setsuna-san?"

It's not like he's hurting from me avoiding him. It gives him more time to spend with her.

"The princess is very unstable and her health is deteriorating. Please don't upset her."

"She's deteriorating because I'm not with her. Leave us!"

The doctor can't disobey the prince. The door shuts and I'm alone with him. I reach for my pad and he takes it from me. He stares at my words. He sits on the couch beside me.

"Why don't you trust me? Why won't you confide in me?"

He leans back on the couch staring at the ceiling. I should tell him what I know so he can stop all this.

THE LAST PRINCESS

"I heard you were getting worse. I wanted to see you but figured you were too weak. But you're purposefully trying to keep me away. Why?"

He turns to me and I keep my head straight. Don't want him to analyze me.

"I don't want to lose you. I know it's tough...what you went through and what you lost but...I don't want to lose you. I don't want you to lose yourself either."

He touches by chin and comes close to me. I put my hands up to push him away.

"And you won't let me even try to help," he whispers. "Tell me what's wrong so I can fix it."

I grab my pad.

"I know about you and Anki-san. She told me that I'm here for appearances. I won't allow you to be king if that's all you're after," I write.

I pass him the pad. After a moment he drops it.

"I admit I fooled around with her. I did up until the point where I went to meet you for the first time. She means nothing to me. Doing all that stuff with her doesn't change how I feel about you. I don't care about being king. I only want to be king cause I wanna help you. Really I just want to be with you. I wanted to try to...be closer with you...know more about you....protect you."

He takes hold of my hand. I want to believe him. I need to but I'm scared. I always felt behind him. I'll always think I'm being replaced cause I'm far from his level.

"I think about you all the time. It drives me crazy how much...how much I like you."

He touches my chin again and comes closer. He kisses my forehead softly. His eyes glare at me half opened and he holds his forehead against mine.

"I'm nothing if I don't have your trust," he whispers to me. "You can't doubt me. You said you would fall in love with me."

My heart thumps again with his words.

He leans back from me and starts laughing. This is so embarrassing.

"I'm sorry, I didn't mean to embarrass you."

THE LAST PRINCESS

I push his hand away. He sits back beside me still smirking.

"I have to laugh to keep myself from feeling ashamed. I really do like you but you're just a kid. And I was about to…nevermind. Perhaps we're just moving too fast with all this. You have a lot of growing up to do and I can't do it for you."

I'm confused. I hope it's coming across that way. I've never seen Kyoya-sama chuckle so much. I grab my pad again.

"I'm gonna get some air."

He heads for the balcony. He's going to smoke again. I wish he'd stop with that. I wanna believe him. I wanna believe in every word. I suppose for now I have to cause he's all I have. Father approved of him so trusting Kyoya-sama is the same as believing in my father. Eventually I would have been in the Niwa family's care. It's just a lot sooner than expected.

He comes back in while I'm stuck in thought.

"I want you to focus on getting better," he says to me. "And if I want to see you then I'll see you, got it?"

I nod to him. He leans down and kisses me again.

"Be a good girl for me."

I nod to him again. Wait! I get up with my pad and run after him. He's so quick to get away. I leave out after him and the guard stops me.

I try to speak but just a weird sound comes out.

He turns around and I start writing. I hold it out for him to read.

"Can I come with you?" I write to him.

"Of course you can."

The guard steps away and I walk to him.

"You're trapped in there, aren't you? There's no need to ask. You can come with me for a bit. Just don't tire yourself out."

He takes me under his arm and walks with me. We go to his office and he starts writing. It's good to know he can work without being distracted by me. I finally get to be in a room of his. I get to touch his books and sit in his chairs. I do it all.

THE LAST PRINCESS

I want to ask him so much. What's his favorite thing here?

"Kyoya-sama, may I have a word?"

The door opens while I'm peeking into a box on his bookshelf. I quickly close it. It's Captain Saki. He looks at me and then takes a step away.

"Please, come in," Kyoya-sama says to him.

"I didn't mean to interrupt."

"She was just snooping while I get some work done."

So he noticed. I take my hand away and move behind his chair.

"No need to be formal," he says to me. "Ayato-san is a good friend of mine."

They're friends. I suppose so. He doesn't even call him by his title.

"Nice to see you again, princess."

He bows to me. I guess since they're friends I should warm up to him.

"Is she still not talking?" he guesses.

"Afraid so."

"We just need to focus on getting her well. I came to say that the...memorial will take place this weekend."

The memorial? So everyone is finally accounted for. They can finally rest. But what if the killer is waiting. What if he wants to kill me so everyone can see.

"Are you alright?" Kyoya-sama leans back to me. "I'll be with you the whole time."

I nod to him. I think I better go back to my room.

"Are you feeling ill? Ayato-san will escort you back. Don't worry."

That's a good idea. His hand lingers on mine as I walk away. I nod my head intensely. I can't go back there. I can't. I don't want to remember. Kyoya-sama puts his arms around me to keep me from shaking. I don't want to see that man again.

He hugs me gently petting my head. Someone thirsty for power wouldn't bother. With him close, everything will be fine.

THE LAST PRINCESS

"I'm sorry I brought it up, sir," Captain Saki says.

I need to tell them everything I saw. If I express my fear, maybe they can help me. If only I could talk again. There's no use waiting. Kyoya-sama's eyes look so worried. He's afraid I won't get better. I really don't know what's wrong with me. I don't cough or sneeze, I just feel weak all the time. I gently push him away and nod to him.

His fingers linger on my cheek and touch my bandage.

"I'll escort her out," Captain Saki tells him.

He reaches out his hand to me as I reach the door. They're friends; I must remember that. I take his hand and he guides me back down the hall.

"If you're worried about going back, I assure you it's safe. No harm will come to you."

He figured it out. I don't want to stress Kyoya-sama with my account of the attack. I'll have to tell Kantarou-sama about it.

We get to my room and the guard opens the door. I step in and walk quickly to the night table. I'm so thirsty.

"Can I ask you something?"

I turn around quickly. I didn't think he would follow me in. I step away from the bed and sit down at the chess table.

"Did you see who did it? Everyone's afraid to talk to you about it but if you could give a description it could help us out a lot."

Should I tell him? I look at him and he stares at me intently as if gauging my honesty even before I say anything. Kantarou-sama said only to discuss the details with him or Kyoya-sama.

I heard the man's voice and saw his shape. That's not enough to say I know who did it. I thought about it before. The killer told me to stay in one spot so that I would be found, but given the size of the woods, I would only be found if he led them to me. Like a trail or…

I shake my head and he sighs.

"Sorry to bother you with it."

I have to talk to Kantarou-sama quickly. I think the killer is close to us. Either in the Han military or the Morinaga military.

"Well get some rest," he says to me.

I wait for the door the close then quickly run to my pad. I have to write down everything. I'll write my account and my suspicions. But can I trust Kantarou-sama? He's an active military member. I should run it by Kyoya-sama first.

Chapter 29: Kyoya

I found peace long enough to fall asleep but it's interrupted. What's with the banging? I didn't plan another catastrophe. I'm too tired to put my robe on. I open the door and she stands with her fist about to knock again.

"Is something wrong?" I ask her.

She's supposed to be resting. How did she even find my bedroom? I look out into the hall. I guess she figured it out on her own. I move aside and let her in.

"Go lay down," I tell her.

She sits on the bed and I join her. I'll sleep with her again. I try to get underneath the blankets and she stops me with her hands.

She scribbles on her pad and hands it to me.

"I need to talk to you," I read aloud.

She scribbles again.

"I want to tell you about that night," she writes.

I didn't think she would bring this up.

She digs underneath her stack of papers and hands me a folded piece of paper. This is her account of the night.

"I know who it is," she writes.

THE LAST PRINCESS

She knows who it is? I'm getting nervous. She can't remember. If she knows Ayato-san's face then it's easy to connect it to me. My hands are shaking just holding her account. In the dim light I see her searching into my eyes.

She's so strong in all this, much stronger than I thought. She put aside her sickness and her fear to investigate on her own.

"You don't need to worry about this," I tell her. "Kan-nii is leading the investigation. He has our best men on it."

She touches my hand and urges me to read her account. I'm afraid to. She brought this to me because she trusts me.

I open up the paper and read on. She talks about how there were screams…a guard carries her away and….a man with a blade dragging behind him is on a hunt. He kills her guard and stabs at her head. He scrapes the blade from her eye to her chin and she stabs him near his chest.

I look up at her and she's focused on the paper. I read on and she talks about how she wakes up with him washing her blade in the creek. He returns it to her and she grabs his mask.

He sealed her voice to keep her from screaming and explicitly said to wait until someone found her. She feels as though she was found in less than an hour. Now she's making a deduction. Sealing her voice and making her wait in a creek to be found. She thinks he lied about watching over her and led the search party to her.

"So you think it was Ayato-san?" I say out loud.

She nods. Damn it! She's too damn smart.

"Setsuna-san, I hope you haven't shown this to anyone else."

She shakes her head.

"I'm a bit disappointed with you."

Her eyes open up shocked with my words. I have to take her off the trail.

"Ayato-san is my friend and a captain in the Han Army. He's part of division that guards the palace and everyone in it. That includes you."

She shakes her head again.

"He's also an expert tracker which is why I sent him to Morinaga under my orders."

Now she's feeling bad. She lowers her head and I touch her shoulder. I'm sorry to do this. She's absolutely right but I can't allow this to continue.

"I know you want to solve this but it's not up to you to solve. I'm glad I know what happened that night but you need to forget."

Just forget and things can get better. If she forgets then her sickness will go away and she can be happy again. I pet her hair and she covers her eyes to cry. I made her feel bad about her accusations.

"Trust me a bit more," I say to her.

She won't stop crying. I lean down to get a look at her face. Her crying sounds painful since she can't speak. I hold her to my chest.

"I'm not upset at you. I don't want you to think of these things."

I need to distract her. I look around to find something but focus in on her face. It must be cause of her trying to talk.

"Your cut opened up."

It should be healing by now. I move her hand away and peel the bandage off. It hasn't even scabbed. It looks a fresh red. What the hell did he have on that blade?

"Just relax and you can get a fresh bandage tomorrow."

I turn away to shut off the light and she isolates herself at the other end of the bed. I see her jerk slightly. She's still crying. There's only so much I can do. I have no idea what's going on in her head. No matter what, I can't let her suspect me. I want to put all this behind us and be a king. I want her to smile again.

I knew this would be hard on her. Hopefully the hard part is over. At least I don't have any more plans.

Chapter 30: Kantarou

Who invited all these damn cameras? Some stunt by one of father's men. They're all watching us as we make the trip to Morinaga for the memorial. I stand outside waiting for the others to leave the car.

"Commander, I'm at the ready."

THE LAST PRINCESS

She's certainly stepped up a bit. It's been awkward between us for some time. She confessed to me and I rejected her but when the massacre happened I was at her side through it. But now she's acting diligent and I never asked her to.

The cameras take notice of us and I step away. Kira steps out frowning followed by Kyoya. He helps Setsuna-san out and she grips his arm.

"Commander Niwa, I suggest we move quickly," a guard says to me.

"Her safety isn't in jeopardy."

She still continues to wear her veil. With the mystique she has about her no one would hurt her. She doesn't have a voice to hate.

It's not until we're on the plane that everyone starts talking.

"Setsuna-san should sit next to me," Kira says.

"Don't be so bossy, Kira," mother says. "It seems to me like she wants to stay attached to Kyoya."

"They've been spending too much time together-"

"You can sit with me, Kira-sama," Yumiko-san says to him.

"No, I have to discuss some things with you," I say to her.

"I'm sure it can be discussed another time."

"If so I wouldn't have made a point about it now."

"I know it's a two hour flight but I rather not be near you."

The nerve of that woman. I approach her and the little princess steps in the way. She pulls my arms and pulls me down between her and Kyoya.

"Isn't she a peacemaker, Kan-nii."

"Shut up."

I'll sit here to calm down. I reject her and she turns bitter. I forget how young she is. She pulls Kira to the next row and starts to giggle with him.

The jet takes off and everyone seems distracted with themselves.

"Setsuna-san," I say to her. "I trust you'll keep your tears to a minimum. This is the first time the public will see you…aside from that other day."

THE LAST PRINCESS

"Don't bother her," Kyoya says. "She can cry if she wants."

Why is she holding my arm? She's gotten entirely too comfortable with me.

"She told me she likes you a lot. Perhaps you should tell her how you feel about her."

I'm sure he's doing this for a reason. She looks up at me smiling.

"I love you."

She looks shocked.

"What's wrong with you?"

"Well what do you want me to say?"

"Tell her the truth."

"Well...I don't mind you as much as I thought I would, little princess."

She hugs my arm.

"When she's able to speak again, she wants to call you "Kan-nii" too," he says to me.

She nods enthusiastically.

"That would be...fine."

"Setsuna-san, why don't you go sit with Kira. I know he enjoys your company."

She nods and moves away.

"What's with all that?"

"Read this," he says handing me a folder piece of paper.

I read it and quickly look up at him. She figured it out. How is this possible?

"I don't want her to suspect you so try being a little nicer. And as far as Ayato-san, he already knows his part. I don't know how but find who did this."

He looks over at me. I get it. I nod in agreement. We need a fall guy.

"She gave that to me a few nights ago. I've been trying to distract her ever since."

"Distract her how?"

He's quiet for a moment. Did he give her stickers or control of the remote. Anything would work on her.

"I let her look at the old albums. Mostly your old albums."

"I suppose we all have to sacrifice. Is that why she's holding on to me so much?"

"She's our family now. She was distracted enough with the notion. But I can't stand being near her."

"Doesn't look that way."

"After the memorial, I'm staying behind to start my position and I wanna have you with me. Kira will keep her busy."

"I'd watch out for him. He has the intention of stealing her from you."

"Are you serious?"

"A twelve year old boy discovering his body would be perfect for her. He can answer her questions," I warn him.

"You're trying to make me laugh."

"Just watch him."

"I'm not worried about little Kira."

Chapter 31: Kira

She's just as good at computer chess. I can't beat her. She laughs each time she wins.

"I wonder what they're talking about," Yumiko-san says.

"Leave us alone and go find out."

"They always seem up to something."

THE LAST PRINCESS

Setsuna-san takes the tablet from me. If she's so curious she should just leave. I'm trapped between the two of them. She's obviously lusting after Kan-nii. That's why she keeps touching her shirt buttons.

I hear a shutter sound. Oh, she just found the camera. She points at me and then herself.

"She wants to take a picture with you," Yumiko-san says.

"Huh? Me?"

"She never got to take photographs, she's just excited."

We take a photo together and she stares at it. We don't look bad together. Before I can speak she jumps up and runs back to Kyo-nii.

I like her. I like her a lot. But she only sees Kyo-nii. If she would just open her eyes, she would see me too.

"I wish her voice would come back. But…she's taking it all better than I thought," Yumiko-san says.

"Okay, just one more picture," I hear Kyo-nii say.

I can't stand him. I get up and walk to the back of the plane. Mother and father are hugging like normal.

"Something wrong, dear?" mother asks.

"Can I talk to father, please."

He releases her and she walks to the front.

"What is it, son?"

"I want Setsuna-san."

He lowers his head and sighs.

"If Kyo-nii won't step down then I'll step over him."

"Try to understand the princess' feelings a little. She just had a terrible thing happen to her. All her life she's been told that Kyoya will care for her. She needs him and she loves him-"

"Cause she was told to."

THE LAST PRINCESS

"It's not cause she was told to. She loves him and he loves her. You can see that, right?"

"But-"

"And she really likes you…as a friend. Don't hurt the princess and don't betray your brother by doing this."

"It's not fair for her to not know. If she knows she has a choice then I know she would choose me."

"And are you capable of leading her country. That's never been your course of study but it's always been his."

He won't even encourage me. He's saying I'm not good enough. I'll stay quiet for now. I know Kyo-nii isn't right for her. I'll make her see it first.

"I'll step down," I say to him. "Sorry."

Kan-nii encouraged me but he said I have to make myself be seen as a man in her eyes. I'll make her see me. I go back to the front of the plane. She still hasn't come back from his side.

"Kira, sit her a moment. Don't worry about your brothers," mother says.

Yumiko-san is crying again. We are heading to a memorial. So I guess there's reason to be sad. I sit down on Yumiko-san's side. Since she's been here she's been a pain but, she's also been very pleasant to me. When I touch her shoulder she starts to wail louder and the others notice. Setsuna-san runs over and they start hugging. What use am I? I don't know what to say.

"Setsuna-chan, how can I look at them again?"

Setsuna-san tries to speak but only whimpers. Mother looks on close to tears. I see Kyoya stand. I have to be a man in her eyes; if I take care of Yumiko-san then she'll know I care for her family.

I grab Yumiko-san from her and hug her across the seat.

"Don't worry; you're not going through this alone."

She stays quiet. After some time she pulls herself away and wipes her tears.

"You're like family so you're not alone, Yumiko-san."

"T-thank you."

THE LAST PRINCESS

Setsuna-san smiles at me. That's exactly what I wanted. It won't take long.

Chapter 32: Yumiko

That was unexpected. That little Kira-sama is gonna be dangerous when he gets older. He made me blush for a moment. Being in the sky again made me think about my first time flying. It was the last time I saw my aunt and uncle. I wish I would have said goodbye appropriately. Since my parents left me, they've attempted to treat me like a daughter. But I could never make them proud, Setsuna-chan either. I don't like that kind of regret. It's the regret I can't fix.

We should be landing soon. Setsuna-chan has fallen asleep next to me. Kira-sama is asleep next to her. When I was crying, I hoped that Kantarou-sama would help me.

He rejected me but hasn't acted any different since then. I've been the one afraid to get back to normal. And really his reason was good. If we started dating people would get the wrong idea. But if he really liked me, he would find some way to fix it.

"Hey."

I look up. He stands in the aisle ushering me to him. I guess he wants to talk. I really would like to speak to him normally. I get up slowing and follow after him. He goes to the luggage room and closes the door behind me.

"Are you going to be okay when we touch down?" he asks.

"I don't know. I was thinking about the last time I saw them. They were on my back so much about doing my best while in your care."

"I made that promise to your cousin. And I suppose if you don't have anywhere to go back to, you'll still be in my care."

He walks pass me and sits on a trunk. I think he's being sweet to me. He seems exhausted. He's been doing a lot lately. He's been trying to catch the murderer while in his own country.

"You've been trying to convince the Morinaga military to take your ideas," I say to him. "Is it not going well?"

"They're stubborn. I tried reaching out to your father thinking he would ally with me-"

THE LAST PRINCESS

"My father? I wouldn't give you any leverage with him."

"You're mistaken. He wants to help me. He wants to help me because of you."

My father still cares about me? He still remembers me?

"He's allowing me to meet with some of the other higher ups so they can hear my ideas."

"That's great," I tell him. "You're so accomplished."

"I want you to come with me. If you can be seen with me, I'm sure people will stop talking down to you."

So that's what he wanted to discuss.

"That would have happened on its own but-"

"I will go anywhere with you, commander."

"It's good you understand. During the memorial…"

I try to look into his face but he turns away. He's shying away from me.

"I know it will be tough for you and Setsuna-san," he continues. "She will no doubt hold on to Kyoya….you can hold on to me if you want."

"Why are you acting so shy?" I ask him. "This isn't like you."

"I just didn't want you to cry again."

"I could never cry around you. I have no reason to."

There's silence. I appreciate every word he said. I'll follow him. I need to do something to distract myself from all this. My father will likely be at the memorial. I am hoping my mother might show up too. It's a broken family but it's my family.

"I had planned this for you for some time. It's your choice if you want to go through it or not."

He hands a letter to me. I open it cautiously and the first words make me gasp. "Accepted"

"You…you got me into college."

THE LAST PRINCESS

"It's one of the most prestigious universities in Han. You can study what you want but don't forget your duty to me."

"Commander…"

I never thought I was good enough for college but he does. I never thought I was good enough for anything but he sees something in me that I don't.

"Thank you," I say to him.

"I'm not all bad."

"I never said you were bad."

I smile at him. If I gain confidence then he'll know I can handle the burden; we can be together.

"And there will be suitable men for you to date," he states.

Date? He says it so nonchalant. He says it feeling nothing for me. He's a damn idiot. Same as me for liking him. I drop the letter and head to the door.

"Yumiko-san-"

"I'll go so let's not speak about it anymore."

I slam the door and run to the bathroom. Why? Why can I never been seen as worthy? There's a heavy knock on the door.

"Leave me alone!"

"Yumiko-san?"

It's Kyoya-sama's voice. I crack the door leaving my head down.

"What did he do to make you so upset?"

His voice is always so gentle. He's always so caring.

"He got me into college," I say to him.

"You poor thing-"

"He's sending me away to get over him. He rejected me again."

It's quiet with just the sound of snores and jet engines. I shouldn't be talking to a prince from inside the bathroom. I step out and wipe my eyes.

THE LAST PRINCESS

"I'll never understand what you see in my brother but did he look at you when he said those words?"

"No, he didn't."

"Then it's hard for him too. If he lets on that he likes you, he thinks you'll be taken away. That's how he's always been. He's been trained to not have a weakness; so he's detached."

He stands with his arms crossed. My problems must be stupid to him. He sighs and I'm alerted that he's so casual.

"A lot will change after this memorial. I'll be staying behind, you'll be going to college in a few months-"

"Staying behind?"

"Yes, I must."

He looks over at me. I don't see how a foreign king can accomplish anything when his only claim to the throne is an engagement.

"That will leave Setsuna-chan all alone," I say to him.

"I'm aware....but I'll make sure she never feels lonely."

That's unfair. She'll just be trapped in another palace. I lower my head. The poor girl will be trapped again longing to see him. I don't even know if they are close to finding the people responsible for the massacre.

"I always wanted to say sorry to you since the night we learned about all this. I want to be a good king for you as well."

Those charming eyes and gentle voice. He's not a snake. He's truly genuine.

"Um...I'll support you."

"Thank you."

Chapter 33: Setsuna

I stand with Kyoya-sama on the stage looking at the hundred coffins sitting underneath us. So this is everyone. The guards, the maids, the cooks, and even mother and father. I talked to my father frankly and he said this would be a possibility. He made me understand his will and the will of all the kings before him.

Kyoya-sama can never fill father's shoes but I don't think father would mind if he tired. I'm the only survivor of that night. It had to be on purpose. I have to get father's will across.

"I didn't think there would be this many cameras," I hear him say.

He touches my head and I straighten my veil. So I'm supposed to just stand here and look sad. That's not what father would want. I pull on his sleeve and he kneels down to me.

"Something wrong?"

The coffins are spread along the palace lawn. Just outside the gates the cameras and people are waiting for the ceremony to begin. I point back to the house. There's no way for him to understand me. I start walking and he just walks behind me. We get to the front door and there's tape around it.

This is my house; I won't let it be a crime scene. I pull the tape off and forcefully throw it to the ground. This house is all I know; it's not a bad house, bad things just happened here.

I step inside and the blood is gone. That's good. I keep walking stopping at every room. I know where everything is. Everything is in its place but…there's just no people.

Kyoya-sama follows behind me silently.

"I'm glad we're alone, I wanted to talk to you about something."

I turn back to him. We're right near the room where we first met. I bet no one has fed the fish. I open the door and the pond is empty.

I sit down on the edge and he sits down next to me. I feel so comfortable around him, not like when we first met.

THE LAST PRINCESS

"I remember I met you here. You made me feel so nervous. You really were the most beautiful thing I had even seen. I never would have thought…I would fall for you, a girl eight years younger than me. I felt myself falling just from you saying my name that first time."

He's staring straight again. He must be about to say something to make me sad.

"I really like you, Setsuna-san and given what's happened I wanna stay by your side but…as much as I have a duty to you, I have a duty to your father and your people."

I agree. I know he has to take the throne soon, even if we're not married. The people will grow restless without a leader; father told me that.

"And also I don't want to make a mistake. We need to cool down a bit. Or I need to cool down a bit."

So he's just gonna start his duties. I know he can't babysit me.

"I'm trying to say that I'm staying behind and sending you back to Han. It may be years before we can be together again."

I look up at him. He can't stay away that long. I like him too much, that's the problem. I didn't give him room to breathe. I'll give him space. I pull on his arm and he refuses to look at me.

"I'm being cowardly by saying all this to you when you can't talk back. I'm sorry."

I try to call out his name but nothing comes out. I wanna speak again.

"Be a good girl," he says. "I need to do this. It will hurt me too, being apart from you. I have to do this so that what happened here will not happen again. Hear me as your future king and your future husband, do you understand?"

I release him. Father would say something like that. This must be why he chose Kyoya-sama. He blindly puts his arm around me.

"I love you," he says to me. "And I'll love you even more when I meet you again."

I try to keep my tears from him. I wipe my eyes on my sleeve but he notices quickly. He pulls me to his chest and I cry. I don't want him to leave me. I've been alone for so many years waiting for him.

113

THE LAST PRINCESS

"If you were to say "don't go" or "please stay" you would cripple me. That's why we have to do this now."

I can't even tell him "I love you." If I don't say it, he won't know. I try my hardest to speak and it just comes out as a scream.

"Don't push yourself. I'll hurry and fix things here so we won't be apart too long. And I'll have Kan-nii helping me so things will go faster."

If Kantarou-sama is here with him that means Yumi-chan will leave too. They're in love after all.

"And I'm going to put Captain Saki in charge of you so try to get along with him."

Because they're friends. I don't want to burden Kyoya-sama. I have to be strong so he won't worry about me. I nod to him. I wipe my tears again and he leans down and kisses me.

"Don't kiss anyone else, okay," he says to me.

He should do the same.

"I'm gonna head back out. Take your time."

He gets up and I'm left alone like before. I wish I could talk to mother. I want her advice. I wonder if she ever cried when father stayed away. I never saw her cry so, she was just being strong.

"You must never burden your king; you must only encourage him," she would say.

She may have been harsh towards me but she was only trying to prepare me.

"It's easier when you're not in love," I heard her say. "But when the man you love is away from you, it makes you feel like a common woman. But you must be strong to make him strong. Because you're the only thing making him feel like a common man. Remember that, Setsuna."

It was one of the rare times she let her hair down and let me brush it. I touch my own hair ornaments. It's all passed down between generations. These robes and hair ornaments are a representation of her. She's here with me.

"That was quite a scene."

THE LAST PRINCESS

I turn back. No....how could he. He takes a step forward with his heavy boot vibrating the floor. Where's Kyoya-sama?

"I'm sorry your lover is parting from you. You seem so sad."

It's the killer from that night. He would come back into this house on the day of the funeral. There's a hundred coffins outside and he walked pass them to get to me; he felt nothing.

"I'm not here to hurt you," he says lifting his hands up. "I came to see how you were."

He takes another step closer to me. I know he's not going to kill me. He just wants to intimidate me. I turn back and look at the empty pond. He sits down right where Kyoya-sama was.

"You're still weak. I saw you wobble on stage. You'll just get weaker cause you're losing even more people now."

I can't let it break me. He passes a jar to me.

"It's for your wound. Use this every night to make it heal. Make sure no one sees you do it."

I take it from him. Why is he trying to help me now?

"And I came to give you your voice back."

I turn to him quickly. I'd be able to tell Kyoya-sama how I feel.

"But in exchange, I still expect your silence."

I get my voice back but I can never say who did this. I have to talk again but to live with the guilt of silence is too much.

"You want to talk to you lover one last time, don't you?"

I nod.

"Then you agree?"

I nod. I stumble back when he lifts his hands to me. He pauses then comes at me again. He turns down my collar exposing my neck. I close my eyes then feel a sharp pain like a needle. He replaces my collar and gets up.

I try to speak but still nothing.

THE LAST PRINCESS

"Give it a few hours and you'll be back to normal."

Hopefully I get to stay by Kyoya-sama until my voice returns. I get up and straighten my robe.

"You're going back to Han afterwards, right? I'll try to pay you a visit."

He walks to the door. I still need answers from him. I run forward and grab his arm. I need to talk to him. He stops and I look around for paper. The room is completely empty.

"I can read lips so go ahead and speak," he says.

"Why? Why did you do this?" I mouth to him.

"Things will be better now, don't you think? For all you know, I did it for you, little princess."

"I never met you before," I mouth to him.

"But…we can go on meeting now."

He touches my chin and I move away.

"I'll never hurt you; you can get that out of your head."

He's confusing me. Killing all the people in this house did not help me. It made me hate being the only survivor.

"What is your name?" I mouth to him.

"Call me whatever you want."

"Are you Captain Saki?"

"Captain Saki?" he repeats. "Do you want me to be?"

I don't want to be correct about my assumptions. I just want to know who this man is.

"Don't make another grab for my mask," he says.

I was thinking about it. I don't want to be alone with him anymore. I want to be next to Kyoya-sama again. He takes a step back then leaves the room.

Chapter 34: Kyoya

This is incredibly boring. It's been going on for hours. I sit on stage with the princess and Yumiko-san while hundreds of citizens march through the yard observing the coffins. Both girls seem quiet. Probably trained not show emotion at a time like this.

I thought this would break them but it hasn't. Setsuna-san continues to amaze me. She doesn't even seem fazed by her second meeting with her parent's killer. I guess she can't speak just yet. I know she'll talk to me as soon as her voice returns.

What's she staring at off stage? She must still have it in her mind. She's staring at Ayato-san while he stands guard. I put my arm around her and she looks straight ahead.

"Kyoya-sama," Yumiko-san says to me. "Is she really okay with you staying behind?"

"There's not really a choice."

"She could stay with you while you work."

"It's safer for her in Han."

"Sounds to me like she'll just be locked up again."

"With a killer on the loose I think that's best."

And I don't want to touch her prematurely.

"She waited a long time for you. And she has so much grief now. Rethink this."

"Yumiko-san-"

"Do you not know how this looks? Just abandoning her and taking the throne-"

"I'm not abandoning her! Stay out of matters that don't concern you."

I put my head down quickly. I can't lose my cool now. I didn't kill them just for the throne, I did it be close to her. She's happy now, even if I don't get to be around her. I did it for her. For Setsuna-san.

THE LAST PRINCESS

She's staring at me with worry. Her small hand slides over mine with a tight grip. I can't lose it in front of all these people.

After the crowd passes through there's silence. Her hand falls away from mine and she stands up. The guards look uneasy. Is she going to speak now? She walks slowly to the end of the stage. Her parent's bodies are right beside her. The cameras flash capturing every moment.

She's braver than I thought. Probably even braver than me. She lifts her veil and there's a worldwide gasp.

"M-my name is Setsuna Asahina. My father was…my father is Hajime Asahina and…my mother is S-shouko Asahina: your king and queen."

Her hands are shaking along with her voice. She's speaking cause she feels a duty to her family. I can't stop her. It's making me sad to hear her voice again. I can hear her pain now.

"I was here on that night. I never left the palace except for that night when I had to run away. It was scary. I stared the killer in his eyes. I fought him and lost to him. He's still alive, probably content that somehow all this is going his way."

My heart sinks with her words.

"But the palace will not falter. Kyoya Niwa-sama is the man my father picked for me to marry and the man that will become Morinaga's king. He will take the position sooner than expected because I am fairly ill since the attack. I have faith in him. And I will guide him because no one knows my father's will and the will of all the kings before him more than me. So…"

She takes a deep breath.

"You will accept him. And I don't want any unrest. The Niwa family of Han were there for me and there for my family in this terrible circumstance. The Niwa family sheltered Yumi-chan. Without her I would have no one. Thank you Kantarou-sama for looking after her…They want nothing but the best for Morinaga…"

It's the first time she's spoken. She's very well trained. At the bottom of the stage I see Kan-nii standing guard with a smirk on his face.

"There was an understanding my father had with them. He explained everything to me. Han is different. It is a stronger nation that shows its power; they're arrogant, entitled but only cause they've earned it. It's a country that lost a lot of men because it doesn't back down from a fight. It's a country with a lot of pride. Kantarou-sama symbolizes his country very well; which is why he will be a wonderful king."

118

THE LAST PRINCESS

I watch her on the big screen. A smile spreads across her face.

"Morinaga is just as strong but doesn't like to show it. It's observant of others so that it can strategize in the best way. It's caring, calculating, subtle, and full of potential it has yet to show. Morinaga is just like Kyoya-sama. My father saw it, which is why he betrothed me to the second born and not the first or the third. I love Kyoya-sama like I love my country and that's why I know he'll make a great king."

I put my head down. Her father believed in me at such a young age. I killed him. I can't look at her. I can't look at any of them. She's smiling at me and I can't take it. Her words are too much right now. I look down at Ayato-san and he signals me to come forth.

I look back at her. She's so beautiful. She deserves so much and I took it all from her. She stares off into the crowd then looks stricken. They're not cheering for her. They're screaming in displeasure. She takes a tiny step back.

I get to my feet quickly and stand behind her.

"It's okay," I say to her. "You did well."

"Traitor!" I hear.

"No," she whispers to herself. "It's not supposed to be like this."

"Fucking traitor!"

She tries to take another step back but I stand still. The crowd is getting out of hand. I thought this was a funeral. Something shoots out of the audience and she's blasted with red paint. It slides down her face and soaks into her dress.

She looks to the open casket beside her and screams seeing the paint on her mother's face. I turn her to me and shield her. Kantarou jumps on stage deflecting the next paint bomb with his sword.

"Saki, right there," he calls out.

Ayato-san pushes through the crowd and snatches the man up by his collar.

"The Han military has no right to be here," a Morinaga soldier calls.

"Why don't you do your job then," Kan-nii calls back. "I will not let her own people do this to her."

I peek down and see her crying still. I walk her off stage and Yumiko-san takes hold of her. They'll be a riot between Han forces and Morinaga troops. I walk back to the microphone.

"What are you doing? They won't listen to you," Kan-nii tells me.

"They crossed a line so I'm going to cross it some more."

I can't stand this. I will not rule a pack of idiots. They will change now. She looked devastated. She has the courage to finally speak and they hate her for it. I can't allow anyone to make her cry like that. She's innocent.

"Your last princess shows her face to you and overcomes all her fear to speak and you call her a traitor!"

There's silence. Now is the time to show what kind of king I will be. I planned on being nice but not after seeing her cry and scream.

"Han has no right here!"

The crowd gets loud again. A rebellion? I didn't expect this. I think we just found the resistance that caused the massacre.

"We are still looking for the murderer that killed all these people. Anyone that speaks against the princess will be detained as a suspect and likely killed. And you Morinaga people have no tact; throwing red paint at a funeral and making your princess cry."

Ayato-san still holds the paint thrower.

"Kill him," I say to him.

He doesn't hesitate. He takes out his knife and slits the man's throat. That should fix things for now. The crowd roars louder and I step off stage. That's real power. That's what I wanted. Watching her tremble angers me. I admit I caused her grief with my plan but I will not allow any more to come to her.

Chapter 35: Yumiko

Never thought I would be back here again after what happened. There's no sign of an attack. With the crowd outside being unpredictable we took refuge in the palace. Setsuna-chan immediately went to her room and ran a bath. I sit at her side watching her take the paint from her ears.

"Are you really okay?" I ask her again.

"I'm fine," she says hoarse.

There's just the sound of water. Her screams are still in my head. I had no idea what to do. She was covered in blood once before and I'm certain this was a reminder. After she left the stage she turned cold. She's been taking everything so well. It can't be long before she lets it all out.

"Please talk to me," I say to her.

"There's nothing to say."

"You got your voice back so there must be something to say."

She shakes her head. If she won't talk then I'll just leave her alone.

"I'll go grab you another robe."

I get up and go to her bedroom. If it had been me, I would be crushed. What makes her stronger than me? I went through some of the same training. Up until my mother's scandal I was treated as an heiress. If anything were to happen to Setsuna-chan I would be the last princess. I was prepared for that. But I can't handle her burden. What is it about her?

"I figured you would be here. Same as always."

I turn to the door. A woman dressed in black steps forward. She's flashy with fur trim and dazzling diamonds. Gaudy, actually.

"Mother?" I guess.

I haven't seen her in years. I figured she would show.

"Always so supportive of little Setsuna."

"She's like my sister."

"If only...then you would be worth something."

"Why are you-"

THE LAST PRINCESS

"I only tease. You got your hands on the crown prince. That's a great come up."

She takes off her hat and I look away. I realize now why I never missed her. She walks around the room slowly examining anything worth money.

"Keep him close and you can be queen one day."

"I don't want to be queen," I tell her.

"Why not? You would have a legacy. You would have money and fame."

"I don't want that."

I just want Kantarou-sama. I don't want the prince or the future king or the commander. She's turned into such an opportunist since losing her royal status.

"I only stopped by to give you a bit of advice. You don't have to scowl at me, dear."

"I don't want your advice. Shouldn't you be more concerned about the loss of your brother?"

"My brother? You mean that prick, Hajime. The brother, the king, that turned his back on me. The brother that wouldn't even let me explain my circumstance. The same brother that exiled me. Fuck him!"

"That's enough," Setsuna-chan steps in. "I won't let you speak of him that way."

Setsuna-chan frowns across the room with just her towel. Mother went too far. Seems no one has respect on this day. I'm so embarrassed of my mother.

"Nice to see you again," mother says to her.

"It isn't. You were told to never enter this house again. Leave or I will have you escorted."

"No need to show fangs. I thought we were family."

"Not with those words you just spoke."

"Fine…don't be so touchy."

Mother slowly saunters out. I sit down holding my head. Even now when I am so shook up, my cousin is calm. She goes to her closet and picks out a robe. I never knew my mother was that bad. What turned her sour? What life has she been living since being thrown out?

"I know she's your mother but I don't like her," Setsuna-chan speaks.

"I know."

"Yumi-chan..."

I look over at her. She struggles putting on her robe. Her hands are trembling. I get up and run to her. I kneel down and tie her sash.

"I'm really sad but...I don't want to think about it. If I do, I'll break."

"I can always put you back together."

We will only feel sad for a moment and then we'll move on. Kyoya-sama is the one that makes her happy. Just the idea of him makes her happy. With him gone, there has to be something to take his place.

"I need to say my goodbyes to Kyoya-sama."

She sits down at the vanity and puts on her makeup. I don't think she'll ever let go of the traditions. Aunt would be so proud of her.

"I'm gonna head to my room and grab a few things," I say to her.

I should take some of the traditions with me too. I look back at her and she's silent going through the motions

Chapter 36: Ayato

It's not necessary for me to visit her again but she's becoming like a little project for me. I stand near her door and watch her cousin pass right by me. With the door open I glance in.

She has her back to me. I step in and close the door. Her head perks up then she turns sharply.

"Real blood suited you better," I say to her through the mask.

"What do you want?"

"Please continue with your regiment. I'll just observe."

THE LAST PRINCESS

She's gotten use to the masked figure. But she's very hard to read. She'll show a fear once but won't repeat it. She screamed for me to stop that night but when I visit her now, she says "what do you want," like I'm an annoyance.

That night she had the best screams. I didn't think they could escape out such a small body. She can definitely take the torture; I guess that's why I like her. I guess that's why I got carried away that night.

"Did you recover from your wound?" she asks.

The wound I got when she stabbed me in the chest. It still hurts. Luckily I'm not an ordinary man. Odd of her to inquire. I walk to her side and watch on as she delicately tries to cover up her own wound. Next she pins up her hair.

"Why aren't you afraid?" I ask her.

"You said you wouldn't hurt me. And you've already killed my family, what else could you do to me."

"Take away your lover."

She stops and lowers down her comb. Just a bluff. I could never get rid of Kyoya-sama. He's the only friend I have. I saved his life and that saved my own.

He came to me with his plan saying I was the only one capable and the only one he trusted.

"I...I wanna be king. I'm ready."

"You can't marry her until she's sixteen and even then you can't take the throne until her father dies."

"Well...I can't make her grow any faster but we can do the second part," he said to me.

I stared at him hard. Kyoya-sama isn't a killer; he doesn't think like one. He's not like me. I dismissed him two years ago. I refused to do it if it was on a whim but then he came back. He planned everything and was certain in his wishes. I had to make his wishes come true.

I had made captain and there was a lot at stake. If anyone found out then we would both burn for it. His family would be disgraced and forever labeled murderers. He planned it well, calculated everything. But he didn't count on this girl not being a naïve little girl. He didn't count on falling in love with her either.

"What do I have to do to stop that from happening," she says to me. "I'll do anything to protect him."

She tilts her head up to me. I don't know why I came here. There's no reason for me to see her again. But now I want to. I always admired Kyoya-sama and respected him. Right now....I wanna feel what he feels. I wanna know why this girl makes him feel so weak. He made me slit that man's throat. It wasn't part of any plan. He just had so much hate for the person that made her cry.

I wanna feel what he feels with her in his life. He keeps her ribbon in his pocket and smiles every time he looks at it. In that video...he showed so much tenderness. He wasn't the man I knew but I wanted to be that man too.

"Kiss me."

"Huh?"

What am I saying? Shock spreads across both our faces. She can't see mine.

"Your face is priceless. Like I would ever. I'll leave your lover alone so long as you keep your silence."

"You support him as king," she guesses. "Is that why you did what you did?"

So perceptive.

"Think whatever you want."

I walk to the door. I close it behind me and take a big breath. I can't take Kyoya-sama's place. I need to know my own. I said such stupid things in there. Good thing it's just between me and her.

Chapter 37: Kyoya

So this was his office. She told me he spent a lot of time here writing. His body was found here. Probably his last words were about sparing his daughter's life. If his soul still haunts this place then I'm sure he's standing next to me. He wouldn't curse at me but just shake his head in disappointment.

I'm not fit to take his place but I will. I don't know much about his country or the kings before him; I spent time learning about my own country's culture. And yet

THE LAST PRINCESS

I wanted to take over this place. I never tried to understand it deeply. I figured she would help me with that.

I walk around his desk and pick up the one picture frame he has. How fitting. It's a picture of Setsuna-san smiling. I can't believe she thought he didn't love her. I hope he told her before he died.

"Kyoya-sama."

I look up and see Ayato-san at the door. My loyal friend. Seems like he'll do anything I ask. He has no morals.

"Time to go?" I ask him.

"No...they're still ushering the crowd away."

"How come you didn't hesitate?" I ask abruptly.

"Hesitate?"

"When I told you to kill him."

"He harmed the princess. If you didn't tell me to I would have done it anyway. Probably not in public though."

I feel sad being here. It's wrong to walk through another man's palace. I could never live here. I'll have to have a new one built after the wedding.

"You seem distracted," he notices.

"I don't know what kind of king I want to be. I haven't figured that out."

"I think you know. You're just worried about being accepted."

"On stage I wanted to show my anger. I wanted to make an example of him. But Setsuna-san is so gentle. I wonder if she agreed. If you could have seen her face when she cried at my chest....you would know-"

"I get it. You'll kill anybody to make her see you as her savior. You like having that little girl in the palm of your hands."

She's not in the palm of my hands; I don't control her. I feel like she controls me. At this point I'll do anything she says to make it all up to her. He starts walking around the room. He touches the bookshelf and blindly plucks a book from it. It falls to the floor.

THE LAST PRINCESS

"He was where you were standing on that night. Standing right above his desk just like that when I entered."

He stops and slowly draws his sword. He looks at it amused then points it at me.

"I wanted to hear his last words so I stopped just like this. He quivered. He asked who I was and I told him, "Kyoya Niwa sent me to kill you so he may have the princess and the throne." And you wanna know what he said."

So he knew right before he died. I suppose that was fair. He knew why and he knew she would go on living.

"What did he say-"

"Kyoya-sama?"

He puts his sword away. The door creaks open and the princess steps in. She's cleared of the paint and put her makeup back on. I smile at her and she steps in happily until she sees him. She hides her smile quickly and moves towards the wall. She's still suspicious of him.

"How are you, princess?" he asks her. "It's nice to hear your lovely voice again."

"Um…"

"Setsuna-san, I already told you that Ayato-san is my friend. There's no need to act so scared of him."

"I know that-"

"And since I'll be gone for a while and my brother will be here too I'm leaving Ayato-san in charge of you."

She looks at me with worried eyes.

"I look forward to it, princess" he says to her.

"Can I speak with Kyoya-sama alone, please?"

"As you wish."

I don't want to be alone with her now that she can talk. I don't want to see her face either. I definitely don't want to be in this room. I walk towards the door and she grabs my hand.

THE LAST PRINCESS

"I always wanted to bring you here. I figured this would be your office one day."

"I don't want it."

"I know. Not after what happened. I didn't think I could walk around the house like normal but…with the blood gone…"

She holds my hand tighter.

"I know you must stay and I know I have to release you but I don't think I can make it without you."

Her voice starts to break and then she starts wailing louder with all her pain. I stand still. I know I'm supposed to hug her but I can't do it here. I have to get out of this room.

"He came to me again. Twice today. The killer."

Twice? I kneel down to her. Why would he come twice? I told him to give her voice back but why a second time?

"He came to you?" I ask her.

"Yes, I think he'll hurt you."

"No one can hurt me."

"He said if I told he'll hurt you but I couldn't keep it all in. I'm afraid of being apart from you. I'm-"

"No man can hurt me. The only one that can hurt me is you," I tell her.

She dries her eyes on her sleeves.

"And…the only one that can hurt me is you," she says back to me. "So that means I have nothing to worry about."

I nod to her. The worst is over with; there's no more I could do to hurt her. Well…leaving isn't helping. I have to talk to him before they all leave. I need to know why he paid her a visit without my knowledge.

"I feel a bit better saying that," she says. "You would never hurt me. And I should believe you when you say Captain Saki is a friend."

"Yes, he's a friend."

THE LAST PRINCESS

I need to get out of this room. I feel eyes on me. I grab her hand and pull her out. I need to get out of this house.

"Wait," she says to me.

She goes back in the room. It feels like that one room has the worst aura. She comes back and hands a book to me.

"This is father's journal. He wrote in it often. He never allowed me to read it. Only the successor can read the words of past kings. The other king's journals are archived but I think you should start with this."

I struggle to take it. His last thoughts are likely written here.

"Go on," she says to me. "Let father guide you."

"Um...I-"

"I know it's all very sudden for you. You didn't ask to take the throne so early. But I believe in you. I will wait patiently for your return."

I take the book from her. I have a lot to atone for. I thought I would be heartless when this time came. When I planned it all I figured I would step into place put on my royal robe and rule but I didn't count on her looking up to me.

"I look forward to meeting you again. Please stay as beautiful as you are."

I haven't been very honest with her but my feelings for her are real. They were real since the day I first saw her. I look forward to marrying her.

She smiles at me and I lean down to kiss her one last time. It doesn't matter what's around us; right now all I see is her. Her dead father can haunt someone else; he's not ruining this moment.

"I...wanted to say...I love you."

Immediately my skin tingles.

"I love you too, my princess. Is there anything you want from me? Just ask me and I will do it."

She shakes her head. Of course it wouldn't be that easy. I stroke her hair until I hear steps behind me.

"It's time to part," Ayato-san says to me. "The jet is ready."

THE LAST PRINCESS

"Is there no more time?" she asks me.

I suppose not. I think I said all I needed to say.

"I'll go get Yumi-chan so she can say goodbye to you."

She runs down the hall with her long sash behind her. Before he can move any further I grab Ayato-san's shoulder.

"I know how you are," I say to him. "She is not one of your play things. Do you understand?"

He nods to me.

"Why did you see her twice?"

"She told you-"

"Why? What did you say to her?"

If I can't trust him then I have to rethink everything.

"You know I would never go against you," he says to me. "I just..."

"I know what you want to say. Stop playing with her."

"You have my word. Sorry."

I release him. He's a strange man. I know he gets some sort of sick pleasure from killing people and tormenting. I have to believe he would never hurt her; he always keeps his word with me.

He knows I'm disappointed, I can see it in his face. I slap his shoulder to snap him out of it.

"I'll speak to you regularly to check on her."

Chapter 38: Setsuna

I hope he stays the same. I didn't want to mention the public execution. I figured he had his reasons. The wind blows fiercely as he hugs his parents and they board the jet first. Kantarou-sama is staying behind too but he refuses to hug. Yumi-chan is hesitant to hug Kyoya-sama but he grabs her first and I smile at their embrace. With Kantarou-sama she walks right by him.

"You have two weeks. I expect you back at work," he calls to her.

"Yes, commander."

"C'mon, let's get going," Kira-kun says taking my hand.

I can't go without saying my last goodbye. I pull away from him. He frowns at me but waits at the bottom of the stairs.

"Take care, princess," Kantarou-sama says to me.

"You too. Thank you for taking care of me."

"It won't be the last time, I'm sure."

"Don't give her a hard time," Kyoya-sama steps in.

We gaze at each other and I feel settled. With a nod I go on my way. Kira-kun walks me up the stairs to the jet and I'm careful not to step on my robes.

"Looks like you just have me now," Kira-kun says to me.

"I know I'm not alone. I have a new family now."

"Well, you and I aren't really family."

"I would like us to be."

I sit down and stare out the window. He sits next to me and Yumi-chan sits across giggling. I thought she would be sad too since she's leaving her love behind. Maybe it's different between them. Kyoya-sama walks off with his brother. I miss him already.

"Don't smother her, Kira," Tomoko-sama says to him.

"I'm not smothering her!" he calls back.

"Leave them be. They'll be separated soon enough," his father says flatly.

"What do you mean?"

"You'll be going off to the military academy soon."

"What! Who the hell said-"

131

THE LAST PRINCESS

"Kira!" his father quiets him. "It's not a choice you get to make."

"Both your brothers went. It doesn't mean you have to join the service," his mother says.

So he'll be leaving me too. Kira-kun doesn't strike me as the type to fight or pick up a weapon. He's not pleased to be going. Now that I can talk again I was hoping to be better friends with him.

He's always pouting when he doesn't get his way. I better cheer him up.

"We'll still talk; don't worry," I say to him.

"I rather talk in person. You just got your voice back."

"Maybe I can visit you."

"You'll have to visit often."

His mother looks on laughing. His father shakes his head while they go into their usual embrace.

"You'll be a man in a few terms," I guess.

And I'll still be trapped in a palace reading books. When will I get to see the world and be around people? I had thought meeting Kyoya-sama would change all that. Everyone still thinks my life is in danger.

"If I graduate from the academy, you'll see me as a man?" he asks me.

"Of course."

"I'll finish quick."

Yumi-chan starts laughing and he snarls at her.

"What's so funny?" he yells at her.

"Nothing, prince," she says.

"He has a motivation for going," his mother says. "How cute."

I don't get what they're saying. When we're in the air everyone settles down. I feel like my sickness has gotten better. I think the memorial helped even though it was a disaster. I saw my palace again just like I remembered it. I saw my parent's bodies and didn't feel any hate from them.

THE LAST PRINCESS

"Are you okay?" he whispers to me.

"I think so."

"I've been trying to understand you. I would be sad if I lost my home and my parents and was left all alone. I'll try to be more sensitive to you."

"But you have been-"

"No...I shouldn't have told you about my brother's whore."

Anki-san....I was hoping to forget about her.

"He won't be seeing her anymore since he's staying behind in your country. But I'm sure he'll find some others. And no one is there to tell you about it."

"He wouldn't."

"I should hope so."

He falls forward when Captain Saki smacks his head.

"Shut it," he says to him. "Stop putting those ideas in her head."

Kira-kun quickly gets to his feet to face him. He's too short to be intimidating. Kyoya-sama loves me. I have nothing to worry about. We didn't discuss that he would stay away from the whores but I just assumed he would.

"Go sit near your mommy," Captain Saki says to him.

With a touch of his sword handle Kira-kun walks to the back of the jet. Captain Saki takes the seat beside me sighing.

"Jealous prick."

"You can't talk to the prince that way."

"I can. I'm special like that."

"Cause you're Kyoya-sama's friend?"

"It's mostly because I'm not afraid of any consequence. It's nice that you're talking to me, princess."

"I'm sorry for doubting you."

"Why so afraid?"

THE LAST PRINCESS

"You remind me of the killer. I don't know what it is but you just do."

"I'm an excellent swordsman, maybe that's it. Kyoya-sama set you straight?" he asks.

"I trust him."

He didn't give any evidence but I just wanted to trust him.

"It's just gonna be the two of us for a long time. I want you to trust me too."

"I'll try."

"Can you start by looking at me then?"

I guess that's a good start. I turn to him and in his eyes I see it. I know it's him. Kyoya-sama says it's not. I have to get over this or I'll ruin their friendship with my suspicions. I have to try to see something else.

"Um…how did you meet Kyoya-sama?"

"Hmph, you really wanna hear that story?"

"Yes. I wanna know why he trusts you so much. Then maybe I will too."

"Very well. I'll start by saying when I was your age, I was in the same predicament."

What's he mean? I don't think he's a royal.

"I had my family taken from me too. Slaughtered in front of my eyes. If anyone knows what you're feeling, it's me."

"Did you see-"

"I saw him. I killed him. And I've been using the sword ever since."

"Not a gun?"

"You see, I liked the feeling of my first kill. I keep trying to get that feeling- that joy back again. So I keep using the sword. No one's been able to give me that feeling."

He reaches to me and touches my bandage with his glove. I wince. Is it bleeding again?

"But I'm getting close."

He's scaring me. How can Kyoya-sama be friends with someone like him? He talks about getting joy from killing people.

He pulls away from me.

"A little too close," he mumbles.

He turns away from me. I guess it's too much for him to continue. Captain Saki is strange.

Chapter 39: Kira

I really think father is doing this on purpose. Kyo-nii stays behind and keeps Kan-nii with him. I get the opportunity to be alone with Setsuna-san and now he wants to send me away. The military academy is four years. I'll be great at it, of course, but I'll miss out. I'll miss out on her.

It's been about three weeks since I got separated from my brothers. I don't miss them. They're both a pain in the ass. There's no one to smack the back of my head now.

It's my last night before I move to the academy. We already had dinner. Father lectured me about controlling my mouth when I meet my new teachers. He says these teachers won't do what I say. I'll be seen as a normal student and not a prince.

I was annoyed by it all at first but if I complete it she'll see me as a man. I got to be with her away from my brothers since we arrived back in Han. She doesn't seem like herself. She just stays in her room all day reading or hanging with Captain Saki.

I can't get any alone time with her; he's always around.

I stand at her door trying to decide what I should say. Confessing seems right but not if her mind is somewhere else.

I knock on her door and wait. Regretting it already.

"Kira-kun?"

"H-hey."

"I thought you would be asleep. You have to get up early tomorrow, right-"

THE LAST PRINCESS

"W-will you miss me?" I ask her shyly.

I'll miss her. I've known her a fairly short time but I would hope she might favor me just a little. When I go to the academy to be amongst all those teenage boys, I'll miss her smile. I'll miss playing chess with her and having someone on my level. Still haven't won against her.

"Yes, of course."

"What will you miss about me?"

She hesitates. I just wanted to feel something from her before I go.

"Your grumpy face."

"Huh?"

"And that face you just made. That's my favorite."

Her laugh is nice.

"Come with me," I say to her.

I take her hand and walk down the hall. Captain Saki can't be far. She says nothing as I pull her away; doesn't tell me to stop or ask where we're going. At each corner I look cautiously; he's gotta be near.

Maybe I'm just paranoid. I open the door to the outside and she stops.

"It's okay if you're with me," I tell her.

What's she staring at? The moon. It's hard to believe she's never been outside. I grab her hand again and lead her into the garden. I stop and sit in front of the big tree.

"I gave it some time cause I didn't want to bother him but I'm getting worried. Kyoya-sama won't answer my calls."

It's always about him.

"I didn't bring you here to talk about him."

"I figured you talked to him for advice or something. I just wanted to-"

"I don't care about him!"

THE LAST PRINCESS

She looks shocked at me. I just don't care about her and Kyoya. They should never exist together. I'm trying to talk to her and possibly tell her that I like her and she just wants to talk about him.

I take a deep breath. She's frightened.

"He's never gonna answer your calls. You already gave him what he wanted so why would he call you."

"C-cause he loves me."

"He doesn't love you. He just loves to use you. And because you wouldn't let him fuck you he's over there fucking every girl he meets. That's all he likes girls for. You're so stupid."

Maybe that wasn't the right thing to say. I said I would be more sensitive and I call her stupid. While I'm contemplating I see her running away from me through the garden.

She can't go without me. I get up and run after her.

"Setsuna-san!"

"Leave me alone!"

The garden is getting thicker. I have to catch up to her. I don't have a lot of experience chasing people. When she's close enough I dive and tackle her into the bushes.

"Get off me!"

I didn't mean to call her stupid and hurt her feelings. I don't know how to talk to girls. I never had one, never been near one. I lay on top of her. It's dark out but I can see every part of her face. Her eyes are my favorite. Her cheeks too.

I lean down and kiss her cheek and she bites her lip trying to hold back tears. Am I that deplorable?

"I like you," I say to her. "Stop being stupid and be my girl."

I stare at her and she stares at me for another reason. It makes sense that she be with me. There's no taking it back now. If I'm supposed to leave a boy and come back a man, I have to let her know my feelings.

"Answer me," I say to her.

THE LAST PRINCESS

"That's enough."

He's always nearby. Captain Saki grabs my collar and stands me up. The princess gets to her feet and grabs hold of his arm. She's wants to be with him over me.

"I'll get your answer when I come back."

"Let Kyoya-sama deliver her answer."

I don't care if he knows. I look back at her and she keeps her eyes to the ground holding on to him. I didn't win her this time but at least I succeeded in getting her attention.

"I like your red cheeks better," I say to myself.

Chapter 40: Kantarou

"You've been so quiet lately," I say to my brother.

"Been talking to myself mostly."

"About what?"

He's been drinking a lot. I rather him drink with me than drink by himself. We sit in his temporary office in the Capitol Building. It's been nonstop meetings since we got here.

"How is Kira doing? He left for the academy, didn't he?" he asks me.

"Surprising he didn't whine about it."

"He needs to be tougher. It should bring him out of that phase of his. I don't want him ending up like you."

He's so flat lately. His eyes are always half open. He takes another drink and I reach across his desk and take it from him.

"What's wrong with you?" I ask.

"You already know."

THE LAST PRINCESS

"You could have stopped it but you went through with it. You went through with the plan. You got everything you wanted. Be a man and accept it."

"I accept it. I'm a monster."

"No one knows except you, me and that weird friend of yours. You're not a monster, you're a king. Act like it."

I sit back down and take the drink for myself.

"Kira made a move on her," he says. "He confessed to her. He should have her. He's a good kid. Once he toughens up he'll be even better."

"I warned you about him. He told me he would take her from you."

"He's calculating; he picked the right time."

This is ridiculous. I can't stand to see my brother slumped down in a chair. We have a meeting with General Yamamoto soon. Only that little girl can fix this. She's his woman so she'll know what to do.

I pull out my phone and call mother.

"Kantarou!" she says into my ear.

"Hello, mother. Put the princess on the phone."

Kyoya's eyes finally open. I put the phone on speaker. He turns away from me but keeps his ears open.

"The princess? She's off with her bodyguard picking flowers."

What a girly thing to do.

"She would love to speak with you. The therapist says she seems sad."

"Why is she still seeing the therapist?" Kyoya asks.

"Uh-is that Kyoya? She would love to speak to you too. I'll have someone fetch her."

I knew he would be curious. It's been six months since he left. Hasn't talked to her since. He won't lose his strength while I'm here. If he wants to become a king before me then he better give me something to light a fire under me.

There's a knock at the door. It must be time for that meeting.

139

THE LAST PRINCESS

"Stay here and speak with her. I'll stall them."

I get up and head for the door.

"Kyoya-sama, I missed you so much. How are you? How is your brother?" Setsuna-san says over the phone.

I look back. He holds the phone in his hand like he's about to talk. He bites his lip and breathes heavily. Can guilt really do this? He has the ability to make everything fine and take all her sadness away. When she's fine he'll stand and lead. But he won't even try.

"Kyoya-sama?"

He throws the phone against the wall. He still can't talk to her. His hands are shaking. All his resolve is crushed.

"Go on. Stall them," he says to me.

I open the door and step out. The princess changed him. I warned him not to care about her. Kissing her was a mistake and caring about her wellbeing was useless. For men like us women are just things for entertainment.

"Afternoon, commander."

Or in my case, I have this. Not really sure what to do with her now. Yumiko-san stands in uniform saluting me. Not sure why I kept her here.

"General Yamamoto has arrived. He's in conference room three."

"Have you greeted him?" I ask her.

"No, I didn't plan on it."

"How long has it been since you've seen your father?"

"Uh...seven years. I already told you, I'm nothing to him."

We start walking. With all the royals in the ground, the people will look for the outcasts to rebuild the royal family. Yumiko-san will be worth something soon. The general may not be her biological father but I'm sure he cares about her.

"Nervous?" I guess.

"A little. Shouldn't Kyoya-sama be coming with us?"

THE LAST PRINCESS

"He'll catch up. Don't say anything unnecessary. Your job is to support me."

Seems she's not use to people clearing a path when I come down a hall. The respect around here has improved. I'm about to orchestrate the capture of the masked man that did the massacre. It's gonna be big. When these hicks know Han men bring results they'll let Kyoya do anything.

We get to the door and she stops. One more step and she'll see him. Too soon, I suppose. Her head stays down and I touch her shoulder.

"It won't take long. Have coffee waiting for me."

"I'll get right on it, commander."

She runs off down the hall. I'll miss her scurrying away. It's best she leaves and find some other man to play with. She deserves better. She's no queen of mine. I couldn't do that to her.

I open the door.

"Commander Niwa, good to meet you."

"You too, General Yamamoto."

"Did you want decaf or…"

I turn around and Yumiko-san stands at the door shocked. Her eyes stay on him with her mouth wide open.

"Yumiko," he says to her.

"Sorry to interrupt. I will prepare both."

"Wait," I say to her. "Don't be rude."

She shakes in the doorway. I examine him closely. He doesn't dislike her like she thinks. Wait a minute…his eyes are watering.

"N-nice to see you again, sir," she says bowing to him.

"It has been a long time. You look well."

"T-thank you, sir."

THE LAST PRINCESS

"You're very lucky the commander took you under his care. He's doing a fine job."

"You can leave now," I say to her.

She runs away quickly. He turns from me quickly taking his sleeve to his eye. I knew it would get to him.

"She was scared to see you again. She thinks you don't like her," I say to him.

"What happened was out of my control. She stayed in the palace and I couldn't. It's nice to see she's doing okay. I hope she hasn't been a burden to you."

"Not at all. We get along well. Soon enough we'll be family."

"Yes, when your brother marries Setsuna-san. Is he running late?"

"Just finishing up a call."

We take our seats. After some time Kyoya comes in. He sits next to me without a word.

"Hello, prince."

"Sorry for being late. I had to follow up on some intel."

"What kind?" the general asks.

"Kantarou will explain."

I guess it's time to start the show.

"Highly confidential," I say to him. "We found the murderer, the one responsible for the royal massacre."

"Found him? Isn't it a group?"

"It was one but he's being guarded as a sort of hero in the lower district known as Highland Row-"

"I want it burned," Kyoya speaks. "The entire district. It will help cut down on our crime rate since that place holds all type of criminals."

"Yes, there are drug dealers and thieves. They can be trailed not burned."

"I'm the king so we do this my way."

"But your reputation-"

"I want people to know that I'm a person that kills anyone that harms my princess."

"But that's close to two thousand people," the general says. "Do you really want to avenge the people that died in the royal massacre by causing a massacre of your own?"

Now is the time to make his choice. What kind of king will he be? With all the guilt he's facing, how will he respond. He can continue wallowing in regret or go forward like the monster that started all this.

"Tell him the killer's name," Kyoya says to me.

I take the photo from my pocket and slide it across the table.

"He's just known as Yee," I say to him.

He's our fall guy.

"I want him brought to me so he can confess. His dwelling examined and his district burned for hiding him," Kyoya says to him. "Can you do this or do I have to bring in my own men."

The general looks at the picture. I look over at my brother. He's pretty convincing. After this he'll be cemented as a leader. The general will have his back and the citizens will grow to respect his cruel ways.

"I'll make arrangements. Once we talk to this man then we'll decide how to punish his district. Maybe we can meet in the middle."

A smile spreads across my brother's face.

Chapter 41: Setsuna

The day is coming. I'm so happy. When I turn sixteen everything will get better. I can leave the palace and explore the world. Maybe even get a job and spend my own money. I've been alone here for a long time. Everyone else is away bettering themselves.

THE LAST PRINCESS

Yumi-chan is in school. She's doing well and calls often; I can't ask for anything more than that. Kira-kun is at the academy. He sends me letters and I write back pleasant responses. I don't know how to talk to him anymore. I feel so confused about what he did. That night I was happy to see the moon with him but he was so mean. He put tons of doubt in my head that I have yet to get over. The kiss…was unexpected.

I felt so tarnished but couldn't tell anyone. I feel like I'm the one that's been unfaithful. It's better to forget it. He said he liked me but I'm sure he's gotten over it.

I see Kantarou-sama often. He visits me and allows me to talk to him more. He sounds like he's gotten stronger from doing his work in two countries. He's more familiar with politics and acting like a leader. I see Kyoya-sama too but just on the television. I watch all of his appearances. It's the only time I get to see him.

For three years Kyoya-sama hasn't said a word to me. I call him and he ignores it. I get someone to call for me and as soon as he hears my voice he leaves on important business. What could I have done wrong? My worried face would just alert everyone.

Since I lost my parents and had to abandon my palace, the Niwa family has been nothing but nice to me. They even scold me when I do something wrong. But when I am close to sadness, they are quick to worry; probably fear I will get sick again.

Kyoya-sama said that he would work hard so we could be together soon. There was this big report a few years ago about how he caught the murderer. A man named Yee hiding in a lower district. I knew it wasn't the real killer. That man entered the royal house on the memorial day and no one seemed to notice. He wouldn't be hiding in a lower district or caught. I bet he's in Han, still watching me. I can't prove it was Captain Saki; I let go of those suspicions after spending time with him. He's my closest friend now.

Captain Saki speaks highly of Kyoya-sama. He tells me all the time about how busy the soon to be king is. I believe it but Kyoya-sama said he loved me. I just don't get how he can stay so far away from the person he loves. I write him letters and try to pass messages through Kantarou-sama but I get no response. I'm sure he'll come to my sixteenth birthday party. Then we can clear all this up, whatever the misunderstanding is.

"Uh-I told you about coming here. This is no place for a girl."

He finally shows up. Captain Saki has been by my side since Kyoya-sama left. He's someone I can count on. I was waiting in his room for him. He doesn't like when I visit the barracks.

THE LAST PRINCESS

"So you were in the shower," I guess.

The towel around the waist is a good indicator. He's not shy about it. He goes to his closet and drops the towel. I immediately shut my eyes.

"How did you get in here anyway?"

"What you're doing is really uncalled for," I tell him.

"It's my room."

"But I'm sitting right here."

"Just give me a sec."

He's entirely too comfortable. With everyone gone he's been my playmate. He watches shows with me and takes me on walks. I can leave the palace just not the palace walls. It's been a big improvement. He doesn't seem to have much of a life outside of guarding me. He goes on small assignments but he's never away too long.

"Something wrong?" he asks me.

"My birthday is coming up soon."

"I know."

"I was hoping we could try calling Kyoya-sama again. I want to invite him to the party."

I open my eyes. Good, he's clothed.

"I'm sure he's busy," he tells me.

"I wanna try. Please."

"Fine, but let's get you out of here first."

If he answers I'll speak fast. I just wanna see him. That's the only gift I want. We leave the barracks and walk along the garden path. This time will be different. I won't mention that I miss him.

He takes out his phone and dials.

I hold it close with two hands.

"Hello."

THE LAST PRINCESS

It's him!

"K-Kyoya-sama, it's me Setsuna."

"I don't have time-"

"Please wait! Please. I just wanted to…"

He's gone. I needed this. I needed to speak with him. I doubt his love for me. My head drops and I try to hold back my tears.

"He's just really busy."

"No, he just doesn't want to talk to me. I wish I knew what I did wrong."

"Nothing," he says to me. "You're perfect. You've always been perfect."

"So I guess he's the one that changed then."

It must be another woman. I get up and run back to my room. I'm such an idiot.

"Oh! Setsuna-san, I'm glad to see you," Tomoko-sama says.

I was almost there. I keep my head down to the queen. She tries to peek in to see my face but I avoid her.

"I wanted to tell you that we'll be having two birthday parties."

"Why's that?"

"Kira's birthday is in a few months so we will celebrate your birthdays together. Should be fun, right? He'll be coming home soon."

I have to see him? I haven't seen him since that night.

"Um…that's great. I need to get to the bathroom. I'm sorry."

I run pass her. Before I get to my room I pass Kyoya-sama's office. The door is always locked. My father's office was his most private place. He said it held all types of explanations.

I try the door again and it opens. That's odd; it really should be locked. The darkness is chilling. I step inside and close the door behind me. He was in this room more than anywhere else. This room probably holds the key to his way of thinking.

THE LAST PRINCESS

With the light on it still feels chilling in here. This room hasn't been used in three years; maybe that's why it's haunting. Books here range from war tactics to botany. I had no idea he likes plants.

Oh! This one is about computer systems. I had no idea he had an interest in software development. It's like I don't know him at all. Never had the chance to spend time with him and figure these things out.

I sit down at his desk. It's relaxing. I wanna believe his presence is here. I wanna believe he's the good person I made him out to be.

Pulling out his drawer I see the peach envelopes and folded up letters. He kept them. I can't believe he treasured them. Sorting through them I find my first one. I was seven when I wrote this.

"Dear Kyoya-sama, my name is Setsuna," I read aloud. "Please be nice to me. I want a friend."

That's all I wrote in my first letter to him. Then I started complaining to him and begging him. He must have been fed up with me before we even met. All I did was complain to him. Underneath I find a journal.

I shouldn't read this but I'm curious. I wrote all of my feelings to him in these letters but he never wrote back. Maybe this holds his thoughts. Just one page and I'll put it away. I want to know what he thinks of me. But this hasn't been written in for three years.

I still want to know what he thought about. I want to know who Kyoya-sama really is...even if it scares me.

Chapter 42: Kyoya

"Please wait! Please. I just wanted to…"

I place the phone on the desk. I just can't speak to her anymore.

"He's just really busy," I hear.

"No, he just doesn't want to talk to me. I wish I knew what I did wrong."

She sounds close to tears. She could never do anything wrong. How could she even think that.

"Nothing. You're perfect. You've always been perfect."

THE LAST PRINCESS

"So I guess he's the one that changed then."

I hate hearing her sad voice. She's been sad since I've been away. I still can't talk to her. Have I changed? I suppose so. I realized that I don't deserve it all. I can't have power and her beside me. She doesn't deserve a man like me. A man that would kill hundreds of innocents then thousands to cover his ass. She deserves to be free.

"You still there?" Ayato-san says on the other side.

"Don't have her call me again."

"I think this time was too much for her. You really should have said something."

"Who are you to tell me what she needs," I say to him.

"I'm here…you're not. I'm the perfect one to tell you what she needs."

I haven't seen what she looks like lately. Kan-nii admitted that she's grown into a beautiful woman. Not sure how she could get any more beautiful. I know what she needs but I refuse to give it to her.

"Just make her stop calling," I say to him.

I hang up and hold my head. Whenever I hear her voice I get a headache. She sent me letters so I know what's on her mind. She's turning sixteen; the magic number. It means we're able to get married…able to have sex and restore her bloodline.

I still love her but all I can be is cold.

At night I lay alone still thinking about the princess' words. I remember when I first found out about her. I was thirteen. Father told me right before I started at the military academy. I didn't think I had much of a position. Kantarou was heir and just graduated the academy. All the focus should have been on him. That day all types of things went through my head.

"Kyoya, come here a minute," father says to me.

Kantarou lowers his sword. Good timing; I was about to be defeated. There's no way I can beat him. He's so much taller and stronger than me. I don't know why he insists on sparring with me.

"What'd you do?" Kan-nii asks.

THE LAST PRINCESS

"I have no idea."

"Perhaps it's that weird friend of yours."

What could Ayato have done now? Father retreats to his office. Before I follow I better ask. Ayato was watching us spar. When I approach he gets up to run away.

"Wait! What did you do?"

"It could be a number of things. I'm afraid to admit," he says.

"Seriously, why do you cause so much trouble?"

"I...never meant to cause trouble for you, Kyoya-sama. I did mark the baby's face while it was sleeping. I stole one of the queen's bras and burnt a few of the roses-"

"Anything else?"

He shakes his head. It's good he's coming to the academy with me. He needs it. I sigh and he lowers his head.

"I'll behave," he promises yet again.

He's a street orphan and now he lives in my palace. He should be more thankful.

"Go wipe Kira's face before someone sees."

I better see what father's wants. I go to his office and step inside bowing.

"Good news, Kyoya!" mother shrieks.

I lift my head. So it's good news. She runs over and hugs me; always smothering me with her bosom.

"This isn't about Ayato?"

"No. But I'm sure whatever he did will come to light soon," she tells me. "Tell him the good news, Eri-san."

She guides me to a chair then stands right next to father. I get the feeling this is good news for them and not me.

"You've heard of the country, Morinaga, correct?" he asks me.

THE LAST PRINCESS

"Yeah, a little."

"The king there, Hajime Asahina, is a good friend of mine. We've always been on each other's side. You know our countries share the same ancestors."

"Um…it would be great to meet a friend of yours," I say to him.

I'm not sure what to say.

"He had an accident a while ago. He's unable to have any more children."

"Are you sending me to him?" I ask.

"In a way, yes," mother adds on. "He has a little girl. She's five like Kira. She's the only one that can carry on the Morinaga legacy."

I look at them confused.

"And she will carry on that legacy with you," father explains. "You're engaged to the Morinaga princess."

"I didn't give my answer."

"You don't get an answer. You should be honored."

"I get they need a mate for her but why not Kira?"

"It's you. That's all there is to it."

"Isn't this exciting, dear," mother squeals.

I'm engaged to a five year old. My role is determined. I'm the second prince; I was supposed to have an open path not be a pawn.

"You don't look happy," she guesses. "Did you fall in love with someone else?"

"No. I just think this is a big thing for you to decide without me."

"Your father and I were arranged. It's how you find an ideal mate."

"What makes you think this five year old is ideal for me?"

"I don't know," father says. "But you're ideal for her. Now that's enough. You won't see her for many years. I respect you enough to tell you."

He respects me enough to tell me. There's no respect at all.

THE LAST PRINCESS

"You can leave now, if you like," he tells me.

I'll gladly go. In my room all I can think about is how I'll never have a life. I'll just be a figure head going to functions and waving to people that aren't even my people.

"I wiped the baby's face. He woke up though....what's wrong?"

Ayato stands at my door. He's not a royal. He's not bound by anything. He can do mischief and not be scolded. He can be whatever he wants when he gets older. All I'll ever be is a foreign husband.

"Kyoya-sama, was your father mad at what I did. I'll take responsibility so you don't-"

"It's not you. Father respected me enough to tell me about my arranged marriage."

"But your brother doesn't even have a wife yet."

"It's unfair. I always stayed out of the way so that he would allow me to be myself. I guess none of that matters."

"So who is it?" he asks me. "Is she pretty? Does she have big or really big boobs?"

"She's five; she's Morinaga's last princess."

He walks in and sits next to me. I intended on playing video games but I'm not in the mood. He picks up the controller and plays in my place.

"Don't you realize what this means," he says to me.

"I can never command a unit in the Han military."

"That's not what you want. That's what your brother wants. What I was trying to say is that if you marry that girl, you'll be a king. And when you're king you can do whatever the hell you want. Even marry your son off to a baby."

"Huh?"

"You'll be supreme. You may not know what you wanna do in your life but at least you can do anything. You should be thanking that little girl."

So he sees it that way. I'm fighting for my own path but what do I wanna be?

"Ayato, what do you wanna be?"

"Simple. You."

He continues playing. I just want to be…able to do whatever I want. I go back to my bed and write an entry in my journal. I hate this nameless princess. I don't ever wanna be put in a room where my will is taken from me. Not ever again.

Chapter 43: Ayato

"Do you have a girl you like?"

"Huh?"

"Do you have a girl you like?" she repeats to me. "You always spend your time with me. I just hope I'm not keeping you from her."

Once again I'm with her picking flowers in the garden. The princess has a big love of flowers. She comes out here to draw them, plant them and pick them. I think that's something I only know.

"I suppose there's one I like."

"Really?"

I sit under the tree and she turns back to me. It's been a peaceful three years. The most peace I've ever had. The big bad wolf everyone is afraid of is me so there's no need to put up a guard.

"Who is she?" Setsuna-san asks me. "Is she a maid or a soldier?"

"Neither."

"Is it the queen?" she whispers. "I won't tell."

"You seem to be in a happy mood. I thought you'd still be sad that you couldn't invite Kyoya-sama to your party."

"It's fine," she says. "I figured out why he's avoiding me."

"Why's that?"

"I won't say. So about this girl of yours. How old is she?"

THE LAST PRINCESS

Has she given up on him? I can't blame her; it's been three years of nothing. I warned him. With him out of the picture that just leaves me.

"She's a nice young girl. Pretty, polite, intriguing, smart. But I like her in a very unconventional way. So I'm not going to tell her how I feel."

"What's an "unconventional" way?" she asks.

When I'm around Setsuna-san I think about her screaming. Her scar has disappeared; I wanna make a new one. But I'm restricted cause I made a promise to my friend. I won't play with her. I kept that promise so far but if she's falling out of love with him and he wants nothing to do with her that leaves it all open.

"Not all love is posies and strawberries."

"You're weird," she says to me. "Do you like this bouquet?"

She holds them out to me. I nod and she gets up.

"Who are these for?" I ask.

"My mother," she says to me. "I can't see her crypt so I've just been placing flowers outside the windows. I figure she stands there watching me."

"You miss your family?" I ask.

I follow behind as she walks back to the palace.

"I do," she admits. "I miss all of them but I've never sat in the grass until I came to this place. I've never picked a flower until I came to Han."

That's why she likes it out here so much. She places a flower under a window and keeps moving.

"The killer told me he did it for me. He implied it at least. I couldn't figure out what he meant. I figured he was a supporter of Kyoya-sama; he never talked about him though. Maybe he did it so I could walk in a garden."

"Well he's dead now. I doubt his intentions were like you say."

"He's not dead, he's here."

"Hm? What do you mean?"

THE LAST PRINCESS

"The man that confessed to the massacre was not the killer, just an unfortunate result of failed intel. The real killer is near me. I'm not sure where he is...."

She turns back to me. Does she suspect? I'm frightened by her big eyes.

"But I'm sure he's happy wherever he's watching from. Everything is working like he planned."

She hands a flower to me.

"Put this under your window so mother can watch over you."

I take it and put it behind me to hide my shaking hand. What am I so afraid of? It's cause for once if I silence a witness I'll be the one grieving. She skips around the corner.

Definitely hard to read. I can't tell if she knows the truth or not. Somehow she knows why Kyoya-sama refuses to speak to her and she knows her parent's killer is still watching over her. The Morinaga military couldn't figure it out so how can she? But...she still stays near me. Perhaps she doesn't mind being liked in an unconventional way.

Her screams snap me out of it. I grab my sword and run after her.

"Setsuna-san!"

She stands backed up against the palace. She looks like she's seen her mother's ghost. I put my sword away.

"Welcome back, prince," I say to him.

Kira, the brat from the past, is her tormentor. He's starting to resemble his brothers a bit; he's gotten much taller. She looks at him with the same fear she once showed me.

"You still hanging with this idiot," he says to her.

"H-he's my bodyguard."

"You don't need him when I'm around. Come play chess with me."

What the hell has gotten into him? I've been to that military academy; it doesn't have the resources to turn a brat like Kira into a man.

"C'mon," he urges her. "We should talk."

THE LAST PRINCESS

I look at her trying to see her intentions. If only I could harm him; I would make him leave her alone for good. She doesn't trust him after that stunt he pulled. Her eyes look scared but she pushes herself off the house and steps closer to him.

"Captain, please take your break now."

"As you wish, princess."

"I don't think they'll be much use for you anymore. You can use your skills to cut my steak tonight," he says to me.

"Captain Saki deserves more respect than that. Three years in the military academy doesn't make you better than him. Apologize," she says to him.

"Why should I-"

"Apologize or I won't play with you."

He grumbles. This will be interesting to hear. That's two bothers she has wrapped around her finger.

"Sorry, captain. I meant no disrespect."

"She's not even your woman and you let her whip you."

"Shut up."

"Kira-kun," she warns him.

"I apologized so can we be alone now?" he asks her.

"Please stay close," she says to me.

I would have even if she didn't ask. He made a move on her last time; I won't allow it to happen again. They start walking and I stay behind. I'm curious what he has to say but I think I know. He wants her answer. Kira has some nerve to move in on his brother's girlfriend. But what he's doing isn't any different than what I'm doing.

She turns back to me with worry. It may not have been my mission when I met her but I'll protect her. Not sure if I can protect her from me though.

Chapter 44: Setsuna

He's definitely changed. I bet when Kyoya-sama was fifteen he looked like Kira-kun does now. He's gotten taller than me and his arms are a bit bigger. Also his voice has gotten deeper. When I saw him for the first time I was shocked; I thought somehow it was Kyoya-sama. But I can't be that lucky.

I walk with him along the palace perimeter. Looking up at him I see him smiling with his hands behind his head. What's there to smile about? I'm extremely uncomfortable. He turns to me and I put my hands to my mouth; I won't allow him to kiss me again.

"You look the same," he says to me. "I thought you'd be wearing normal clothes by now."

"These are normal clothes."

"Your grandmother's clothes. You'd look better in a dress. Then I could see what's under there."

I cross my arms to hide from him. So he hasn't dropped his...what do you call it....attraction for me. He was supposed to be my friend. I'm disappointed that we can't be.

"So....I won't draw it out. I'm curious about your answer."

"I'm engaged. You know that."

"Yeah, I know that."

"And Kyoya-sama is your brother-"

"I know that too."

I haven't even thought about it cause there is nothing to think about. Kyoya-sama is my boyfriend and will be my husband.

"I'll give you more time," he says.

"I don't need more time! Kyoya-sama will be my husband."

"Even though he's been ignoring you ever since he took his place as acting king for your country."

THE LAST PRINCESS

"How did you know that?"

"This is my palace remember. I've kept my eye on you," he says.

We get to the entrance door and he steps in front of me. Everyone knows Kyoya-sama has been ignoring me. They've probably all been laughing at me this whole time. I look up and see a hand outstretched to me.

"Come on, let's play. I bet I beat you this time."

I sigh; I feel so defeated. I take his hand and pull up my robe to walk up the stairs. He snaps me forward into his chest and puts his lips close to my ear.

"I would never ignore you, Setsuna-san. The whole time I've been away I thought about you," he whispers.

He looks over me and then separates. Captain Saki must have shown himself.

"That's more than I can say about my brother."

He goes inside and I'm frozen. I tried to hide it. I tried to be positive but three years with no words is too long. And from what I read in his journal I know why. So why am I still holding on to him? My life has always been about Kyoya-sama but knowing that I'm nothing to him....knowing that he lied about his feelings for me...

"Are you okay, princess?" Captain Saki asks me.

"Kyoya-sama holds many secrets, doesn't he," I say to him.

"What do you know?"

"I want to confirm it all myself."

I step inside the house and follow Kira-kun to the study. I haven't played chess with a person in a long time. Captain Saki is terrible at it. I'm gonna beat him.

"Kira."

We both look up and see his mother.

"You come home and see Setsuna-san over your parents."

"Hello, mother. You look young."

THE LAST PRINCESS

"Oh, you think so. I lowered my wine intake while you were gone. I don't have a little boy to worry about."

She grabs his cheek and he shakes her off. She reminds me that he's just a boy. He's only acting like a man. I laugh watching them.

"This shirt looks good on you," she says to him. "You're dressing yourself well-"

"You're interrupting! Can we catch up later?"

"Interrupting what?"

She looks over at me and I lower my head.

"He wanted to play chess," I say shyly.

"That can wait. Since you're both here I wanted to tell you the details of the party. Follow me."

I rather not be alone with him. He continues to mumble and I walk after her. He's right about one thing, his mother always looks so young. She's near fifty but she looks half of that.

While I was here I compared the queen to my own mother. Tomoko-sama is a young spirit. I like that she's in love with the king and has so much fun being queen. When she walks she's so sensual; nothing I could recreate.

"Setsuna-san, keep up with me," she calls back to me.

"Yes, queen."

I run to catch up with her. She puts her arm around me.

"He's not bothering you, is he?" she whispers. "Kira has always been brash. You're no doubt seeing that first hand."

"It's um...nothing."

"If you're uncomfortable let me know. Eri-san and I were hoping sending him away would cure him of his crush on you."

They knew? Am I the only one that didn't? And I suppose they were trying to protect me by sending him away.

"What are you whispering about?" he asks behind us.

THE LAST PRINCESS

"Nothing, dear," she shouts back.

She leads us to a room and I sit next to Kira-kun while she talks to her court ladies. She calls this the "party planning" room. Fabric samples and pictures of guests line the walls. I don't know any of these dignitaries. Some of them are supposedly from Morinaga.

I haven't gone back to my country since I was labeled a traitor for allowing Kyoya-sama to take the throne and his forces to come with him. But through some magic of his own he's loved by them. Loved for dropping crime and making things safer. It means changing a lot of people's rights but they've allowed him to do it.

He really is amazing.

"I can't believe you're older than me," Kira-kun says to me. "I'm far more experienced."

"Experienced how?"

"Hmph, I bet you'd like to find out. I could show you when we're alone."

"What use is that expensive academy if you can't learn manners."

"I learned something I already knew," he says. "In Han, women don't talk to their men like that. It's you that needs to learn our way of manners."

"I'm not from Han. In Morinaga, women are treated with respect and only give it to men that deserve it."

"What's got you so snippy?" he asks me.

He touches the strand of hair near my ear and I get up quickly. His mother sends the court ladies away. His touch makes me feel disgusting.

"What's going on?" she asks us.

"Kira-kun has been acting inappropriate," I say to her.

She looks over at him and he shrugs it off. I'm not imagining it; he's been inappropriate since he confessed. She touches my shoulder and I start to breathe again.

"What's been happening?" she asks me.

"Before he left for the academy he confessed to me and kissed me. He wants me to forget about Kyoya-sama and be with him. He's been pressuring me for an answer but I said "no." He won't believe me."

THE LAST PRINCESS

"Do you really wanna be with a guy that used you to get your throne? I bet he incited those people on purpose."

"He did not!" I scream at him. "Kyoya-sama isn't to blame for any of that!"

He stands up kicking his chair away. Inches from my face I look into his eyes with his mother tugging me back. I won't back down.

"He's been ignoring you and you cry all the time about it. Why should you be with him when I'm right here saying I want you!"

"Cause I love him."

"You love him cause your dead father told you to."

I release my blade on my arm and hold it to his neck. His mother pulls me away fiercely. Just his fear is enough; I don't want to hurt him.

"Setsuna-san, stop," his mother says to me.

"Don't say another word about my father," I warn him.

I retract the blade and he falls back towards the wall.

"I'm sorry," I say to the queen. "I'm going to my room."

Kira-kun is brash. I hate that he says what I don't want to hear. It may all be true. I close the party planning door behind me and lean against it. I'm a mess. I could be put on trial for treason for threatening the prince. Father....father should have never came out his mouth. I love Kyoya-sama not cause I'm supposed to; I love him cause he's my hope.

"Princess."

I look up alarmed but it's only Captain Saki.

"I know what I'm about to ask is against your code or whatever it is you follow but...."

"I'll do anything," he says to me.

"Can we leave, please."

"I-"

"Please, for just a while. Please, captain. You've been with me for three years. Can't you just-"

"I'll take you. Go to my room. We'll leave as soon as it gets dark."

"Thank you, captain."

Chapter 45: Ayato

When she talked about running away my heart, the one I assumed was missing, skipped. But this is hardly rebelling. We haven't even left the capitol. We're in a hotel that overlooks the palace.

I covered her up in my coat. She holds it close looking out the window. By morning we'll head back but for now, I'm enjoying myself. Being alone with the princess is nothing new but it feels different when we're outside the palace.

"You should eat, princess."

"I'm not hungry."

"Will you tell me what happened then? You obviously have something on your mind."

"I don't want to talk about it."

I'm keeping my distance. I'll have to stay in this chair all night watching over her. She turns from the window and I see her tears. It's not my place to hug her; I stay seated. She made me pull the couch up to the window just so she could watch. "Watch what?" I asked. And she simply responded, "everything."

"I had hoped my first day outside the palace would be with Kyoya-sama."

"Forget about him for now. Aren't you happy to finally look at a street?"

"I...am."

She turns back to the window and I see her smile in the reflection. The rain is keeping us from exploring. So many places I could take her if she agreed to change out of her royal attire.

THE LAST PRINCESS

"I don't think I've ever used an umbrella," she says to me. "It's nice that people share. But...I think it would be fun to walk around without one."

"Have you ever been in the rain?"

"Only felt it from my window. Mother didn't want me to get sick. I told her, "it's just water." She scolded me. Tomoko-sama feels the same. She doesn't want me to get sick."

Since she's a princess I assumed she was spoiled. She gets the best education, the finest food and servants. I've noticed she won't use servants and when people say the wrong thing she never corrects them. Binding myself to the chair isn't working. I get up and stand beside her.

"It's unfair what he's done to you."

He shouldn't have taken everything from her and left her with no replacement. I look on and she takes a book from the coat. It's his journal. Many times he would ignore me to write in it. That's the one from his adolescence. She hasn't read the one he writes in now.

"I don't blame him. I understand it all a bit more," she says to me. "He...wanted to be free but it was taken away from him."

"He was young when he wrote that."

"But it's still his feelings. He's actually a good writer. He said he would pretend to love me and follow orders. He would win my favor to make our parents happy then cast me aside so he could follow his dreams. That's exactly what's happening."

It's better she find that journal than the newer one. I can't deny what she's saying; there's proof in that book. As his friend I should find a way to fix this but I keep thinking about how nice she looks crying.

"He wrote about you too. You were a troublemaker," she says.

"That's putting it lightly."

I sit down on the couch next to her. When I was her age I was in the academy hiding my ways and studying to pass a psych test. I got away with a lot of things cause Kyoya-sama had the influence to hide it all.

"You never told me how you two met. You told me about your family but-"

THE LAST PRINCESS

"After I killed my family's killer I left and moved on the streets. I didn't want any questions. I was declared missing."

"You were homeless?"

"For a bit."

I look out the window and I feel her eyes on me. I'm not trying to get her sympathy. I never needed anyone's sympathy; that's why I ran away. The story hasn't been told since it happened.

"It was in this city," I tell her. "I stole food and money. Slept wherever I could. Then one day the royal family went out for a tour of the city. I knew all about them. Kyoya-sama was my age and I had it in my head that he was like me. I wanted to be friends with him."

I admired him before I even knew him. His life seemed so easy. His parents and all the Han people loved him. They loved him just cause he was alive.

"During their tour there was an assassination attempt on him-"

"On Kyoya-sama!"

"Yes. I killed the guy; stabbed him in the face but got shot in the process."

She looks worried. I reach over and touch her cheek. It's nice to know she would make that face for me. I turn to her and she allows me to get closer; probably distracted.

"I woke up surprised I was alive and Kyoya-sama was by my side. He thanked me and visited me every day until I got better. And then the king asked me to live with them. He said he would take care of me since I saved his son's life."

"Did they know you were the missing boy?"

"Of course he researched me before he made the decision. He told me to serve Kyoya-sama well. I already planned on it."

I'm too close to her. I pull away and focus on the window.

"Thank you for telling me," she says. "I know why he trusts you so much. But it seems unfair. He didn't want to be with me so he left you to do it."

"It doesn't mean I didn't enjoy every minute of it."

THE LAST PRINCESS

"Why would you enjoy being my bodyguard? You haven't seen any combat since you started."

"Somehow I've still been fulfilled."

I keep sneaking gazes at her. I know I'm wrong.

"I've enjoyed it too," she says to me. "You're a lot of fun. You were always good at making me forget…you know."

It feels right to ask. I take a breath and turn to her again. She doesn't even realize I'm asking to be with her.

"Would you be alright if it stayed like this?" I ask her.

I don't even recognize my own voice; it's timid. I don't want to know her answer. I get up quickly and walk back to the chair. I could never be with her. Aside from the promise, I'm just too different.

"Ayato-san."

I turn quickly hearing my name. No one calls me that except Kyoya-sama. I haven't been sweet Ayato since my parent's murder. When her voice says it, it feels like layers are being stripped from me.

"You can't replace him," she says softly. "My heart still wants Kyoya-sama even if he doesn't want me. I know I've spent more time with you than I have with him but… nothing can replace what he means to me. He is my hope."

She made her decision. I can't convert my feelings for her then. I can't play nice and take Kyoya-sama's place. Calm down. Don't be rash. I sheathe my sword away from her eyes. I can't hurt her for her words although I want to.

I'm trembling cause I want to strangle her for rejecting me. She's rejecting me! The one that's been by her side this entire time. The one that's covered Kyoya-sama's ass with so many lies. I've suppressed so much of myself just to see her smile at me. I….can't do this anymore.

"I accept your choice," I mumble.

"Choice?"

"I have to report in. I don't want to waste people's time looking for you. Stay here and try not to get noticed."

"Alright."

THE LAST PRINCESS

She will scream for me tonight. I'm turned on just thinking about it.

Chapter 46: Setsuna

How can anyone go to sleep when there's so much happening out there. The lights never turn off in this city. This is enough for me. With Kira-kun in the palace I felt so trapped. No matter where I went there was a reminder that Kyoya-sama abandoned me. Kira-kun says it plainly and this book says it all too.

It's been a while. Captain Saki should be back by now. He must be in a lot of trouble for taking me and he can't get off the phone. It's my fault. He would never say that though. He's....very protective over me.

It can't go on being just the two of us. He's not my love, he's just my guardian. And maybe what I said made it seem like he wasn't doing a good job. I often miss these social cues.

I'll sleep by the window; he never said it wasn't okay. I drag the blanket from the bed and get on my knees to pray. All I want is what I was promised. It sounds selfish, I know but....

It got darker. I stand up and look around. The city lights illuminate the room but it's still not enough light. I always had this fear of complete darkness. Feeling around for the furniture I make it to the bed then grab the lamp.

"You leaving the palace is like an invitation for me."

No! I swing the lamp back as hard as I can. It crashes against his face but he's unfazed. I swing again and he grabs my wrist. His grip is so tight. I drop it.

"You miss me?" he asks.

It's been so many years. Did my parent's killer come cause I finally left the palace.

"Captain-"

He covers my mouth with my back to him. I can't see him but I'll always remember that dark voice. If I'm calm maybe he'll talk to me rationally like before. Why did I leave the palace? They kept me inside for a reason.

I stay still and he releases me. No screaming. I just need to see what he wants. Captain Saki will be back soon.

THE LAST PRINCESS

"What brings you outside your fortress?" he asks me.

I tilt my head back. He's checking around the room. I turn and face him cautiously.

"I just needed some space."

"I must say it's really good to see you," he says.

"This can't be the first time you've seen me. You've been watching me, right?"

"You think you're that special."

"Aren't I?"

Just need to keep him talking. Captain Saki will hear and save me. I search the room for him. He's stopped. This can't be good. He charges at me with his sword and I fall back to the bed. I have to stay calm. But his blade is right at my neck.

His body hovers over me; it's the closest he's been. He seems different than the last time we met. He's lost his cool and collected demeanor.

"You think I can't kill you," he says.

"I think you can but you don't want to."

"You're right. I don't want to. I'll make you scream. I'll make you scream for the rest of your life. You're gonna always remember what I'm about do to you."

I look into his eyes and I know what he's thinking. He can't do that to me. He drops the sword and pulls the ribbon from my hair.

"Please stop."

"Yes, keep saying that."

I can't stay calm anymore. I push at him. When I release the blade on my arm he dodges then grabs my arm violently.

We roll across the bed as I kick him. It's not strong enough. My only defense is ripped from my arm. At the edge he turns soft. Touching my face gently

"You're just like those flowers you like so much. Let's see what's under the first petal."

THE LAST PRINCESS

He pulls out a small knife. I push at his face and he points the knife inches from my eye.

"Put your hands above your head and don't move them."

Would obeying make it any better? Whether I fight or submit it won't stop what he's about to do. I raise my hands above my head. His expression is covered but I'm sure he's pleased.

I start crying when he pulls at my sash. I close my eyes expecting him to kiss me but he cuts me on my shoulder. I open my eyes and see him studying me. Intrigued by every part of me. He pulls at more of my layers until he stares mesmerized at my exposed skin. He's not doing what I feared. Maybe if I say the right thing he might give up on all this.

"I know you don't want to hurt me," I whisper.

"But I do."

"Maybe we could be friends."

"Is this really something a friend would do?"

The knife is cold. He traces a heart on my stomach; it tickles.

"You love me, don't you? Is that why you did it? You wanted to keep me away from my family so you could be with me," I ask him.

"No. I started to love you after."

His voice sounds different there; soft and familiar.

"Don't think you understand!" he screams.

He's swift cutting my arm, then my stomach. He's making little incisions everywhere. Not enough to kill me but just to leave marks. I keep my hands in place thinking it can get worse if I move them.

"I didn't say I understood," I plead with him.

He moves down to my legs and I shut my eyes again. He cuts my thigh and I scream.

"Tell me that you like this," he says.

THE LAST PRINCESS

He kisses my thigh sucking the blood. I cringe and hold my mouth. He can't do this to me. Where is Captain Saki? Why won't he rescue me?

He moves up my thigh kissing my underwear and I snap up. I kick his chest and we struggle again. Who is this man? It can only get worse.

I grab his mask and tear it away from him. He swings blindly turning his head away. Am I gasping for air out of shock? No. Have I really been cut? I touch my neck and feel blood. I'm dying, aren't I?

It's all blurry but I see him fighting to save me. Cursing and panicking; he does it all like he cares about my survival. Who is this man? I don't think I'll get to find out.

"Setsuna-san," he cries out.

Please Kyoya-sama. I need you.

Chapter 47: Kyoya

"Thank you for giving me a lift back," she says to me.

"What were you doing in Morinaga anyway?" I ask.

"Visiting my father. I spent most of my break with him."

She's smiling. It's nice she can get in touch with her family again; there's hardly any left. Yumiko-san rides with me in my jet. It's rare that we're alone together. Seeing someone outside of politics is just what I need right now. Family is the only thing I can trust; they're the only ones I can be honest with for the most part. I consider Yumiko-san like my family. Very unexpected.

I've put it off long enough but it's time to go see Setsuna-san. She'll be excited to see me I'm sure. I could stay away for a lifetime and she would still welcome me.

"I...haven't seen Kantarou-sama in months. How is he?"

She may not want to hear this but she should be over him by now.

"He's been trying out some women. He's expected to be married at thirty. So he needs to be seen with a steady woman about now."

"Oh? Why thirty?"

THE LAST PRINCESS

"It's just customary."

A servant delivers my tea. Been trying to cut down on the alcohol. I'm going to be married soon; I can't keep pushing down my feelings.

"I...um...."

"You're not over him are you?" I ask her.

"No, I've been dating too. But does he plan on loving any of these girls?"

"No, it's more about the image. He'll probably pick a small woman. She'll have to be accomplished but not more accomplished than him."

It's not going to be her. He should have set her straight already.

"Well you're a good example of arranged marriages working out. I'm sure he'll find the right one," she says to me.

"You don't sound satisfied-"

"I love him okay! I'm not satisfied with him being with someone else."

"You really want to be queen?" I ask.

"It's not about being queen-"

"But it is. Kantarou isn't a simple man that you can just date. Give up on him."

She turns away from me. Guess we'll be flying in silence.

"Setsuna-chan tells me everything," she says to me. "But she's been oddly quiet about her relationship with you."

I wish we could fly in silence. Two hours to sit through her questions. She'll be relentless.

"I know you haven't visited in three years. Have you been calling her?" she asks me.

"That's not your business."

"How isn't it?"

"Because what goes on between me and Setsuna-san is between me and Setsuna-san. She knows that. That's why she hasn't been talking to you."

THE LAST PRINCESS

"You wanna play it like that, huh?"

"Don't interfere."

My last line made her scared. I'm sure no one knows we haven't been talking. Yumiko-san reminds me of the press. They have the same questions. I slump down in my chair; I'll just pretend to be asleep.

I spoke about giving up and letting Kira have her or letting her pursue whoever she wants but I can't do that anymore. I'm learning to live with what I've done. I couldn't have done that with her at my side. After this time, I realize that I miss her. I stayed away to satisfy my own conscious.

Three years haven't been spent alone. I had women satisfy me but they never meant anything. I'll have to teach the princess how to do it. She should be old enough.

"I know you're not asleep," she says to me.

"Me pretending should show you that I don't want to be bothered."

When we land the guards take hold of me and rush me to father's office. I'm sure there's a lot to yell at me about. He doesn't like how I'm running Morinaga and I'm sure mother will chime in on how I don't visit.

Inside mother's crying and father is holding her. Not their normal loving embrace.

"What's going on?" I ask.

"Close the door."

Nothing made me shake this much in years. I know Kira was supposed to be coming home. Did something happen to him?

"Is Kira okay?" I ask

"It's Setsuna-san," he says to me.

Setsuna-san....

"She tried to kill herself," he says to me.

My head throbs with Ayato-san's warning. "I think this time was too much for her. You really should have said something." He warned me. Staying away was selfish; I thought about what I needed and refused to acknowledge her. Mother keeps crying

THE LAST PRINCESS

"Is she okay?" I ask him.

"She had an argument with Kira. I took his side and she ran away," mother cries out. "I should have comforted her."

Father touches her shoulder to calm her. I need to know if Setsuna-san is okay. Why am I just finding out about this. Phone lines aren't safe.

"She ran away with Captain Saki. He said he would keep her away for the night to cool her head," father tells me. "He stepped away to alert the palace and when he returned to her, that's when he found her…with her throat slit."

No….that's not like her. She's always been strong. She would never. I try to stay calm but I just want to run to her. She wanted to speak to me; I never thought she needed it.

"Is it true you haven't talked to her since you left?" he asks me.

"I-"

"After what happened to her, after knowing what she's been through you forget about her?"

"I don't need to hear this from you. Just tell me where she is."

"How could you-"

"You were the one that wanted this to just be for show. I don't need you on my back about how I treat her! Now where is she!"

"Kyoya, don't," mother cries.

"I'll find her myself."

I leave the office and Ayato-san stares at me. I pause and then we both start walking.

"Nice to see you again, Kyoya-sama."

I don't even know where her bedroom is. I keep walking despite that.

"What's been going on?"

"She's been doubting you for some time now. She confirmed it all when she found your journal."

THE LAST PRINCESS

My journal. I always keep it with me. I look over at him to elaborate.

"The one you kept as a teenager," he says. "She read all of it."

"Where is she?"

I stop. I just need to know where she is. Those words were from a me that didn't know her.

"She's been sneaking off to your room lately," he says to me.

I take one step to reach her and stop. He was with her this whole time. Looking back at him I scan his eyes to make sure all of this is the truth.

"I'm sorry about what happened. I've always been afraid of getting too close to her," he says to me.

"I know you've done your best."

But I know all this is a lie. Setsuna-san would never try to harm herself. She didn't try it after her parents were murdered; she wouldn't try it now.

I'm suspicious of him for a reason. I know he wants to play with her. Since their first meeting he's had some type of attraction for her. I figured he would have some self-control; his promise to me should trump his own desires.

When we were at the academy we were surrounded by all types of willing little girls and women. They patrol the town looking to claw into a young cadet and ride it out until he's successful.

I remember he was acting odd for about a week. I knew him well enough to pick up on his subtle changes. One night, while we were at the academy, I followed him. He snuck out of the gates and went into town, right up to this apartment.

"Ayato," I call to him as he opens the door.

"I knew you were following me," he speaks amused. "Come inside."

I follow him in. Who's place is this? Why does he have a key? He goes to the kitchen and pulls a soda. Why lead me here? Is this some sort of hang out? Looks like a lady's place.

"What are you doing here?"

"I know you're not like me but you've always been accepting of me. Since we're out of the palace I can do a lot of things."

THE LAST PRINCESS

He walks over to another door and opens it smiling. I immediately hear whimpering.

"What have you done?"

Inside is a woman tied up to her bed naked. Cuts all over her body. She turns away seeing two of us.

"Her name is Saya. She's been letting me explore her body."

"No," I say to him.

"What do you mean "no"? I said she let me. She saw my uniform and invited me up right away."

She had no idea who she was messing with. I grab the blanket off the floor and cover her up. How can I fix this?

"You can't do this to people," I tell him.

"I was just going to kill her when I'm done. It won't cause any problem for you."

"No," I say to him again. "You're at the academy to become a person that protects people. You can't torture them."

"If we release her, she'll tell."

She shakes her head furiously. She will tell but I don't want to kill her. I'll have to figure something out.

"I thought you accepted me," he says.

"I do accept you but you told me you would stay out of trouble."

"I know! I just….I needed this."

I better keep quiet. I close my eyes as he throws a lamp across the room.

"Everyone else there is so content looking at magazines and kissing and whatever. I just-"

I grab his shoulder before he can throw something else.

"You're mad at me, aren't you?"

THE LAST PRINCESS

He hugs me and I sigh. I can just try to control him the best I can. He was doing well but every now and then he has to release his frustrations. He's some sort of psychopath but he's my friend.

"Kyoya-sama, I tried."

"One day we'll get you a nice girlfriend and she'll accept you. And you can do whatever you want with her. So save it all for someone special, okay?"

"Okay."

"And we're gonna let Saya go. She won't say a word cause she knows you have no problem tying her up again."

He lets go of me.

"I'm not mad at you. But next time tell me. I'll find a willing participant."

"She was willing-"

"I'm sure she was. Now let her go."

He struggled with his desire to kill her and my order to let her go. In the end he released her. Looking back at him now we seem the same just twenty-three instead of fifteen. Since I found out about his ways I knew I always had to keep him close. If he's away from me his actions will be unpredictable.

"Are you behind this?" I ask him.

Just like I've neglected to see Setsuna-san, I've neglected him as well. His eyes widen and he looks down to the floor.

"You know I would never hurt her," he says.

"Why's that?"

"Cause I've sworn to protect her. She's your future wife and-"

"And?" I urge him.

"You know the rest."

"You love her too?"

His idea of love and affection are different. He keeps his head down. I can't focus on him anymore. I take off towards my room.

Chapter 48: Setsuna

They're all growing nicely. I think I have a talent for growing plants. Reading those botany books really helped. Whenever he comes back he'll be happy to see full grown plants on his balcony. Down below I see some guards checking in the shrubbery. They're looking for me.

About a week ago I woke up in my room with bandages all over me. I survived. That's twice I had that sigh of relief. The killer wasn't near me this time; I was alone. When the king asked me what happened I lied. Seemed easier than telling him that the killer returned. That would mean Kyoya-sama made a mistake and he would be hated for it.

So I'll keep it to myself. I'm still covered in bandages but no one can tell because of my robes. The king said not to tell anyone my story. The birthday party is coming up soon and it would only make the palace look bad if they knew the princess was suicidal.

There's so much I can't say and it's starting to hurt. Captain Saki hasn't been near me much. I overheard a palace guard say that he was in a lot of trouble for taking me away and allowing me to hurt myself. I want to apologize to him but I'm not allowed to leave my room. I manage to sneak into Kyoya-sama's room often. They never look in here.

It's not Captain Saki's fault. I don't want them to punish him.

I stay low on the balcony. It's dangerous for me to leave the palace but I still want to know what's out there. Also…I want to understand that man, the killer, a bit more.

I turn around to go back inside.

"Uh!"

Am I dreaming? I stand stiff not believing my eyes. I imagined his face before but it seems so real now. Kyoya-sama stands in the doorway just like I remember him. Handsome like always and powerful with his hair slicked back and his tie loosened.

"Setsuna-san," he says to me.

My heart beats uncontrollably.

THE LAST PRINCESS

"I'm sorry. I shouldn't be here."

I push pass him and run for his door.

"Stop," he calls to me.

I fumble with the door knob. When I get it open his hand slams it. I tremble underneath his frame.

"Please, just talk to me. Are you okay?"

It's been so long but his voice erases all my doubt. For so long I just wanted to run into his arms. Am I even allowed? Feeling my hesitation he takes the lead like he always does. He reaches for my hand and leads me back to his chair. He sits down and stands me to look at him in between his legs.

His hand grazes my neck touching my bandage and I shiver. I haven't felt his soft touch in so long.

"Why did you do this?" he asks me.

"I…don't know."

I can barely focus. His hand traces me; he moves the hair from my ear and tilts my head to look at him.

"You've been lonely, haven't you?" he asks.

I nod.

"You've missed me?"

I nod and my eyes start to water. I can't believe he's here. I fall to him and cry on his shoulder.

"Kyoya," I cry to him.

"I know."

"Why did you abandon me?"

The tears won't stop. I spend what seems like hours crying into his shoulder. My makeup stains his expensive clothes but he doesn't say anything. He just allows me to cry.

THE LAST PRINCESS

"Those are some pretty plants you have out there. Did you grow them for me?" he asks.

"Yeah," I sniffle. "They're like the ones in your books."

"This whole time, you haven't forgotten about me?"

"Of course not! I thought about you every day."

I pull away from him and see him smile.

"I thought about you too-"

"Then why-"

"It's complicated. Right now, I'm just happy you're alive."

Complicated? What's so complicated about talking to me? He grabs my chin and pulls me to look at him.

"You really are beautiful," he says to me. "It's nice to look at you again-"

"I won't forgive you."

"Forgive? What do you mean?"

"I won't forgive you for abandoning me."

"Then I'll work hard to make you fall in love with me all over again."

He pulls me closer to his face and I stare at him. Still I love him. I love him despite everything. But I hate him for leaving me. But I love him for coming back. It's all so confusing.

"I'm having a palace built just for you. When we marry I'll move you in and let you decorate. You won't have to hide your interests anymore."

My own palace. It sounds like a dream. A place for me to start my legacy.

"It will have a garden and lots of birds and butterflies. I figured you would like that."

His voice is like a whisper tempting me to forgive him. He's just trying to make me forget. His whispers come close to my face. I pull away when he tries to kiss me. I refuse to forget how I spent every night yearning for him. He can't take all those tears away with a promise of birds and butterflies.

THE LAST PRINCESS

"I'm sorry but I can't let you abandon me and think a kiss makes up for it. I'm going to go back to my room. I'm supposed to be under surveillance."

I push away from him and close his door behind me. Part of me wanted to kiss him and stay but I couldn't. Then he'll know what he did was okay.

I stand at his door for some time and the smell of his cigarettes comes to me. It's like he's right on the other side of the door calming his nerves.

Chapter 49: Yumiko

It's so ominous around here like someone died. I can't find anyone. I'm told Setsuna-chan is sleeping at this hour. Its only 3pm so I don't believe that. The palace is hiding something.

As much as I want to see her, my legs are taking me another way. The birthday party is soon so we're all reuniting at the palace. Kantarou-sama must be here somewhere. He's not in his usual places.

"Welcome back, pretty lady."

I look up. I know I'm supposed to feel protected around him but he creeps me out. Captain Saki stands looking at me; I swear it always seems like he's checking me out.

"Setsuna-chan isn't allowed visitors. Has she been okay?" I ask him.

"Of course. I'm I charge of watching her after all."

He wanders to my side and I pull away.

"You're boobs have gotten bigger," he says to me. "Setsuna-san will look like you soon enough, right."

Such a creep. But somehow it's flattering. I thought I was looking a lot shapely lately.

"I know what you're really looking for," he says.

"And what's that?"

"My commander."

178

THE LAST PRINCESS

"Well, tell me where he is."

He walks off silently. Is he taking me there? I contemplate following him then he runs around a corner. He's probably playing with me.

"Wait," I call back to him.

When I turn the corner I bump into him.

"Or maybe it's this way," he says to himself. "He's in the middle of a marriage meeting but is it in the east wing or the west."

"He's in a marriage meeting now?"

He nods amused. So there's a prospective mate in the palace. I'm sure all the women he meets are pretty; what's his preference? Blondes maybe. I've been wearing this purple dye too long. Would he like my natural black hair?

"Well let's get going," I tell him.

"What do you plan on doing when we get there?"

I don't know. I just want to see it for myself. But I get the feeling the captain is playing around. We've been traveling around in circles.

"Do you know where we're going?" I ask him.

"I'm just wandering around on purpose."

"What! Why?"

"Cause I can't play with Setsuna-san. Genetically, you're second choice. Sexually active too; we'll find out later where that comes in."

"Who said I was sexually active?"

"A man can tell. And with you…a man imagines."

He walks backwards still checking me out. I hope Setsuna-chan doesn't go through this. It looks like we might be getting somewhere. This is the security wing.

"You won't be able to intervene but you can watch the recording."

He opens the door and signals the men away. The room clears out and it's just the two of us. He sits down wheeling himself to the back of the room. On the monitor I see Kantarou-sama. He looks different outside of uniform; nervous too.

THE LAST PRINCESS

I sit down ignoring the weird captain. Kantarou-sama says something but I'm unable to understand. The king stands next to him and they exchange in a foreign language.

"What are they saying?" I call back.

"This should be fun. During marriage meetings the participants speak Hangese."

"Do you speak it?"

"Surprisingly, yes."

He wheels his chair next to me. I feel like I'm spying. Like I'm some crazed jealous ex-girlfriend. I wasn't even good enough to be his ex.

"Why does it have to be a Han woman? Yumiko-san was sufficient," he says to me.

"Really? He said that!"

"Haha, no. He just asked why the woman is running late. He says it's disrespectful."

That sounds about right. I can't believe any of his translations. I really thought Kantarou-sama would think about me and say all these other women don't compare. Hearing him speak in his country's language makes me feel like he's very different from me. Of course he would be expected to date a woman from his country.

The woman enters. She's small and very pretty. Beautiful wavy brown hair and simple style. Her skirt touches her knees and her heels are low. She's not the most fashionable but I think she has the edge.

"She's apologizing and he's telling her to forget it and sit."

She looks nervous.

"What's her name?" I ask him.

"Chiyo."

I don't need him to translate anymore. Kantarou-sama smiles at her and I'm certain he likes her. He even laughs with her while she gives a shy giggle. I get up and leave. I'm done. I have to be done.

"You look so sad," the captain says stretching out the door.

THE LAST PRINCESS

"I just need to move on."

"I can help with that if you want."

He's offering a rebound. All the men I met in college were rebounds. The captain is handsome in a gothic sort of way but it's too close to the family. And it would be entirely too slutty of me to be with him.

"Why don't you wear that royal dress of yours and tie your hair up and-"

"You trying to make me look like Setsuna-chan?"

Really gross. Why would Kyoya-sama choose this guy to guard her?

"It's a stretch but-"

"You're disgusting."

"I'm sorry," he says tilting his head. "I assumed you didn't have morals. Well...the offer's still open."

I will never take that offer. I'm not that desperate. It's flattering to know I can catch a captain's eye. I go up to Setsuna-chan's room. Now it feels like all the guards are checking me out; must be his words in my head.

"Setsuna-chan," I call at the door.

She opens it fiercely.

"Yumi-chan!"

She hugs me tightly. I guess it has been a while.

"Come in," she says to me. "I had no idea you were here."

"I came with Kyoya-sama," I tell her.

She turns silent. Don't tell me he didn't see her yet. She goes back to her bed and sits.

"Is it true he hasn't seen you this whole time?" I ask her.

"He's been busy. But I rather talk about you. I got your last picture. You looked so happy on the beach. I wish I could go to one."

"I was just hanging with some friends."

THE LAST PRINCESS

"You have more than one friend?"

It's time to enlighten her a bit. I collapse on her bed and she starts stroking my hair. I can tell with her line of questions that she's always admired me; always wanted to see what I see. But it's overrated.

"How many friends do you have?" I ask her.

"Well there's you, Tomoko-sama, Eri-sama, Ayato-san, Kantarou-sama, Kir.....I mean..."

"Kira-sama, right?"

"I didn't mean to say him."

"You two aren't friends?"

"No," she mumbles.

"What aren't you telling me?"

I sit up and she turns away. I know he liked her but she seemed oblivious of it.

"I don't get along with Kira-kun anymore."

"What did he do?"

"He's been mean and he's trying to break me and Kyoya-sama up."

"That's bold of him."

"You knew that he liked me, didn't you. Why didn't you say anything?"

I figured it was innocent. She seems traumatized by it.

"You're a pretty girl," I tell her. "Boys will like you; boys that aren't your boyfriend. You'll need to know how to handle it."

"How do I handle it?"

With the way Kyoya-sama's been acting it seems he feels comfortable in his position; he thinks she'll always be interested in him. Time to shake him up a bit.

"Go see Kira-sama," I tell her.

"But I don't-"

182

THE LAST PRINCESS

"And perhaps if Kyoya-sama finds out, he might get jealous and know he can't keep his eyes off you."

"Make him jealous? But that's not fair to Kira-kun."

"Just give Kira-sama a little of what he wants but not all."

She stares at me confused. This is how I would handle a man that can't behave. He needs to be shaken up.

"So how has it been with that guard of yours?"

"Captain Saki? He's a great friend."

"He doesn't seem weird to you? Ever done anything inappropriate?"

"No. Well maybe sometimes but it was funny. Like one time when Kantarou-sama came back to the palace. I made tea for him and we replaced his sugar with salt. He drank the whole cup with a bitter face. When he saw us laughing at him he chased after us. Captain Saki got away but I was caught. I couldn't stop laughing and...Kantarou-sama just smiled at me. I see why you like him. Kantarou-sama is really nice."

Talking about him makes me want to take the rebound offer to clear my head. I should be giggling with her but I can't.

"I meant did the captain make you uncomfortable in any way? Does he touch you too much or..."

"No, he's actually afraid to show affection for me. Whenever I hug him he hugs me back but quickly pushes me away like he's disgusted. Sometimes he likes to touch my face but then he'll pull away quickly too. He seems hesitant."

She talks with so much concern for him. I feel like I missed so much from being away.

"I know a bit about his past so I feel like I understand him a little. Perhaps he's afraid of having family or close relationships."

"It's not worth trying to understand him. He's just a guard."

"He's my friend. Kyoya-sama's friend too," she tells me. "I feel the difference between our old palace and this one. Did you know Kantarou-sama wanted to become commander of the palace guard since he was a little boy? He always wanted to be the one to protect his family. And Tomoko-sama, she told me she just wants to make her sons feel like normal people and not princes."

THE LAST PRINCESS

She sees the Niwa family as her family now. She doesn't have to spy on them to understand them. The Niwa family likes to talk. She seems happier here. I can't mess that up by ruining Kantarou-sama's marriage or sleeping with her bodyguard.

"What happened to our palace will never happen here," she says.

"Cause the killer, Yee, is dead."

"It's just that....no one would dare stand up to this place."

I felt accomplished as the commander's assistant but since leaving his side I feel like I've fallen into my old self. Nothing makes me special anymore. Men just want to have sex with me; they don't want to know me. The commander had dual intentions but he always stopped himself.

"Yumi-chan, what's wrong?"

"It's good to see you're well. I'm gonna head back to my room."

I've been trying to figure out what's wrong for a long time. Best answer I have it that it's me that's wrong. Outside her door the guards stare at me again. This is getting uncomfortable.

"Yumiko-san!"

It's the commander storming down the hall. He wants to put me back to work but I can't work for him anymore. I run down the hall before he can reach me.

Kantarou-sama keeps calling after me. I turn the corner and push myself to the wall. Why does he keep teasing me and putting my hopes up; it's painful. I hide my face in my hands and breathe in.

When I lower my hands I see him frowning at me.

"I'm not in the mood to work today-"

"Why's that?" he asks.

"I just can't."

I keep my head down hoping he won't notice my awkwardness.

"You'll work for me until I say you can't. I should be the first person you see when you return home."

THE LAST PRINCESS

"This is my home?" I ask him.

I've never heard him say that. He shuffles around the hallway nervously. I try looking into his eyes and he dodges me.

"Wherever I stay is considered your home. And when I leave here, you'll come."

"How's that gonna work with your new wife?"

"What's that have to do with it?"

He doesn't get it. Just moments ago I heard him speak foreign words to another woman. I don't want to be a mistress.

"I can't work for you anymore and if it means I have to leave the palace then I will."

His head snaps back to me. I know he doesn't like things not going his way but I have to do this.

"You don't have that option," he says coldly.

"I'm not your prisoner."

His boots thump towards me and I straighten up against the wall. I hold my gaze with him and he grabs my chin harshly.

"If I have to make you one, I will. You're not leaving," he says snarling.

He shoves my face away. I watch him walk down the hall and grab my chin in disbelief. That's not like him. Something has to get through to him. He can't have it all. He can't have a queen on one arm and me on the other.

"Get back to work," he calls back.

Chapter 50: Kira

"So Kira, one more year until graduation. Have you thought about what you want to do after?" mother asks me.

Is that what she called me in here for? This is the whole "what are you doing with your life" meeting. I can do anything; I don't need to explain that to her. I'll just behave because the tea is good.

THE LAST PRINCESS

"I'll wait for father to tell me."

"He has no plans for you. You can pursue whatever you want."

I'm sure she's saying that wrong. Father has to have a plan for me. We continue sipping tea while she smiles at me constantly.

"What is it?" I ask her.

"I'm just so proud of you. You're a very striking young man."

"I already know that."

"You can have any girl in Han," she says leaning over to me. "Why Setsuna-san?"

"I'm not talking to you about this."

"Better me than-"

The door opens and Kan-nii steps in. I was wondering why there were more places set. Mother backs away from me and stands to kiss my brother.

He sits next to me. I haven't seen him in a while; I don't miss him.

"Something wrong with your mouth, brat," he says to me. "You don't greet you oldest brother."

"If I wanted to talk to you, I would greet you."

He slaps my head. I expected as much. I move my hair into place and the door opens again. Kyo-nii is here too! I had no idea he was back in Han. He sits down on my other side and immediately starts drinking.

I always wondered if Kyo-nii knew what I did. Does he know I confessed to Setsuna-san? And on top of that….does he know my words caused her to run away and try to kill herself. No one has talked about her suicide attempt. No one told me, probably figured I wasn't important enough, but I overheard the guards talking outside her door.

I want to see her and talk to her. It wasn't me that pushed her to it; it was Kyo-nii. Mother seems happy with this little reunion but I'm on edge. I look over at Kyo-nii and he's calm.

"Kira," he says to me.

THE LAST PRINCESS

I feel my heart jump. I look to him slowly and he's smiling at me.

"I wanted to tell you how proud I am of you," he says. "I know the military academy isn't easy."

"I was meaning to say the same thing," Kan-nii jumps in. "Good job."

They're both proud of me? They've never said that to me before.

"You'll have your pick of what country you'd like you work for. You'd be a great asset to Morinaga."

"Um…thanks."

"It's so nice to see my boys," mother says.

"Enough of this," Kan-nii slams down his cup. "Why'd you call us here? No one has time for your senseless tea parties."

"It's your father that wanted to speak to you. The tea is just to calm your nerves. Nothing seems to work on you though."

"This can't be good. Sounds like he's about to announce his upcoming expectations," Kyo-nii says taking another sip.

"Who's heard this speech more, you or me?" Kan-nii says to him.

Father never announced his expectations of me before. I've proven myself by attending the academy. Perhaps he has plans for me.

The door opens once again and father steps in. He stays standing. Mother pulls on his arm to sit but he grips the back of his chair firmly and stares hard at all of us.

"I'm disappointed in all of you," he says. "I'm lucky enough to have three sons but none of you know how to play your part."

"Tell us how to be better," Kan-nii says leaning back in his chair.

Sarcasm, I bet. Mother's eyes warn him not to kid around. My brothers don't seem shaken by any of this. They must have these conversations with him all the time. I can't look father in the eye with that hard look of his but my brothers have no problem.

THE LAST PRINCESS

"I've given you ample time to pick a wife," he says at Kan-nii. "You're lucky I gave you a choice and you piss all over it. You've insulted every one of them and left me to clean up your mess with their fathers."

"Bring me someone that's a challenge-"

"Shut up!"

Father looks at me then turns quickly to Kyoya. Is there nothing to say about me? That's good to hear this time.

"What reason could you possibly have to neglect the princess all this time?" he asks him.

"I'm running her country. She knows that," Kyo-nii says to him.

"And since when have either of you talked back to me!"

"I get that I'm your son but I'm a king, same as you," Kyo-nii says.

He stands suddenly to meet father's level. How could I think I was better than my brother? He has nerves I've never seen before.

"No one needs to worry about Setsuna-san but me."

"If that's the case, will she succeed in killing herself next time-"

"Darling," mother says touching father's hand.

"Perhaps I should give her to Kira since he has an interest in her."

"You threatening to take her from me?"

Damn! This is not the time to bring me into this. My brother looks down at me and I avoid his eyes. I'm not ready to challenge him.

"You still trying to control people. Setsuna-san is on my side and she always will be. She has the only claim to the throne and even if you could somehow cancel the arrangement you made with her father, she would still choose me. She will choose me no matter what."

"Don't you-"

"No! Don't you stand there and lecture me about how I should treat my wife and how I should conduct my life. You will never sit me down and take away my will again."

THE LAST PRINCESS

It occurs to me why Setsuna-san hasn't given up on him yet. He's a man in her eyes…the man I can never be. She's seen the man that I've never gotten the chance to see. I've only seen Kyoya as my brother but I see him as a king now. And I had the nerve to take his wife from him. I don't have a chance with her.

"Darling," mother says again. "Let's take a break from all this."

"At the party, you will announce your queen," father says to Kan-nii. "And you," he says at Kyo-nii.

Kyoya sits back down and takes a sip of tea. Is he trying to piss father off on purpose?

"You will follow what I say. You're no king yet."

When the door slams I'm snapped out of what I hoped was a dream. I've never heard father talk like that. My brothers don't seem rattled.

"Time for a drink," Kan-nii offers.

"The tradition continues," Kyo-nii says. "You should join us," he says bumping my shoulder.

"You're a man now, right?" Kan-nii teases. "You must be since you're stealing women that don't belong to you."

Kyo-nii hasn't said anything. I look over at him and he's still silent. Why won't he reprimand me?

There's a knock at the door. It opens slowly. Father forgot to say why he was disappointed in me.

"I'm sorry to interrupt," I hear.

"Setsuna-san, you didn't have to seek me out," Kyo-nii says standing.

She takes a step back. I thought she would be all over him but she's distant.

"Kira-kun, do you have a minute?"

She wants me? I immediately stand. I'm ahead of him then. All eyes are on me as I walk over to her side.

"What took you so long?" I ask her.

He can't count me out just yet. I'm still a threat. And if she wants me then I'm not giving up. With the door closed behind us I take her under my arm.

"Can we play a game of chess?" she asks me.

"Of course. I have a set up in my room."

Chapter 51: Kyoya

"So there's this one. She works at some computer company."

Kan-nii slides another picture to me. Not a good idea to be drinking while helping him pick a wife. I lean over his desk. All these women are acceptable. They have good jobs and good looks. They'll probably agree with everything he says.

"You could pick anyone at this point. You're not gonna like any of them."

"I would rather be engaged to the princess. She's quiet and stays out of the way."

"Do I have to look out for you too?"

"Not like that."

I don't want to think about what Kira is doing to her. I feel like I know her well; she wouldn't do anything to hurt our relationship. But I don't know what kind of girl she's become. I haven't been around to spot the differences.

"I care about the princess a lot," he tells me. "I mean that now. Every time I came back to the palace she would come to me and listen to my stories. She got what I was talking about more than a person my own age. I told you a long time ago not to get too attached to her but I realize now that it was out of your hands."

"Thanks-"

"But I don't see how you could leave a girl like that alone and crying for you, even with all the guilt you had."

"This isn't supposed to be about me."

"She came to me once crying at my door. She asked if you were okay. She was making all sorts of stories to explain why you wouldn't talk to her. She thought you were dead or in love with someone else. I told her you still loved her but felt like I was lying."

Didn't expect to hear this from my brother. I take another drink. I haven't had a proper conversation with her. I'm putting it off hoping things will return back to normal.

"I don't believe she would try to kill herself," he says to me.

"Me neither. But I won't know what happened until she tells me."

"Now seems like a great time."

He points behind me. The princess stands outside peeking in.

"Always snooping," he says to her. "Just announce yourself like a normal person."

She steps in shyly. She looks the same in a lot of ways. Still dresses in her traditional clothes. But she's taller and more developed. I stand up and she takes a step back.

"Let's have a talk," I say to her.

She nods. We walk down the hall far from each other.

"I was just helping Kantarou pick his wife. Can't say I'm very useful."

"I didn't mean to interrupt."

"No, it's okay. I wanted to talk to you."

"Does jealousy not work on you?" she asks abruptly.

She stops suddenly and waits for my answer. Has she tried to make me jealous?

"You're not jealous, are you? You think I'll always be here waiting for you and so you treat me poorly. You were supposed to realize-"

"Who's teaching you this?"

"Yumi-chan."

THE LAST PRINCESS

I don't like games and Setsuna-san is terrible at them. I touch her shoulder and she stares up at me. I'm not jealous cause I know she loves me. And also I would take out any man that tries to take her from me. I know who is a threat and who isn't.

"You and I don't have to play these kinds of games. Just speak honestly to me like you have been."

"Did you fall in love with someone else?" she asks.

"No."

"Did you start to hate me?"

"No."

"Do you think I turned ugly?"

"Absolutely not."

I take her chin in my hand. She has turned more beautiful. She looks away and pulls a book from her side. So this is about what she read.

"You found my journal. You are pretty good at snooping."

"Were you just saying words to please everyone?" she asks. "Me, my father, your father, my people."

This isn't the place to discuss it. I try to pull her forward and she stays in place.

"Come with me back to my room," I say to her.

"What then?"

"I'll tell you everything."

In turn, she better start talking too.

Chapter 52: Setsuna

"I've been drinking," he admits.

THE LAST PRINCESS

Why did he have to mention that now that we're alone in his bedroom. He walks from the door coming towards me in the middle of the room. I close my eyes but he keeps walking.

"What's the occasion?" I ask him.

"Just a bit stressed. I am hoping to clear a few things up with you."

He collapses on his bed. This is so casual for Kyoya-sama. I step closer to him. He holds his head like he's in pain.

"I love you!" he shouts.

I take a step back startled.

"I never stopped loving you. And I know what you read in that journal. That's how I use to feel. I didn't want to be your husband. But when I met you it's all I wanted."

I look down at the book in my hands. It's possible he's a different person now. Is it some coincidence that things turned out this way? I step closer and put the book beside him. Since he's this casual, his behavior is unpredictable.

"When I met you and we were alone I had to fight my urges. There were so many parts of me that I didn't want you to see. Even now there are so many parts of me I don't want you to see…so it's like there's nothing to show."

"Um-"

"I didn't talk to you because I felt like I didn't deserve you. That's all there is to it."

So that's it.

"Were you faithful?" I ask him.

"No."

My heart immediately aches. I can't see his face and I don't want to. In my head I knew that was the case but hearing him admit it without hesitation is breaking my heart.

Without realizing it I'm backing away from him. I'm trying to escape because it's hard.

"Come here," he says to me.

193

THE LAST PRINCESS

Still lying on the bed he lifts up his hand beckoning me.

"Come here," he repeats. "I know you're upset."

I shake my head. I back all the way to the door and slide down to sit. I don't know him at all. I cover my face and start to cry.

"Setsuna-san."

I feel his arms around me.

"I'm sorry," he whispers.

"You're so unfair."

"I know you still love me."

Why do I still love him? I wish I didn't. Crying into his chest is nostalgic. He's been there for me during some really hard times. And before I met him, the idea of him got me through some hard times.

He tilts my head to him and wipes my tears with the swipe of his thumb.

"For a while I wanted to give you away and let you be free. I knew Kira made a move on you. I always thought he was more fitting."

"I don't want Kira-kun!"

That attempt at jealously just blew up in my face. Kira-kun just got the wrong idea.

"I slept with other women cause I was lonely. Those women didn't admire me or look at me with such big eyes."

"You let me down."

"I know. Will you give me another chance? Will you still marry me?"

Even after what he did I know the answer. I nod to him and he hugs me. He grazes my neck and I take hold of my bandage. It still stings a little. He tries to get a closer look and I turn away.

"Since we're being honest," he starts. "Tell me who put all those cuts on your body."

THE LAST PRINCESS

He doesn't believe my suicide attempt. I turn away from him. It's all supposed to be a secret. I don't want Kyoya-sama worrying about my parent's murderer on the loose. And also...I was hoping to meet with him again to find out why he saved me.

"It was me," I say to him.

"You really tried to kill yourself?"

"Yes. As soon as I was left alone I did it. I...I never thought I would see you again. That's why I did it."

If he sees my face he'll know I'm lying. I dive back into his chest again.

"Don't worry," he says to me. "I won't leave you alone again."

Chapter 53: Kantarou

How can I enjoy an event like this? So many people are in the palace for this party. The main level was sealed off but I have a guard in every hallway and stairwell to make sure no one strays. There's got to be somewhere I missed.

"It's obvious what you're doing," Yumiko-san says behind me.

"I thought I told you to examine the buffet."

"I already ate."

"That's not what I meant."

There's people here from all our allied countries. Our prime minister is at the bar and the Morinaga general is mingling. I stand behind the stage watching it all.

"It's obvious you're trying to distract yourself," she says to me.

Kira and Setsuna-san sit on stage. He's ogling her and she's smiling despite it. She's never been around so many people before.

"Go back to the buffet," I tell her.

"Did you pick someone yet?"

THE LAST PRINCESS

I rather not think about it.

"That's not your concern."

"It's Chiyo-san, isn't it?"

It is. Chiyo-san is the quietest person I've met with. But all those meetings were secret. She must be spying on me. Speaking of Chiyo-san, I should greet her. When my eyes spot her Yumiko-san slaps my arm.

"Don't be immature. You're not seventeen anymore," I tell her.

I look back at her and her face is contorted trying to fight off tears. Now isn't the time for this.

"You can't have both of us," she says to me. "If you announce your marriage to her then I'm leaving tonight."

"I told you, you can't."

"You can't have both of us! Get that through your thick head."

She storms off. I've grown to like Yumiko-san. I've even grown to like her emotional ways. She gets me but she can't be with me. If I wasn't the crown prince it would be different. Since she's not a royal she has no concept of what duty is. If she understood my duty, she would get me a bit more.

I see no reason why she can't continue to be my plaything. This marriage is just a business deal. I step down to the people and make my way to Chiyo-san.

She's a smart quiet girl. Twenty-five and just finished her masters in sociology. Her humanitarian side will compliment me well. She can do all my community outreach for me. It's a good choice. And she's good looking so she'll make me a really pretty daughter and maybe some sons.

"Kantarou-sama," she says as I approach.

"Thank you for coming to the birthday celebration."

"Thank you for inviting me. It's my first time seeing the princess. She's really something."

"That she is. You received a call yesterday about the proceedings?"

"Yes, I am very happy you picked me."

THE LAST PRINCESS

It will be final once I announce it. She's acceptable but I don't like having things set in stone. What if she's a bitch? I won't be able to change my mind. I haven't seen every side to her. But what's it matter. It's just for show.

"Don't speak about it," I say to her. "I'll make the announcement when I am ready."

"I look forward to spending more time with you once it's announced."

"Do yourself a favor and keep this professional."

I need a drink. I grab a glass from the waiter and make my way back to the stage. This is as good a seat as any.

"Thank you for guarding the party," the princess says as I sit next to her.

"Of course."

"You don't look so good."

She lowers the drink from my face. She should save all that concern for her own husband. I haven't seen him make an appearance yet.

"I think I broke your cousin's heart," I tell her.

"You already broke it. But you made a promise to me."

"I want to keep it but-"

"But you can't have both."

"What makes you think I want her?"

"Cause…"

She lowers her head and starts playing with her fingers. Out with it.

"I think you would be good for her. You make her feel more important and confident. And if you two are together, we would be even more like family."

"I'll be your family no matter what. But things are not going to work out between me and your cousin. You have to let that promise go."

"I would if you really wanted me to. You want an excuse that will allow you to keep her close."

How does Kyoya put up with all her perceptive skills.

THE LAST PRINCESS

"Maybe I do," I admit to her. "Your love and your duty happen to be the same thing. We all can't be that lucky."

"Can you stop boring her," Kira says stretching over her. "I swear you're becoming like my big sister."

"Don't mind him," she says pushing him away. "He snuck some wine."

"Kantarou whines too much," he says laughing.

I'd slap him if we weren't in public.

"Take some advice from me for once. Do whatever the hell you want. That's what you use to do. I liked that about you."

"Kira-kun, you're causing a scene."

"Sorry, dear. A kiss would shut me up."

"Princess, why don't you go tidy up since you lost your appetite."

He has his eyes closed with his lips puckered. She gets up quietly and I take her seat.

"Remember what we use to do at boring dinners," I tell him.

I grab his hand and pull his finger back. He mouths a scream and straightens up.

"Okay, I'm sorry."

"Don't disrespect her again," I warn him.

"We have a thing."

"There is no "thing" between you and the princess. There are a lot of girls that came here just to get a look at you. Why not try to bed one of them."

"You encouraged me to be with her remember?"

"But if she doesn't want you, back off. She wants to see you as family. She's trying to replace what she had. Don't push her."

"Whatever."

He goes back to sipping his cup. So much growing up to do. I'll have to make a call to make sure he has a tough time when he gets back to the academy.

THE LAST PRINCESS

"Thinking about girls can make you go crazy, right?" he asks me. "The ones that just take off their clothes make it fun but the ones you care about are hard to handle."

I'm surprised how he understands it. It's exactly how I feel.

"What do you know about the girls that take off their clothes?" I ask.

"You didn't warn me they would be fighting to get a piece of me. But still....I like Setsuna-san."

"Give it up."

"Show me how and I might try."

I'm asking him to play by the rules and I won't. Since when have I cared about people's feelings and expectations. I don't play by the rules. If I want a queen to do my public service and a woman to entertain me then I'll have both. Fuck the rules.

"You'll give up on Setsuna-san because she's a nice girl."

I scan the crowd and see Yumiko-san prowling the buffet. She's eating slowing while checking all the guests. I'll make her come around.

I keep thinking why I want to hold onto her so much. Never knew who she was prior to that first meeting. Waiting to see Kyoya's bride I looked across the table and saw this beautiful woman. Our eyes met and she stared shocked; couldn't believe I didn't take my eyes off of her. She seemed so funny to me and out of my world.

Being crown prince I was always molded to be a king. And as a king, my enemies will threaten the things I love. I took charge of my family's safety myself. They were all I could care about. From talking to Yumiko-san I started to care about her too. I don't want her to leave.

I always get what I want. This is no exception. Kira takes after me in a lot of ways. Hopefully he knows how to be selective when imitating me.

Chapter 54: Setsuna

It's such a fun party so far. People are smiling at me and I get to look them in the face for the first time. A lot of Morinaga's big leaders came just to apologize to me about what happened at the funeral. But there are also people asking about my future husband. He's yet to show himself today.

I step outside the birthday room and go into one of the closed off hallways. The guards take notice of me and let me pass. With the birthday hall in the distance I can still hear the laughter. My parents never gave me a birthday party. They would acknowledge my increase in age but wouldn't make a big deal about it; they wanted to continue hiding my existence.

The Niwa family is so loving. I never knew family could be like that.

I stop at an open door to the courtyard. No one is supposed to be this far away from the birthday hall. Kantarou-sama told us all to stay alert. I peek out and the familiar smell of cigarettes comes to me. So he's been here this whole time. Kyoya-sama only smokes when he's stressed. He's been stressed a lot lately.

I wish things could become normal for us again. I really am happy he's here. But thinking about him with someone else makes me feel like I don't belong near him anymore. Since he told me about his unfaithfulness I've been avoiding him. Is it alright to love him still?

He breathes out heavily and I grip the doorway. The training I had didn't include any of this. Mother's lessons mentioned nothing about how to deal with a lack of trust.

"Can I have a light?"

Someone else is there! I grip the doorway harder. Where did that woman come from? She sits down next to him on the step a few feet from me. Can't judge what he's thinking by staring at his back.

"Smoking isn't an attractive habit," he says to her.

"That hasn't stopped you from looking good."

He looks towards her and hands over his lighter.

"You don't recognize me?" she asks.

"I do. You're a reporter on the evening news"

"So how come you're not star struck?"

"I hate reporters."

THE LAST PRINCESS

Is there some kind code I can't break? Every woman that's near him is a potential affair. Their words sound normal but what if there's something underneath it all.

"So let me ask you-"

"Don't," he silences her.

"Just a quick question-"

"Nope."

"Are you really going to marry the princess?" she asks in a rush.

I listen closely for his answer. He puts out his cigarette and stops completely. I wanna know what he has to say.

"Stop fishing for a story," he tells her.

"Are you saying you don't plan on marrying her? Or perhaps you'll marry her to take the title and-"

"Say whatever you want about me but leave the princess out of it."

"I see-"

"And also, relinquish that recording device to the guard that will be escorting you back to the party."

He's good. Kyoya-sama has always been very astute. Oh! He's getting up. I back away from the door and start running down the hall.

Hearing the door close I run faster and duck into the nearest room. Not ready to talk to him just yet. He was alone with a pretty woman and had no interest in her; it's somewhat reassuring.

What room is this anyway?

"Did you need me so urgently that you had to barge in here?"

"Captain Saki!"

I haven't seen him since the night we left the palace. He turns around from the toilet zipping up. Still so comfortable around me. I had no idea this was the men's room.

THE LAST PRINCESS

"I haven't seen you since the night we left the palace," I say to him.

"Not my best night."

He hasn't looked at me since I walked in. He stays at the sink washing his hands. I know he got in trouble. Maybe he hates me for it.

"We shouldn't stay in here," he says.

"No, we can't leave just yet. He might still be out there."

"Who you hiding from now?"

"…Kyoya-sama."

He opens the door and looks out. Something is definitely odd with him. He's normally happy to talk to me and engage me. While I've been avoiding Kyoya-sama, maybe Captain Saki has been avoiding me.

He opens the door and waves me to follow.

"I'll escort you back to the party," he says dryly.

"Wait, what's wrong?"

"What do you mean?"

I tug on his sleeve but he still won't look at me. He really doesn't like me anymore.

"I'm sorry if I got you in trouble. Has the king been too hard on you?"

"It's nothing I can't handle."

I tug on his sleeve again and no response. I didn't even realize I lost a friend. My hand drops from him and he walks on. He doesn't care about me anymore.

"I-I'm sorry," I call to him. "I really am sorry. I've been selfish to you and-"

He quickly turns back to look at me. I don't want to lose a friend. There's not a lot of people I can count on; he's always been good to me. But these stupid cuts and that stupid man that came and gave them to me make it seem like the captain isn't good enough.

He stares down at me seeing me close to tears.

THE LAST PRINCESS

"You would really cry for me, princess? I've wronged you in so many ways."

"No, you haven't. I just want you to keep being my bodyguard and my friend."

He slowly steps closer to me. I raise my head to look up at him. Whatever he says, I'll take it. If he doesn't want to be around me anymore, I'll respect his decision.

"Even if you can't see me, I'm always watching to make sure you're safe."

"But we don't even talk anymore."

"You have Kyoya-sama for that," he says.

"You're my friend in your own right. And last year on my birthday you stayed with me the whole day. Now-"

He plants his hand on my shoulder.

"Happy Birthday, Setsuna-san."

He leans down and kisses my cheek. My face gets warmer. He stays close to me inches from my face. Can he hear my heart beating faster?

"If you want me near you, I won't let anyone take me away," he whispers.

"Am I interrupting?"

"Kyoya-sama!"

I quickly push the captain away. Kyoya-sama steps down the hall. Each step makes me scared. Has he been spying like I do with him.

"You two are so close," he says to us. "It's to be expected, I guess."

"I was just leaving," Captain Saki says.

"No," I say to him. "You don't have to go."

"Kyoya-sama can escort you back to the party. You don't need me."

He's shying away cause Kyoya-sama is here. I look back and forth. This must be a part of his punishment. I grab the captain's sleeve to keep him from leaving.

"Have you been mean to him?" I ask.

THE LAST PRINCESS

"What?"

"Captain Saki is our friend. What happened wasn't his fault."

"I get that you're fond of him but I left him near you cause I was away. Now that I am back, he knows to go back to his other duties. I don't blame him for what happened. You told me that was all your doing."

"Well...what if I don't want him to go back to his other duties," I tell him.

"He won't grow as a captain unless he does."

I guess that's true. He will never be promoted just being my bodyguard. It's selfish of me to keep him near me cause I like him and trust him. But does that mean I won't get to see him again?

I look back at Captain Saki and he stares down at me.

"Kyoya-sama always knows best," he tells me.

I know he's right. I drop my hand from him. I have to believe in what the captain told me earlier. "If you want me near you, I won't let anyone take me away." Yes, I will believe him.

Kyoya-sama comes to me and takes my hand. He turns me away as Captain Saki walks off.

"I didn't think you two would hit it off. You had so many worries about him before."

"I should head back to the party."

His grip tightens.

"Why have you been avoiding me? I thought you would want to spend time together."

"I just wanna head back to the party-"

"Talk."

I tense up. I don't know what it is but Kyoya-sama seems so much scarier these days. In his interviews he's sharp and ruthless. Maybe I'm thinking about that. I clear my throat nervously.

"I still haven't forgiven you for....a lot of things."

"What can I do to help?"

"I don't know. I just wanna get back to the party."

I break away from him and run down the hall. I'm not ready to be near him. Definitely don't want to be alone with him.

Chapter 55: Yumiko

What am I supposed to be looking for? I'm not military trained so why put me on security duty. I keep telling him, "I'm studying fashion design" but he never listens. Still insists on making me do things unrelated to fashion.

The ladies here have some pretty nice dresses.

"Um, excuse me."

Especially this one. I love the white beading at the bottom contrasting with the blue dress. And the bust line is pretty too. Oh….it's her.

"You're Yumiko Yamamoto-san, princess of Morinaga."

"I'm not a princess."

"My name is Chiyo Subera. It's really nice to meet you."

"It is?"

"Yes," she says smiling. "When you started at the university I really wanted to be friends with you but I was a bit too shy. I never would have thought I would be…chosen by your boss."

She went to school with me? It's a big school so it's possible. She's adorable; that's very different from me. Unconsciously I am sizing her up. Why did he choose her?

"He's not my boss," I correct her.

"Then what is Kantarou-sama to you?"

Ugh, it's that cute head tilt. I use to be able to do that. Since when does Kantarou-sama like cute girls.

THE LAST PRINCESS

"Uh...he's like..."

She's the one that should be explaining her position, not me. I was here first. She stares at me with her stupid head tilted as I stammer.

"Okay, he's my boss," I sigh.

"I guess I'll be your boss soon. And I know you're not a princess."

She smiles and takes a shrimp from the table. She's gonna be a problem. I take back what I said about the dress. She turns around flipping her wavy brown hair at me. I have to get rid of her. Kantarou-sama cannot have a woman like that.

"Why the sullen look. It's a party isn't it?"

I am done watching this buffet. It brings nothing but bitches. My mother stands in front of me flashy as ever. She wears a low cut red gown. It's a beautiful gown but she makes it look ugly.

"I couldn't help but overhear. Is that woman Kantarou-sama's choice?"

"Yeah."

"And what are you doing to stop her?"

"Nothing. He's not into me like that. He just wants me to work for him."

That's what I gather. He's intent on keeping me under him in a way I didn't have in mind.

"Maybe now you'd like some advice from me," she offers.

I don't want to interfere but it's gonna kill me to watch him marry her. I look up at the stage and see him laughing with his little brother. There's so many sides to him; he's allowed me to see them all. If he shows all that to Chiyo-san, there'll be nothing special or unique between us.

"Introduce me to him," she says to me.

"Really?"

"Yes, let's go."

She grabs my arm and heads for the stage. I'm tempted to go with this plan of hers. Before I can change my mind she starts making a scene.

THE LAST PRINCESS

"Prince, it's lovely to meet you," she says climbing the stairs.

He stands up alerted. He takes notice of me and relaxes. Mother goes right up to him and hugs him.

"Who is this woman?" he asks me.

"My mother-"

"I'm Ju Mei Asahina-Yamamoto. Thank you so much for taking care of my daughter and that lovely niece of mine."

She backs away from him and gives Kira-sama a flirtatious wave. He straightens up in his seat. It's embarrassing but I wanna see where she's going with this.

"It's been no problem taking care of her," he says to her. "She's a lovely woman."

"So nice to hear you say that. Cause of my reputation, I thought no one would make an honest woman out of her. It's often the case with being labeled a bastard child."

She grabs my hand and pulls me forward. I bump into him and he braces me grabbing my shoulders. I haven't been this close to him in a while. I miss his cologne.

"Your mother told me you were making your marriage announcement today. Please let me do the honor," she says.

No, don't do this. She's gonna ruin everything the king has planned for his country.

"Mother, don't-"

"Sorry to interrupt the birthday party, everyone," my mother says turning to the crowd. "But when I heard the good news, I couldn't keep it in."

She raises her hand to display us like some sort of art piece. I push away from him and try to reach her.

"Kantarou Niwa-sama has just asked for permission to marry my daughter."

The crowd cheers and claps. I turn back to Kantarou-sama and he looks down at me pissed off. Any backtracking now will make people not take him seriously. So much hate in his eyes.

THE LAST PRINCESS

"You have my blessing, prince. You have my country's blessing."

He grabs my hand and pulls me behind the stage curtain. The crowd starts whistling. He pulls me further from the stage then out into one of the hallways. He's silent until we reach his office. He throws me in and slams the door shut.

"I didn't tell her to-"

"Do you realize what you've done!"

I stumble back as he approaches me. I bump into his desk and quickly move around it. There's no telling what he'll do.

"You just cost the palace billions of dollars. The Subera family has money, more money than your entire country. And what do you have? Nothing but a bastard title."

He's never called me that before. He keeps approaching and I back against the wall. I don't think he'll hit me. That's never been his style. But he's furious; I can tell by his breathing.

"Kantarou-sama, I didn't know she would do that. I just wanted to introduce you to my mother. I'm sorry," I beg him. "I'll talk to Chiyo-san. I'll apologize to her and make it better."

"You'll get on your knees and beg for her forgiveness."

"I will."

"This isn't about your feelings or mine. It's about the future of my country. That's something you'll never understand."

He turns around and heads back for the door. Am I that bad? I fall to the floor crying. I was happy when all those people cheered for us. They didn't mind us being together. He's the only one against it.

"Do I really have nothing to offer you? Not your country but you. Do you really not want me?"

I hug my knees and cry into my dress. I have to leave the palace tonight. I'll have to beg Chiyo-san to marry him, the man I love.

I feel his warmth above me and open my eyes. He's kneeling down to me. His eyes look pained too. I reach out and touch his cheek. His eyes gaze into mine.

"Isn't it enough to just be near me?" he asks softly.

"No."

"It has to be."

"It's not enough. I can't watch you be with her. I want you to be with me."

He leans in and kisses me. I wrap my arms around him and he pulls me to sit in his lap. For a while we kiss behind his desk. Our minds empty of any worry or reality. But when we part, it all sets in.

"I want you to listen carefully and keep this between us," he says.

I nod to him.

"I love you," he whispers to me. "And it's because I love you that I can't marry you. You have to step aside. We can only have our moments in the dark."

"Kantarou," I say tearing up again.

He places me on the floor still gasping for air between cries. I'll never get to be with him. The door slams closed and I fall to his carpet with my head right where he would put his feet.

Chapter 56: Kyoya

I followed right after her but she's yet to step back into the party. She stands at the doorway looking in at all the people that came just to see her. I step behind her and she doesn't notice.

Setsuna-san always seemed smart and wise for her age. She's effectively punishing me for what I've done. And because she's a bit older, I can't win her back with a kiss. She'd rather cling to Ayato-san and worry about her relationship with him than her relationship with me. She thinks I'm not capable of jealously but…I think he's a threat.

I can't let him know that.

When I saw him kiss her in the hallway, I wanted to grab him by the neck and strangle him. She was blushing and that made me even angrier. We've never fought over a girl.

"Can I escort you in?" I ask her.

She turns around stumbling away from me. I hold out my hand to her and she just stares.

"I'm not ready just yet."

I look into the room and see Kira on stage. Mother hugs him and makes her speech to all her guests.

"He needs his attention too. How considerate of you," I say to her.

"I'm afraid he might cause a scene if I go in. Like announce his love for me."

"You have your pick of lot of men."

She keeps her eyes away from me. I miss looking into her big eyes.

"I don't see it that way."

"How close are you with Ayato-san?"

"He's just my friend."

"Does he kiss you often?"

She turns back to me smiling. Don't tell me. She wouldn't pursue him.

"All the time," she says staring at me. "I spent a lot of time with him. Naturally we've gotten closer."

She's lying. She's feeding off what I say to make me jealous. These games don't suit her at all.

"We spent a lot of nights together and we would watch movies and sneak snacks from the kitchen. He's a lot of fun. And I like him a lot. Especially when he kisses me."

"Here's the thing you should know about me," I say leaning down to her. "I will kill any man that tries to take you from me. So think carefully about what you're saying."

"W-we spend a lot of time together but it's just as friends," she stammers. "It's never been anything more than that."

"Good."

THE LAST PRINCESS

But she likes him enough to protect him. I'm on the fence about whether he should keep guarding her. Since she's sixteen now I can be more public with our love. I want to take her back with me but I need protection for her. He follows my orders blindly and that's what I need but…can he control his emotions?

The crowd starts clapping listening to mother talk on stage. I grab Setsuna-san's hand and pull her forward. Now is as good a time as any to start being public.

"Oh, the two lovers emerge. I've been looking for you," mother announces.

I pull her on stage and keep her beside me. The clapping goes on and on and I feel the sweat on her hands.

"Thank you all for coming to celebrate my brother's birthday and my princess' birthday," I say to the crowd. "I've spent a lot of time away trying to get Morinaga back in order after the tragedy. And she's been waiting patiently for me while recovering from her heartache."

It's a great story. The princess has lost so much but she holds on to me. Her people trust me because she sees me as her only hope. They see me that way too. It all worked out perfectly.

"I've done my best for you but I feel like it's never enough," I tell her. "I can't stay away from you much longer so please give into my selfishness and come back to Morinaga with me."

The crowd claps and screams their support.

"Welcome back, princess," I hear.

"She's a queen now," I correct.

I'm a king with everything. The Han people love me and the Morinaga people love me. Setsuna-san loves me despite everything I've done and everything I've done that she doesn't know about.

I'm on top of the world now. Finally I have my path. I turn to her in front of everyone and hug her close. She looks frightened.

"How about a dance," mother suggests.

I've never danced with her before; I know she's trained. I lead her off stage and the crowd separates. With all eyes on us she stuffs her face into my chest.

"Why so shy?" I whisper.

THE LAST PRINCESS

"They're all looking at me."

"Cause you're a queen."

I shuffle across the floor with her and she holds onto me tighter. She stays at my chest listening to my heartbeat. I missed being romantic with a woman. Sex was nothing compared to having her in my arms.

"Happy birthday," I whisper to her. "Sorry I didn't get you a present."

"You are my present. All I wanted was to see you."

"I have to give you more than that."

I slide my hand to her lower back. She's picked up a curve or two. I know one way to make her forget about her trust.

"Stay in my room tonight," I whisper to her. "I'll give you another present."

"I'm not old enough for that."

"I think you are. Aren't you curious?"

I kiss her neck and she turns her head away. What's this? She's still wearing a bandage. But she cut herself weeks ago.

"Why are you still wearing a bandage?" I ask her.

"It still hasn't healed."

Hasn't healed? I take my hand from her back and peel the bandage away slowly. It's fresh red. It's just like the cut she got on her face years ago.

"Ayato," I breathe out.

He did this! He cut her!

"Tell me what happened that night you left the palace," I say deeply.

I'm having trouble controlling myself. I want to run and punish him but I need to know for sure. I need to hear it myself.

"I already told you-"

"Tell me the truth," I say squeezing her hand.

"You're hurting me."

THE LAST PRINCESS

"Tell me the truth now."

The crowd cheers on and I hide my face against her neck.

"They look so good together," I hear from the crowd.

"I already told-"

"The truth, Setsuna."

What's she hiding from me? She's not supposed to lie to me.

"I was in a hotel room with Captain Saki."

"And what did you two talk about?"

"We talked about what I read in your journal. We talked about his past, about how he met you. A-and he asked….if…."

"Tell me," I urge her.

"He asked if I would be okay if it was the two of us and I said no. He seemed sad after that and left the room. I waited for him but he didn't come back."

"And how did you get all the cuts?"

I lift my head scanning the room as I twirl her around. Where is he?

"The masked man came back," she says softly. "He did it. But I don't think he meant to hurt me. He said he loved me. I didn't want to say anything because I didn't want people to know you killed the wrong man."

"You're not protecting me by hiding things from me. Don't lie to me again."

The song ends and I grab her hand and lead her off the floor. The crowd cheers as we exit.

"Save it for your wedding night!"

I keep tugging her behind me and she struggles to keep up. I need to trap her some place so I can confront him. But knowing him, he's close. I turn around and Ayato-san stands at the corner. He knows I know. And he knows I'm ruthless when it comes to Setsuna-san. She's yet to see him.

I keep her turned away while we stare each other down. He's never challenged me. What's gotten into him? If I send him away, he'll be unpredictable.

213

Only Ayato-san and I know the details of the royal massacre. He was the tool and I was the one directing him. I have to work on controlling him again. I can't let my emotions ruin my plan.

I think about our years together. He's never been in love. And I know how sweet Setsuna-san can be. I left him to take care of her and he's been pushing down his feelings the whole time.

With her still turned away from him I start to speak.

"Ayato-san walked away that night because you rejected him," I tell her.

"I didn't."

"He wanted to be with you and you told him you wanted to be with me. Didn't you?"

"He's my bodyguard-"

"You're much more to him than you think. Tell me you'll never fall in love with him."

He looks shocked. I want him to hear it. If he hears it for himself then he'll give up and things can go back to normal. He'll punish himself and I won't have to.

"I can't say that," she softly.

"What?"

"If you would have stayed away a bit longer, I might have. I'm sorry."

Chapter 57: Ayato

I think I heard her correctly; I'm so shocked.

"If you would have stayed away a bit longer, I might have," I repeat in my head.

"I might have….I might have," I repeat again.

Setsuna-san runs away from him without seeing me. So I had a chance. I never thought she saw me that way. Maybe she was starting to.

THE LAST PRINCESS

Kyoya-sama walks up to me in my daze.

"Don't look so smug."

He punches me and I fall to the floor. Still smiling. I can't believe I had a chance. He kicks me and I lay still. I can tolerate a lot of pain. This doesn't hurt at all. For once I'm on the same level as Kyoya-sama. Setsuna-san likes me.

"Why are you smiling?" he asks leaning down to me.

"S-she likes me."

"So what. You think that means you can have her?"

"I-"

"She will always be at my side. And you will sit there with your sword in your hand and do nothing."

I try to sit up and he slams his hand on my face to push me down.

"I'm taking you out of the palace guard."

"No!"

I slap his hand away and sit up. If he takes me out the palace guard I won't get to see her or him. I won't have anyone. There are a lot of secrets between me and him. If anyone were to find out about the things we've done, we promised to go down together. That's why he'll never tell her what I did.

"I'm the best one in the palace guard. Even better than the commander. You know that. And without me guarding her, she'll be in danger."

"The only one that's ever tried to harm her is you."

It was only because she made me angry.

"Seems removing you would solve a lot of things."

"You're finally jealous of me," I say to him.

"Jealous of you? What could I possibly gain from being more like you?"

"Setsuna-san's love."

THE LAST PRINCESS

He punches me and I spit out blood. I figured he would do that. I sit up again and wipe the blood from my face. For a guy that hasn't been in combat he's pretty strong.

"You're supposed to be my friend," he says to me. "I had your back so many times. I covered for you so you could be yourself. Remember Saya."

I remember her. After that day Kyoya-sama knew the extent of my disorder. He hand delivered people for me to experiment with. He accepted how I was, laughed with me, and held me when I cried.

There were moments when I remembered my parents and cried. Nothing could make me stop. I thought….I'm just like the man that murdered them senselessly. And I'll just breed another when I take someone's parents away from them. I didn't know Kyoya-sama well at that time. It was the day I moved into the palace.

"I heard all about you," his mother says to me. "Mind telling me your name?"

He has a hot mom. I look over at him and Kyoya-sama shakes his head in disapproval. So I shouldn't look at her chest.

"Ayato Saki," I tell her.

"You're so handsome. Just like my Kyoya. Looks like you'll be my forth son."

"I'm not looking to be your son. I already had a mother. I just want to stay near Kyoya-sama."

"You sound like a loyal friend. Welcome."

She walks off with her baby trailing behind her holding her dress. He's not quite a baby but I bet he acts like one.

"Be more respectful to my mother," Kyoya-sama tells me.

"Sorry. She seems like a nice lady."

"She is. It was her influence that allowed you to stay. My father is really against it. Says you'll be a bad influence."

"Oh…"

"But don't let that stop you. Just be yourself."

THE LAST PRINCESS

I start walking with him down the hallways. There are infinite hallways. I look out the large windows and see a big open garden. It's so different. He walks these halls like he owns them.

"W-what do you do all day around here?"

"Study."

Twelve year olds have to do more than study.

"You'll be studying with me," he tells me.

"O-okay."

"But how about we play some video games first."

I never played them before. I bet he has the best ones. I try to hide my smile. He makes me feel normal.

"I'll race you," he says looking back me. "Take a left at the corner and go upstairs. It's the first door."

"Um, you mean now?"

He's already taken off. I run after him and feel so happy. I see him up ahead but I'm not far. I breath heavily but it's the happiest I've been.

"You're too slow," he calls back to me.

"Look out!"

He bumps into a man and falls down. I kneel down to him.

"What did I say about running in the hallway?"

"Sorry, father."

The king looks down at me and I stare back. I would never bring any harm to Kyoya-sama. I'll be good.

"Ayato-kun, have you settled in?" he asks me.

"Uh, yes, sir."

"It's nice to see Kyoya with a friend."

We both look at each other embarrassed. I'm happy to have a friend too.

THE LAST PRINCESS

When night time comes I'm left alone in my room. It's a big room. Not sure what to do with all this space. I'm afraid to close my eyes; if I do, this might all go away. My eyes flicker then finally shut.

I'm awakened by my own screams. Kyoya-sama's arms hold onto me. I slow down and stay silent.

"M-my mom."

"What about her?" he asks.

"I miss her. I…I killed the man that took her from me. I think she might have still been conscious when I did it."

"So are you regretting what you've done-"

"I liked it," I admit to him. "I feel like I woke up when the sword went through him. But what if she sees me now. She would hate me."

I sit up and wipe my tears. It's what I've been afraid to tell him or anyone. It wasn't for defense. That man never tried to attack me. I killed him cause I didn't want him to get away. I enjoyed it. It made me happy being covered in his blood. I wonder if he felt the same being covered in my mother's.

Kyoya-sama sits next to me on my bed. I wonder what he thinks.

"You and I will be friends for a long time," he says smiling. "Nothing you say or do will stop that."

"But…why?"

"Who's to say I'm not like you."

His words made me want to serve him. Looking back at him now, I've never seen him have so much rage towards me. Kyoya-sama has had it all his entire life. All I want is to have that girl. He'll always be my friend. Nothing I say or do will stop that. So if I go after her, we'll see who comes out on top.

"Still won't drop that stupid smile," he says to me. "Fine. You can stay in the palace guard."

"R-really?"

"If you hurt Setsuna-san again, I will kill you myself."

"I'm only allowed to die by your hands."

THE LAST PRINCESS

"It would be a pain if any of this got out," he says to me. "Silence the reporter peeking out that room."

How did I miss that?

"You're skills aren't as sharp as they use to be," he teases. "Maybe you need to get some practice in."

"I'll take care of it."

I snap up and grab the door before the woman can close it. I'll have to be careful about this. It will just make the palace look bad if someone ends up dead.

"I have this wonderful drink I want you to try. You'll forget all your worries."

"I'm gonna report what I heard."

Kyoya-sama steps up behind me. It's the bitch from the evening news. She got herself a real story just now.

"I told you to stop fishing for a story," he says to her. "We have this drink that can turn you brain dead and another that can make you forget the last two years."

I'm prepared to give her either one. As long as I get to force it down her throat, I'm happy. He steps in and before she can shriek he covers her mouth. Oh, this is surprising. He's never been very hands on.

He looks over at me and I pull a vial from my side. Never know when it will come in handy.

"Another secret between us," he says to me.

I nod to him. He holds her down and I open her mouth wide.

When it's done he walks the woman back. The guests should be leaving soon. I missed most of the festivities. I hope Setsuna-san had fun. She always wanted a birthday party.

She looked so pretty on stage. She couldn't stop smiling and I couldn't stop staring. I better do my last perimeter check. It's been such a long day; it's been a good day though.

I can't wait to see Setsuna-san again. If I talk to her a bit more and make a move, she'll fall for me. She doesn't care for Kyoya-sama anymore.

THE LAST PRINCESS

"Excuse me, Captain Saki."

I turn around. Normally I have a thing for crying distraught women but she just doesn't do it for me. Yumiko-san walks towards me. I examine her to make sure she wasn't attacked. Her dress is intact.

"I know you're supposed to be on duty but…is your offer still open?" she asks softly.

"What offer?"

She sniffles and comes closer to me. I remember the offer; I just want to make sure she does. Kantarou-sama must have finally finished breaking her heart.

"I'll wear the royal attire and put my hair up," she says. "And…you can call me whatever name you want. It'll…it'll be between us."

"Really now?"

She's already ashamed, I can tell. Her shame is not my business. I lean down to her ear.

"I'll come to your room right away, Setsuna-san," I whisper to her.

She sniffles and walks pass me. It really has been a great day. Yumiko-san seems to have fallen into the darkness, my territory. After a few rounds with me, she'll snap out of things. I'll enjoy playing around with her in the meantime.

Chapter 58: Kyoya

I wonder if she put all these plants on the balcony to improve my air quality. Seems like something she would do. She doesn't like that I smoke, I can tell. But today was stressful. Today rattled me.

I breathe out trying to avoid the plants; I want to keep them alive as long as I can. The things she's touched are the only things I can look at to remind me that we're still in love. Fishing through my pocket I find her ribbon. When I pulled this from her hair on that first night, I decided that I would love her.

It's not just some silky red threads, it's her innocence.

THE LAST PRINCESS

There's a knock at the door. I put the cigarette out and head back inside stuffing the ribbon in my pocket. Hope this isn't about that reporter woman. I open the door and stare down at her.

"I hope I didn't wake you," Setsuna-san says to me.

"Is something wrong?"

"You said I could stay over. Or maybe that's not the best thing-"

"Of course you can stay. Come in."

Did she come to get the present I talked about? Surprisingly I'm not in the mood. I close the door behind her and she waits in the middle of the room.

"It was a fun party, wasn't it?" she says to me.

As long as she enjoyed herself. I walk pass her and go to the closet. Her words still sting. I can't blame her for it but it still stings. I guess this is how she felt imagining me with someone else.

I take off my tie and begin to undress. It's quiet. I turn back and see her watching. Don't tell me she's interested. I'm looking right at her and her eyes are focused on my body.

"What are you thinking?" I ask her.

"I always wanted to see how you take off your suit. How you hang it and care for it."

"I wondered the same about you."

"With me it's more complicated. I have to take each layer off then fold it and when I'm all done I have to pray and thank my ancestors. I have to do the same when I put my robes on too."

"All that?"

"But if I'm really tired, I just sleep in them. Mother would never figure that out. She would come in some mornings and I would jump out of bed like I had gotten up early to prepare myself. She seemed so impressed by me."

"Can I watch?" I ask her.

"Hm?"

THE LAST PRINCESS

"Go ahead and get undressed."

She shakes her head. It's was worth a try. I wanted to experience her traditions a bit more. I continue to undress while she watches me.

"Dancing with you was fun," she says.

"Glad you enjoyed it."

"But it didn't end well. Can we try again?"

"At the next event."

"How about now?"

"I'm really not in the mood now. It's been a long day."

She puts her head down. What am I doing? She's trying to get closer to me and I'm turning her away. I put my shirt away and pause. We can't keep avoiding each other because of the hurtful things we've said.

"I'm sorry for what I said. I could never fall in love with anyone else-"

"You don't have to be sorry for anything," I tell her.

"But...I hurt you."

"You can hurt me all you want. It's nothing compared to what I've done to you."

She slams into me from behind holding me tightly. I touch her hands as she holds on to my stomach. I turn around and kneel down to her. She's still the sweet girl I remember.

"Don't make that face," I tell her. "You've done nothing wrong."

"I only wanted you. I swear."

I'm the one that's at fault. I actually did something. But her thoughts of someone else make her feel as guilty and wrong as me.

"But I really am close to him. He's like my best friend. He's all I had while you were away and Yumi-chan was away and-"

"I get it. I left him with you so I get it. Don't beat yourself up."

THE LAST PRINCESS

"I really do love you," she says to me. "It was hard but I never stopped loving you."

"Is it possible you've turned even sweeter than before. Let me have a taste."

I kiss her and pull her close. We've talked enough; I just want to feel her now. When I back away she licks her lips and comes at me again.

"I'm sorry," she says shyly. "I didn't mean to."

"Come to bed with me."

I take her hand and she follows behind with her eyes on the floor. I won't get carried away; at least I will try not to. We both sit down in silence. It's not my intention to have sex but she pulls her robe off her shoulder and I'm immediately stimulated. It's mesmerizing just like when I pulled the ribbon out her hair. It's arousing to see a part of her that no one else sees.

But there are just bandages underneath. White bandages wrap around her arms and across her chest.

"None of them have healed," she says to me. "I'll be scarred for the rest of my life unless…he's nice enough to give me that salve again."

I was turned on at first but I can't stand looking at her like this. I reach out and touch her shoulder and she winces with pain. He told me about his special blades. He likes to stare at his work so he coats his blades with a serum to allow a wound to heal without closing.

"I must look disgusting."

"Not at all. But you're still in pain. I don't want to be too rough with you."

I turn away from her to cool myself off. I was thinking we might do something. Her kisses are just too hot; such a tease.

"You're still as gentle as I remember," she says to me. "But you're also quite scary too."

"Sorry if I said-"

"No, it's okay to show yourself to me."

It's okay? She says the words I always wanted to hear. It's nice of her to say but I know it's not okay.

"You're really doing a great job," she says softly behind me. "I watched all your appearances. Everyone loves you. They see what I see."

"And what is it that you see?"

She doesn't see all of me, no one does.

"My hero."

I immediately breathe out. I look back at her and see her smile. Even after what I've done, even after I abandoned her she still sees me that way. I take her in my arms and hold her tight. I don't want her to see me cry. It's easy to tear up.

"You mean everything to me."

"Show me," she whispers.

I peel away from her and look into her eyes. They belong to a woman. I hope she knows what she's saying. As I move she moves with me. Backing up towards the middle of the bed and laying down.

"Show me I mean everything to you," she whispers in my ear.

I can't hold back anymore.

Chapter 59: Kantarou

"Yumiko-san!"

I pound on her door. She normally comes at the first knock. We have a breakfast to go to. It's father's follow up meeting where he continues saying how disappointed he is.

I got a taste of it last night. After that red slutty woman announced my marriage to the wrong woman he screamed at me till he went hoarse. I couldn't hear him at that time. Kept thinking about how much Yumiko-san cried. It's a sound I can never forget.

"Yumiko-san!"

THE LAST PRINCESS

Even though I got the reality of things first, it's still hard to hear her cry. The sooner she gets back to work, the sooner we can normalize all this. I'll get to look at her and look out for her.

The door cracks a little.

"Commander," she says.

I push the door open. She must have had a tantrum in here; it's a mess. She's a mess too. Normally she's always put together.

"What's the occasion for your royal robes?" I ask.

I can't tell if I caught her in the middle of taking them off or putting them on. Her lipstick is smeared all the way to her ear. She puts her head down trying to wipe it away. I know she was trying to escape. Does she plan on going back to her country like that?

"Just trying them on. Why are you here?"

Things are starting to make sense. There's a bottle of wine at her nightstand. I didn't know she drinks. I step closer and pick it up. She was upset enough to start drinking. A cheap bottle but it'll get her drunk. She sniffles grabbing the bottle from me.

"Why are you here?"

"We have a breakfast to go to. My father wants to speak with you. Get ready."

"Speak with me?"

"You should know why. I tried to cover for you as best I can-"

"I need to face him and apologize. I get it."

"Hurry and shower. You look a mess."

She walks off to the bathroom. I didn't mean to have her crying all night and drinking. We've been apart for months at a time. I assumed she had a better handle on our situation.

I plan on paying her well and making sure she's taken care of. She just needs to be my assistant. She's the only one I can tolerate being around in such a fashion. And when she understands her position we can continue our relationship in secret.

THE LAST PRINCESS

I wander around her room kicking around the mess. Last time I was in here was when she asked my opinion on a dress. We were heading to the military ball. She loved being out in public with all the cameras. Took the spotlight off me. The reporters asked if we were together and I shook my head saying she was just a kid. Denying it to no end but desperately wanting to....to....

"You don't have to wait for me."

I look back and see her damp. A towel barely covers her. I've known her for three years. I was attracted to her since the moment I looked at her. We've gotten pretty close but always just short of intercourse. It would just make her confused.

How can a man sit idly by when a woman looks like that and the doors are closed. I approach her and she pulls her towel closer.

"We're already late so it's fine to fool around for a bit."

"Do you not remember what happened last night?" she asks holding up her hand to me.

I stop and think. Last night I said what I needed to say. I won't marry her but I'll still have my fun with her.

"We have an understanding," I clarify.

"Yes, that you'll never marry me."

"That's correct but it's fine to-"

"No! You can't keep doing this. Our relationship is either on or off. And you made it clear that it's off."

"Cause I won't marry you doesn't mean-"

"I'm not gonna be your mistress!"

She....she has the nerve to yell at me. She has the nerve to reprimand me and deny me. I take a step closer to her and my boot crunches on something. Looking up at her I see her staring at my foot in horror. She runs into the bathroom and locks herself in.

"What's the big deal?" I question.

I lift up my foot and reach down. A used condom wrapper. She was with someone last night.

THE LAST PRINCESS

"Yumiko!"

I bang on her bathroom door and she doesn't answer. Who was she with? I have to know. There were so many people here last night; I can't narrow it down.

"Who were you with!"

"It's not your business," she yells from the other side.

Someone touched her. Of course that's my business. They did it in my palace, in the room I gave her. I bang on the door harder and I just hear her crying on the other side.

"Stop it," she says sobbing. "You're only hurting me. You can't break my heart and then act like you still own it. Please, just go."

I'm only hurting her? Does she think I'm not hurt too? I can't help what both of us were born into.

"Please, just stop all this," she says.

"Who was it?" I ask again softly.

"You don't get to ask that."

I don't get to ask? I care…she has to get that. I'm hurt that she would lie down with another man in my house. Stupid woman doesn't get that I have to do my duty as crown prince but I still want to be with her despite that. I'm trying to make it all work. I'm trying to make it work for her.

"You're supposed to be my woman."

"You're a liar."

"Fine," I say to her. "Let's be done with it then. It's obvious you'll never be able to understand what I've been trying to tell you."

"Please, go."

"For the record….you were plenty good enough for me. You just didn't know how to act like it."

I say it's over but I don't know if I can just give up on her. I've never had real feelings for a woman before so I don't know how to get rid of them. Never felt jealously; always felt superior to every man. But there's a man that she would choose

227

to lie down with over me. I take the long way to the dining area thinking about all my words to her.

"So it looks like everyone's running late," Kyoya says to me.

"Um, yeah."

"Good morning, Kantarou-sama," the princess says to me touching my arm.

He opens the door the dining room to let me in. Seeing my face he closes it.

"Setsuna-san, go in and save a place for me."

She goes in and he stays next to me in the hall. Is it that easy to tell I'm uneasy.

"I heard about your little debacle last night," he says to me. "It will go over like a prank. Some desperate attempt by the exiled woman."

"After that false announcement, I took Yumiko-san aside to make things clear. I told her I love her but I'll never marry her. I assumed she would grow up a little and get that we could be together in secret."

"No woman wants that," he says.

"You somehow get to have everything you want. Why can't I?"

"A lot was sacrificed so I could get my way. Don't think it's easy to live with," he tells me.

So I have to sacrifice to get my way.

"Like I told father, you can't control people," he says opening the door. "Yumiko-san is not someone you can control like you want to."

That's becoming obvious. Inside mother sits at the head of the table with father. Kyoya takes his place next to Setsuna-san and Kira scoffs from across the table.

"Sorry for being late," I announce.

"You're not the latest," father says. "Where's Yumiko-san?"

"On her way."

I sit down next to Kira and across from Kyoya. Let's get this over with.

THE LAST PRINCESS

"Setsuna-san, you're really glowing. You must have really enjoyed yourself last night," mother says to her.

"Nothing happened!" she screams at mother. "I kept my hands to myself."

"Dear? Did something happen last night? The two of you left so suddenly."

"Don't tell me," Kira says to her. "You did it with Kyo-nii?"

"I did not!"

Her face is so red. Looks like everyone was fooling around last night. Kyoya touches her hand and she lowers her head.

"What's it like being with such an old man? I bet he forced you," he teases her again.

"Kyoya-sama is not old and he didn't force me. A-and we didn't do anything."

"That's enough," Kyoya quiets her. "Now isn't the time for bickering."

"We have more pressing matters than the princess' chastity," father announces.

"Did he remember to call you by your name?" Kira teases again.

"Shut up!"

"Settle down, Setsuna-san," father calms her. "Don't make me tell you again."

"Sorry, king."

It's quiet as we all take a sip of tea to calm our nerves. Kyoya looks pleased; I wonder if he did deflower the princess. All must be forgiven between them. But she's so short compared to him. I wonder how it looked. Did she even know what she was doing. There's a knock at the dining room door.

"Kantarou, please open the door," father says.

I thought we had servants for that. I push my seat back. Father must be saving his rage for Yumiko-san. He looks pleased so far. I open the door and immediately hear giggling.

"Uh-"

THE LAST PRINCESS

"Good morning, Kantarou-sama."

"Uh….C-chiyo-san?"

"Let her in, dear," mother calls. "I invited her for breakfast so we can all meet her."

I didn't expect to see her so soon. She snatches up my arm startling me. She was different in the meeting. Very distant and quiet. She knew I was a big deal. Now she's smiling and holding me like I've known her for years.

"I can sit next to you, right?" she asks me.

"I…guess."

I lead her in. Kyoya keeps his head down and Setsuna-san hides her face behind him examining her.

"So rare to see my Kantarou with a young woman on his arm. I like this look," mother says.

"It's quite a match," father adds.

Chiyo-san steps over to the other side of the table. Her heels echo as she walks. It's all I hear. I feel so out of it.

"It's wonderful to meet you, princess. My name is Chiyo Subera." she says bowing in front of Setsuna-san.

The princess stares confused then touches her shoulder.

"No need to bow. I'm not your princess."

"But you are. You're a wonderful figure in Han. Everyone admires your courage and perseverance. It's really an honor to meet you and to see how much you've grown since that day we all got to look at you."

"There's no need to try and win my favor."

"But when I marry Kantarou-sama, we will be like sisters."

"You have a lot of training to go through before you'll be accepted. Your grand display at to say your name to me is not something a queen would do."

"I look forward to your teachings," she says smiling.

THE LAST PRINCESS

"M-my teachings?"

The door opens again and Yumiko-san steps in startled. She finally got herself cleaned up. I'm tempted to stand but remember we're supposed to be done with each other.

The ladies take their seats across from each other. The sound of heels echoing makes me feel like something bad is about to happen. Chiyo-san sits down taking my arm again.

It's quiet again. I reach to have my tea but this woman is grabbing me too tightly.

"I'm sorry for last night, Chiyo-san. My mother just misunderstood."

"It's easy for someone to misunderstand. You two are too close. Anyone could mistake it for dating."

"That won't be the case anymore."

Yumiko-san glances over at me. This isn't what she wants. She doesn't want to see another woman latched onto me. I try to shake off Chiyo-san but she grips me tighter. This is just hurting her. I don't want to hurt her. She'll just do something unlike herself.

"I agree with Chiyo-san," father says. "You spend too much time with Yumiko-san. We don't want people to misunderstand like last night."

"It won't be a problem, king," Yumiko-san says to him.

It's like she's close to tears. I guess we have to end it. That's what she wants.

"Kantarou, perhaps you and Chiyo-san would like a stroll through the gardens," mother suggests.

"Yes, that sounds lovely."

My body moves on its own fulfilling everyone's expectations. I look back at her and she won't even look at me. She wipes her eye and I want to run back to her. Chiyo-san pulls me away.

"I can't wait to see your gardens. I'd like to have a real tour of the palace. I'll learn it all soon enough but I'd love to have my hubby show me around."

231

"You're not the same girl I met in the meeting," I say to her when we're finally alone.

I shake her hand off me and step away. I would have never picked her if I knew she'd be this clingy and pompous. It's like she has an agenda. No one plays me.

"I admit I was nervous then."

"You are here, not cause I like you. You're here cause I need a woman to stand next to me and blow kisses to my people. Do you get that?"

"You love her, don't you? The disgraced princess."

"Who I love isn't a concern of yours."

"Could you think about me a little," she says to me. "I was forced to marry you. The situation is no different than what Setsuna-san is going through and I know you're fond of her. I want to be in love with the man I marry. I'm trying. Why won't you? Do you really just want to stand next to me and not feel anything for me?"

So there isn't an agenda.

"You already picked me so can you try to have a relationship with me and treat me like a woman and not an object. Be nice to me and let me enjoy having such a handsome man to hold on to."

She has a point. My mind is so set on someone else; I haven't been being fair to her.

"Sorry," I say to her. "I can see how this must be an exciting time for you. So what do you want to see first?"

"How about your room."

"Hm?"

I know that look. Lips slightly parted and hips sticking out. Her finger rests on her top button. Yumiko-san has already made her choice. She's not waiting for me; she doesn't want to be with me in secret. I wonder if she did the same thing to seduce a man last night.

"Don't be that kind of girl," I tell her. "That kind of girl gets no respect from me."

Chapter 60: Setsuna

"I think I'm happy now," I say to him.

"That's nice to hear."

Kyoya-sama is out in the garden with me. He sits under the tree writing while I sketch the new flowers. I always wanted to do this with him. I can't stop smiling. Just weeks ago it was Captain Saki sitting in his place….This is much better.

"If you're happy, I'm happy. Thank you for not giving up on me," he says.

I wanted to but I just couldn't. I look back at him shyly. He's worth the wait. When he catches me looking I snap forward.

"Are you ready to go back with me?" he asks. "You should know a king can't leave his country unattended for too long."

"Everyone was very nice at my birthday party but I'm afraid if I go back they might….call me a traitor again."

I love my country so much but I've been fearful of going back after how I left. I left twice in a hurry because I was threatened.

My shoulders stiffen feeling him close to me. He sits down hugging me from behind.

"No one would dare say a harmful word to you. I'll protect you."

I feel safe in his embrace.

"I thought you might be a bit hesitant. I set up an interview so that your people can get to know you better."

"An interview? What will they ask me?"

"Just simple questions so they can see what kind of person you are. Of course they'll ask you about me and the kind of person I am."

"I've never done an interview."

"I'll be right beside you. And if it's something you don't want to answer, I'll tell them to back off."

THE LAST PRINCESS

"My mother never did interviews. She wasn't very close with the people."

"I know they'll love you."

He hugs me tighter. I would like my people to know I care about them. I want them to know my parents cared too. They were just so bound by traditions and didn't say it.

"It sounds like fun."

"I'll go finalize the details. I'll be right back."

So nice of him. He cares about my legacy. An interview will be fun. My teachers schooled me about dealing with the public. I haven't had a teacher in so long. These past few years I haven't been gaining knowledge, just experiences. It's what Kyoya-sama wanted for me.

"Hello, Setsuna-san."

I snap out of my daze and see Captain Saki sitting in front of my sketch subject. How did I not notice him?

"Um, hi. I haven't seen you since the party. Have you been doing your other captain duties well?"

It's odd to look at him. I confessed something terrible to Kyoya-sama. I don't know why I said it; it just awkwardly came out. My mouth felt so dirty after saying those words. I don't like Captain Saki like that.

"I had more fun guarding you. But I do get to practice my combat skills a bit more."

"Well, what have you been doing?"

"Patrolling the capitol mostly."

He tilts my sketchbook down to see. I've shown him my sketches before. I surrender the book to him and he goes through the pages.

"You seem happy with Kyoya-sama near you. I was afraid to interrupt."

"It's okay to show yourself. I've missed you."

"Have you now? I've missed you too."

THE LAST PRINCESS

He stops at a page and stares. I look forward and grab the book from him. I sketched some other things in there.

"Who's that?" he asks.

"That's my parent's killer."

I didn't want to forget what I saw so I sketched him. I spent days trying to get it right. He holds out his hand and I willingly pass him the book.

"Why remember such a thing?" he asks me.

"It's just. . .I met him multiple times. The first time was when he broke into the palace and killed everyone. He was deadly but after that day when I met him again he was different. He talked to me more….admitted things to me. I know he felt in charge somehow but when I last met him he felt pained."

I touch my neck remembering how frantic he was when he cut me. It was an accident. He didn't want me to see his face.

"I think he knows me."

"Are you looking to see him again?"

I nod.

"Why?" he asks me.

"I never got an answer for why he did it."

Here I am talking to him like normal again. My comfort with him has returned.

"I'm going on another patrol tonight. Did you want to come with me? I can sneak you out."

"But the last time-"

"I won't let you out of my sights."

Tempting but I'm not supposed to leave. That rule is crucial since I got hurt last time.

"Come," he says to me. "Maybe we'll find some answers."

"I don't think I should."

THE LAST PRINCESS

"We haven't been able to have any fun together like we use to. I could take you to a movie theater-"

"A movie theater? Really?"

"I'll come get you later. I have to find some clothes for you to wear."

"I didn't agree," I tell him.

"I know you're coming," he says standing up. "You can't resist a chance to see the real world."

That's very true. And I would love to go to a theater. He reaches down his hand to me and I take it. I've never worn the clothes girls normally wear; mother was always against it. He pulls me up and I brush the dirt off.

"You can't tell anyone. Not even Kyoya-sama," he says to my ear.

I don't want to lie to him.

"Setsuna-san."

I push Captain Saki away as Kyoya-sama approaches. He might misunderstand. He stares at us and I take another step away.

"Ayato-san," he says. "I haven't seen you in a while."

"I've been on patrol."

"But you still find your way here, looking at my girlfriend."

"It's what she wants. I'm pretty good at giving her what she wants."

I feel like there are daggers being thrown between them. They just stare at each other talking in monotone voices.

"Um-"

"Come, Setsuna-san," Kyoya-sama says to me.

I step over to him and he pulls me under his arm. I think I missed something in their conversation.

"I'll see you later, princess," Captain Saki calls to me.

I'm still debating that.

THE LAST PRINCESS

Kyoya-sama walks me back inside. He's quiet walking me to his office. I always thought he would be the one to take me outside the palace and roam about the city with me. He's never offered. Everyone is so intent on keeping me inside and watched. But Captain Saki isn't like that. He's right. I can't pass up this chance to see the real world.

We go to his office. He lets me hang around him while he sets up the interview details. It's nice to see him work. He has a wonderful telephone voice and great posture. I guess he had a lot of classes too when he was growing up. I remember negotiation class, tons of etiquette classes, and my defense classes. I stand looking at his books on the shelf while he works.

"Kyoya-sama," I call to him.

He keeps writing.

"What kind of schooling did you have?"

He looks up from his book. I just wonder if all this is natural for him. I see him read and write so much; I know he's smart.

"Same as you," he tells me. "Etiquette classes, history classes, I did a lot of math too."

"And your degree?"

"Political Strategy."

"Oh, so that means you have a very calculating mind."

"Yes, I would hope so."

"Is that why you write so much?"

"Why the sudden interest in my schooling?"

I'm being a burden. I turn around hoping he'll ignore my question. I stare at his shelf glancing back to see if he went back to work.

"It's cause you feel like you don't know me very well, isn't it," he guesses.

I nod. That's exactly it.

"I write cause I have a lot of thoughts. I remember things better and it helps me be more consistent."

THE LAST PRINCESS

"That's very interesting."

"It's also like therapy. I'm not always upfront with my feelings so I write them down and later figure it all out."

"Oh, okay-"

"So I rather you not read my journals."

At that time I felt like I didn't have a choice. There were no responses from him. I doubted him and just wanted to believe in him again. Still....I invaded his privacy; feel bad about that.

"If you want to know my feelings, just ask me," he continues.

There is something I want to ask.

"How come you haven't permitted me to leave the palace?" I ask him.

"I'm just being careful. I don't want anything to happen to you."

I remember the captain told me that Kyoya-sama had an assassin after him. Maybe that's why he's nervous about taking me out. Or it could be related to me coming back in cuts the last time.

"Captain Saki told me he saved you from an assassin," I say to him.

I look back at him and he smiles. That can't be a happy memory. He laughs; it's nice to hear his laugh. I always see Kyoya-sama composed. While he's distracted I move closer and stand at his armrest.

"I forgot all about that. Yes, that's how we met. That was around the time our fathers starting meeting to discuss the details of our engagement. A lot of people were against it even before it happened."

"So someone wanted to kill you for it?"

"Yes…but he saved me. He killed the man and ran back to me. Pushed through all the guards and came straight to me with blood all over him. "Prince, are you okay? Are you hurt?" he asked me. He was bleeding from his stomach but ignored it just to talk to me. He has a terrible scar there."

He stops completely looking forward like I'm not even here.

"He became my best friend," he continues. "I love him like a brother. I guess that's why I couldn't send him away."

THE LAST PRINCESS

"He loves you too. He always speaks highly of you."

"He's a good guy in some ways but….he's also a very sick man."

"What do you mean?"

"He's just not someone you should get close to. I understand the situation while I was away but…I don't want you to be left alone with him."

But that's exactly what will happen if I go out tonight. He's probably speaking out of jealousy. Captain Saki isn't in love with me like he thinks; we're just friends. I nod to him saying I'll do what he says. I guess Yumi-chan's advice worked. But he didn't get jealous of Kira-kun; he got jealous of his best friend. I don't want this to be something that rips them apart.

"I better leave you to your planning," I say to him.

I turn to leave but he pulls me back by my waist. He twists his chair around away from the door and pulls me to sit in his lap. This is embarrassing. Moments like this should be shared between adults; that's why I feel so embarrassed.

"I know all you want is to be free. To wander around town and country without a leash."

"I understand."

"Do you know how scared I was when I heard you almost died? I never felt so afraid. I promise I'll consider it but not now."

He'll always be too afraid to let me out. The killer still hasn't been caught. He knows that now. Obeying him and staying inside is the right thing but if I go with Captain Saki I might get answers. I might meet that man again and I really want to.

"That's fine," I say to him. "I understand your feelings."

But I'm leaving tonight.

Chapter 61: Ayato

I always wanted to see the princess outside of her robes. Not a big selection here. Her cousin's wardrobe is way too revealing. She needs to hide herself, not stand out. Maybe if she covers her shoulders with this sparkly little thing.

THE LAST PRINCESS

I don't have much time. Can't believe I have another chance to be alone with her. This will be different. I know she likes me; she's just hiding it from me. Now would be the perfect time to confess to her in person. I have to do it before she goes through with the wedding.

"What are you doing?"

"Hm?"

I look back. Yumiko-san steps into her room. Makes no difference. She dressed up as Setsuna-san for me, now it's time for Setsuna-san to dress up as her.

"How much of a pervert are you? What do you need with my clothes?"

"I thought we agreed not to ask questions."

"Whatever."

She falls down to her bed straight into the pillow. Something must have happened. Not my place to care. I take another glance. Nope, I'm not in the mood for sex right now. Might be getting it from the real thing soon enough. No, no, that would be too soon. Kissing will be for today. We can save sex for another time.

I'm attracted to the princess. I like her spirit immensely. Physically I'm into her too but mostly, I like being near her. If she doesn't want to kiss I'm fine with that. I want to hear her sweet voice say my name again.

"What are you smiling about?" she asks me.

"Life is going well."

"For you maybe."

I dig deeper into her closet and find a dress. It's small; this might work.

"Can you stay over tonight?" she asks me. "I need you to clear my head again."

"I'll be on patrol."

"Then how about now?"

Maybe it's a good idea to let some nerves out before I meet with the princess. Don't want to come on too strong. I drop the dress and approach the bed. No...I can't do it with her dressed like that. I can't imagine it.

THE LAST PRINCESS

"Go change," I tell her.

"Seriously?"

"Go change. You want your head cleared, don't you?"

"I can't believe I have to do this again."

It was good the first time. I could picture Setsuna-san right in front of me. She gets up and goes to her closet. I sit and watch each detail. With her back to me I picture Setsuna-san. I close my eyes and her words come to me. I remember the first time she was nice to me. When Kyoya-sama left she was scared to be around me. Thought I was the killer. But I stayed close to her and didn't realize she let go of her animosity for me. One day she let me know in a big way.

"I have a surprise for you," she says pulling my arm.

I follow her down the hall unsure of what's ahead. There's no way she could plan a surprise without me knowing. I know what she's doing at every moment. We stop outside the dining room and she waits.

"What's the meaning of this?" I ask her.

"Are you ready?"

Is she planning my execution in there? Her words are always cold towards me like she wants to kill me.

"Close your eyes," she tells me.

I do as she says. The doors creaks open and she pulls me forward. She fumbles putting me in a chair. I have excellent hearing. A plate is put in front of me. She adjusts it many times.

"Okay. Open them."

When I open my eyes I see a cake in front of me. Chocolate with the words "I'm sorry" etched in white icing. She smiles next to me clamping her hands closed in front of her face.

"Do you like it?" she asks nervously. "I baked it for you last night."

"What are you sorry for?"

"For not making you a friend sooner. I really like you. I hope you can forgive me for being so cold."

THE LAST PRINCESS

She puts her arms around my shoulders and I immediately stand and hug her properly. She's so small in my arms. I wonder if this is what Kyoya-sama feels when she's in his arms. It's warm, very pleasant. I don't feel a bit of rage or frustration.

"There's nothing to be sorry for," I say to her.

I sniff the top of her head and my mind immediately remembers my promise to Kyoya-sama. I push her away and sit back down.

"Let's eat," I say to her.

"I'm a pretty good cook so I'm really confident you'll like it."

She pulls her chair next to me then concentrates cutting a piece. I lean over and kiss the top of her head without her noticing. I open my eyes and see Yumiko-san in front of me struggling to put on her layers. I get up and grab her from behind imaging Setsuna-san.

"I'm not done yet," she tells me.

"It doesn't matter. I'm just going to take it off."

I pull her to the bed and it feels better than the first time. My head only pictures the girl I want. I did a number on Yumiko-san. Her head has to be clear by now. It's enough to put her to sleep. I sit up from her bed and put my clothes back on. It's late so it's time to get going.

I walk down the hall with the little dress hidden behind me. The halls are empty. Just guards on patrol. Kyoya-sama is probably distracted doing work. He'll have no idea I'm getting her on my side.

"I don't want to play with you tonight," I hear down the hall.

"Why not? I'm gonna be going back to the academy soon. You haven't received enough of me."

"Not tonight, okay."

"It's cute when you play shy."

Kira is bothering her again. She's trying to close her door on him but he's strong enough to keep it open. I have to get rid of him. She takes notice of me when I walk closer. Her eyes lock on to mine and she smiles knowing I'll take care of things.

"I think it's time you leave, prince," I say to him.

THE LAST PRINCESS

"You again."

He backs up and I block the door. I push the dress to her and she retreats back inside.

"This isn't your business," he tells me.

"Her safety is always my business."

"Then what made you drop the ball when she hurt herself."

I grab my sword instinctively. No, I can't hurt him. He's Kyoya-sama's brother. He has a mouth on him though. Wouldn't mind silencing him for a bit.

"Don't hurt him," she appears from the room. "Maybe he could come with us."

"Don't say unnecessary things."

"You're sneaking her out again?" Kira guesses.

"He's taking me to a movie. Did you want to come?"

"Princess, you really should-"

"I'll come," he answers.

This just became a babysitting job. I was supposed to make my confession tonight. Kira looks over at me smirking. I'll ditch him soon enough. She closes the door on us and I size him up.

"I promise your final year at the academy will be tough," I tell him.

"I'm sick of hearing about that. I'm better off at a real school where I can use my brain."

He slumps down on her door. I heard he was doing so well. He's not enjoying it.

"All people do is compare me to my brothers," he says.

"That's cause you're not an individual. You're so focused on how you can please your daddy. Neither of your brothers cares what he thinks-"

"That's not true-"

"They respect him and follow orders but they don't care what he thinks."

THE LAST PRINCESS

He puts his head down thinking. I sigh and lean against the wall beside him.

"You're wrong," he says to me. "That's not how it works. You just don't want me to break your stupid record."

"The target skill challenge? Do I still hold the number one spot?"

"Not for much longer," he challenges me.

He gets off her door challenging me with a grin. Whatever. No one will ever surpass me with knife throwing. Kyoya-sama has a real burden with a brother like him.

"I keep telling you, you're not necessary anymore," he says to me.

"I have the perfect test. Wanna see something?"

I knock on the door.

"Princess, can I come in?"

"Sure," she answers.

"Uh-what about me?" he asks her.

"No!"

He's the unnecessary one. I go in and lock the door behind me. She stands at the mirror with the dress on. I've never seen her outside her robes. I can see her arms and legs. She still has bandages down her arms but I can see what her body looks like. She's small. Hasn't developed a chest like her cousin.

"It looks weird," she says.

"You look beautiful."

She spins in it.

"It's so light. It's like I'm wearing nothing. It's not dragging and…I don't look like my mother. I don't know who I look like."

"It's just for one night."

She stares at herself in the mirror. She looks like a girl for once. I watch from afar as she takes down her hair. It falls touching her lower back.

"Does it look okay?"

THE LAST PRINCESS

She turns to me with her hair whipping in the air. I'm mesmerized. Taking her out her robes is making her stand out more. It's making me love every inch of her.

"I'm really excited to go to a movie theater. Please sit between me and Kira-kun."

"Why did you invite him?"

"When he doesn't get his way he complains about it. And this is supposed to be a secret, right?"

"Right."

"Can we go see some animals too? Like cats and dogs and fish."

She runs up to me with so much hope in her eyes. I'll try not to let her down. I nod and she hugs me tightly. I dive my nose into the top of her head and smell her hair. My hands slide around her and I can feel her frame for once.

"Thank you," she says to me. "Kyoya-sama is scared to let me leave. He thinks I might be attacked again but....I'm safe with you."

I bite my lip to keep from blurting it out. I love her.

"We should get going. There's a short window of time," I tell her.

"Hold on. I forgot to pray."

She runs back to her bed kneeling. I've watched her pray so many times. Thanking her ancestors for everything she has. Asking her parents to watch over her, watch over the Niwa family, Kyoya-sama and even me.

I don't know who I would pray to. When I'm not near her I do wish for her happiness and safety. I wish the same for Kyoya-sama. But I know that Setsuna-san is going to end our friendship. I need both of them but when I fell in love with her it started a countdown to the end. If only I could be him, then I could have it all.

She stands up and runs back to me. I open the door and Kira stares at her mesmerized.

"Uh..."

"Tonight is a secret, okay," she tells him.

He nods stupidly. I can't go on with her not hearing my feelings. I want her to hear them and believe them. I want to give her a choice. She can continue being a trapped princess and live with Kyoya-sama or she can be free by choosing me. She'll know tonight.

Chapter 62: Setsuna

"Setsuna-san, wait up."

I can't believe we made it out. It's so dark out but the lights are still strong. I run ahead of them. I feel so light. I can run now and spin without tripping over my clothes. I hold my hat down as I run. It's the first time feeling the wind in my hair.

I stop and let them catch up. I'm happy but…I wish he was here giving me this feeling. He's still stuck at his desk working. Lying to him is hard. He told me to stay inside and he told me not to be alone with Captain Saki. But he doesn't know how unhappy I am just sitting there.

A woman walks by with a dog and I kneel down to it. It's my first time seeing a dog. I grab its face and she pulls him away.

"Calm down," Captain Saki says to me. "Don't overwhelm yourself."

"But did you see it. His face was so wrinkly."

"We're trying not to stand out," he tells me. "Just don't act like it's your first time on the street."

"It's better if she holds onto me," Kira-kun comes forward. "People will just think we're on a date. If she hangs on to you people will think it's a kidnapping."

"She'll stay near me where I can protect her," Captain Saki says.

"I agree with the captain. We have to be careful."

I hope he understands exactly what I mean. My parent's killer can't be too far. If I can sneak away, he might show himself.

We walk the street to the theater. No one pays any attention to us. Kira-kun is walking ahead like he's being noticed but he's not. He tilts his head down and waves the approaching women off although they pay no mind to him.

"It was supposed to be the two of us. I don't feel like looking after him. And all he does is whine and complain."

THE LAST PRINCESS

That's how he's always been. I expected some changes since he came back from the academy. The only change is that he knows how to act tough.

"I get the feeling you don't like Kira-kun too much," I say to him.

"I never have. He's spoiled and acts entitled. That's why he thinks he can just have you."

I look up and see Kira-kun just ahead. I'm trying to keep my voice down but the captain doesn't care.

"Truth is he's the unnecessary one. He knows it. He thinks having you will somehow give him some validation or some usefulness in being the third son."

If that's true then he must feel so bad when his brother's receive so much attention. All he wants is to feel important. That's why he acts how he does. I catch up to him and grab Kira-kun's arm. He tries to push me away but quickly stops seeing that it's me and not a fan.

"What-"

"You're really getting a lot of attention," I tell him. "I didn't know you were so well known here."

"It's my city so of course I'm well known."

Everyone deserves to feel important. I'd give it up if I could. All it's given me is a lifetime in shackles. Kira-kun wants so much attention but I'm sure he'll regret it when he gets it. I have a way to give him what he wants.

"Wait here," I tell him. "I want to give you something."

I go back to the captain and whisper my plan. He has no problem with it. I wave back at Kira-kun and he looks at me confused.

"Prince Kira!"

I step back and a flood of people run up to him. He gets surrounded and I step away. That should be enough attention for him. But as a result...I'm left alone with the captain.

"C'mon, the theater is this way."

Walking with him I think about Kyoya-sama's words. Why did he say Captain Saki was sick? I know he likes to battle. He told me stories about his kills but it didn't bother me; he kills bad guys. Would it be rude to ask? Probably.

THE LAST PRINCESS

"Can I ask you something?"

"Yeah," he says to me.

I can tell he's on guard. I don't want to distract him.

"Kyoya-sama said-"

"We're here."

Is that what all the sparking lights are for? It's amazing. There's even a spotlight in the sky. So many people too.

"Looks like a premiere. We're better off seeing an older movie."

"A romance, please."

"A romance? Looking for lessons?"

"Well...yeah."

He laughs and takes hold of my hand. It's not weird to be alone with him. We do this all the time. We approach the crowd and I have my first experience waiting in line.

"So how does this work?" I ask him. "Are these people going to see a romance movie too? Will there be enough popcorn to go around?"

"We wait here and then buy our tickets with the cashier. Snacks are optional once inside."

"Do you have enough money?"

"Just calm down, Setsuna-chan."

"What did you call me?"

"We're trying to blend in. I'm just addressing you like a normal girl."

It feels odd. Normally I'm "princess" or people say my name with formality. This is the normal girl experience. I look down the line. There are lots of normal girls here with their....boyfriends.

I left Kyoya-sama in his office. He has no idea where I am. I was wrong for lying. As exciting as this is, I should go back.

"I don't think this is right," I say to him quietly. "Kyoya-sama-"

THE LAST PRINCESS

"Don't worry about him. He's fine."

"He's gonna be so mad."

"No matter what you do, he can never be mad at you. This is what you want. If he can't give it to you then I will."

He puts his arm around my shoulder and pulls me close to him. Still feels wrong. The line starts moving and it's our turn to buy.

"You sure you want a romance?" he asks me.

"Yes."

Inside is more exciting. He guides me away from all the commotion and we go straight to the theater. It's kind of empty. We sit in the back and I marvel at the big screen.

"I'll be back," he says to me. "Just wait here."

"Uh-huh."

I'm good at trivia. I read the screen but don't know any answers. Seems different than what I studied; I don't know anything about actors. Oh! Could there be actors in the theater right now watching their own movies. I see a couple up ahead and a man sitting alone. No movie stars here.

"Hey."

"Uh?"

A boy sits next to me. Does he recognize me? I tilt my hat down and look away.

"Are you here alone?" he asks me.

"I um....my um....bod-I mean friend is here."

"Well, he's not here now."

"He um…"

Oh my gosh! What's wrong with me? I don't know how to act with the public. I'm so nervous. He's a boy about my age. I don't really know what to say.

"Do I look like a teenage girl?" I ask him.

THE LAST PRINCESS

"Yeah, that's why I'm talking to you. You don't have to sit alone. You can sit with me and my friends. We're just down there."

I look ahead. There's a girl down there. They all look my age.

"I'm Bunji."

"Bunji-kun?"

"Yeah, what's your name?"

"Setsuna."

He looks above me like he's seen a ghost.

"Move away from her. She has a thing for older men."

Captain Saki leans over me and Bunji-kun goes back to his friends. He wasn't a threat; he didn't have to chase him off.

"Should have known I couldn't leave you alone without the boys coming out."

"He was nice."

"Don't get too close. And don't give out your name."

He sits down next to me and hands me a soda. He's always protective.

"I do not have a thing for older men," I say to him.

He starts to laugh. I know Kyoya-sama and him are twenty-three. So that's seven years. My mother and father were ten years apart. The age gap is common in arranged marriages.

The movie starts. It's very sweet in the beginning but with this one scene I see them stare into each other eyes in front of the roaring fire. There's no talking but she starts taking off her clothes.

I quickly shut my eyes.

"Why bring me here? This isn't for kids."

"You said you wanted to learn."

He keeps laughing at me. I don't want to learn this stuff. When I open my eyes the scene is over and I notice the captain is closer to me. He has his arm around

THE LAST PRINCESS

me stroking my shoulder. I look down and see the teens doing the same thing. Uh! They're kissing too. What kind of place is this?

"Do people always mimic movies when they watch them?" I ask him.

"Seeing other people in love just puts people in the mood."

Is that what's going on with him? I stay quiet and he slides his arm around my waist. My face feels warm. He sniffs the top of my head and I pull my arms close.

"Um-is there a bathroom?"

I jump up and exit the theater. What's going on in there? He's not acting like a bodyguard. Normally he doesn't want to hug me or touch me. What mood is going on in there?

I stand outside the doors breathing out heavily. I can still hear the movie in the background.

What if Kyoya-sama was right? What if Captain Saki is in love with me?

"Hey, are you alright?"

I straighten up hearing his voice. I can't look at him. He appears right in front of me.

"Hey," he says again.

"I'm not enjoying it like I thought I would."

"Too much for you? It's fine. We can see something else."

"No, we should just go home."

"Not just yet. I wanted to talk to you about something."

I don't feel so comfortable anymore. My head is spinning with possibilities. What if he loves me? What does that mean to me? What does that mean?

"You're a pretty girl," Yumi-chan once told me. "Boys will like you, boys that aren't your boyfriend. You'll need to know how to handle it."

How do I handle it?

"Are you hungry?" he asks me. "Let's get something to eat."

"O-okay."

THE LAST PRINCESS

We walk out the theater. There's still a crowd outside. I'm so distracted; I can't take in the view anymore. Looking up at him I feel so scared. Captain Saki is my friend. If he loves me then....I would be happy. That makes me sound terrible. I love Kyoya-sama; there is no one else.

I start to cry and stop walking. He notices quickly and leans down to me.

"What's wrong?"

"I know," I admit to him. "I know....you love me."

"So....why are you crying about it?"

"Cause I'm confused. I'm happy that you love me. You make me feel so normal. You've been the only one to...to let me be free. I-I love you too."

He gets surprised and he hugs me. The smell of him makes my heart flutter. No, I need to make myself clear. I love him like my best friend. I know his love is different.

Under the night sky he continues to hug me. I wipe my eyes and clear my throat.

"I love you a lot but...like I told you before, Kyoya-sama is my love, my husband."

He pulls away and I wipe my eyes again. This is so tough. I don't know why it's tough to say how I feel. Maybe I don't want to acknowledge that I can see myself with him.

"I'll give you a choice," he says to me. "You can marry Kyoya-sama and be a queen still trapped in your own palace. Or you can be with me and just be Setsuna. I would take you away and you could go wherever you like, be whoever you want. And I would love you and marry you."

A choice? I finally have a choice. I can't believe I'm even considering. No! I love Kyoya-sama. He will be my husband.

"Don't talk about this again," I say to him.

"Just let me know your choice before the wedding. I know what you're feeling. You just won't admit it."

"Please, don't-"

"You feel doubt. You've felt doubt for the last three years. But you've never doubted me."

"Let's not talk about this, please."

He stands up and I keep my eyes from him. Yes, there's plenty of doubt. But I made my choice a long time ago.

"I should get you back," he says. "I'm glad you know my feelings. I didn't mean to make you cry."

"You son of a bitch!"

Kira-kun comes towards us. I pull my hat down.

"How could you ditch me? What did you two do?" he asks him. "I'm telling when we get back."

"Show some consideration for the princess," the captain says flatly. "She just wanted to see some lights."

Kira-kun looks over at me and I nod.

"We can go home now," I say to him.

The captain walks ahead and we follow him.

"Please, don't tell anyone about tonight," I say to him.

"For you, okay. Did you have fun?"

"It was....enlightening."

"We should go out just the two of us next time. We don't need the captain."

My heart feels heavy. I've wronged Kyoya-sama. I need to speak to him. Or maybe, this can be another secret. I look up at the captain. They're best friends. I don't want to be the one to drive them apart.

Chapter 63: Kyoya

It's finally time to head back. At least I'm not going alone. But no one knows how to show up on time. I bang on her door.

253

THE LAST PRINCESS

"Yumiko-san," I call through the door. "I told you seven a.m."

"Uh, just a second."

She opens the door frazzled. She's traveling in her royal robes? I thought she hated wearing those things.

"Just let me shower and I'll be out."

Looks like a fresh hickey on her neck. She looks nervously behind her. What man could she be seeing? I don't think my brother is in there. She closes the door and I lean against the wall. What am I being nosey for? Kantarou has feelings for her but it's over between them. Perhaps I'm just concerned; I want her to make the right decisions.

"Hey," Kantarou says approaching.

"Oh, morning. I was just trying to hurry her along."

"She's not use to getting up early."

Maybe he shouldn't be here when that guy comes out.

"Can you make sure she's taken care of?"

"I thought you two ended things."

"This is just between us. Make sure she's okay. What captains are you taking?"

"Just Ayato-san and some guards. She'll be fine."

"What do you think they'll ask her in the interview?" he asks.

"You two are a big rumor. They'll ask her about that. I'm working on a way to get her status back. I'll coach her on what to say."

"She'll like that. Let me know if there's anything I can do."

He takes a step away and I grab his arm. He's so plain about all this.

"Kan-nii?"

"What is it?"

"This is really what you want?"

THE LAST PRINCESS

"Chiyo-san will be my wife but I still want to make Yumiko-san happy however I can. And right now that means leaving her alone."

I let go of him and he walks off. This is so unlike him. He's not being selfish for once. I support whatever he does but father won't. I don't need to know who's in there with her. That's her choice.

I walk down the hall. I'm surprised Setsuna-san didn't run to me this morning. She should be excited about going back to her country. She's been shut in her room for the last few days. I'm told she gets depressed sometimes so I leave her alone. There's probably a lot on her mind; she's still scared about returning.

She stands outside her door with a bag in hand. Of course she's prepared; she's always considerate with these things.

"Are you ready?" I ask her.

She nods quietly. I reach my hand out to her and she ignores it. I guess she doesn't want to hold onto me. I start walking away from her and she grabs me from behind.

"I forgive you," she whispers.

She forgives me? Is she talking about the sleeping around? I don't care if she ever forgives me; I know I was wrong. What makes her forgive me now?

She's done something.

"Thank you for forgiving me. Hopefully we don't have to have those feelings again."

I turn around and she nods still holding onto me. Close to tears I see. She's feeling guilty about something.

She stays close to me as we walk to the runway. Keeps her head down and holds onto my sleeve. The press takes pictures from the gate; it makes her hide her face more. Yumiko-san joins us still frazzled. It's another farewell moment. Mother and father hug me and the girls. Kantarou looks like he's on patrol and ignores us.

"Will you make sure the flowers are taken care of?" Setsuna-san asks him.

It breaks his concentration. He turns to us and smiles at her. She lets go of me and stretches her arms out to him. Dropping his persona for a moment, he kneels down and embraces her.

"I'll miss you," he whispers. "Be good."

THE LAST PRINCESS

"You too."

Yumiko-san is next in line. He suddenly pulls her close. He has to know there are cameras here. I see him whisper in her ear and she blushes instantly. They separate and she stares at him shocked.

"What are you doing?" father asks with anger.

They keep staring at each other until Yumiko-san nods. They separate and he goes back to ignoring us. I'm not very emotional about any of this. I'm leaving what was once my home and I'm going back to a place that I have control over. The best thing is, I'm taking Setsuna-san with me.

Because I'm taking her, I'm taking him too. The bodyguard who put all those cuts on her body. I've never seen him fall for a girl. I'm just letting it happen so I can examine things. Ayato-san stands at the base of the plane smiling at her. Both girls seem awkward. They both stop prior to getting on.

"Get that grin off your face. You're scaring them," I tell him.

It is a weird sight to see him smiling. I wanna know what's on his mind. The girls sit close to me in the back of the plane. Ayato-san stays near the front. I doubt either of them will tell me what's going on.

"I've been practicing my smile like you told me," Yumiko-san says to me. "I'm just wondering if it's necessary to smile all the time. If they ask me about the royal massacre should I smile to show I'm okay or cry to show I'm sad?"

"What do you feel when the subject comes up?"

She lowers her head thinking about it. I'm not trying to have them play characters during their interview. The people will love them as they are. Setsuna-san reaches over me and touches her hand.

"I feel okay," Setsuna-san speaks up. "Mother and father told me it's fine to move on. They said they're happy knowing I'm alive and that you're with me."

"I'm not as spiritual as you are. When I think about what happened on that night, I feel like such a coward. I was here while you were there fighting for your life. I was here while you were injured in the woods and-"

"I'm happy you were here," Setsuna-san says to her. "When I heard everyone was gone, I wanted to disappear too. I was scared to be the only one left. But then I remembered you were in Han with Kyoya-sama. I had a reason to go on."

THE LAST PRINCESS

They both start tearing up. I sit still as they hug over my seat. I'm glad I was convinced to save Yumiko-san. Makes me feel like I'm not a complete monster.

"That's why I'm so thankful to Kantarou-sama. He kept you safe."

"And he brought you back to me," Yumiko-san cries.

They continue hugging. Ayato-san stares back. Seems the sins of that night will never go away. I assume he's getting increasingly guilty about it since knowing the two girls. I could be wrong.

"Looks like you found your answer," I say to Yumiko-san. "You have a reason to cry and a reason to smile."

They separate and wipe their eyes. I get up and walk to the front of the plane. They need some time to themselves.

We're in the air now. Nowhere to run. Time to get some answers to some awkward questions. I close the curtain and sit down next to him.

We're quiet for a while. I'm hoping he'll speak first.

"I haven't been fair to you. It's the first time you've liked a girl and I'm not talking to you about it."

"It doesn't seem like something we can talk about."

"Pretend she isn't my girlfriend. Tell me about it."

He looks over at me confused. I just want to get what's going on in his head. When I understand his emotions I'm better at controlling them. After a pause he drops his guard.

"I don't know when it happened," he starts. "My heart jumped at little moments. Those moments kept happening and it took over my whole body and I couldn't ignore it anymore."

I pass him a drink. He takes it and drinks quickly.

"She showed that she cared. If I wasn't around she would ask where I was. If I got a scratch on my arm she would bandage the little thing. Make me get well cards when I got sick and slide them under my door."

He smiles remembering. He's having all the experiences I've missed out on being away. I thought I could handle hearing it all. I have to take my emotions out of it. I have to hear more.

THE LAST PRINCESS

"And every year her smile got so much brighter. She started to forget about her family and some moments she forgot about you. But every time she did, she felt so bad about it. She would beg me to call you and you would never answer. Then she would cry and I would hold on to her and try to distract her with a story. And I would tell her each time, "Kyoya-sama loves you very much." Pushing down my own feelings."

I pour a drink for myself.

"So when I asked her if she wanted to be with me and she denied me, my instinct was to hurt her. And I did. I'd done so much for her."

"If she denies you again, will you hurt her?" I ask him.

"No. I could never hurt her. That time I thought she was saying that she didn't like me but....she was just saying that she doesn't choose me."

We stop talking for a while and just drink. We both dropped our guards to have that conversation. A normal man would send him away feeling threatened. But he's right. He's the best one in the palace guard. As king I may have to take care of things secretly. That's something he can do. If I didn't love Setsuna-san it would be easy to give her to him. That's not going to happen. It's getting harder to turn a blind eye.

I need to make Setsuna-san's feelings for me stronger.

"I know it was hard for you to talk to me but thank you for it," he tells me. "Even in this situation that we're in, I can only be honest with you. I'm sorry I developed feelings for a girl that was promised to you. I tried not to… for your sake."

His voice is low and he won't look at me when he says those touching words. He's being honest but he's omitting things. That's fine for now.

"Sorry I hit you," I say to him. "I didn't have time to situate my emotions."

"It's fine. I really deserved it. No harm will come to the princess, you have my word."

"And Yumiko-san too."

"Of course," he says smiling.

"When we land they'll be a lot of press. Keep your guard up. Don't do anything reckless. The public doesn't know you but they'll take an interest quick."

"I'm just a bodyguard."

THE LAST PRINCESS

The curtain parts. Yumiko-san stands with her head poking through. She keeps her eyes down. I check his face for clues but there are none.

"Kyoya-sama, can we review some of the questions before we land?" she asks shyly.

It's good she's taking this seriously.

"Sure, I'll be back in a moment."

She nods and vanishes. I may have picked his brain too much but it can't hurt to dig a bit more.

"Why is she acting so strange around you?" I ask him.

"Cause she feels shame."

"Shame?"

"The commander broke her heart. So she's trying to get over it by having rough sex."

I immediately tighten my fist.

"With you?" I clarify.

He nods. I don't want her to be with a guy like him. I picture her being tied up and…

"This stops now," I warn him.

"It was her idea-"

"I don't care. Leave her alone. I don't want her messing around with you."

"What do you mean?"

"Cause you'll hurt her and she'll let you. You know what I mean."

I get up and swallow the rest of my drink. There's so much to take into account. I have to start writing. I knew Yumiko-san was hurting but I didn't think she would rebound like this. I should talk to her soon before she makes a mistake.

When did I start caring? She's Setsuna-san's cousin; she'll be my family soon. But besides that, she's a nice girl that I spared. Kind of troubled but a nice girl.

"I thought I was helping her," he says to me.

"Young girls make a lot of mistakes at her age and it's normally selfish men that lead them to it."

Saying that out loud makes me think about Setsuna-san. She's young too. I was selfish for staying away from her and I assumed she took it well. I mean, I know the suicide attempt was bogus.

She's been so sweet to him and he's fallen in love with her. Has she....No, I don't want to think about it. She would never be with another. She was so awkward when we were in bed together; no experience there. She freaked out right after I touched my pant zipper. Then she ran to the balcony and started talking to herself.

"You're really good at understanding people," he says to me.

But I don't even understand myself. And Setsuna-san eludes me as well.

Chapter 64: Setsuna

The crypt is about half a mile away from the palace but still within its walls. It's the first place I wanted to go. I know it makes no difference whether I talk to my parents in my bedroom or in front of their tombs. I just want to know what it feels like to be surrounded by their ashes and the ashes of the Asahina family before them.

It feels peaceful. Not many people would think that while in a crypt. Yumi-chan might like it here too but she's too scared to come down. Kyoya-sama and the others are upstairs waiting for me. I denied the guard cause I don't want anyone to hear my thoughts.

"Hello, mother and father. It's me, Setsuna. I'm your daughter or use to be. I feel you watching me. I don't know if you're satisfied with me yet. Kyoya-sama is great."

He really is great. He understands what it takes to be a king. As queen I'm not sure what use I will have. It's kind of daunting to think of my future. I really do think Kyoya-sama will leave me again. He'll keep me in the palace cause he thinks I'm safe and travel the world without me.

I'll always be guarded and never get to be free.

"Would you be mad at me if I didn't become queen?"

Of course they would. Captain Saki's offer is tempting. It's what I've been thinking about and crying about the last few days. He can give me the freedom I want.

THE LAST PRINCESS

But then I see Kyoya-sama's face and feel like a terrible person for considering. Going with Captain Saki would be the easy way out.

"If I want to be free, I can't wait for someone to give it to me. I have to break out on my own. I keep thinking I'm letting you both down. Every decision I make needs the approval of so many people and I don't like that."

I drop my head on father's stone casket. I wish he could talk to me.

"You're gone now. You don't have the burden of royalty anymore. I wonder if you still feel the same way about what I should do with my life."

Hearing footsteps I stand up. I guess I've been here too long.

"I figured I should try," Yumi-chan says.

She steps down the stairs cautiously. It's dim lighting down here. I go over to her and grab her hand on the last step. She always insists on wearing heels.

"Did you want privacy?" I ask her.

"No, don't leave me here alone!"

"Hehe, I won't."

She kneels down in front of them. We're quiet. She must be talking to them. She never got their approval either.

"You're on the right track," I tell her.

She opens her eyes.

"I don't think so," she says quietly. "I lost some of the morals they tried to put in me. I disrespected my family."

"What do you mean? You being here is not disrespecting-"

"The robes we wear, the ones that use to belong to the Asahina women before us, I sullied them. You and your innocence, I sullied that too."

"Yumi-chan, what did you-"

"I'm sorry," she says crying. "Kantarou-sama turned me away. And as soon as he did I felt lost."

I reach over and hug her shoulders. It's not like her to cry.

THE LAST PRINCESS

"I just wanted to forget him and feel good again so I…purposefully lost myself. Wanted to forget who I was and just feel good again."

I rub her shoulders and she cries more and more. She puts her head on the stone coffin and I move her hair from her face. I want her to rely on me like I rely on her.

"What did you do?" I ask her again.

"Your bodyguard has a thing for you."

She knows too! Does she know the offer he made me? I stay quiet.

"I dressed up as you so he would have his way with me. I sullied my robes, I let him call me your name, I….I'm sorry."

She had sex with Captain Saki. I don't really understand. So he kissed her and…my mind's going blank. Does it mean they're in love with each other now?

"You should stay away from him," she tells me. "He's obsessed with you."

"I don't know what to say."

"I feel so stupid for all this. I had it in my head that I would be with Kantarou-sama some kind of way but it can never happen. I've just proven that I'm just some whore from Morinaga, just like my mother."

"No, don't think that. You're not her. You're a person that's trying to get better."

I give her my sleeve to wipe her tears. She takes it then gets to her feet.

"You've always been so strong."

I wouldn't be here asking for guidance if I was. With her tears dry my mind goes back to Captain Saki. He would really pretend to be with me by being with my cousin. Am I supposed to feel flattered? I don't. I feel….jealous. They kissed and hugged. He did all that with a person he wasn't in love with. I shouldn't feel jealous. This is crazy.

"Can we head upstairs now? This place is creeping me out," she says to me.

I take her hand and help her up the stairs. At the top I see Kyoya-sama and Captain Saki. I run to Kyoya-sama immediately. I'm starting to understand why he called Captain Saki a sick man. I have to put that in my head so I won't think about him. Yumi-chan wanders to Kyoya-sama's side too and hugs him. He's surprised by it.

"I take it you both made your peace," he says to us.

"I want to review for the interview again. I have to get it right. I need a second chance."

"I'll help as much as I can."

He rubs my head. I pull my eyes away from the captain.

"Can you keep yourself busy?" he asks me. "I'll be with Yumiko-san for a while."

"It's okay to walk around your house?"

"Of course. It's your house too."

The palace he's building for us isn't finished yet. But there's a guest house he's been staying in. Yumi-chan and him go in a separate car to his office in the Capitol Building. I'm left with Captain Saki heading to the house. Kyoya-sama seems to trust him. He's leaving me with a "sick man." A man that's in love with me. He must trust him despite all that.

Kyoya-sama always knows best. He doesn't see the captain as a threat so maybe I shouldn't either. This is the first time I've been alone with him since that night at the movies. I look out the window to distract myself. I want us to take the longest route possible; I want to watch the trees pass by.

"Beautiful, isn't it," he says to me. "It's nice to come back here. I'm glad it's under happier circumstances."

"Y-yeah."

"Nothing has to change between us. You can talk to me like normal."

"How can I?"

"He knows."

"Does he know what you offered me?" I ask.

"No….that's between us of course. If he knew he would just stop us. Makes me wonder why you haven't told him."

263

THE LAST PRINCESS

"I..."

"I'm happy you're considering."

"I'm not! I just don't want to bother him with stupid things," I tell him.

Forget the long way; I rather be away from him. He was with Yumi-chan. I just don't understand that. I've never seen the two of them talk. She says she loves Kantarou-sama and Captain Saki says he loves me. So why are they together? I have to ask this in a crafty way.

"Yumi-chan told me you've been helping her through her breakup. I didn't know you guys were friends."

"She told you?"

"Yeah, she said you helped her feel better."

"How?"

Do I have to say it? I'm trying to leave that part out.

"She just said you guys were talking. Did you give her some good advice?"

"She said we were talking?" he questions.

I keep my head towards the window. I'm not a very good liar. I nod to him and he starts laughing.

"I can tell you're lying. Does it bother you that I'm sleeping with her?"

"Are you in love with her?" I pull away from the window.

"You don't have to be in love with someone to sleep with them. Kyoya-sama could tell you a lot about that."

"Ugh...don't bring him into this. I don't want you with my cousin. I order you to stop."

"You order me-"

"Yes, I order you. Do you not work for me?"

He laughs at me again. I've never given him an order. Of course he wouldn't take me seriously.

THE LAST PRINCESS

"Yes, I work for you. I'll take your order if you tell me honestly why it bothers you."

I'm not sure myself.

"You…you've never shown an interest in girls. I don't think you have her best interests in mind."

"Go on."

"Uh…That should suffice," I say to him.

"Are you jealous that I gave her some attention?"

Maybe that's it. I nod to him.

"I'll leave her alone."

So he accepts it. He's not going to tease me about it.

"The last thing I want is for you to feel uneasy. If anything I do makes you feel uncomfortable tell me directly."

"T-thank you."

The driver slows and I realize that Kyoya-sama's new palace isn't far from my old one. I assumed he would model it after his home in Han but this place is small just like my old palace was. He gets it; he understands my family's vision. Everything is to remain small.

When the car stops I grab the handle and he blocks my hand.

"Never a good idea to get out the car first," he tells me.

He switches back into bodyguard mode so quickly. The door opens and he steps out with his sword. His hand reaches back to me.

"Take my hand," he says.

I have to believe that even though his feelings for me are cloudy he'll always put my safety first. The house is small; it's like something a normal girl would live in. I wish this small house could be our palace. He walks me up the walkway slowly.

"Why are there so many guards?" I ask him.

"It's your first time back. Can't be too careful."

THE LAST PRINCESS

"Is my life in danger?"

"The interview will create enough chatter for us to be certain."

That's very calculating of Kyoya-sama. This is my first time entering his house and he's not here escorting me in. All the moments I expected to have with him have Captain Saki instead.

The door opens for us and the servants bow to me in the foyer. I was hoping we wouldn't have servants. They're all pretty girls. Not that I don't trust him; I just wanted a normal house. I would cook for him and do laundry like a normal girl. I guess that's what Captain Saki is offering me. This appears to be more of the same.

"Welcome Princess Setsuna," they say in unison.

I don't feel well. I need to be by myself. There's a whole house to explore but I stay in Kyoya-sama's room touching up my drawings. I wish there was someone I could talk to about this. I'm scared that my life with Kyoya-sama will be more of the same. But I want to be with him. Maybe I could talk to him about what I feel; maybe he'll compromise just a little bit.

I look at my sketches; it makes me happy to see the flowers and birds. But I'm looking at them caged too. We're all hidden behind the palace walls. Everyone thinks we're delicate but no one wants to let try to be strong.

It gets dark and I see the moon perfectly from his window. That always got me though my lonely times. No matter where we are in this world or out of this world, we all see the same moon. Kyoya-sama looks at it just like I do.

"You're still awake?"

I turn around sharply. Oh...it's him. Kyoya-sama steps into the dim room loosening his tie. He drops his jacket on his chair and sits down on the bed.

"I heard you locked yourself in here as soon as you arrived. Is something wrong?"

"No."

"Tell the truth."

He continues taking off his clothes. He's peeling off his layers so maybe I should too. I scoot closer to him.

"I don't mind living with people but I don't like servants and guards. I thought cause this place was small it would be different."

THE LAST PRINCESS

"I'll consider cutting it down a bit but you'll be taking away jobs these people need."

"Oh! I didn't think about that."

That was selfish of me.

"It's alright," he says. "It's just the two of us so it does seem excessive to have so many guards and maids. But royal houses have to employ a lot of people. We can afford to and they feel pride in working here."

"You're so smart about these things."

"There's this one girl....Her father was the one that tried to carry you out that night. She begged me to let her be a servant. She wants to continue where her father left off. Although she just does laundry here, she's extremely happy doing it."

I shouldn't be so quick to turn the servants away. I remember that guard. He found me and tried to save me. "You have to survive," he told me.

"You are a figure that keeps them strong. There were a lot of people that lost their parents that night, their sisters, brothers, and friends."

"But I survived-"

"And they look to you for strength."

"But they called me a traitor."

"Some people don't want Han influence here, that's true. But that's not going to stop us."

He puts his arm around me. It would be selfish of me to leave it all behind. I lean closer to him as he rubs my head.

"How are you liking our bedroom?" he asks me.

"Our bedroom?"

"Yes, this whole house is ours. There's never been anything that's belonged to both of us."

"I...I like it."

"I'm glad I got this time with you. It'll be a lot of commotion soon. Everyone will be looking at us."

THE LAST PRINCESS

"I know."

"This may not be the most romantic place but I wanted to rush home and give you this. You'll have to forgive me if I'm a little nervous."

He reaches in his pocket and shows me a small red box.

"We've been through a lot," he says turning to me. "And we'll continue to….but we'll do it all together."

He grabs my hand and pulls it to his face. I wince when he kisses it.

"I love hearing your answer so I'll ask you once again."

He opens the box and I gasp. It's a ring with the Han gem from the story. The gem that led the trapped princess out the cave. I cover my mouth in disbelief. It's a stone ring but so pretty.

"Will you marry me, Setsuna?"

"I-"

"I promise to make you happy. I know you want to be free and wander the world. I can't permit that just yet. It's not what you want to hear but I want to be honest with you."

So it will be a life of being trapped. He slips the ring on my finger and smiles. It feels like he's asking me as man and woman. I look into his eyes and I see he's scared. He thinks I'll say "no." I could never deny such a sweet man.

"Thank you for being honest. I should be honest too."

I take a big breath.

"It's daunting to think of what lies ahead. But I want to go through it, only because I'm with you."

He crashes into me kissing me fiercely. I put my arms around his neck and embrace my own hands. The stone feels so cold on my finger. He's promising that one day he'll lead me out.

"I love you," he whispers to me under the moonlight. "I'm so lucky to have you as my first and last love."

"I'm lucky too."

Chapter 65: Yumiko

Okay, I can do this. I've drilled enough; there's nothing left to practice. I didn't think I would be doing this alone. Kyoya-sama and Setsuna-chan are having their interview in a separate area.

I wish I could talk to him. He's so cool about all this. Last night he stayed with me until I was settled with it all. We went over Morinaga's history and how to be charming.

"You're gonna sweat the makeup off. Calm down, sweetie."

"Sorry."

I take a deep breath. I need to talk to someone to calm my nerves.

"Is my cousin close?" I ask the makeup lady.

"No, the princess and prince are upstairs."

I was expecting an outdoor interview. The breeze would put me at ease. Instead we're stuck inside this hotel. They say it's safer. No one is after my life. I'm not worried about an assassination. I'm worried about looking like an idiot on live television.

"We're ready for you," someone pops in.

I grip my phone in my hand. His number is the one I want to call. If Kantarou-sama was here he would call me a fool for caring what these commoners think. Maybe I need to hear that.

"I'll be out shortly. Can I have some privacy?"

I'm left alone in the makeup room. Can't seem to dial his number. We're not supposed to be communicating. Right now I just need some encouraging words. He'll be able to give me that much.

"H-hello, Kantarou-sama."

I wait on the line. Please say something to me. We should still be friends after all this. He knows what I'm dealing with here.

THE LAST PRINCESS

"Disgraced princess, is that you?"

That woman! Chiyo-san is answering his phone. I wasn't even close enough to answer his phone. They're close now. When did that happen? I hold my mouth to keep from screaming.

"Your interview is about to come on. Feeling nervous?" she asks me.

"W-where is he?"

"Busy."

"Put him on the phone, please."

"I said he's busy," she repeats.

"He'll make an exception for me."

"You're right and there lies the problem."

I hold my fist tighter. Who does she think she is? Kantarou-sama would never like someone like this. She must be hiding it from him.

"He's forgotten about you," she continues. "It wasn't hard for him to forget. A little touching goes a long way. I touched places you never knew existed."

"Just put him on the phone!"

"You had so much time with him. He'd be yours if you would have put out-"

I hang up and slam the phone to the floor. Damn her!

"Yumiko-san."

I don't need this right now. I go to the mirror and stare into my eyes. I can't show a tear. It can't get to me. This is my second chance. My chance to be called Princess Yumiko again. I don't need him. I know I don't need him. I'm good enough on my own.

Who am I kidding...I'm a loser. Last night, he tried so hard to make me feel better. I wondered why he cared so much. Setsuna-chan should be his concern not me.

"You're getting in your own way," Kyoya-sama told me last night. "Just let people get to know you. There's nothing wrong with how you are."

"They think I'm just like her."

THE LAST PRINCESS

"You're nothing like your mother," he told me. "You're a much more beautiful woman."

"Why are you trying so hard?" I asked him. "You're trying harder than me."

"You are a part of my house and my family, so I care."

"But-"

"You need to stop all this self-sabotage. I'm trying to give you a chance to erase all the shame she's done. Don't play the victim."

He's so straightforward. I look into my eyes again and…I see a Morinaga woman. Cheeks rosy, hair held up and adorned. A pure woman. Or….pure at heart.

I go into the interview as poised as possible. The lights don't bother me and the chatter is fine. Whatever they're saying about me isn't my concern. The interviewer sits down in front of me.

"Nice to meet you," he says. "I'm Jay Yuki."

"You're from New News Now."

"You watch me?"

"All the time. I love your commentary."

This must be Kyoya-sama's influence. I didn't know I would be getting such a young reporter. He does the pop culture section. Could he be making me into a pop icon?

"I was nervous about meeting you," he says to me. "I guess it's the getup. My grandma dresses like that."

That's why I hate dressing like this. We sit across from each other and the makeup artist touches me up again. Kyoya-sama warned me that they might make up their own story based on my words. I have to be genuine.

"We're starting in three minutes," I hear.

I can still hear Chiyo-san's voice. Probably lying in bed with him right now. I was with another so I should be okay but…

"So how are you liking Han?" he asks first.

THE LAST PRINCESS

Did the interview start? I see the camera's blinking and it's really quiet on set. I smile and look to the camera. Easy question.

"It's a lovely country. I'm thankful for the acceptance of the Niwa family, my university and all the citizens."

We practiced that one. I smile at him and he continues on.

"But it's radically different from Morinaga, don't you think."

"Different but similar. There's nothing keeping the two countries from getting along."

"You've even spent some time serving in their military-"

"Not directly," I say to him.

He's trying to trap me. Kyoya-sama said they would imply something treacherous as often as possible. So far this is going exactly like he said it would.

"I was Kantarou Niwa-sama's assistant. I served him, not the military."

I smile reluctantly. Sounds like he's my boss; that's all they need to know.

"We're getting into this a lot sooner than I thought. No need to beat around the bush then," he says. "Everyone wants to know your relationship status with the crown prince."

"He….he's a lovely man. He taught me a lot. He's going to be a great king."

"You didn't answer the question. What's your relationship?"

"We're just friends."

I'm not a fan of Jay Yuki anymore. He's not taking me seriously as a figure of my country. He's trying to make me into some tabloid title.

I know what I'm supposed to say but it's not like me at all. It's best to dodge it.

"Just friends? Really?"

"If all you want to do is gossip, we should end this right now."

"I'll back off. Forgive me."

THE LAST PRINCESS

I wonder if he's watching me. He's probably laughing at me. I bite my lip but quickly correct myself. Body language experts will be dissecting all this.

"Wait," I interrupt him. "Stop asking questions and let me talk. I have something to say."

"Uh, go right ahead."

"I only wanted to introduce myself. I'm Yumiko Yamamoto, age twenty. I study fashion design. I like pop music and sci-fi movies. My mother was exiled years ago for having an affair with an unnamed man and I lost my status as princess. She was labeled a whore and I believe that is wrong and unfair. She never got a chance to explain herself to anyone, not even her brother. So I'll explain it now."

I take a deep breath. All I can say is the truth. If I'm like her, it's not in the way they think.

"She married the general because she was supposed to. She loved him because he was kind and had a strong sense of duty. But....her love was a man she met prior to all that. She was with him in secret because she was not allowed to be with him in public. They had their moments in the dark. I'm a product of their love and I'm not ashamed of that."

"Oh...so what's his name?"

"It doesn't matter."

I don't know his name, I never will. I take another breath. Time to confess. Time to let them know who I am.

"I understand why royals have their relationships in secret. It's flattering to be chosen; I get it now."

"What are you saying?" he asks. "Is this about you and the prince?"

I pause thinking if I should say it. I keep picturing him with Chiyo-san. I desperately want to ruin it all. I wanna say that I was his first choice. I wanna prove I was something to him. But would that really satisfy me. It would just make him hate me.

"This isn't about your feelings or mine. It's about the future of my country. That's something you'll never understand," he said to me.

No, I understand but I thought I was more. I feel my eyes tearing up. I get what he was trying to do but I can't do it. My birth father, whoever he was, had it hard.

He had to watch the woman he loved parade around with someone else. He had to be strong to do it; I'm not.

"I love Kantarou-sama," I admit to him. "But there's no future between us. He set me straight years ago. He told me to get over my stupid crush but it's hard. I answered the question everyone wants to know. Now…I hope you find me interesting enough to ask something else. What's your next question?"

"Um….well…we have to go to a commercial break. We'll be right back with our special on the returning royal family."

Chapter 66: Setsuna

Yumi-chan did amazing during her interview. I can't tell what Kyoya-sama is thinking. Since it ended he's had his hand to his chin and hasn't said a thing. She wasn't supposed to say she had feelings for Kantarou-sama. That will take away from his engagement to Chiyo-san. But I'm glad she did it.

"I guess we'll be next," I say to him.

He still doesn't break his concentration. The woman touches up his hair and he still doesn't move.

"This could work," he finally says. "She can be seen as a normal girl. Everyone has had a crush, right?"

I nod to him. There's a lot of people running around preparing the set. We sit secluded in the makeup room.

"Who was your first crush?" I ask him.

He chuckles.

"I don't think I had one."

"Really?"

"People have had crushes on me but I was too focused to like someone else. I like the feeling though."

He reaches over and touches my cheek. Kyoya-sama was my first crush. I liked him before I even knew what he looked like. He's handsome but even if he wasn't I would still like him. He's getting so much attention from all the girls around here. I've watched news reports while he was away where the women would drool over him.

I'm lucky he would show feelings for me. I do think about his affairs; it creeps into my mind a lot. But I find myself forgiving him because I've enjoyed all my time with Captain Saki; it's like I had an affair too.

"You are Ayato-san's first crush?"

"Why do you still permit him to guard me?"

"Cause he's motivated to protect you. I feel it's all harmless. You make me feel very secure in our love."

The captain is right outside the door. He's the only security we have during this interview. Kyoya-sama likes it that way. It's good I make him feel secure. I must not be showing my doubt.

"You're very beautiful, you know. When the public sees the older version of you, boys will want to be with you and girls will want to be like you," he tells me.

"That's not true."

"It is. You'll see soon enough."

The door opens and it's our turn to start. I'm excited about it. Kyoya-sama takes my hand and leads me to the set. He whispers some words to the captain and then walks on.

"Princess, wonderful to meet you."

"Um, hello."

"I'm Lisa, I'll be interviewing you. I hear this will be your first time. I'll make it easy, okay?"

She's nice. I'm glad she's nice. I sit down closest to her and Kyoya-sama keeps his hand on mine.

"Are you okay?" he asks me.

The spotlight turns on.

"I'm okay," I tell him.

THE LAST PRINCESS

"We begin in two minutes," I hear.

I glance around the room and my eyes spot the captain. He smiles at me with his hand on his sword. I'm the first girl he's liked. That means he's given this a lot of thought. When he sees me with Kyoya-sama his eyes don't show any hurt or jealousy. Is he so certain that I like him? Everyone thinks they know me and where my heart lies.

"You look great," Lisa-san says to me. "I really love your hair. I hear you do it yourself."

"Yes."

Everyone stops moving and it gets really quiet.

"I'm here with our returning princess, Setsuna Asahina-sama. I'm so happy you've allowed us this brief time with you."

"Oh, are we on?"

"Yes."

"Oh….um….I'm happy to be back."

"We're happy to have you. You'll be here permanently?"

I look over at Kyoya-sama and he nods to me.

"Yes," I say to her. "There's a new palace being made."

"And the other palace will be a monument."

"I have no problem staying there but…I do understand if others aren't that comfortable."

"You have no problem?"

"No. It was my home. I still see it as my home. The palace did nothing wrong. It still stands. I don't sense any spirits in it."

"Oh well, you're a really strong girl."

"Thank you. I visited the crypt a few days ago. No bad feelings there. Everyone is happy."

"How do you feel when you think about that day?"

THE LAST PRINCESS

"Curious," I tell her.

"Is everything settled in your mind since the killer was captured and killed?"

He's still out there. Kyoya-sama squeezes my hand. I can't speak about it.

"I...I don't know."

"Well I'm told you'll be going on a visit to Highland Row, the lair of the killer."

"I am?"

"Yes, the district is in quarantine, a way to punish all the conspirators. It's a pretty controversial issue. Most people are for it but some are against it."

How come I wasn't told about this? Those people in that district aren't conspirators. They have nothing to do with it. There was only one man and he did it all by himself. There's people still being punished for it.

"You had no idea?" she guesses.

"I...I um-"

"While she was in Han part of her recovery relied a lot on making her forget," Kyoya-sama says. "I purposefully wanted to keep anything related to that case away from her. She's much better now because of it."

"Well we will all see when you take your tour if you agree with the treatment of the conspirators. It's been a real hot button issue. Your opinion will mean a lot."

"I support Kyoya-sama. If he feels it's necessary then it is."

How are they treating these people? Are they just being watched or are they being beaten too. How could he keep this from me? He knows he caught the wrong man. As soon as I told him he should have let those people go. I have to say I support him but I don't.

"Quite a shock for you, it seems," Lisa-san says to me.

"It is."

With all the prepping we were going through, why didn't this come up?

"We'll take our first break. More coming up with our returning princess, Setsuna Asahina-sama."

THE LAST PRINCESS

With the cameras cut Kyoya-sama takes his hand away and drinks his water. He has nothing to say to me. I look over at him and his face is calm.

"We'll talk later," he says to me.

"Why would you keep this-"

"We'll talk later," he repeats. "Now isn't the time."

"May I escort you to the restroom?" the captain comes forward.

I think that's best. Kyoya-sama looks like he'll snap at me if I keep asking.

"We'll be back in four minutes," I hear.

I take one look at Kyoya-sama; he doesn't stop me from taking the captain's hand. He leads me down the hall until it turns vacant.

"You know about all this?" I ask him.

He nods.

"What's going on? There are people being punished for the murder?"

"The convicted killer, Yee, was from the poor area called Highland Row. The story goes that he was encouraged to do it from this small community of people. They all supported him so they all get punished for it. They're labeled terrorists."

"That doesn't make sense."

"They're quarantined to keep their ideals in one place. There's a tall fence to keep people in and out. Nothing cruel is being done to them; they're just being contained."

"Show me."

He takes out his phone and within seconds shows me pictures. I hold my hand to my mouth. They're being starved out. There are children there, and elderly. There are families being punished for no reason.

"Like the woman said, if you support this, it means you support Kyoya-sama's way of doing things. It means he can keep doing this. You have the power to validate every cruel thing he does. He expects your support."

"He kept this from me cause he knew I wouldn't agree."

"You have to. If your country is to be stable, you cannot doubt him with this."

"This is your advice to me?"

"I would never steer you wrong. I'm telling you how to keep these people from rebelling. He doesn't want to trap these people. It's a test to see how far he can go. It's an important test."

I can't support this. The captain grabs my shoulder and leads me back to the interview room. It's so strange; we talk like normal when there are so many blurry feelings between us. When I'm confused, I'm so use to asking the captain for help. He knew to come right away.

He puts me back in my seat and goes back to his corner. The captain's always been honest. Kyoya-sama is turning into quite a snake.

"So what's the relationship like between you two?" she asks next.

"I…I love Kyoya-sama."

"What do you love about him?"

"He's um….he's very smart and a good judge of others. He's kinda closed off with his emotions but that makes the moments when he smiles and laughs really special."

"That's very sweet."

"He um…grew up kind of similar to me. Studied a lot and um…"

"No need to be nervous."

"Sorry."

What I really want to say is how much of a liar he is. I don't want to sit next to him right now.

"But truthfully I feel like I don't know him very well," I admit to her. "He's reserved and won't show all his sides to me."

"That's something every woman struggles with. Your relationship with the prince seems similar to what I go through with my husband."

"You're married?"

THE LAST PRINCESS

"Yes. Speaking of which, when do you two plan on marrying?"

"I don't-"

"In about a month," he cuts in.

I look at him sharply. A month! That's so soon. I had no idea. We only just got back together. I was thinking there would be years before we decided on that.

So much I don't know about.

"You believe in getting married so young?" she asks me.

I have to agree with him but I don't want to encourage other girls.

"My situation is different than the average teenage girl. Kyoya-sama will be my husband. That was decided a long time ago. It makes no difference if we marry now or later."

"But now is fine with you?"

"Yes."

Now is definitely not fine with me. I'm marrying a man and I know nothing about him. It's so scary. The interview carries on with basic questions. He answers them and I smile. I feel out of it. I need to be alone again. I need to figure all this out.

He grabs my hand and smiles to the camera. He laughs and comes off very charming. I'm starting not to trust him. My life with him will be about validating his cruelty. Nodding and saying "I love my husband."

"Have you two thought about kids?" she asks.

I snap back to the present.

"In time," he answers. "I'd like to have five kids. Three girls and two boys. But she's entirely too young to have children."

Marriage then kids…I can't do it. I look over at the captain and he mouths something to me. I can choose. I'm certain that's what he said. I'm considering. I regain my composure and finish up the interview.

We all leave the hotel and head back to the palace. Yumi-chan squeezes in next to me as I sit next to Kyoya-sama. There's plenty of room on the other side of the limo. She's staying away from Captain Saki.

THE LAST PRINCESS

There's so much on my mind. I can't hold it in.

"You're a liar," I say out loud.

Each one of them looks over at me.

"You're such a liar!"

I turn to Kyoya-sama.

"I said we'll talk later," he says calmly.

"No, you'll talk now. How could you keep so much from me? How could you not tell me we're getting married until you announce it to the world? You didn't even ask if I was ready."

"Setsuna-chan," Yumi-chan takes hold of my arm.

"I agreed with everything you've done, everything you said only because we were on camera."

"That's good-"

"No! I don't have to marry you if I don't want to. And if you keep treating me like I'm just some character in your journal, something you can predict the outcome of, you will be sorry."

He finally looks over at me. He stares into my eyes challenging me.

"I keep things from you just like you keep things from me. I'm only trying to protect you," he says to me.

"I have no idea who you are. I refuse to marry a stranger."

"Stop the car," he calls forward.

The car pulls to the side and he opens the door. He's kicking me out. I get up and he holds his hand stopping me.

"You two, find another way back."

Yumi-chan looks over at me. He's kicking her and the captain out. He wants to be alone. He's going to yell at me. I don't mind getting out too. His rage will be harsh.

"And try to keep your hands off each other."

The two crawl over him and he shuts the door when they're outside. I move further from him to the other side of the car.

"I refuse to marry a stranger too," he says to me.

He lights up a cigarette and I push further away from him. The car takes off. I look over at him cautiously. What will his next words be?

"Seems we have a lot to discover about each other."

Chapter 67: Ayato

It's good she's standing up to him. The princess has a strong spirit; she doesn't like being told how to act anymore. He hasn't seen that evolution in her like I have.

"What now?" Yumiko-san asks. "Is there not a backup car?"

"There isn't. You're from here. You should know how to get back."

I can't wait to hear what they talked about.

"Give me your phone. I'll call a cab," she says.

"What happened to your phone?"

"I dropped it."

"Let's just take a bus. It'll be good to sightsee."

"Not with you dressed like that."

What's wrong with how I'm dressed? It's normal to see a man dressed in military uniform. She's dressed as some costume character. Now that I look at her, I'm getting turned on. Setsuna-san told me to stop that. She's jealous that I would bed her cousin. I'll happily bed her when she's ready. Getting really close.

"Stop looking at me like that," she says to me. "I refuse to sleep with you anymore."

"I was about to say the same thing. I'm ending it."

THE LAST PRINCESS

"I ended it first!" she screams.

"Why did you tell Setsuna-san about it? You said it would be a secret."

"Why did you tell Kyoya-sama about it?"

She stares back at me with her hand on her hip. She was the one shamed, not me. I have no problem telling him.

"He asked," I admit. "He told me to stop before you get yourself hurt."

"He did? So....he cares?"

"Of course he does. You're a commodity now. So why did you tell Setsuna-san? That had to make you look bad."

"Well....she asked too."

She did!

"I told her what a pervert you are. And that she should stay away from you."

"It didn't work."

"Whatever. Just call a cab. People are starting to stare."

He dropped us off at a pretty secluded place. There's an elderly man pushing a cart with his groceries down the road. She's just looking for attention; no one is paying us any mind.

Setsuna-san needs time to let out all her frustrations.

"Hurry up and call. I wanna get out of this outfit."

"Follow me."

He wouldn't be walking home groceries if the store was far away. We start walking in the opposite direction. She whines for a bit saying her feet hurt.

"So....did you see my interview?" she asks me.

"Of course."

"How was it? Good? Interesting?"

"Hm....you did okay. Trying to best the commander's fiancée I could tell."

THE LAST PRINCESS

"Huh?"

"Why else would you say you love him without admitting that he loves you back? You're trying to get the people to be sympathetic to you. When his engagement goes public, they'll hate her."

"I...didn't think of that. Really I just wanted to say how I feel. It all feels like some big crush on an older man."

"He'd be lucky to have you."

"Really?"

"Yeah, you're squishy in the right places."

"Shut up about that. Where is this stupid town? My feet hurt."

"Up ahead."

Just need to get her somewhere safe until this fight blows over. We left a pretty major city to do the interview but this place is like a ghost town.

"This looks like Seran. It's a dingy old town."

"You know of it?"

"At my high school kids from here were bussed in. Such a poor town."

Perfect place to hide out. Even here they don't pay any attention to us. If she mentions her feet hurting one more time I swear I'll start dragging her.

"I heard of this place," she says. "Some kids would take the bus here just to eat. It's supposed to be a pretty good diner."

"Fine we'll eat here."

I open the door to the diner. The bell brings all eyes on us. She steps in behind me and they start to gasp.

"Yumiko-sama!"

They're harmless. I back away and they flood over her.

"We just saw your interview," they say to her.

"Oh, we were just hungry so-"

THE LAST PRINCESS

"Have a seat."

I sit at the counter away from her and keep an eye on things. She's smiling as they fawn over her. She's getting the attention she wants.

"And what will you have?" the woman asks me.

"Something heavy."

"I know the perfect thing. You um…are with the Han military?"

Curious old woman. I nod to her.

"I'm a captain in the palace guard. Just watching after her at the moment."

"I respect what you do. If only Morinaga had a stronger palace guard."

"There wasn't one to begin with."

"Very true. But I hear Prince Kyoya is changing that. He's a good man."

"You're a supporter?" I guess.

She nods and goes back into the kitchen. If there's going to be a palace guard in Morinaga, I'll probably be the commander. But then again, I rather guard the princess personally.

Hearing her stand up to him made me so happy. She's doubting him so much now. She's learning that he hides things from her and does things without her consideration. She'll make the choice soon enough. So far, being with me is looking pretty good. Once she sees the devastation going on in Highland Row, she'll see he's not the man for her. I'm even crueler than him but I'm better at hiding it.

I'm better than him in that regard. I'm use to the shadows; I know how to keep my bad deeds secret. She hasn't brought up a single thing I've done.

Tempted to tell her. I'm really curious if she would accept me….all of me. Perhaps I should find that out before we run away together.

"Here you go," the old woman returns. "Something heavy."

A hamburger and a milkshake.

"You just made my day," I tell her.

"Just keep guarding our princesses well."

THE LAST PRINCESS

I eat keeping my eye on Yumiko-san. That guy's getting a bit too close. She should have picked up on some tips while being the commander's assistant. Looks like she's too distracted. I get my plate and clear a path to sit next to her.

When I sit down the crowd disperses. I always have that effect on people.

"You did that on purpose, didn't you?" she says.

"Can't be too careful. Even around hicks."

"They're not hicks. They're my fans."

My phone rings. I forgot about the check-ins. I can handle this while finishing my milkshake.

"Yes, commander," I answer.

She jumps in her seat and pushes closer to me. I switch the phone to the ear away from her. It'll be the normal "everything is fine" routine.

"You're the only contact I have. I expect you to call me before I have to reach out to you."

"Sorry, sir."

I still haven't gotten use to him being my boss. I knew him before he became the commander. He's always been Kyoya-sama's tall older brother to me. He teased us about being so close. Use to walk into our sleepovers and throw cold milk on my face. Figured he was jealous cause he didn't have a best friend but before we went to the academy he said, "You better take care of my brother."

"Where are you now?" he asks.

I can only tell the truth.

"We were headed back from the interview when Kyoya-sama and Setsuna-san got in a fight. He kicked me out the car with Yumiko-san."

"Kicked you out?"

"It's all under control. I'm watching her. She's right next to me."

"Let me talk to her."

I hold the phone out to her and she looks at it like it's him. She stares hard and bites her lip. I push the phone to her again and she turns away.

286

THE LAST PRINCESS

"She doesn't want to speak," I tell him.

"Put me on speaker. I don't care who's around."

I do as he says.

"Yumiko-san," he speaks.

She turns back to the phone still looking at it like it's him.

"I wanted to congratulate you. You did very well. I'm proud of how you conducted yourself. I….thought you would need encouragement but….you were fine on your own."

She holds her mouth.

"You're stronger than you think. But like I told you before you left….you can call me if you need me. I'll always make time for you."

She takes her hand away and snarls like she's about to say something. She turns away again.

"Check in when you're back in the palace," he says to me.

"Yes, sir."

I hang up and go back to my burger. This place is pretty good; they know how to make a heavy burger. Should have asked for rare.

"You're not gonna ask me what's wrong?" she shoots back at me.

"Since when have I cared."

"Hurry up and finish that. We need to talk."

I was the one that had sex with her to clear her head. Now she wants to talk. The old woman gives me a burger to take home. I drink my second milkshake while I walk with the newly spoiled princess. She wants to take a long way back so she can tell me her feelings. She's babbling about something as we walk through the town.

"Wait what was that last part," I interrupt her.

"Chiyo-san answered his phone. Weren't you listening?"

"Which number did you call?"

"T-the zero zero zero number."

THE LAST PRINCESS

That's a secured line. That's how he contacts me. The commander wouldn't lose sight of that phone. If his fiancée got her hands on it then she's sneaky. I don't know if he's sharp enough to notice that.

"This happens to coincide with my job so I'll help you," I tell her.

"Help me?"

"I'll research her a bit."

"But she's all the way in Han. How can you?"

"I command a unit, you know. They're watching the palace."

"You command people? I've never seen you do it."

I'm more of a hands off captain. They're fine teaching themselves. I can have that woman tailed as soon as I make a phone call.

"You know I've never really talked to you before," she says to me. "You're pretty cool when you're not being creepy."

"Don't think you know me cause I'm nice to you."

We keep walking and it turns residential. Time to call for a ride. Enough time has passed for those two to argue and hate each other.

"Wait, look there," she says to me.

"What is it?"

She stops and holds my arm. I see it; I should have seen it first. A man pokes his head from and alley way. Seeing us stopped he ducks back in.

"He was in the diner," she says to me.

It can't be a coincidence that he's here looking suspicious. I grab my gun and point it at him. When he peeks back out he raises his hands high above his head.

"Come with me," I tell her.

We approach him and I see him shiver in the spring heat. He's just a punk; some nerd type. Looks harmless but can't be too sure. I put the gun to his head and he whimpers.

"Yamamoto-san," he cries.

THE LAST PRINCESS

"Stop," she says to me.

I move away and he stands straight staring at her. They look about the same age.

"Do I know you?" she asks.

"W-we went to school together."

"High school?"

He nods.

"I-I just wanted to say you were great in your interview. Y-you've always been a princess. If…if the prince can't see it then you don't need him."

I wish I could walk away from this. I turn my back to them. This must be the best day of his life since she's looking at him. I bet he likes her. I can relate to his nervousness. When Setsuna-san smiles at me I lose all composure; I forget what I'm about to say. I use to watch her from afar too. It was fine to be close to her but I watched from afar so I could see what she's like when she's not on, when she's not happy.

"Thank you for your kind words," she says to him.

"We have to go," I interrupt her.

"I'm applying to the palace guard," he tells her. "I'm gonna make sure what happened doesn't happen again."

He really thinks he can stop it. To him it doesn't matter. He's just saying he wants to protect her. I look back at them; he seems like the type to get strong just to protect her.

"I hope you make it-"

"Hisoka. My name is Hisoka Ui."

"I'll remember that. I hope you make it Hisoka-kun."

"Now, Yumiko-san," I say back to her.

So distracted that she's getting attention. She'll need a bodyguard of her own soon enough. We start walking away and she stays smiling.

"I really think my head is clear. Thank you captain," she says to me.

THE LAST PRINCESS

"I don't care."

"The feeling is nice. I hope you can experience it some time. When you can let go and feel satisfied with yourself. When you can stop tying your existence to other people."

My eyes immediately look over at her. She does seem blissful. My existence tied to others? She means Kyoya-sama. I want to be him; life would be easy if I was him. When I'm in my own head I'm not normal; I'm an outcast. When I'm in my own head, people die.

I want to be with Setsuna-san. When I'm with her I don't feel any angst; she takes it all away. But then that would mean tying my existence to her. Am I scared to be alone now? I think I might have another violent episode.

"We should hurry back," she says. "Looks like a storm."

"I don't mind getting caught in it."

Chapter 68: Kyoya

As soon as we got home I went to the shower. It feels nice to get out of the suit. The weirdest thing is she's staring at me shower from a crack in the bathroom door. I'm pretending not to notice.

She was so feisty in the car. I didn't know she could make me so nervous. It's so cute to hear her scream at me. I can laugh now but in the car I was sweating.

She doesn't have to marry me if she doesn't want to. Why wouldn't she want to? I take a minute to calm down. When it's time to talk she's on the other side of the car.

"Uh....Setsuna-"

"I'm sorry," she says to me.

"There's no need for that. We obviously need to talk."

"No, it's fine. Everything is fine."

THE LAST PRINCESS

"You're upset about the interview. I didn't consider any of that an issue. I figured you would just agree with me on those matters. I know you want to get married. You were very excited when I gave you that ring."

"What about the other thing?"

"What other thing?"

"Those people. You're quarantining people for ideals they don't have."

"What makes you so sure?" I ask her.

"Cause it was all done by one man and he has no ideals at all. He's just a murderer."

Whenever I lock eyes with her she turns away.

"Are you afraid to have an argument with me?" I ask her.

"I'm not arguing-"

"Look at me."

Her shoulders stand up just hearing my voice. What have I done to make her afraid of me?

"It's fine. I'll agree with everything you do. It's what I'm supposed to do. I'll get used to it."

"It's not what you're supposed to do-"

"How isn't it? I said "I support you." I said it blindly and I'll continue to say it blindly."

Her voice starts off angry and then gets quiet. It's fine to argue with me. Maybe she thinks it means we'll break up.

"I rather not talk to the back of your head," I say to her.

"I rather you not see my face."

"I know you're used to being by yourself when you encounter some new emotion. You can't do that now," I say.

I touch her shoulder.

"Don't touch me!"

I squeeze close to the door on my side of the car. She's never pushed me away like that.

"I'm sorry," she whispers.

She turns back to me clutching her ring.

"I've been feeling doubt," she admits. "I just….I just feel like I can't handle it. I can't play the princess anymore. At first I thought that was all I was, all I could be. That's how my parents made me feel. But I'm more than that."

I scratch my head nervously. Is she asking to leave? I can't permit that.

"You don't think I'm smart, do you? You don't think I have a brain?"

"That's not true."

"I felt hurt when I was blindsided during the interview. I felt like you only see me as a figurehead or a symbol."

"That's not true."

"I trained to be a leader just like you. I understand it. You don't have to keep things from me."

She slides closer to me. Her eyes are searching mine. Searching for what, I wonder.

"I think you're a great king. I wouldn't take that away from you but you need to realize…I can."

She's threatening me.

"All I'm trying to do is be on equal ground with you. I can handle whatever you tell me. I can make my own decisions about it. And I will support you but you need to know how I feel first."

"I understand. I'll try to include you more."

I assumed she enjoyed the docile role. Most women like a man that can handle everything. She smiles at me and I see the girl I'm used to. She can't be serious about taking my position away from me. I need her to get stronger feelings for me.

I open my eyes in the shower and see her still watching me. I can't figure her out. Why did she say, "I don't have to marry you if I don't want to?" It's like she was

THE LAST PRINCESS

warning me. I'm pushing her closer to….leaving me. I haven't even considered that a possibility.

I have to face her. When I step out the shower she hides behind the door frame. She's definitely going through her curious phase.

"Can I watch you shower now?" I ask.

"Huh! What? N-no."

"C'mon, I wanna finally see what's under there."

She steps into the doorway with her head down. Her sketchbook is under her arm. So she's been drawing me. I cover up with a towel and walk towards her. She's still.

"There's absolutely nothing," she says holding her arms across her chest. "You're better off looking at Yumi-chan."

"What makes you think I like girls like her?"

"Everyone does."

Yumiko-san is sexy but she's far too annoying to be with. All last night, Yumiko-san talked and whined and gossiped. So many times she asked about Kan-nii and I had to put her back on track.

"You're my type," I tell her.

I tilt her chin to make her look at me.

"How'd you get so many muscles?" she asks staring at my chest.

"You attracted to guys with muscles?"

She blushes and I hug her close.

"You're still wet," she mumbles.

"The house is empty. How about we both hop in the shower?"

If I can get her to have sex with me, she'll be more obedient. I'm certain she'll forget about any doubt in her mind. She pushes me away putting her sketchbook between us.

"Why do you keep pushing me away?" I ask.

THE LAST PRINCESS

I haven't had sex in three months. Something has to be done about that. I take a step closer to her and she runs out the room. Her tiny feet thump down the hallway. She stays hidden the whole night.

Close to midnight I walk around. Yumiko-san should be here by now. I walk pass her room and hear the two girls laughing. They're happy being back in their country.

"So um....what's it like being with Captain Saki?" I hear Setsuna-san say.

She knows about it. Why would she be curious?

"Don't make me answer that."

"Is he sweet?"

"No. He's the strangest man I've ever met. He helped a lot though. But it's over now. That was just a short chapter in my life. I like the single me."

"So you guys aren't boyfriend and girlfriend anymore?"

"We never were. He was just something to fool around with."

"That's not nice. You shouldn't fool around with his feelings."

"There were no feelings."

She's so sensitive to Ayato-san. She understands his delicate emotional state without even knowing the story behind it. Maybe that's just the kind of person she is.

"I told you, you have to leave that guy alone. He's obsessed."

"He's my friend. I don't mind how he is. If he thinks you don't accept him it'll just hurt his feelings more. And when his feelings are hurt he likes to be alone."

"I guess I've wanted to talk to someone about it. He's not all bad. He is a good kisser," Yumiko-san says.

"You kissed him?"

"He kissed me. He's really energetic when he's into it. He says really sexy things and has a nice motion about him."

"Um…"

THE LAST PRINCESS

"You're the wrong person to talk about this with. This is extremely awkward for you." Yumiko-san asks her.

How is it awkward for her?

"It's weird to think of him that way. He's my friend. He always wears a uniform. I can't imagine him naked."

"I liked it when he wore the uniform. It reminded me of…yeah, we should stop talking. Stop trying to picture him naked!"

"I'm not!"

I'm the one that had to tell him how sex worked. He didn't get the concept of it so when we were younger we watched tons of porn. He still didn't get it so he went on his own and started binding women and experimenting. Now he has a "nice motion" about him. Am I supposed to be proud?

"So….you wore the robes and pretended to be me. Did it work?"

First I'm hearing of it. He was with Yumiko-san to satisfy himself. He really wants Setsuna-san. Why would Yumiko-san go along with it; her self-esteem must have been shot. Things are definitely getting out of hand.

"He was really into it," she admits. "It was….good. Are you sure you wanna hear about this?"

"I know he's in love with me. This isn't surprising. The thing is….Kyoya-sama knows; he knew before me. But still he lets the captain guard me."

"Cause he trusts you."

"It's like you said. He thinks I'll always be here."

"Won't you?"

I'm getting nervous listening.

"Well anyway he trusts the captain too, although I don't think he should," Yumiko-san says to her.

"He really shouldn't."

"Did the captain make a move on you?"

"No. He never has."

"Do you want him to?"

"D-don't talk like that!"

"Why do so many boys like you? If you went to high school all the girls would be jealous."

Yumiko-san's gossiping has come in handy. Setsuna-san sounds so much different than she did when I first met her; she's mature now and having mature feelings.

The door opens quickly and I stare at Yumiko-san.

"Stay quiet," I mouth to her.

"I'm gonna get us some drinks. Stay here."

She walks out and closes the door. I have nothing to say. I retreat back down to my room.

"Kyoya-sama," she calls to me.

"Don't say anything."

"I won't. I want you to be with her. But you should know…she's thinking about him."

Chapter 69: Kantarou

"We'd be in so much trouble if someone saw me in your room."

"But you keep coming."

"Cause you never stop me."

She runs to me and I take her in my arms. I haven't seen Yumiko-san in months. Finally she has a break from school. Her scent comes back to me and my guard goes down.

"I'll give you my first night but I have to see Setsuna-chan."

"The little girl is fine."

THE LAST PRINCESS

"I have to make sure. And plus I miss her."

I don't plan on letting go tonight. I refuse to tell her that I missed her. We fall to the bed and I lay still with her. I just want to sleep with something warm in my arms.

"Commander, you're never this grabby."

Her chest is the warmest part. I push my head against it and nuzzle close.

"I don't feel like a commander when I'm with you."

"Is that a bad thing?"

"No, that's exactly what I want."

I wake up. She's at it again. I sit up in my bed and push my hair away. Dreaming about her is nice; I can still feel her warmth.

"Why are you going through my closet?" I ask.

"Good morning, Kantarou-sama. I was just picking out your outfit for the day."

"I wear a uniform every day."

"And I'm picking it out to you."

She's so annoying. Mother invited her to stay in the palace and every day she gets on my nerves. Chiyo-san is becoming less and less ideal. I haven't announced anything but I know I have to go through with it. Why'd I have to wake up from that dream?

"Today I was hoping to have lunch with my parents," she says.

"Fine with me."

"I want you to come too."

I lie back down and cover my head with the pillow. It can't just be me; other people have to see how annoying she is. My phone rings on the nightstand. I reach my hand out and connect with hers. Pushing the pillow away I see her reaching for it.

"Don't ever reach for my phone again," I warn her.

"S-sorry."

THE LAST PRINCESS

"Leave. I have business."

The phone keeps ringing while she walks to the door. When the door closes behind her I answer it.

"Commander speaking."

"I'm checking in."

"I get that. What's going on?"

Captain Saki is on the other line. He doesn't take any of this seriously.

"I'm taking leave."

"Why?"

"Psychological problems. Kyoya-sama approved it."

"Kyoya isn't your boss. I am."

"Believe me, it's for the best."

"What replacement do you have?" I ask.

"None."

Typical of him. Doesn't care for the big picture.

"Whatever. I'm going there anyway."

Anything to get away from Chiyo-san. I've been waiting for an excuse.

"I knew you would have my back. It might interest you to know that they'll be forming a palace guard in Morinaga."

"Not without my input. Take your leave. I'll be there shortly."

Yumiko-san will be there. I know she doesn't want to speak to me. After all I said I feel like I made a big mistake. I don't want to marry a woman I don't have feelings for. Appearances are meaningless; I don't care anymore.

When Yumiko-san spoke in her interview it made me want to change the formula of things. I was happy for the people to know but it wasn't one sided. There was love between us from the beginning. At first I faked it to keep her away from Kyoya's plan but then it all got real. I just don't know when it happened.

298

She'd be a good queen but it's too late for that.

I get up and see the uniform Chiyo-san laid out for me. I push it aside and grab a new one from the closet. After getting dressed I open the door and see her standing.

"I'm going to Morinaga," I tell her.

"Perfect. I'll come too."

"You won't."

"But people will need to see us together. And traveling to your brother's country will be perfect. I can help Setsuna-san plan the wedding."

She follows me down the hall and I stop.

"You're getting in the way," I tell her. "If you continue to get in the way, I'll have you kicked out of here."

"I'm coming with you. I won't leave you alone with her."

"Are you making commands at me?"

I turn back and see her.

"You may not like me but you need me."

I need her money, not her. I'm starting to think the money isn't so important.

"Don't follow me," I say to her.

If I can get the pilot to wake up I should be there in a few hours. Breakfast can be eaten on the plane. I'll have my clothes sent over later. My phone rings again.

"Commander speaking."

"Are you trying to lose Chiyo-san?" father screams.

"Huh?"

"She says you've been being mean to her. If you're going to visit your brother then she goes with you."

"I'm going on business," I tell him.

"She goes with you."

THE LAST PRINCESS

She called him that fast. She has the old man wrapped around her finger. He wants her money too.

The plane ride is unbearable. She keeps talking about how she wants an interview of her own. She wants the people to know about our love. I just want her to go away.

"What's Morinaga like?"

"Quiet."

"I had a feeling it was like that. It's such a small country-"

"No, you stay quiet."

I'll gladly guard the princess if it means I can escape from my future wife. Chiyo-san takes a drink from the attendant. Maybe now I can go back to sleep.

"You don't talk about yourself much," she says.

"Ugh."

"Is it that you don't have much of a personality?"

"Yeah, that must be it. You really can do better. Now can you shut up so I can sleep."

"You're so anxious to dream about her. I heard you say her name when you were asleep."

"So?"

"What is it about her? You have to know she's just a kid."

She keeps asking about her. It's not her business. Probably I did say Yumiko-san's name in my sleep. She admitted to the world that she loves me. I'll be expected to respond. Not sure what to say. Things were so much easier when no one knew and we could sneak into each other's rooms after dark.

"Probably she just seduced you."

She's still talking.

"She's inconvenienced us a lot. How are you going to respond when people ask what you feel for her?"

300

THE LAST PRINCESS

"I'll tell the truth."

"Kantarou-sama-"

"You'll never succeed in controlling me. You should just stop."

"I'm not the bad guy here. You promised to marry me and you're thinking about other women."

So I'm the bad guy. I never said I loved Chiyo-san nor had any intention to. I was honest with her from the beginning. Now that she's here she feels she can make demands to me and act like we're in a relationship.

"I promised nothing." I say to her.

"But-"

"And if you keep talking back to me I'll throw you off this jet!"

She sinks down into her seat. Women are so damn annoying! This whole be married at thirty thing is a pain. I get the reason behind it. I have to command and my queen has to win everyone's heart. Setsuna-san gets it; she was trained to understand it all. We talked about politics several times. She understands what a queen is there for. She would have been a good candidate.

I'm told Yumiko-san had some of the same training; she should get it too. No....she's not from Han. Morinaga can break tradition and have a foreign royal but I can't do that here. Dammit! I keep going back and forth with this. I can't be with her but I want to and I'm desperately trying to rationalize it.

"You're not very nice," she says to me.

"I know that."

"Can I just talk to you?"

"All you do is talk."

"Please just listen."

She sits across from me nervously drinking. I can tell she doesn't drink wine often.

"I really like you. I always have ever since the king announced you would succeed him. I was there in the capitol on that day. You looked as sour then as you do now."

301

THE LAST PRINCESS

I was eighteen years old then. It was right after I finished the military academy. I had to greet the people but all I really wanted was to gain rank and become commander.

"You stood next to your brothers and looked so cool. Kira-sama attempted to run off stage and you grabbed him by the collar and brought him back."

He cried about it. Back then father was away so much. Kira called me "father" for a few years. So what if she likes me; I don't care.

"What's your point?" I ask her.

"I…just want to be yours. Please consider me seriously."

I heard that once before. Back when I didn't realize I cared for Yumiko-san.

"I'm sorry but I like you," Yumiko-san once told me. "I don't want you to see me as a mistress. I want you to see me as good enough to walk beside you and sit across from you. When I kiss you…my feelings are real. I'm so disappointed when you stop."

"I should have known you couldn't handle it."

"Please consider me seriously."

My mind keeps going back to her. She confessed to me and I denied her. I let her in but I never told her my feelings. I never made her feel secure. I only approached her like she was my mistress. I ruined it all.

Chiyo-san hides herself behind her hands. I am the bad guy here.

"Come sit next to me," I tell her.

She quietly gets up and sits next to me. Perhaps if I pretend I'll slowly develop some real feelings for her. I put my arm around her.

"Don't talk so much and I'll consider it."

"Really? Are things really over between you and her?"

It has to be.

"Yes. I have you now."

Chapter 70: Kira

Everyone's in Morinaga except me. When did that become the cool place to hang out? Everything Kyo-nii touches is cool. He turned that backwards country into the most interesting place in the world because he's on track to becoming a lovable dictator.

All the while I'm stuck at the academy. I'm so far behind. Setsuna-san was supposed to wait for me. When I finish up here she will see me as a man. She's such a fickle girl. She won't give me any attention after leading me on for so many years.

The break is over so I'm back in class. Back with the so called future defenders of my country. The first days back are just a gossip fest. Everyone keeps talking about my brother's stupid interview.

"Can you believe in a month he'll be married?"

"I wish I was Setsuna-sama. She gets to marry our handsome prince."

"Kyoya-sama is the most handsome, isn't he?"

"Definitely."

"Shut up!" I scream.

So much damn chatter. The girls look back at me.

"What's his problem?"

"Probably jealous."

They have no idea who I am. Who I am doesn't mean anything. I'm the third prince. I'm so far in age from my brothers that I have nothing in common with them. I met Setsuna-san, a royal that could understand me, and she's captivated by Kyo-nii like all the rest. Somehow she's captivated by the captain too.

All those girls up front and none of them look back at me. Handsome runs in the family; I'm just as handsome as my brother but no one bothers to look at me.

At break I head to the telephone lounge. We're not allowed to have phones so this is my only connection to the outside world. My one call a day normally goes to mother but…I feel like it can't hurt to try someone else.

I dial Kyo-nii and feel stupid for doing it.

THE LAST PRINCESS

"Kira, is everything okay?" he says on the other end.

I don't normally talk to him. I don't know what to say.

"Um..."

"Did you call for Setsuna-san?" he guesses.

"I-I'll speak with her but I wanted to talk to you first."

"Really...figured you still hated me."

"Hate? I-I don't hate you."

I never said I hated him to his face. It's starting to get loud in here. More people crowd the room to get a phone.

"I hate it here," I say to him.

"Too tough?"

I hold the phone closer. If anyone were to hear, they would call me a coward. I...I want to give up.

"It's meant to be tough, you know. Only thirty percent of my class made it to graduation."

"It's not that it's too tough, I just...don't belong here."

"You'll never know where you belong. It's up to you to create that place."

"But I-"

"Kan-nii wanted to be a commander because he always wanted to be in charge. He created that environment for himself. Strived for it."

"I don't want to be a commander. I don't even want to be king. I just want to be important."

"You're plenty important," he tells me.

"You know I'm not."

"What do you think boys do to feel important?"

I've been watching them. They brag about how far they made it with girls. I tried that. Made it seem like I slept around and knew how to satisfy a women. I've never even kissed one. Setsuna-san was my first kiss. It was so easy to talk to her and feel like I was somebody around her.

The girls here won't even look my way.

"You'll figure it out," he tells me. "I'll have to introduce you to someone when you come for the wedding."

"She's going through with it?"

"What makes you think she wouldn't?" he asks.

Cause of all the terrible things I said about him.

"Congratulations, I guess."

Just cause she marries him doesn't mean I have to give up on her. Kinda feels that way though.

"Don't be so jealous," he tells me.

"I'm not jealous-"

"Kira-kun?"

That's her. I straighten up. She's really here. All I wanted was to talk to her while I was away but she would never talk to me. She must like me again.

"S-setsuna-san?"

"How are you? How is school?"

"Everything is going well of course. If you heard otherwise they're lying."

"Hehe. I envy you."

"Why's that?" I ask.

"You get to make a name for yourself independent of your title."

That's not the case. She probably sees me as a hero. I can't let her down.

"How many friends do you have there?" she asks.

None.

"A few. It's hard to trust people when everyone knows I'm a prince."

THE LAST PRINCESS

"You have to be selective. That makes sense."

"Why are you talking to me now? You avoided me for so long?"

"You are not my biggest issue," she says to me.

"Uh..."

She breaks my heart instantly. I'm not even on her radar anymore.

"I guess you have bigger issues being a princess. Like your wedding."

The boy next to me immediately looks over. I said a buzz word.

"Don't remind me. You're coming, aren't you?"

"Of course I'll be there, princess. I'll be one of the groomsman."

"Since when do you call me "princess." Did you forget my name?"

Another person looks over. I think I found a way to get some attention. I know the princess. Being the third prince hasn't given me much but being Setsuna-san's brother-in-law is getting me tons of attention. I hear whispering.

"That's Kira Niwa. He's related to the royal family, right?"

Damn right.

"Have you gotten over that little crush you have on me? We should clear that up before you get married."

"Huh?" she says confused.

I lean back in my chair and all eyes are on me. More whispers arise. If I'm good enough for Setsuna-san, I'll be a treasure to any one of these girls.

"I gotta go. And don't worry. I'll make it to Morinaga for your wedding."

"Um...okay," she says to me. "I'll see you then."

I hang up the phone and they all look at me. I can milk this even more. I have pictures of Setsuna-san from the birthday party. Everyone continues with their conversations; I leave out and slam the door behind me.

I walk quickly back to my dorm. Where are those pictures? They're from mother's personal collection; never released from the public. I know the masses will be here any minute.

THE LAST PRINCESS

"Excuse me."

I look back at my door. How did a girl get into the dorm? She's a tall one too.

"What is it?"

"I overheard you in the phone lounge. Are you Kira Niwa of the Han royal family?"

"I am."

The rooms floods with all types of people. Girls and boys looking everywhere. I pull out my desk drawer and as the girl comes towards me she notices the pictures.

"Is that the princess?" she squeals.

"Uh, yeah. It's the album from our birthday party. Did you wanna see?"

I think I did it. I created an environment where I can feel important. My room is full of my people. They're gawking over me…well mostly Setsuna-san. They know who I am now.

"You kind of look like Kyoya-sama," a girl tells me.

"No, he looks like Kantarou-sama."

The chatter goes on as the pictures circulate. There's one girl that doesn't look enthused. She sits in the corner looking at one picture angrily.

"It's getting late," I announce. "You all should go before curfew."

The room clears out and I go to the girl in the corner. She's too distracted to see we're the only ones left.

"Hey," I say to her.

"The princess should have died that night."

"What?"

"No good has come from her surviving," she snarls.

"What do you mean? Kyoya is the leader of Morinaga. It's basically our country now."

307

THE LAST PRINCESS

"You want a country to vacation in, that's fine. But he's pulling Han forces away from his own people. Why should I be here fighting and studying just to end up protecting the princess' people."

I never heard someone talk so angrily about the princess. Han has plenty of forces; we're not stretched thin. I guess Kyoya hasn't communicated that the countries will merge.

I can't get a good look at her. She has blond curly hair covering her face. No one should hate the princess; she's harmless.

"There are plenty more that think just like me," she says.

"I doubt that…"

I watch on as she crumbles up the picture.

"She should die," she says again.

"Kyoya will still rule her country."

"Then it'll be a conquering and we can purge their people out. What he's doing to those people in Highland Row, he'll do everywhere. And all that will be left are survivors pledged to Han."

Does she realize who she's talking to? I won't let anyone hurt the princess. We're not conquering anyone. Kyoya is just fulfilling a promise. Seeing their interview, I understand what he was doing. I understand the importance of their love even thought I don't like it. I can't let anyone speak against her.

But I'm not tough enough to make an impact. This girl seems hardcore.

"You should go," I tell her.

She stands up and moves her hair away. There's an actual girl under all that hair. I turn my head away. She's….kinda cute.

"If you don't fit in with the Han royal family you can just join another. I'm Naoko."

I would never betray my family.

"Leave," I tell her.

"I've known who you are this entire time," she says at the door. "And I know you feel like an outcast. I've watched the last three years."

I lift my head up see her. I'm not that kind of outcast.

"Whatever group you are a part of, I will stop them. No one will harm Setsuna-san."

"We'll see how that goes. I'll visit you again. Goodnight, prince."

Chapter 71: Kantarou

"It's nice to see you," Kyoya says to me.

"I wish I could reunite with you without the shrieking."

"Oh my gosh, Kyoya-sama, it's so good to see you. You were amazing in your interview," Chiyo-san squeals at him.

He nods at her but before he can speak to me she squeals again.

"Setsuna-san was amazing too. Kantarou-sama was talking about getting me an interview. I'm sure you have connections at-"

"Very nice to see you, Chiyo-san," he cuts in. "Can my brother and I have a minute? You're welcome to go wherever you wish."

"Sorry, I can't do that. I stay by his side."

She grabs my hand. He looks over at me with his eyebrow raised. I really don't know how to handle this girl. I shake her off.

"Go," I tell her. "Stop interfering in my business."

"But we're a team. Whatever Kyoya-sama has to say to you he can say in front of me."

"Go!"

"I-I'll just have a look at the gardens."

She clams up and heads back out the front door. I hold my forehead but it doesn't stop throbbing.

"Very interesting relationship."

THE LAST PRINCESS

"I don't know what I'm doing," I admit to him. "I hate her. I really hate her. She's the most annoying thing I've ever met."

"But...."

"I'm trying to play the gentleman."

I sit down on his couch. She's supposed to be queen so it shouldn't matter but it's so hard to sit next to a woman I despise. She tries to take my control away. Trying to say what I should wear, who I should talk to and how I should treat her. When she quiets down I remember the girl I met in the marriage meeting. Quiet, gentle, and with a cute laugh.

"Nothing is public so just deny her."

"I figured I would pretend and feelings would come."

I sat next to her on the plane and put my arm around her. She went on and on about how we should have a palace for the two of us.

"You know, you've never had a steady girl. You always said they were annoying or didn't understand you."

Except Yumiko-san.

"Maybe you're better off alone than feeling miserable."

"Since when are you the big brother. I'm supposed to be giving you advice."

"Could you?"

He sits down and starts to rub his chin.

"I'm really glad you're here. You'll be guarding Setsuna-san now?"

"Yeah."

"Watch her closely. I think….she's hiding something. Just the other day she said, "I don't have to marry you if I don't want to." I wanna know what other choice she has."

All she talked about while he was away was how much she wanted to marry him. Seems he's under a lot of stress. Why aren't any drinks being served? Is it such a small house that servants can't fit.

"Why'd you send Saki away? He's pretty close to her."

THE LAST PRINCESS

"Haven't you heard? He's in love with her. And she…might be in love with him."

He keeps his head down. Ashamed of the words he's forced to say.

"Why didn't you send him away sooner?" I ask him.

"I didn't send him away. He asked for time off. I need him so…I'm hoping this just blows over. Her words….what she said to me…."

She must not be in the house if he's talking about it.

"You're being blind," I tell him.

"No! I'm just trusting her."

We didn't use to have women, now we're both having problems.

"Where is she anyway?" I ask him.

"She wanted to go back to the crypt. She took Yumiko-san with her."

I guess I'll have to meet her again.

"We're short on rooms. You and Chiyo-san will have to share."

"No."

"You have another arrangement?"

"Put all the girls together. I rather have a room to myself."

"You just wanna watch them fight over you."

Chapter 72: Yumiko

"I'm glad you went back to the crypt with me," she says.

"It was calm just like you said. I can't get use to that stone statue of your mother."

"It's nice they used her scowling face."

That's how I'll always remember her. There's no food allowed in the crypt so I'm extremely hungry. We're in the car taking the short ride back.

THE LAST PRINCESS

"I'm gonna call ahead and get the cook prepared. Do you want something?"

"No, we can cook our own food."

"But we don't have to."

"I want to," she says to me.

She's the one that had all those cooking classes, not me. Wait...I didn't get my cell phone replaced yet. I have to tell Kyoya-sama so he can get me a secured line again. I'll have to explain why it's broken. It was a small hissy fit after hearing Chiyo-san's voice. As long as I stay in this palace, I should never see her again.

"Um...I meant to ask you something. Did Captain Saki say anything weird to you?" she asks me.

"No."

"He's gone. He just disappeared."

"Probably some official business. Just let him go."

Doesn't seem like she wants to. Maybe I should warn Kyoya-sama a bit more. She lowers her head like she's sad.

"Setsuna-chan, you should calm down on the whole making him jealous thing."

"I'm not trying to make him jealous."

"You have to know you're being pretty obvious about your fondness for the captain."

She turns away from me and looks out the window.

"You love Kyoya-sama, don't you?" I ask her.

"I do."

"Then think only of him. He's a good man. Lots of women would love to be in your position."

She turns back to me with tears in her eyes.

"Yumi..."

I reach over and hug her. I don't know what she's feeling. She won't say.

THE LAST PRINCESS

"I....I love Kyoya-sama but I find myself thinking about the captain a lot."

"It's normal at your age. Don't beat yourself up. They're both attractive men but…you have to know the captain is a sick person. He's no one you should be thinking about."

I didn't know how sick he was till I slept with him. He cut my thigh and sucked my blood. I still have the mark.

"There's nothing wrong with him," she says to me.

"There is. I don't know the whole story and I don't think we should."

He was pretty rough with me all while yelling out Setsuna-chan's name. He never saw me once; all he saw was her. I don't see how Kyoya-sama can know about that and still permit him to guard her. Perhaps Kyoya-sama is sick too.

We pull up to the house and she dries her eyes.

"This stays between us," I say to her. "I would never tell your secrets."

"Thank you."

I'm thinking I might have to say something to protect her. The door opens for us and I lead her out the car.

"So what do you feel like cooking?" I ask her.

"I was thinking something with lemons."

"You're cooking lemons?"

"You'll see. It'll be tasty."

I open the front door and stop.

"Hello, disgraced princess."

Chiyo-san is here. Setsuna-chan looks up at me. I don't have a nice thing to say. She leans over the couch like she owns the place.

"Oh I didn't see you there. Welcome back, Setsuna-san."

"What do I say to her?" she whispers to me. "Do I kick her out?"

"Just go upstairs," I say to her.

THE LAST PRINCESS

She runs up the stairs. Chiyo-san stands and stares me down. Damn! She's always so fashionable. These are my respectful, talk to the dead clothes.

Wait…if she is here that must mean Kantarou-sama is too. I look around. He's not here now. She steps around the couch. Why do I feel like the one that doesn't belong? This is my country and my palace guest house.

"What brings you here?" I ask her.

"I go where my hubby goes."

"You guys have gotten so close."

She steps closer to me flipping her hair over her shoulder.

"You got a problem with that," she says.

She's trying to intimidate me. It's not worth getting in an argument with her; looks like she's expecting it. Since the interview I felt so free. I can't let her or her hubby take that away from me.

"Just the opposite," I say to her. "I'm happy for you. Now please excuse me."

I move pass her and take a step up.

"That was some trick you pulled in your interview," she says.

I stop in my tracks.

"What trick?"

"You just made yourself look pathetic. You cling to Kantarou-sama cause you miss your precious title. It's pretty obvious."

I turn back to her. I have never seen him as an opportunity to get my title back. It's never been like that.

"I love Kantarou-sama. His titles mean nothing to me."

"Your love for him ends now."

She's insecure. Perhaps they're not as close as I think. She stares me down thinking her eyes will keep me in place. I can't bother with her.

THE LAST PRINCESS

I head upstairs. Why is he here? What business does he have in Morinaga? Midway up the stairs the dining room door opens with chatter.

"You're going to have to redesign the entire palace. Too much exposure. A sun roof is an assassin's best hiding spot," a familiar voice says.

"Since when are you an architect."

I turn around and see Kantarou-sama enter with Kyoya-sama at his heel. Chiyo-san quickly grabs his arm pushing Kyoya-sama out the way.

"Yumiko-san," he says to me. "How have you-"

She pulls at his arm trying to pull him away as best she can.

"Nice to see you, commander," I say to him.

"We should talk about-"

She pulls hard at his arm again. He shakes her off angrily and takes a step up the first stair. I step up away from him. We can't get any closer. I run the rest of the way to my room and shut myself in.

"It's so hard to see him," I say to myself.

"Chiyo-san's things are here," Setsuna-chan says.

What are her bags doing in my room? I go forward and Setsuna-chan is already opening the bags.

"Don't do that," I tell her.

"There are only three rooms here. I guess she'll be staying with you."

"Huh? No, she'll probably stay with Kantarou-sama."

"Maybe it's too soon for them to sleep together."

They're already sleeping together. That's what she told me. How else would she have access to his phone?

"Ugh! Why is she even here to begin with? What business does she have in my country?"

"Kyoya-sama said our return has made a big impact on the media. Maybe now Kantarou-sama will announce his engagement."

THE LAST PRINCESS

That doesn't bother me. Or maybe it does. He looked so sweet on the stairs just now.

"Where the hell did the captain go?"

I need a distraction.

"If she stays here then I'll stay too," she tells me.

"Thanks."

There's a knock on the door.

"It's me," I hear.

I open the door and Kyoya-sama stands against the wall. Checking up on me again.

"Dinner's in a few."

"I won't be going," I tell him.

"I thought you were over this."

I wave him inside. He steps in and I shut the door.

"Don't make me do this," I say to him.

"What am I making you do? I'm just offering you food. I know you like food."

"You're gonna make me sit at the table with her and act all normal and have to listen to-"

"It'll do you some good to listen."

"And you put her in my room. Why?"

"Yumiko-san," he says exasperated. "I'm not going to baby you. Come down to dinner."

He leaves out.

"He's so fatherly to you," Setsuna-chan says. "You should come down. I'll sit near you."

I have to change first. I can be as fashionable as her. I'll make her know she's no bother to me. I'll show both of them.

"Plug in my curling iron," I say to her. "We got work to do."

"But I don't know how to curl-"

"You're gonna learn."

Chapter 73: Kantarou

I sit on the bottom of the stairs waiting for her to come down. She looked at me like she didn't know me. When she said "commander" it didn't sound the same.

I have to admit, I don't know much about my feelings. I keep thinking my life has to reflect my duty but she's the exception. I can't stand not having her in my life. She has to know that.

"AHHH! You burned me!" I hear.

"I'm sorry. I'm really sorry."

"Go get some ice!"

What's going on up there? I hear a door slam and tiny steps come down the stairs. The little princess sees me, bows her head then continues running to the kitchen.

She hasn't said a word to me. I thought she missed me. She runs back with an ice tray. She lifts up her dress to run up the stairs and I grab her arm.

"Did you lose your voice again?"

"Uh…hi."

"Thought you'd have more to say to me."

"I can't right now. She needs ice."

She takes off up the stairs. Once she's upstairs I hear the door slam.

"Ready for dinner," Chiyo-san appears in front of me.

THE LAST PRINCESS

"Oh…yeah, I guess."

"I observed the cook. I made sure she'll give you the biggest steak."

"That would have happened on its own. There's no need or you to interfere."

"You should sit in the dining room with me."

"Just go ahead."

I'm hoping to see her when she comes down. Chiyo-san sits on the stair with me holding my hand.

"I…I put up my hair. Do you like it?"

"I hadn't noticed. I'm not the type to notice those kinds of things."

"Yumiko-san looked nice with her hair up today."

"She wore her hair down. She always does."

She gets up quickly and walks to the dining room. She's never so quick to leave. I guess I found a trick. Wait….I get it now; her feelings are hurt.

"Chiyo-san," I call after her.

I enter the dining room and she has her head down on the table. In all the training I had, there was no mention of how to be sensitive.

"I should ask you now….should I just stop trying?"

"What do you mean?"

"Should I stop trying to get you to like me? If you want I'll call the whole thing off. It'll be my choice. I'll make sure you won't look bad."

A chance to get out of it. I can finally be by myself again. But….she's crying. I don't think Chiyo-san is a bad person. My actions have caused her to feel insecure.

I sit down next to her.

"I have a habit of…not making people feel secure. It's my job and I'm bad at it," I say to her. "I think only about what I want and how I want it to happen. I know I've hurt you time and time again and I'm sorry."

THE LAST PRINCESS

She lifts her head up and I see her tears. I don't think she's strong enough to be queen. Perhaps I don't need a queen just yet. My father is still alive and shows no sign of slowing down. It might be time to break tradition and refuse the marriage. Thirty is just an age; it's no deciding point.

"I'm calling it off," I say to her.

"What?"

"How about we become friends first instead of rushing off and getting married. I would love to spend time with you outside of your obligation to be my queen. I would love to meet the real Chiyo Subera, the girl I met in the marriage meeting. I know that's the real you."

I pass a napkin to her and she wipes her eyes. After her eyes are dry she nods to me. So we have an agreement.

I move the hair from her face and she smiles. She has a nice smile. I lean forward and kiss her forehead.

"Oh my gosh! I'm sorry."

The princess stands in the doorway with Yumiko-san. They both look shocked. Her eyes quickly look away.

"What happened to your forehead?" I ask Yumiko-san.

"Not your concern."

She goes to the seat furthest from me.

"You can't get over her, can you?" Chiyo-san whispers to me.

"I guess so. No need for you to feel jealous about it."

She sighs.

"You're such a stubborn man."

"I know."

Chapter 74: Setsuna

"A surprise for me?"

He nods. What's the occasion?

"I just wanted to take you somewhere special," Kyoya-sama says to me.

"Does that mean we're leaving the house?"

"Yes."

A chance to leave the house with him. I wonder what prompted this. He's been so unapproachable as of late. He's planning our wedding and keeping up with the politics of the country. I'm surprised he has time for me.

I have noticed something about him. No matter how busy he is, he comes home to spend the night with me. Sometimes I never see him but I can tell he's been here. It makes me feel like he won't forget about me.

He's putting the finishing touches on his outfit now. He puts his shirt on so carefully; he never misses a button.

"Thank you for always coming home to me," I say to him.

"There's no place I'd rather be."

I stare at him feeling happy. He really heard my concerns. Since we had that talk after the interview he's improved a lot. He tells me where he's going and asks my advice on decisions he has to make. He's opened up a lot too. We watched a movie together the other day and I heard him laugh so hard he cried.

I see Kyoya-sama more and more. But still…I wonder what the captain is up to. He's been gone for three weeks now. During that time me and Kyoya-sama have gotten to understand each other a bit more. We still need more time but the wedding is approaching. He says it will be in a few more weeks.

"I'm happy to come home to you," he says putting on his jacket. "You're my wife."

"Uh-not yet."

"I've always seen you as my wife."

THE LAST PRINCESS

I touch my ring nervously. It's weird to hear it. I think I'm blushing.

"It's good we get this night out. They'll be a press tour in a few days. We're expected to go on a tour of Highland Row. The outside at least."

The so called "Killer's Lair." It's the area under quarantine for harboring a terrorist that's now dead. I read up on it since finding out. He turned a district already full of scavengers into a prison just by putting up a tall fence. The people there have turned destitute over the years believing that they really are terrorists. My reaction during the tour will be key.

He comes back to me while I'm distracted and sits next to me on the bed.

"Something on your mind?" he asks.

"Just wondering what the surprise is."

There are a lot of things but I don't want to bother him.

"I've had something on my mind," he says to me. "I hope you don't mind talking about it."

He wants to confide in me. I sit attentive. Of course I'll listen. I'll try to help as best I can. He turns to me.

"I really want to have sex with you."

"Uh-"

"I feel like it's time."

"W-what makes you think it's time? I-is there some kind of t-time frame for this sort of thing. I wasn't made aware."

"Just calm down," he says taking my hand. "I know you're scared. Just tell me why and I'll try to make it better."

Why do we have to talk about such adult things? I want out of this conversation.

"You know I cherish you. I wouldn't hurt you. We'll go slow," he says softly.

"I know. Can we not talk about this?"

"I think we should."

THE LAST PRINCESS

"I really don't want to."

Please just let it go. Why is it such a big deal? Ah!

"You're gonna cheat on me aren't you!"

"No-"

"If I don't give you what you want you'll just find someone else again. You said you wouldn't! You said you loved me!"

"Calm down," he says grabbing my shoulders. "I'm not gonna cheat on you."

"I'll do it, okay. I'll do it so you'll stay."

"Setsuna....stop talking like that. I love you. I just want to feel more of you. Feel a bond between us. And plus...I'm really attracted to you. I just want you to know that."

He lets go of me and stands up. All I see is his broad back.

"We'll do it when you're ready. I won't bring it up again."

He walks off and the door closes behind him. What was I saying? I panicked thinking I'd be left alone again. I should have heard him out instead of jumping to conclusions. He thinks I'm so immature. He'll always see me as a kid cause I'm still so far behind him. Have I come any closer?

It feels awkward being around him now. We ride in the car together and sit on opposite sides. He's thinking about sex. I've never thought about it. He yawns and I hold onto the door handle. Is he going to jump at me?

"Pretend I didn't say anything," he says.

"How long have you wanted to....you know?"

"I guess.....since I kissed you the first time."

The recorded kiss? That was so long ago. I remember it clearly without it being replayed over television. He was sweet then. His lips were so gentle. I had never been kissed before so it felt like he was going slowly to teach me. I touch my lips remembering. It was nice being so close.

I move closer to him and he puts him arm around me.

THE LAST PRINCESS

"Maybe we could try," I whisper to him.

"I don't think we should try here. A little too public."

I look pass him. We're here!

"The aquarium!"

"It's all ours for the night. No press, no civilians, no guards."

"Really?"

How did he know I like fish? There are all types in there.

"Will we get to see sharks?"

"Of course."

"And turtles?"

"Let's see when we get inside."

Everything is blue. The ceilings are made of water and the ground too. I put my face to the glass as a school of fish floats by.

"This is amazing!"

"This is only the entrance."

He takes my hand and carries me deeper inside. Finally I get to experience the outside world with him. I'm very happy. He gives me a tour and I get to see the fish I've read about. They're beautiful in person.

The tour ends with a table and chairs set up in the glass room. We're surrounded by water and pink fish.

"It was hard to think of the most appropriate thing to eat in here. So I just bought fruit you like."

"Thank you," I say to him. "Thank you so much."

"I understood what you meant. I can't keep you inside forever just to protect you. It's fine if you go out with me sometimes."

I sit down with him and I can't stop smiling. He smiles too.

THE LAST PRINCESS

"The cherries are my favorite. There's a tree back in the palace garden. Captain Saki use to put me on his shoulders so I could reach them. Then we'd eat them under the tree and bury the pits."

Thinking about him makes me wonder where he is.

"Do you know where he's gone? He disappeared so suddenly. Is he okay?"

"He's fine."

"Did he say where he went?"

"It doesn't matter where he went," he says sharply. "Stop thinking about him so much."

He's upset at me for asking. I take a sip of pineapple juice and watch him from behind the glass. After a few minutes he holds his forehead and drops his grape.

"I'm sorry. I didn't mean to snap at you. I know he disappeared suddenly. He's fine. Just taking some time off."

"Oh…okay."

"Kantarou is supposed to be guarding you. He's a bit distracted so you probably didn't notice. I'll have to talk to him about that."

"He seems like he has more important things to do than guard me. I feel safe for the most part."

"You're not. I don't mean to scare you but I've been listening to the noise. There are people that want you dead."

"B-but why?"

"My people are aggressive in nature. They've seen their country conquer and flex. They don't know diplomacy, they know force."

"So?"

"So…they see me being here as a conquest. And with you dead, there are no royals left. So….I would take the country with no force at all."

"Is that what you're doing?"

"Of course not. Why do you think I'm working so hard to protect you? I wanna make these people believe that our countries can merge together. Be partners.

THE LAST PRINCESS

So you and I need to remain strong in the public eye. No matter what you feel about me, you must always support me in public."

"I don't agree with what's happening in Highland Row."

"I know that. And I'm the only one that should know that."

I understand. I get the feeling my mother was the same way. Tomoko-sama too.

"The wedding is very important. It should calm these people down."

I nod to him.

"I'm fine so long as Captain Saki is near. Hopefully he won't be on leave long."

I take another sip of pineapple juice and see him squeezing an apple to death.

"You....you make me wonder where your heart lies," he says softly.

"What....What do you mean? My heart's always been with you-"

He slams his fist on the table.

"You expect me to believe something you don't even believe!"

"Kyoya-sama-"

"The day I kissed you, I had your heart. I was all you had and all you needed. When you got attacked, you called for me. You wanted me to protect you. Now you just call for him!"

He slams his hand again. He's scaring the fish.

"You love him, don't you?" he asks me.

I don't want to answer. I take another sip and he slaps the glass away from me. It shatters against the glass wall.

"Answer me," he says staring.

I'm scared. I don't want to answer. I don't want to admit it. I bite my lip to stop myself from speaking.

"Answer me! Don't you have the nerve to tell me to my face."

THE LAST PRINCESS

"I-I don't love-"

"Don't lie to me!"

What happened to make him so upset? I didn't do anything wrong. He's never looked at me like that before. He snarls again bringing up his anger. I run for it.

I can't face him. I can't tell him what I've been feeling. I run to the doorway and look back. He flips over the table and runs towards me. Where can I hide? I hike up my robe and keep running. I never thought I would have to run away from him physically.

I turn left at the turtle tank and run over the sting ray bridge. Sounds like he's stopped. Guess I'll be hiding here forever since I refuse to face him. He's always so calm even when he's upset. Now he's out of patience.

Looking around I see I ended up at the dolphin tank. There's one right behind me. So happy in there; they're so happy swimming and bumping into each other. I touch my hand to the glass and it's immediately pulled away. I fall to the floor with Kyoya-sama staring down at me.

"Don't run from me," he says.

"I-I didn't mean to-"

"I can't hear you."

He comes closer to me forcing me to go between his legs. I try to push back to get distance but he follows me.

"What were you saying?"

"I didn't mean to run. You're being really scary."

"I'm just fed up with you. You're not such a good girl. I'm really disappointed."

"I am good-"

"You're not!" he screams. "Do I have to show you what happens to bad girls? Maybe then you'll learn."

He pulls at my collar and I slap him. We're both stunned. I've never hit him before. I'm not the one that should be begging right now.

"Back away from me!"

THE LAST PRINCESS

He obeys and gets to his feet. His cheek is so red now; suddenly my hand stings. No more running away. If he's ready to listen then I'll talk. I stand up.

"I love him, okay. Is that what you're waiting to hear?"

"How could you-"

"No! How could you! You can't blame me for loving him. I had everything taken from me. I was left alone. You came and hugged me but left me."

"I-"

"He was there for me. He was there every time I needed him. Always joking with me and smiling."

"I-"

"I called you every day. I reached out for you and you pushed me away. "It's complicated" you said. Well it just got more complicated."

"You don't know what I was going through."

That's how he's going to defend himself. Nothing he went through could compare to my unhappiness. Last I checked he still had a family and a home to call his own.

"You don't know what I was going though. And if you would have asked maybe I wouldn't have fallen for someone else."

It's liberating to say. I have been afraid to argue with him. We won't get anywhere in our relationship unless we expose the hard feelings.

"Maybe I wouldn't think about him so much and wonder if he thinks about me. I wouldn't try to picture him naked or wonder what it would be like to kiss him."

I hold my mouth closed. How can I admit all this to him; I never even admitted it to myself.

He starts to pace the floor holding his head. I hurt him. I know I did. It's not that I don't love him. I reach out for him and he turns away. His shaking hand takes a cigarette from his pocket.

He lights up as he walks away from me. I ruined it all.

"I didn't mean to," I call to him. "It just happened."

Please don't go. I wanna choose him. As soon as I drop my head I hear a banging sound. His monstrous grunt echoes down the hall.

I run after him and see him banging his fists against the glass. It's cracking.

"Kyoya, don't!"

He screams louder. I'm not strong enough to push him away.

"Kyoya!"

I hold onto him, hug him and listen to his racing heartbeat.

"Kyoya, stop," I whisper to him in tears.

As soon as I cry he stops banging. He pulls himself away and continues smoking down the hall.

"We're going home," he calls back to me.

I follow behind him cautiously. It's hard to look at him now. The Kyoya-sama I know doesn't have rage like that. He's gentle always. I look back and see the cracked glass; he really could have hurt the fish.

"Uh!"

I bump into him. He holds his hand out to me. After all that he still wants to hold onto me. Does he forgive me or at least understand me? I grab his hand and he leads me out.

Chapter 75: Kira

"I'm looking for Naoko-san?"

"Who?"

"T-the creepy looking girl with the curly blond hair."

Should have thought this through. I found out she comes to the knife throwing range after classes. There are some pretty seedy people out here. This tall guy blocks the path into the range. He must be security.

THE LAST PRINCESS

"She's busy. And she wouldn't wanna talk to a runt like you."

"I think she would."

She and whatever group she's apart of are a danger to Setsuna-san. I thought about it for a few days. It's something I should tell the teacher or my brother about but no…I can handle it myself.

"Step aside," I hear behind him.

He moves away and I see the curly haired girl. She smiles at me while pushing him out the way.

"Prince, you really sought me out?"

"Don't go thinking you're special. I just wanted to talk more."

"So you've been thinking about me?"

"More about what you said."

She pulls a knife from behind her back and I step back.

"Go a round with me. If you score more points we'll talk some more."

I'm terrible at knife throwing. Easier to just pick up a pistol.

"Don't come all this way for nothing," she teases.

She pulls me back inside the range. It's a jungle landscape. Ninjas drop out of trees and then go back in. A monkey appears too; I guess I'm supposed to avoid them.

She passes me knives with yellow handles. Her knives have green handles.

"I don't get the point of all this. You being crazy automatically gives you the upper hand in knife throwing," I tell her.

"Eyes straight, prince."

She throws the first one. She gets it right in his eye; she's good. Everything speeds up and she still nails them all. I'm running out of time. I better just throw. By the time I throw the first one the course stops.

"You're terrible," she tells me. "How are you even passing?"

"Knife throwing isn't part of my curriculum."

THE LAST PRINCESS

"Don't you want to be a soldier?"

"No."

Never crossed my mind.

"You should. You'd be great at it. My aim is to command my own unit in black ops."

"You mean like assassinations and stuff?" I ask.

"Yeah, and you can be in my unit. It's all about being in the shadows."

"I'm well known so-"

"Are you? This is your forth year here and no one has said anything to you about being a prince. And a few days ago people were in your room all excited that you know the princess. Do they even remember who you are now? Or did they just scream at the pictures and run."

Some of those people are in my class. They've been staying quiet about the whole thing. She thinks she can analyze me. I'm not so simple just cause I'm invisible. Why am I even talking to her anyway? I exit the range.

"Prince, wait."

"Don't follow me," I call back.

"Why did you come to see me?"

I stop walking. She's right behind me. I have to say something or she will start thinking she's special.

"I want to make sure no harm comes to Setsuna-san."

"I can't promise that. It's not like I run the faction."

"She's a member of the Niwa family. Attack her and you'll be committing treason."

"I wouldn't harm her personally."

I head back to my room.

"I'm invisible."

THE LAST PRINCESS

Doesn't matter how smart I am or how many knives I throw. I'm nothing to my family, to Setsuna-san or my country. Since I came to this place, Naoko-san was the first one to notice me. I went to talk to her today partly because of the haunting words she said but also cause I wanted someone to talk to. Don't even have a roommate cause of security reasons.

While everyone's out having fun and eating dinner I'm stuck here. It's my choice, I guess. What's the use of going into the crowd all by myself?

"Prince," I hear at the door.

What's she doing in the boy's dorm?

I open the door quickly. She's gonna get both of us in trouble.

"Why did you really seek me out?" she asks me.

I pull her inside and close the door. I'm…happy she came. It feels better to talk to her in private.

"You said you would visit again. You were taking too long."

I lay back down on the bed. She joins me right away.

"Chairs are for guests," I scold her. "You can't just-"

"Stop yelling. You want someone to hear."

Her hair is right near my face. We both stare up at the ceiling. I touch a strand. It springs back into place. I remember Setsuna-san had the silkiest black hair. This curly hair is different.

"You're not from Han, are you?" I ask her.

"I am. I've lived in Han my whole life. You don't see much outside your capitol."

I suppose that's true. I've never seen a blond curly girl but that doesn't mean they don't exist.

"Han is a vast country. You call it yours yet you've seen so little. Stay part of the royal family and you'll continue to see so little."

"I'm not leaving my family-"

THE LAST PRINCESS

"I'm not asking you to," she says to me. "I'm asking you to leave your useless title. You can join the black ops with me."

"I'm not a soldier."

"Then what are you then?" she says rolling over to me.

"Just leave me alone."

"I'm not going to leave you alone."

She reaches for my hand and I pull it away.

"Don't misunderstand. I just want us to be partners. And neither of us will have to go through this alone," she offers.

I roll over avoiding her. She's telling me everything I want to hear but she's not the person I want to hear it from. I have no idea who Naoko-san is. She's no princess.

"Why me?" I ask her.

"Does it matter?"

But….I'll probably never get a princess. I roll back around to her.

"We should get to the mess hall before they run out of food," I tell her.

"Do I get to sit at the prince's special table?"

"I guess there's room for one more."

I agree with her in some ways but I'm not going to become a soldier. There's gotta be something I can do to make things safe for the royals.

She's smiling. She looks like a such a girl when she smiles.

"Don't look at me like that," she says.

"L-like what?"

"I just want to be your friend, got it."

"I wasn't even looking at you like I wanted to like-"

"Let's go. I'm hungry."

THE LAST PRINCESS

This final year I won't have to be alone. I don't want to join the black ops but I need to have some plan when I get out of here. Naoko-san has it all figured out. I have no idea what made her seek me out. Is it that she sees something in me? If I take my eyes off the princess, maybe I'll see something in Naoko-san.

"Naoko-san," I call to her.

She's about to leave out the door.

"I'll consider your partnership."

Chapter 76: Kyoya

My mother's not a total airhead. She's father's queen; she sits quietly and lets him make all the decisions. She nods at everything he says even when he's wrong.

"I'm your father's strength and weakness. He has to be the one to balance it," she told me.

I get that now. I lay with Setsuna-san in our bed. I haven't been sleeping much. The last two days I lay restless as the sun rises.

She doesn't have to marry me if she doesn't want to. That's cause she has another love in her life. I bet they've conspired against me; they're planning to run away together. Is she really gonna abandon me and her country? Maybe.

She snuggles closer to me; her head lies on my chest. I haven't said a word to her since that night. Don't know what to say. I understand it. They spent a lot of time together. Each time I ignored her I pushed her into his arms. Mostly I'm mad at myself. But she…..she was supposed to wait for me. Just like she always has.

"Mother," I hear her say.

She talks in her sleep when she's holding things back. Her mother must be on her mind. Slowly she'll guilt me into forgiving her without even knowing it. It was me that left her with nothing.

I push her away and throw on my robe lazily. Once outside I light up a cigarette and cross the lawn. The palace is in the distance. There's no construction today. Construction is slow because I'm trying to make it comfortable for both of us.

THE LAST PRINCESS

The one thing I wanted was a replica of the room I met her in. It's finished. I go through the vacant halls and stare inside the bare room. I stood here as she glanced over into the pond. All I could see was her back.

"So this is her," I said to myself. "My future wife and the girl whose life I'm about to ruin."

She turned around and it was like the whole room turned into a meadow. She looked at me doe eyed....she always looks at me doe eyed.

"Kyoya-sama?" she said.

I'll always remember the excitement I felt when she said my name for the first time. We've come so far from that. Traveled so far from that time of her innocence.

Ayato-san isn't to blame. I shouldn't have fallen in love with her either. Wasn't part of the plan.

"Kyoya-sama?"

I look back and see her standing in the doorway. She left without putting on her robe or putting up her hair. She stands shivering in her thin nightgown.

I turn my back to her and put my cigarette out quickly. When she comes close I take off my robe and put it around her shoulders. We both stare into an empty pond.

"Are you okay?" she asks softly. "You haven't been sleeping."

So she noticed.

"I'm confused. I figured you would want to help me. In a way, since my father died, you've been my guardian. I've looked to you for all types of help. And while you were away, I know Captain Saki cleared everything with you first. Tomoko-sama did too."

I made sure every decision went to my desk first; it took priority over everything else. I was aware of what was going on....just not aware of her feelings.

"You're mad," she says crying.

I don't want to hear her cry again. I turn away from her and leave out the door. She's not allowed to leave the palace walls so I'll just stay outside of them for a while.

THE LAST PRINCESS

"Kyoya!" she screams.

I stop walking.

"Don't leave me," she cries.

"Go back and get cleaned up. No one wants to look at your crying face."

What a stubborn girl. She refuses to leave me alone. I walk across the lawn and back to the guest house and she follows. While in the shower she peeks in at me. If she's not settled she won't let go. Her sniffling is annoying.

When I open the shower door she scurries away to another hiding spot; she has so many. There's other places for me to stay but if I'm caught sleeping somewhere else, it will just make a scandal.

I tie my towel tightly around my waist and go to the closet. She's there. She hands me my black suit with a smile. Can't look at her the same. I take the suit and close the door on her.

"Where are you going?" she asks from inside. "Can I come with you?"

"You know you're not allowed to leave."

"But I'll be with you so-"

"I need some time away from you."

The closet door opens swiftly and she stands in tears.

"But-"

"Stop all your crying."

I turn my back to her and continue dressing. When she cries I feel bad. I've never been hurt by a woman before; I'm not sure how to handle it. I just need to get away from her. She continues to whimper even when I'm done.

"But I just want to talk you more," she whines.

"I think you've said enough."

"It's not fair of you to punish me. I've done nothing wrong. You're the one that-"

"You really think you've done nothing wrong."

THE LAST PRINCESS

She'll throw my sleeping around in my face just to cover herself. I've stopped all that. I'm not the one that fell in love with someone. Best to leave before I say something hurtful. I make a move for the door and she holds me back; she grabs my hand and pulls it close to her.

"Please don't go," she says to me.

"Let go."

"Can we please just talk-"

"Let go," I repeat to her.

She keeps pulling on me to get me to stay.

"You won't even try to help me. I don't want to love him; I just want him to be my friend."

That's nothing I can help her with.

"Kyoya-sama," she whines.

I can't stand her right now. That tiny voice of hers prefers to call out his name. How many times has she pulled on his arm and begged him to stay.

"Setsuna, let go."

"No!"

"Let go of me!"

I swing my hand back to push her away. She falls to the ground holding her face. I....I hit her. I didn't mean....

I didn't mean to hit her I just wanted to get away from her. Her crying is just unbearable for me. I kneel down to her and reach out for her reddened cheek.

"I didn't mean to-"

She jumps up and runs out the room.

"Setsuna!" I call after her.

She's off to another hiding place. I would never hit her. It's just....I don't know how to deal with this. Before I leave out I rip a page from my journal and write her a note. I can't come back to her until I figure this out.

THE LAST PRINCESS

I'm mad at her cause she wasn't how I pictured her. She didn't turn out how I had her planned. I was supposed to be the one manipulating her and she's manipulating me. I just wanted to be a king but I'm something else now. I'm living the life of a common man. I'm jealous and incompetent; my shirt buttons aren't aligned.

I laugh to myself. Look at me. I'm living in a small house, my girlfriend loves another man and I can't dress myself. This is the first time I've felt like a regular man. I guess I should write to her with these feelings.

Maybe I should stop trying to control her and just see what happens. I wonder if I showed her the real me if she would like it. Could I tell her I've never killed a man but had my best friend do it for me? Would she like me if I tell her I've tortured men just for practice? Had sex with women cause I was bored and dumped them right after.

If I told her I touched her the first night she slept over, right after she said, "I want you to help me be free," would she still love the Kyoya she sees.

I rip up the letter. I can't say any of that. After all I've done, this is a small punishment. I'm done blaming her, done blaming myself. I'll just win her back.

Chapter 77: Kantarou

I knew she would come around. Acting cold just makes her come to me to warm up. She feels the same way; misses having me in her life. I take a handful of her silky black hair.

"Why are you crying?" I whisper to her.

I move her hair and see it's longer than usual. Women often times do these things with hair.

"Yumiko-san," I say to her.

She refuses to take her face off my chest.

"What's wrong?" I ask her. "Something I did?"

337

THE LAST PRINCESS

She shakes her head. I hold her close. She's lost a lot of weight; girls like to hear that, right? Her whimpering slows down. I always have that effect on her. Now that she's calm she'll tell me what's wrong.

I stroke her hair and she finally moves her head off my chest.

"L-little princess!"

I jump out the bed quickly.

"Kantarou-sama-"

"Why are you here? Are you trying to cause a scandal?"

That's why she was so thin. It's a damn child. She sits up in the bed. I've never seen her with her hair down; it's so long.

"You're supposed to protect me so I came to you."

I switch back to commander mode.

"What happened?"

"Kyoya-sama hates me."

"I'm not here to protect you emotionally. As long as he didn't hit you, I'm staying out of it."

She holds her cheek shyly. Lover's quarrels are to be expected. I assumed Yumiko-san would come see me since I broke it off with Chiyo-san. The two of them are giggling about dresses and ignoring me.

"He....has a temper," she says softly. "I didn't expect that. He's so calm all the time."

"Did you say something to make him mad?"

She nods. Time to switch back to brother mode. I sit back down. Kids need so much guidance. I'm the oldest so I have to guide all of them.

"I told him I'm in love with Ayato-san."

"Are you?"

THE LAST PRINCESS

She nods. She's doing nothing wrong. My mind wandered a lot when I was sixteen. But I'm not gonna let her go after that creep. I'm not very good talking to girls so how can I word this.

"I'm not gonna sway you either way. All I can say is that my brother loves you a lot. And….I've grown to love you too. I want you to be a part of my family so I can continue protecting you. I want to be your big brother."

She smiles. Don't make a big deal out of what I said.

"When we were younger, Kyoya would always isolate himself. He likes to be alone. He figured if he would do well in his studies and go to the functions, father and everyone else would continue to leave him alone."

"But you two seem close."

It wasn't always like that. He ignored me when he was little. I would try to get close to him but he looked at me like I was father. He didn't know I was on his side from the beginning.

"We both had the same upbringing. I was always being pulled into meetings with father where he would tell me what path to take. When Kyoya was about eight, father started pulling him into these meetings. He couldn't handle it at first. I grabbed him under my arm and did something to distract him. I starting spending more time with him and got to understand him. He writes everything in those books cause he refuses to speak about his feelings. If he experiences a weird feeling and doesn't have time to write, he will show his temper."

She made him scared so he lashed out, I guess. How would I feel if Yumiko-san told me she was in love with another man? It bothered me enough when she was sleeping with someone else.

"When he met Saki, he changed a lot. He finally had a friend. You know how they met, right?"

She nods.

"He built up the courage to ask father if he could visit the hospital while the Saki got better. Father said "no," then mother stepped in and brought him to the hospital in secret. I stood with her and she was so happy to see Kyoya laugh with another boy. To finally hear him share his feelings. She wanted to keep Saki around no matter how much trouble he was. I don't know why they get along so well but they're inseparable. And if you love the captain then it's tearing both of them apart. He won't let either of you go. So he's probably in constant pain."

339

THE LAST PRINCESS

I'm not trying to make her feel bad.

"I didn't mean to," she says. "I didn't mean for any of this to happen. But he ignored me for three years."

"He had his reasons-"

"What reasons?!"

"Selfish reasons."

I warned him but the guilt was too much for him. If she doesn't stay with him, I'll be a bit disappointed. I've grown to like Setsuna-san very much.

"No matter what," I tell her. "I'll be here for you. Nothing between us will change."

She tears up again. I didn't mean to get the tears started again.

"Kantarou-sama."

"Enough. I got enough of your snot on me. Just stay here."

I hate crying women. Since it's a small house I have to share a bathroom with everyone. Hopefully I beat the women to it; they take forever. In the hallway I see Yumiko-san at the bathroom door. She stops with her fingers on the handle.

"You should go first," she says. "You probably have a meeting-"

"No...nothing like that. You can go first. You look amazing already so not sure what you'll be doing in there."

"Always the charmer."

We could always go in together. She hasn't talked to me since I arrived here. She's not going in. Does she still want to talk?

"I-I broke things off with Chiyo-san. I didn't want to be with someone I didn't love."

"She told me. Since you two broke up she's been pretty nice to me."

"I wasn't fair to her. I kept thinking about someone else."

"Who?"

"You know who. I only had you as my assistant cause I wanted an excuse to keep you close. You were terrible at it. Still don't know how to make a decent cup of coffee."

She smiles. So maybe we can start talking again. I take a step closer to her.

"I miss having you in my life," I tell her.

"Commander-"

"Don't call me "commander" anymore. You're special to me, you know that."

"After how you tossed me away, told me to step aside, how could I possibly know that."

She steps in and slams the door.

Chapter 78: Setsuna

Today I'm nervous; I feel like something bad is about to happen. I get to leave the palace walls but I'm not going to see a pretty site. Kantarou-sama rides with me with a frown on his face. He seems nervous too.

We're headed to the capitol building where I'll switch cars and ride with Kyoya-sama. I haven't seen him since he hit me. He said he needed space; I should have given it to him. He's only been gone a day; if it hasn't been enough time he may hit me again.

"Will you stay close to me today?" I ask him.

"Of course but there's nothing for you to worry about."

"Don't these people hate me?"

"Probably but they'll never get close to you."

Is that supposed to make me feel better? They're my people and they think I've abandoned them. I never identified that man as the killer; it's all made up.

"You look so worried," I say to him.

THE LAST PRINCESS

"Not about this."

"Then what is it?"

"It's...."

He takes a big pause. Kantarou-sama has never shared his problems with me. I don't think he shares them with anyone.

"It's nothing to talk to you about."

"It's about Yumi-chan, isn't it," I guess. "She told me you broke the engagement with Chiyo-san."

I don't think she wants to be with him. She's too hurt. I don't know how her heart works. When Kyoya-sama wronged me I still loved him but I didn't forgive him so soon so he would learn a lesson. Maybe she's doing the same thing.

"She still likes you; she just wants some time to explore. She was talking about putting a fashion line together and going back to her high school to talk to people."

"Really?"

"Yeah, she has plans now."

"And I don't fit into those plans."

"Just support her. It's really good to see her doing well. She really hit a low point when she slept with...."

Oh, I wasn't supposed to mention that. She told me never to mention it, especially to him. He doesn't seem to be letting my trail off take effect

"Go on," he says.

"Me. She slept with me."

"I know she's been sleeping around. Who is it?"

"I can't tell you. Anyway it doesn't matter. She stopped."

"If I knew who Kyoya slept around with would you want me to tell you?"

THE LAST PRINCESS

No, of course not. It's easy enough to picture a beautiful no good woman that would kiss a taken man. I'm not curious at all. But it would give me an idea as to what his type might be.

"Can you not bring that up," I tell him

"Hmph…I didn't mean to make you feel bad. You're the prettiest girl he's been with."

"Really? Well….you're one the prettiest guys she's been with. She was thinking about dating this local boy she met. He's from her high school."

"Name?"

"Hisoka. She said he'll be joining the military then the palace guard."

"A child. What is he like twenty?"

"Maybe she prefers someone her own age."

"Trying to make me feel old."

I wasn't trying to. He is sort of old. He's quiet the rest of the way. We arrive at the capitol building and he steps out. Now I'll have to see him. To keep him at ease I won't mention anything about that day.

"Princess, come," Kantarou-sama calls back at me.

I step out and he walks me over to the next car. It's just me here. No sunlight because of the darkened windows. Seems like time that could be used for myself. How should I greet him?

The door opens. I keep my head down to block the sun. The door closes and I see his shiny shoes. I look at his shoes a lot; I know it's him.

"Um, good morning, Kyoya-sama."

"Good morning," he mumbles.

The car starts up and we start the trip south. I've never been to the lower districts. I'm told they are provisioned to allow the lower class to have a comfortable lifestyle. I look out the window at all the sights.

"I got something for you," he speaks.

"You didn't have to."

THE LAST PRINCESS

I turn back to him and he holds a box out to me.

"The aquarium is being repaired."

"Were the fish okay?"

"All except one."

Someone got hurt. Maybe the glass shattered after we left.

"Maybe you don't mind nursing it back to health."

He put a fish in that dark box! I take it from him and rip the wrapping paper. The tape tears away and I'm left confused. He smiles at me and I love him even more.

"A shark," I say to him.

He got me a stuffed shark. It fits right in my arms like a baby. Such big eyes and exaggerated teeth.

"Thank you," I say to him.

"No fish were hurt. No need to worry. I'm sorry if I scared you that night."

I nod to him. Of course he's forgiven.

"And it wasn't my intention to hit you. I would never hurt you; you have to know that."

His voice is so sweet. It's easy to tell when he's genuine. I hug the shark close and he reaches over and pets his head.

"Can we get a real pet?" I ask him.

"You're easily distracted."

It really is a long ride. Now that we hold hands again it's fun. Today's going to be a great day. Nothing bad will happen.

"I thought about it for a while," he speaks.

I look back at him. When did he get so close to me? I lean back to the window and he leans in. I put the shark between us and he takes it from me.

"W-what?" I ask him.

THE LAST PRINCESS

"I was immature," he says to me. "We're both young in love. There's bound to be mistakes."

"Y-yeah."

"But it's easy enough to figure out what your heart wants."

He kisses me. It starts light but then he pushes himself deeper. His body covers mine and my heart flutters. All at once I feel his protection, his love, his obsession, and his warmth. In his embrace with his lips on mine, I feel his love for me.

I start to cry. He pulls away and I'm in silent tears.

"Did you feel something?" he whispers.

I nod.

"That's all that matters to me."

I nod to him again. He leaves me alone for the rest of the ride allowing me to hug my shark close. I cried cause of all the love I felt from him but also….I cried cause of all the pain I made him feel. And also….briefly, I wondered if Ayato-san could make me feel that.

"When we start our tour, I want you to look concerned but feel satisfied with everything," he says to me. "Make sure you stay near me but if I walk away stay near Kantarou."

"Okay."

"If you're asked to speak, say they deserve it."

"What? No, I can't."

"I'm not going over this with you again."

"Those people are not terrorists. Do what you want but I will not say those words."

"Setsuna-"

"I won't."

He sighs and goes back to thinking. He's asking too much of me. I rather stay silent.

THE LAST PRINCESS

"Can you say, "Kyoya's doing the right thing." Can you say that at least?"

"If I have to. That's vague enough."

We arrive and I see the tall steel walls. It's as high as the buildings in there. Barbed wired fences and cameras on the posts. The press is already here. Our car pulls into a circle of theirs.

"There are so many people here," I say.

"Only one station had rights. The others are just piggybacking."

He pulls out his phone and starts talking. He wants the extra cars to disappear. So stern when he gives commands. Part of the thick wall has a chain linked window. I stare close and see a girl inside. Tattered clothes and muddy face. She's younger than me.

"Oh my."

"They'll leave soon," he tells me. "I gave Lisa-san the exclusive since she was so kind to you."

"She was nice."

"I reward people that treat you well. It will be good for her career."

He has so much power. More than me it seems. I hear the cars leaving now. Just with a call he made people disappear. Father couldn't even do that.

"Um....have you met her husband?" I ask him.

"I met both of them before I chose her to interview you. He's nothing special. He fixes printers."

"I would like to meet other couples."

"In time."

That's what he always says. He opens the door and reaches his hand back to me. Time to start smiling.

"Setsuna-sama, I'm glad you made the trip," Lisa-san comes up to me.

"Nice to see you again."

THE LAST PRINCESS

Kantarou-sama appears beside me. She seems a bit intimidated but smiles at me and continues forward.

"And the commander is here," she says. "You were the one that designed the containment."

"It's my pleasure."

"Such a talented family."

We walk along the perimeter as she talks. I take a peek behind us and see guards trailing. She stops at one of the windows.

"It's nice to see the school yard is still in place," she says.

There are children in there running around and playing soccer. All their clothes are tattered.

"I guess they don't know the seriousness of things. Don't know how their parent's ideals have put them in danger. Regicide sympathizers have no place in a kingdom, don't you agree," she says to me.

She looks cautiously at Kyoya-sama then scans my face for an answer.

"Yes," I say to her.

"Setsuna-sama!"

One of them notices me. A young boy runs up to the window. His muddy fingers grab the chains reaching out to me.

"I saw you on t.v. the other day. You came to free us."

"Back," Kantarou-sama says slapping his sword on the fence.

"I came to make things better," I call out. "I promise you."

"Stop," Kyoya-sama whispers at me.

I break away from him and claw onto the fence. Lisa-san's camera looks on. I don't care. I have to have some power here to make things better.

"I came back to make things better," I say to him.

"Princess," Kantarou-sama warns me.

"I'll be your queen soon. I'll find a way to remove all these walls."

THE LAST PRINCESS

Kantarou-sama quickly slides his sheath between us. He pushes me away with his sword. He's harmless; why can't I get closer to him.

"You think I haven't tried," Kyoya-sama says behind me. "I see their faces every day. It doesn't get easier to look at. But look closer."

The boy runs away and joins the others. Kantarou-sama flips his sheath over and I see a knife stuck in it. That little boy tried to kill me.

I step back and Kyoya-sama holds my shoulders.

"Best not to get too close," he says to Lisa-san. "But you can continue."

"That was....um."

She's as stunned as me. My life really is in danger. But why would these people hate me.? I want to help them. They go back to playing soccer so easily.

She clears her throat and we start walking again.

"Are you okay?" Kyoya-sama whispers to me.

"I could have died."

"My brother will always protect you. You don't have to worry about that. He's commander for a reason."

He really is good. I should pay attention to what Lisa-san is saying. It's something about the construction.

"It only took two months for this to be constructed. It was a fast and accurate process."

"V-very impressive," I say to her.

I'm stilled stunned from before; I'm not present at all. As we walk the perimeter there are more chain linked windows. I grab Kyoya-sama's arm each time.

"Don't be afraid," he tells me.

This glimpse in has a temple. I wonder if they still have service there. That's the place of our ancestors; it's inside this prison too. I bow my head and pray.

"So everyone wants to know if you feel these people deserve...."

THE LAST PRINCESS

Please allow me a way to fix all this. Tell me how to support my husband and protect my people. Han ways are just so different. Their justice is harsh. Their punishments are cruel cause they feel pride in it.

"Setsuna-sama," she calls to me.

No answers come to me. They never do. The ancestors never talk back; they want me to figure this out myself.

"Kyoya-sama is doing the right thing," I say to her.

She wraps up production after getting her answer. The guards relax a bit and I step away and look into the opening. The temple is pristine compared to everything else. They still worship; they're praying for answers. It's been about three years and it looks like a decade of decay in there.

"Why the windows?" I say to myself. "It's hard to look in and out."

"Princess," I hear.

I look back. No one behind me said that.

"Princess," a raspy voice says again.

A rose peeks out of the whole. Someone's standing on the side. I can't see him.

"Take it," he says.

"Who are you?"

"I'm glad I get to see my princess in my lifetime."

"You still see me as your princess?"

"Of course."

I take the rose from him. It's just the bud. It's nice to see a flower. Something pretty can grow in there.

"When you pluck a flower you should grab the stem so it can support itself," I tell him.

"Where's the fun in that?"

"You have no appreciation for flowers."

I look down at the bud. Roses will dry and still look pretty. I'll keep it.

"I never said I did."

I stare into my hand not noticing the chain fence creaking back. He pulls me in and smothers his hand over my mouth. The rose bud drops. Something is seeping into me. I take another breath and I feel lightheaded. Reaching out for the temple does nothing.

Chapter 79: Kyoya

"Did you see what just happened?" Kan-nii asks me calmly.

"I did."

"Why aren't you running in there to get her?"

"Why aren't you?"

We both know the answer. Seems we were the only ones that saw. If we alert everyone else then that camera will turn back on and this will become a national emergency. Kan-nii turns away quickly. With his back to me he speaks.

"You know they'll kill her," he whispers to me. "We don't have time to waste."

"But we can't barge in there and alert everyone that Setsuna-san is inside Highland Row."

"Then I'll go in myself-"

"You're too well known. Walk back to the car as if she's in front of you. Get in and stay there. I'll get rid of the news crew."

I got someone that can handle this. I pull out my phone and dial him; he always answers on the first ring.

"Kyoya-sama," Ayato-san speaks on the other end. "I was gonna check in with you a little later-"

"You need to come back now."

A guard comes up to me and I signal him away. No one must know about this.

THE LAST PRINCESS

"Now? Did something happen?" he asks.

"Setsuna-san's in danger."

"You're at the quarantine site-"

"She's inside. Someone took her."

"I'm on my way," he says.

"Wait. No one must know about this. No uniforms involved. Do you understand?"

"I know what I have to do. I'll track her, find her and kill anyone that gets in the way."

He knows how serious this is. She's an easy person to blame. I turn to the chain linked window. I should have kept her closer. It's my fault.

"Kyoya-sama," Lisa-san calls to me. "Setsuna-sama was just here, wasn't she? I wanted to thank her."

"I'll thank her for you. She was a bit shaken up so my brother took her back to the car. We're going to head back to the palace so she can rest."

"It's understandable. I'm a bit shaken up myself. I've never seen a soldier act so quickly and quietly."

"My brother will appreciate the compliment."

"I'm told the ratings were excellent. Setsuna-sama really is good on camera. The audience finds her adorable, and loyal."

"Very accurate. Since the story is done it's best you and your team get out of here so the security can resume."

"Of course. Thank you so much. I hope you allow me to interview her again."

She bows and goes back to her news van. As they pack up I walk closer to the gate and stare inside. She started to pray while she was standing here. It's the temple that prompted her. I never met a more spiritual person. But I believe she talks to her ancestors so much because she never had anyone else to talk to when she was trapped in her palace.

351

THE LAST PRINCESS

Someone must have spoken to her while she was here. Maybe she thought she could save them. I push on the fencing. It has some give; likely secured from the other side. I gave them a view to the outside cause I didn't want to be cruel. I'll be sure to take them all away when she gets out of there.

They're all still watching me; I have to continue to stay calm. I walk back to the car and stop the driver from getting in.

"Go back with the others. Kantarou will drive."

"Yes, sir."

He scurries off. I look back and see security has resumed. The guards pace back and forth and take their place inside the tower.

"So who's going in there?" Kan-nii asks as I open the door.

"Ayato-san."

"I see why you keep him around."

I step in the car and lock the door behind me. My hands are shaking; I guess I'm angry.

"Hey," he says to me. "It's okay to let it out. I know you're angry at me. I should have watched her closely."

"You're not to blame."

"Still I'm sorry."

"She could die in there."

Die. Saying it makes it all come out. She could die. I wouldn't be able to see her again. I grab my mouth to keep from screaming. Panting heavily I look over at him.

"It's okay," he says to me.

I scream all my frustration.

"If she dies, I'll kill all of them. I'll burn this country to the ground!"

I hear her voice calling me. She's asking me to save her. And I'm here. I should go in there myself. He stops me from jumping out. I scream louder pushing him away.

THE LAST PRINCESS

"She needs me! I have to go!"

"Kyoya!"

I break away from him. I know I can't do anything. I know. I smash my head on the window and he pulls me back to him. Cradles me in his arms like we're kids again. She's my love; I want her beside me.

"I can't lose her," I say to him. "She's my-"

"You won't lose her. Put some faith in her. She's a tough kid. And put some faith in Saki. You know he always comes through for you."

He's right. I'm nothing if I don't keep my composure. I have a strong team. He'll come through for me. I'm such a coward for sitting here and letting him go after her. She's already torn; she'll love him even more. She won't see me as her hero for much longer.

"Let's get home and wait this out. I'll pour you a strong drink."

"No, I wanna remember all this."

"At least have a smoke."

"No, she hates when I smoke."

I pick her stuffed shark off the floor. She'll be back. I wanna she her smiling face again. I wanna see her hold this toy in her arms and smile at me.

If she's taken from me then I'll fall into darkness and take this country with me.

"You can drive now," I tell him

As the car drives away my heart feels heavy. I guess it's twice I've abandoned her. How can I make all this up to her? She's supposed to be confined to the palace. I should have never allowed her to leave. That's the only way to keep her safe.

She doesn't want it but I have to chain her there. I close my eyes refusing to look back at the hell I created.

Chapter 80: Setsuna

"Why would you bring her here? Do you know how much trouble we'll be in?"

"Trouble? They'll kill us to get her back."

"Then why bring her here!"

"It's not my idea, okay. We'll just kill her before the soldiers come in."

"She's still our princess!"

"She's that monster's slave. She's no longer our princess."

I don't know where I am. I woke up some minutes ago but feign sleep so they don't bother me. Sounds like two men arguing. One is sympathetic and the other is harsh. This appears to be an apartment; it's small.

"Yee," the sympathetic one says.

Yee? That's the name of the false killer that was executed. I believe it's a last name; they could be related.

"The princess is innocent," he continues.

"Innocent?"

"Just look at her. Killing her won't bring your father back."

His father! No wonder he hates me. He thinks I'm responsible for his father's death. Footsteps come closer. I close my eyes.

"She's just a kid," the sympathetic one says.

"Just go. And don't tell anyone."

Yee doesn't sound like the man that grabbed me. Maybe he was disguising his voice earlier.

"I'll go get some food," the sympathetic one says.

A door closes. I guess I'm alone with Yee. I continue to feign sleep and he drops down close to me. I can smell mud from his boots.

THE LAST PRINCESS

I open my eye slightly. Seems like a slender guy. He has tattered clothes too. I can't see his face just yet.

"You always wanted to meet her," he mumbles. "Why, old man?"

He places a gun down near my face. I look down the barrel; this can't be the end. He leaves his hand on top of the gun.

Should I talk and reason with him? Would it be best to run? I can't lose my head with this. I've had training. He doesn't look too hardened. He's tapping his fingers on his gun and mumbling to himself. Shows he's hesitant with all this.

Before I speak he gets up quickly taking the gun with him.

"What am I doing?" he says pacing. "I can't hurt a girl."

He's behind me; I can't see what he's doing. He grunts and the door slams shut. I wait and hear silence. I lift my head and look around. It is an apartment; definitely appealing to squatters. I guess that's how these people live.

"You're safe for now."

I jump up quickly. A little girl lays on one of the mattresses across the room. It's wrong to assume she's harmless.

I stand defensively thinking she'll make a move. She looks about my age; maybe I should relax a little.

"He's Goto Yee, son of the man you killed."

Goto Yee?

"He's harmless. He won't hurt you."

"He's the one that took me."

"No, that was Taiga. He's the one you should look out for. He runs the resistance that's gonna take down your pretty prince. He uses Yee to get sympathizers."

I run for the door and pull at it. It's locked.

"No use," she tells to me. "You won't be leaving until Taiga sees you."

I run over to the window and look out. It's too far up. To get out of here I'll have to confront them.

THE LAST PRINCESS

"Taiga only says bad things about you."

Maybe she can prep me to deal with them. I walk back to her slowly. She probably needs a place to stay so she's caught up in all this. She stays on her mattress looking away as she talks to me.

"What kind of man is Taiga?" I ask her.

"Big."

I figured that. He pulled me in this place with no effort at all.

"He does whatever he wants," she continues.

"He's your leader?"

"Yeah, but he doesn't care for us. I'm only here because...."

Something going on between her and the resistance leader.

"If you get out of here, you have to help me," she whispers to me. "Taiga is..."

"What about him? I'll protect you, don't worry."

"He brought me here cause I'm next."

"Next?"

"Next to carry his baby."

I won't let that happen. That man is archaic. Being locked in the cage is making him act like an animal.

"What's your name?" I ask her.

"Miyuki."

"I'll get you out, and I'll take care of Taiga."

"Don't bother talking to him. If you say the wrong thing he'll snap."

Talking is all I can do. If someone was coming to save me there would be more of a ruckus out there. I stand up from her and have a look around the apartment. The living room is full of cots and mattresses.

I have experience talking to a killer. I'm not afraid of Taiga.

THE LAST PRINCESS

As I walk around I spot another room. There's a dresser in the way. Tall buildings normally have fire escapes; it could be in this room. I push hard and move the dresser out of the way.

"What are you doing?" she calls across the room. "You can't go in there."

"What's in there?"

"Taiga's apartment."

She hides under her blanket and I open the door. It's a much nicer apartment. So he lives here.

"Miyuki-san, push the dresser back in place."

"If you're not here when they come back-"

"It's okay. Just trust me. I'll bring help."

This other apartment seems well-kept. Why would they all crowd into one place when there's a well-kept apartment next door? The resistance leader must like his space. She pushes the dresser back.

I run to the kitchen and search for a knife. Nothing. So no one here cooks. I have nothing to defend myself. Kyoya-sama made me take off my arm blade just in case the reporters saw. I'll have to make a run for it. The guards will notice me as soon as I get to one of those windows.

I try the front door and it opens to the hallway. Exit is this way. When the two guys were talking earlier, they said to keep my presence a secret. I guess that's why there's no one here.

I walk down the hall and peek around the corner; stairway is clear. I go down the next two floors and still nothing.

I'm almost out. I take the next flight down and hear screaming. That could be Miyuki-san. They came back too soon. I'm almost out but I can't leave her; I promised to save her.

I have an idea; time to play the princess again. I run back up the stairs; the screaming gets louder.

"I don't know where she went. I don't know who you're talking about."

That's Miyuki-san. I stand outside the room. Sounds like just one person is in there. Slamming the door open brings all eyes on me.

THE LAST PRINCESS

"Get your hands off her."

"What! Get back in here."

He approaches me with his gun still in hand. She said he's harmless; I have to believe her. I raise my hand to him and he stops in his tracks.

"Yee-san," I say to him.

"How did you-"

"Of course I know who you are. Put the gun down before you hurt yourself."

"What!"

"Do what I say. I'm your princess, aren't I?"

"No, you're-"

"You may be behind steel walls but you're still in Morinaga and that makes me your princess. Now put the gun down."

He backs up one step at a time and places the gun on the table. I'm surprised that worked. If I can reason with him he'll let me go.

"Why do you want to keep me here?" I ask him.

"It's not me," he says with his head down. "I know you want to free us from this prison. You're the only one that knows my father was innocent."

"Yes, I know he's innocent. I'm sorry he had to die."

"I'm sorry your father had to die too."

I step inside. I always felt bad that someone died and had their name ruined cause I didn't say anything. I want to make it up to Yee-san and everyone here. There's no need for a resistance; these are my people.

"Seems like we're both apart of that monster's game. Prince Kyoya."

"Huh? Kyoya-sama isn't to blame for any of this."

"His men planted evidence in our home just before the arrest. It's him."

"It's not him. I know your father was framed but it wasn't Kyoya-sama that did it."

"He's brainwashed you."

"He hasn't."

Kyoya-sama is just trying to help. All he knows is his Han ways. I plan on teaching him more kindness so he can let these people go.

"After all that happened, who's sitting on the throne benefitting from everything," he says to me. "Prince Kyoya. And you want to marry him and cement it all. Marry him and I'll see you as my enemy."

This is how people feel about him. They don't know him at all.

"Don't take anything personal. What Taiga has planned is to hurt him not you."

I won't be around to meet him.

"Miyuki-san, come with me."

She stands and steps over her blankets. I reach out to her and she retreats backing into the corner.

"Miyuki-san," I call out to her.

She shakes her head and falls down to her mattress. Something pushes against my back and I know it's him. He feels huge; I'm afraid to turn around.

"Setsuna," the familiar raspy voice says.

I've never heard my name said like that.

"You're a feisty one, aren't you."

His hand pats the top of my head.

"I like feisty."

"Taiga-san?" I guess.

"Just Taiga is fine."

His hand is large. He moves from my head to my neck.

"Watch Miyuki," he says to Yee-san. "I want some alone time with Setsuna."

THE LAST PRINCESS

I look over at her and she's in tears. I can handle this. He pulls me out into the hallway and guides me by holding my neck. Now the halls are full of people. They all go where he goes. Looks where he tells them to look. It's easy for a strong presence to rally broken people. Taiga's no hero.

"See your so called people," he says to me.

It's hard to look at them. More people squatting inside apartments. How can I call myself their princess when they're living like this? How can I save them when they think I'm the enemy. In the middle of the hallway he lets go.

There are a lot of them. Now they're venturing out their rooms.

"You have to believe in me," I say out loud. "I'm the only one that can save you. You say the prince is cruel but I can fix him, I can fix this. You won't suffer anymore."

"What do you know about suffering," Taiga whispers in my ear.

I turn back to him fiercely. Finally I can see his face. What can I do against a man that size.

"You don't know suffering. I'm gonna teach you."

I take a step back as he approaches me. The first strike hits my back. I turn around and see a woman with a belt. More approach me with belts in their hand. I'm whipped while Taiga laughs over me. I fall to the floor guarding my face. It continues and all I can do is cry.

Mother and father, I let them down. My people hate me. They yell harsh words at me and whip me. My mother's robe is being ripped to shreds.

"Okay, that's enough," Taiga says to them. "I don't want her to pass out."

Mother's robe is ruined. It was her favorite one. Green was her favorite color. He grabs my hand and pulls me back towards his apartment. I go limp and see them all staring. They hate me because they think Kyoya-sama is a monster. He's not.

The last face I see is Miyuki-san. She stares at me in tears. The door slams shut and I'm alone with Taiga.

"You're not going to break me," I say to him. "I can handle anything you throw at me."

He smiles and starts to undress. No, I can't handle that.

THE LAST PRINCESS

"Bedroom's through that door. Go ahead in."

He turns his back to me and grabs a drink from the fridge. I get to my feet and stumble to the bedroom.

"It's good you understand."

I'm only looking for a weapon. I close the bedroom door and collapse on the bed. My body hurts so much. It's like all the cuts I had previously opened up again. No, I can't give up.

I pull out a few drawers and see nothing. How can I fight him without a weapon? There's no fire escape so I can't get out.

But I can't sit here and let him have his way with me. Even if I survived, I would be sullied. Loud music comes from the other room; it's rock music.

I can't stay. A guy that big will rip me apart. Pushing up on the window does nothing; it's stuck. I bang against it and still nothing.

"Please, someone help me," I say out loud. "Where's Kyoya-sama?"

Where's Captain Saki?

The door slams open and the rock music comes into the room. Taiga stands smiling at me.

"I'm a traditional man, so come near the bed. It's time for your second round of suffering."

"No."

I push up on the window again and it opens. I jump out and he grabs me by my waist. All that's below are bushes; I might survive the fall but likely not.

He keeps trying to pull me inside as I push myself out. I'll take the fall. Just let me fall. He grunts harder and flips up my robe exposing my underwear.

"Fine, we'll do it here."

Taiga falls back and the struggling stops.

"You know I'll always come to save you."

Who in the world…I look up and see a man holding on to the pipe.

THE LAST PRINCESS

I pull myself inside and a man climbs into the window. It's the masked man; the man that killed my parents. He's here to save me.

I don't know what I should feel but I run forward and hug him. He pushes me behind him and takes out his sword.

"Don't distract me," he says to me.

He pushes me back and directs Taiga's gaze away from me. Taiga charges at him and they struggle. Taiga's too strong. The masked man will be killed. I want him to win.

"Please, be careful," I call to him.

The masked man lunges his sword and Taiga snatches it away and throws it into the headboard. If it's a fist fight, the masked man won't win.

Taiga pummels his stomach over and over again and throws him to the floor.

"This your champion, princess," he laughs.

He steps over him and walks back to me. I run to the sword and try to pull it from the headboard. Even if I pry the sword out, I could never kill a person. He's getting closer. I crawl over the bed and go to the masked man's side.

"Wake up, please," I say to him. "You're stronger than this."

I'm pulled away. Taiga throws me back to the bed and lays one last stomp in the masked man to keep him still.

"Let's continue your suffering."

He grabs my neck and I claw at his arms. I can't push him off; he's too big. His other hand pulls at my sash.

My eyes search for the masked man. He's still lifeless.

"Help me," I struggle to say. "Please."

Move....just move. I know it's wrong to rely on him. My memory is still vivid. He's the one that took my parents from me. Killed everyone in my palace. Slashed my face and body. Said he loved me. That's why he came.

I turn my head away and Taiga releases my neck. He senses my surrender.

"You mean everything to me," Kyoya-sama once told me.

THE LAST PRINCESS

I want to see him again. I want to have my first time with him not this behemoth. I want to hug the shark he gave me. I cover my eyes and cry.

"You're so tense. Not use to being touched," he says in my ear.

So slimy. His tongue circles the outline of my ear as I push him back.

He raises his head and licks his lips. Please don't try it again. He chuckles and stops abruptly. Blood spills out his mouth and splashes my face. He hurls more and more and falls on top of me. He's dead?

The masked man continues thrusting his sword into Taiga's back over and over again. I close my eyes and hear his roar each time he stabs into Taiga's back.

"Princess," he finally says. "Did he hurt you?"

He kicks Taiga's body off me.

"You saved me?"

"If this is his lair it's not safe. Follow me."

He helps me up. I fall into his chest; I'm so thankful for him.

"I never thought it would be you. I'm so happy to see you."

"Don't distract me," he says pushing me away. "You're not safe yet."

Chapter 81: Ayato

I don't know what to say. I don't know how to make things better. Finding her and saving her was my priority; it will always be my priority. Yes, I had to kill and I would have continued to kill to save her. But look at her.

I gathered her limp body and brought her to the temple. We are near an opening but we can't leave this place, not while there's still daylight. She sits against the alter with her knees pulled to her chest. I keep my distance. I am not Ayato now, just the man that continues to murder in front of her.

Back in the apartment, I stabbed the man that tried to rape her. Stabbed him until my blade had no solid surface to puncture. She lay covered in his blood. It wasn't a turn on this time. I wanted to rinse it all off and make her clean again. She had suffered enough.

"There are people out there," she tells me.

"Then they'll die too."

"No, you can't. They're my people."

"These people are savages. Don't claim them as your people. Do you realize what he was about to do to you. What your people were gonna allow him to do."

I open the bedroom door cautiously. I'm tempted to burn this place down but Kyoya-sama said to be discreet. A fire here would spread to the whole district.

She groans behind me; she's limping. I go back to her and she hugs her arms close hunching over. She avoids my eyes. I'm not the enemy this time.

"Your back?" I guess.

She nods. Looks like they were aggressive. But she's still standing.

"I'll be fine," she says to me. "You'll get me out of here?"

"Yes."

"But why? Who sent you?"

"Nobody. I just saw you were in danger."

"So you're always watching?"

"Is that a problem?"

"For now….no," she says shyly.

My head must still be rattled from that boot to the face. It looks like she's smiling. For once she's happy to see me. Can't get distracted.

She stays close to me and we head for the front door. It's quiet. I open to door to the hallway and all the other apartment doors open. Harmless tenants wanting to know the fate of the large man's encounter.

A shot fires and I push her back.

"That was probably Yee-san. Don't hurt him."

THE LAST PRINCESS

I can't listen. I go into the hall with my sword swinging. The gunman retreats into the apartment next door. I leap across the hall and cut down a makeshift family then another. Every one of them falls.

My head hurts but I can't rest. Not till they're all dead. I pant heavily and approach the last apartment. Setsuna-san peeks out.

"Stay inside. I have one more."

"No, don't hurt him. I owe him."

"You owe him nothing."

I kick the door in and shots fire. I dodge and run towards him. He fires another shot above my shoulder just as I pin him against the wall.

"Stop it!" she screams. "Please don't hurt him."

"Setsuna-sama," a girl says in the corner.

"Miyuki-san, it's okay. We're gonna get out. Taiga's gone."

They're not getting out.

"Princess, no one here will survive," I say to her.

He's trying to weasel away. I slam him against the wall.

"Is he your bodyguard?" the girl asks.

"No, he's just helping me. We can trust him."

The girl refuses to leave her corner. Setsuna-san's heart is too soft. These are not her friends or people for her to save.

"Stop moving," I say slamming him again. "You shot at me so my patience is short."

"You're the one I saw," he mumbles. "You framed my father."

So this is the boy. If I knew he saw me I would have killed him then.

"You work for the prince, don't you?" he continues.

I look back and see the princess trying to coax the girl out of her corner. She can't hear us.

THE LAST PRINCESS

"Yeah, that was me. Your dad was my fall guy. I'm the one responsible for the royal massacre. I'm the reason you're stuck behind these walls. Kyoya-sama ordered all of it. So you can die knowing the truth."

I take the gun from his hand.

"Wait," he pleads. "Does the princess know?"

I guess I'll give him a bit more truth. Mostly cause I don't want her name caught up in this.

"The princess is innocent. It's just greedy men trying to get what they want. Will that help you rest in peace?"

His eyes float over to her. He starts to say her name and I shoot him in the stomach.

"Goto-san!" the cornered girl screams.

The girl finally comes from the corner in tears. This boy must have meant something to her. Fine. They can die together. I shoot her in the heart. She falls just short of my boot. The princess collapses crying. I scoop her up and head out.

So now we're here. She cries silently and I stand away trying to think of the best thing to say. She's watched me kill in front of her again. I killed people she desperately wanted to save.

"I'm sorry," I say to her. "It had to be that way."

"It had to?"

"Yes."

"What kind of world do you live in where people have to die! Where you have to take their lives!"

I turn away from her. I should go back to silence.

"Miyuki-san was just a girl. She asked me to free her. Why did she have to die, huh?"

I had to kill them; they knew too much. No one must know the princess is in here. But it's more than that.

"They hurt the person I love so….they had to die."

366

THE LAST PRINCESS

I look back at her shyly. It's a familiar feeling. I loved my mother dearly so when she was taken from me I had to kill the man responsible.

"Don't say stuff like that. You don't love me. This is not what love is."

"I'm here….where is your prince?"

I don't want to have a fight with her. I'm trying to get her tears to stop. I step closer and sit down next to her. She stays still.

"Everyone feels they can talk bad about Kyoya-sama. None of you know him."

"Do you?"

"No….but I know he's a great person."

"You want to believe he's a great person because that's what you've always built him up to be."

"Yes, that's true," she admits. "Still….I love him."

Just a few more hours and we can get out of here. The sun's setting.

"I don't get you at all," she speaks to me.

"Hm?"

"Why did you take my family from me? What did you gain?"

I don't want to answer. I was just fulfilling my friend's request. I always do what he says.

"I just wanted to."

"Why did you come tonight?"

"Cause you needed me."

She sighs and hides her face again. I can't give her a clear answer. Maybe I can try to ease things.

"Your mother….she…"

Her eyes look over at me.

THE LAST PRINCESS

"She...um....she yelled at me just before. She said "don't you dare harm my daughter. Setsuna is my world." I could tell she really loved you."

The princess starts crying again. I know it's something she always wanted to hear. She always wanted to know if her mother loved her.

"I'm gonna go find some water."

I get up and she grabs my leg.

"T-thank you for telling me."

She lets go and I wait outside the temple. I don't know what's going on. I use to love seeing her in pain but I'm the one that caused it all. I don't want to be the one that makes her cry. I want to see her smile again. Am I becoming sane?

I know I can give her a happy life. I'm feeling desperate thinking she'll deny me. But I can never sell out Kyoya-sama. That's the only thing I could do to destroy the clean image she has of him. If only there was a way to have both of them. I have water with me but I'll just wait a bit and let her calm down.

I pull out my phone and take a walk around the perimeter.

"Is she okay?" Kyoya-sama asks me.

"She's fine. I got to her in time."

"Thank you," he says to me. "I owe you."

"No, you don't. She's a bit shaken up. She started to sympathize with her captors and it didn't help that I killed them all in front of her."

"Well...at least she's safe."

"The group was run by a man named Taiga and he had the Yee boy with him."

"Lots going on in there I don't know about."

"They're both dead. Anyway I'll try to be in by midnight-"

"Hey, what's wrong? You sound kind of dull," he notices.

"Just...I feel like the bad guy. She hates me."

"She doesn't know who she's talking to. Of course she would hate a killer."

THE LAST PRINCESS

"Kyoya-sama, if she found out that-"

"She's not going to."

I feel less comfortable keeping things from her. Less comfortable with her not knowing who I really am.

"I have to go back in. We're in a temple."

"I know where you are. When you leave out the opening I'll have a car west of there."

"Got it."

"Ayato-san, you have never let me down. Thank you. Keep her calm so she won't think about what she saw."

He hangs up. I could never let him down.

Back inside she's drying her eyes. I pass a water bottle to her.

"You're always near," she says. "Who are you then?"

"No one you would know."

"Does Kyoya-sama know you?"

"Don't think so."

"I can't tell if you're lying."

"Part of my talent."

She laughs. I actually made her laugh.

"I'm starting not to care. Not that I forgive you but…you coming today meant a lot. I screamed for someone to save me. Never thought it would be you."

I sit down next to her.

"I have a bodyguard but he's on leave. If he was around I never would have gotten abducted."

"You have a lot of faith in his skills."

"I do. He's never let me down."

THE LAST PRINCESS

"What's his name?"

I just want to hear her say it.

"Captain Ayato Saki. Everyone calls him Captain Saki. I don't think he likes his first name too much. I think it's a pretty name so I wish I could call him that."

"Maybe he doesn't want to feel the closeness that comes from using a first name."

"I….don't want to give him the wrong idea. There have been some confusing feelings between us."

"How so?"

"We spent a lot of time together and without knowing it we moved into more deeper feelings."

"You love him?"

She pauses. I want to hear it. I look at her closely and she blushes.

"I….do."

We both turn out heads away. She loves me. I wanna hold her in my arms now and kiss her but I can't. I straighten my mask so she won't see my expression.

"Then why not be with him."

"Cause I love Kyoya-sama too. I'm really torn. Ayato-san is offering me a life away from all this. I could go to school and live in a small house; it all sounds wonderful."

"Then choose him," I urge her.

With our heads turned away she continues confessing. My heart feels like it's detaching from me.

"But….Kyoya-sama is so great to me. I feel so special in his arms. He understands me and what I've been though. He protects me in a different kind of way. I have to be married soon and I need to make a decision before then."

"I'm sorry you have to go through such grief."

"I'm told it's normal for a girl to have these feelings. Finally I'm like a normal girl," she laughs. "But it's still hard."

THE LAST PRINCESS

I turn back to her. She really is smiling. I scoot closer to her. I want to be the one she chooses.

"It's nice to see you smile."

"Can I see you smile?" she asks.

An attempt to get me to reveal myself. I can't do that.

"This whole thing is a mess. And it all started with you. Frustrating to know you did all this and don't even have a motive. I have no answers."

"The answers will become clear soon enough. Maybe it will help you with your decision."

She turns back at me staring into my eyes.

"I really thought you were him," she says to me. "From the moment I met the captain and looked into his eyes I knew you were him. But…you're not. Maybe it's just some fire you guys have in common."

"Probably we're both crazy about you."

I touch her cheek and she blushes again. I want so badly to kiss her. I may not have another chance. I pull a scarf from my neck and hold it to her eyes.

"Cover your eyes," I tell her.

"Why?"

"I think it's what we both want."

I know there's confusion. I'm mixed up too. She sits still as I approach her with the scarf. I put it around her eyes and tie it tightly. Since she's blind now I pull my mask down.

"You took your mask off, didn't you?" she guesses. "You're afraid for me to see your face-"

"Can I kiss you?" I ask her.

I sound so timid again. What will she decide? Will she acknowledge the love of a crazy man? No answer. I turn my head away but look back quickly. Her mouth is slightly parted. Is she waiting for it?

I move closer, close enough to put my breath on her nose.

"What's your answer?" I say to her.

"Don't ask me," she whispers.

I tilt my head down and breathe on her lips. She stays still.

"I'm right here if you want it," I whisper back.

Chapter 82: Setsuna

It's over. The nightmare is finally over. I can see the palace in the distance. The lights to the guest house are all on. The masked man carries me in his arms through the dark woods. There's a big fence up ahead and he's walking confidently like he'll pass right through it. He's the enemy to the palace but he doesn't act like it.

Although my memory is vivid, I find myself wanting to forgive him. Keep thinking it's not his fault, at least not directly. I was so happy that he came through the window and kicked Taiga away. My fondness started to grow. He saved my life, that's how I see it. But is my life really worth the deaths of so many?

I couldn't kiss him like he wanted. That would be unfair. I felt his desire for me but didn't want to return it. At that time, my mind was focused on Captain Saki. I desperately wanted him to be the one to save me. To sit me down and comfort me and….ask me to kiss him. But Captain Saki is gone.

Somehow it's not awkward to be carried in his arms. We've been entirely too casual. I've admitted things to him that I thought would never come out.

"I'm sorry I killed," he speaks. "I know you don't like that."

"You plan on repenting?"

"It never occurred to me. I have no problem with what I did but you do so….I wanted to say sorry."

"Sorry won't bring them back," I tell him.

"Neither will your tears."

We come to the wall and he pulls on a handle. So he was walking straight for a door. He's been to this place before. Knows the secrets the guards know.

THE LAST PRINCESS

There are no guards on patrol. That's normally how Kyoya-sama likes it. Says he doesn't like eyes on him. I wonder if anyone knew I was missing.

"Thank you," I speak.

"You're very welcome. I'll always come for you."

We're almost to the back door and the light inside turns on. He throws me into the bushes and jumps away. The back door opens with a cloud of smoke. It's cigarettes.

"K-kyoya-sama?"

He turns to me and leans down quickly. I can't believe I get to see him again. He tosses his cigarette out and wipes the dirt from my face.

"Setsuna-san."

He holds me tightly. I touch his face and feel tears. He's crying.

"I'm so happy to have you back. I couldn't go on without you."

I pet his head and he continues to cry. It's rare for him to cry over me. I do mean everything to him.

"Are you okay?" he asks. "Are you hurt?"

"M-my back hurts."

"I'll fix you. Don't worry."

I get to my feet and lean on him. He's panicky for once. Flustered too. Mumbling all his concerns.

"Did you know where I was?" I ask.

He pulls me inside and closes the door.

"You thought you could save them so you went in. You're lucky you found a way out."

"That's not-"

"Don't mention it to anyone. I have enough trouble controlling the media's attention."

THE LAST PRINCESS

He doesn't want me to speak about it. So he doesn't want to know who took me or what happened. Doesn't want to know who brought me back.

He's acting odd. He runs a bath for me to ease my pain then leaves the room. I take off my robe and look at the damage.

"It's ruined."

It'll have to be burned. Anytime a royal robe is beyond repair it has to be burned. And my hair clips are dirty. Taiga's blood got everywhere.

I sit in the bath and hug my knees. Knowing their names makes it so much harder. Taiga probably wasn't a bad person. He was fighting to free his people more than I was. And Yee-san didn't hate me like I thought. He just wanted someone else to validate that his father wasn't a killer. They're together now but I'm not sure if his father wants that.

The worst part is that I made a promise I couldn't keep. I told Miyuki-san I would lead her out. We were almost there and…she got killed like the rest of them. It was all just to save my life. How can I live with that kind of guilt? Kyoya-sama was the one that put them in there and I have to become his queen if there's any chance of getting them out.

"I keep seeing their faces," I say to myself.

"What faces?" Kyoya-sama says stepping in.

"Nothing."

He approaches me and leans down to the water. He starts to wash my face.

"I can do that-"

"No, I want to."

"I've never seen you do this kind of thing."

"I'm capable. I'm not as high-brow as you think."

I think he just doesn't want anyone else to know I was missing. He continues to bathe me. He looks so uncomfortable looking at all the scars on my body.

"When we met, you had flawless skin," he says to me. "Now you're all mutilated."

"I don't mind. It's small compared to real grief."

THE LAST PRINCESS

"Still….I wish I could take it all away."

He crashes into me hugging me tightly.

"Um…Kyoya-sama, you're gonna get wet."

"I don't care."

I pet his head but he still cries. I've never seen him shed so many feelings. This man is gentle despite what everyone says. Even if I'm the only one to see it, that's enough for me.

He stays close to me until it's time for bed. My shark lies beside me. With the covers pulled up he kisses my forehead.

"Um…you're not going to sleep?"

"No, I'm going to step out a moment. Go ahead without me."

He's still upset. He'll smoke the entire night. There has to be something I can say to him….but he doesn't want to hear the truth. There has to be a reason for that.

I get out of bed and go downstairs. He's probably hanging at back door. I slide the door open and see him standing in the middle of the backyard. Why's he all the way out there?

Before I call his name I stop myself. He starts pacing and I see someone out there with him. No visible face but wearing all black and….long hair.

"The masked man!"

T-they know each other. I stop myself from stepping out. There has to be some other reason for that. There's no way they could know each other. I mean, how long have they known each other? That would mean Kyoya-sama knew what he did….no, maybe they became friends without Kyoya-sama knowing. Why would they be friends at all?

I need to get closer but it's bare out there; nothing to hide behind. I keep squinting to see them. Why would they know each other; I need to figure that out.

Oh, I bet once I was taken the masked man came to Kyoya-sama to get some reward money. They're doing a money exchange. That makes perfect sense. The masked man is always watching so he wanted to capitalize and get money. Kyoya-sama has no idea who he's talking to.

THE LAST PRINCESS

"Little princess."

"Huh?"

I turn back and Kantarou-sama stands above me.

"Shouldn't you be in bed."

He moves his hand to close the door but stops. He sees what I see now.

"Does Kyoya-sama know who that man is? That's the killer."

"What he's doing isn't a concern of yours."

He closes the door.

"Kantarou-sama, you have to warn him."

"You've had a long day. Haven't you accomplished enough mischief."

"I wasn't...."

Is he gonna pretend he doesn't see anything?

"You've had me and Kyoya stressed out the whole day cause you chose to disobey my orders. You had no business going in there."

"I...."

What makes them think I went in on my own?

"Just go to sleep and stop making trouble for me."

Seems like no one wants to listen. I go back upstairs and hide under my blanket. Kyoya-sama seemed so comfortable talking to the masked man. It had to be some sort of money exchange. It's the only thing that makes sense.

I sleep but wake up with the same questions on my mind. It's like nothing happened yesterday. Yumi-chan has no idea I was missing. She's chattering at the breakfast table with Chiyo-san.

"W-what are you guys doing?" I ask looking over.

"Chiyo-san is gonna help me with my collection," she tells me. "I'm gonna design uniforms for my old high school."

"Oh, that's great."

THE LAST PRINCESS

It's just girls at the table for now. They continue talking like I'm not even here. It's nice for Yumi-chan to have a friend with the same interests as her. They would have never met each other if not for the same love interest. I think they both love Kantarou-sama but they ignore him every chance they get. How does that work?

The servant brings out the food without the others being present. Yumi-chan and Chiyo-san eat quickly while giggling with each other. Before I can speak again they get up.

"We're gonna head to the fabric store," Yumi-chan tells me.

"Can I come?"

"You stand out too much."

"Oh."

"Why don't you spend the day with Kyoya-sama? Give him a break from planning the wedding."

I guess I'm a bit jealous. Yumi-chan has another friend to play with. She's stopped fighting the battle to get me to leave the house. I sit at the table alone and nibble on my biscuit.

Is this how it's always gonna be? We eat breakfast together and then everyone scurries off leaving me to wave at them from the window. Chiyo-san knows how to drive too; they can go everywhere without me.

I grab the fruit bowl and head to Kyoya-sama's office. The door's cracked a little. I can hear him and Kantarou-sama.

"I have to move everything up. I want the wedding to take place as soon as possible. Forget blessing the venue."

"I'll call mother and father and make arrangements for Kira," Kantarou-sama says.

He's pushing it forward. What's the rush about? The door opens and Kyoya-sama looks down at me.

"Y-you missed breakfast so I brought-"

"Thank you for seeing me but I have to leave out."

I move aside and he steps away from me.

THE LAST PRINCESS

"Have a good day," I say bowing my head to him.

He stops and walks back to me. I see his shiny shoes.

"Go prep the car," he calls back to his brother.

We're alone in the hallway now.

"I think I will take some cherries with me. Thank you for being so sweet."

"Why are you pushing up the wedding date?" I ask him.

"No use in waiting. I'm just the acting king at the moment. I won't have any real power until we marry."

"You're planning something worse for Highland Row, aren't you?"

"Have you been eavesdropping?"

"No," I tell him. "It's just you've been too calm about the whole thing. You're planning to get rid of all those people cause you want to punish them more. I wish you wouldn't."

"I know what's right. I thought you trusted me."

I keep my head down to him.

"I'm sure you heard some pretty mean things about me while you were in there. But you know it's not true."

He kisses my cheek and walks off. With everyone gone it's just me. There are guards outside but only me in the house. I open the back door and a guard blocks my way.

"I just want to sit outside," I tell him.

"I can't permit that."

"Please."

"I'm sorry, princess. You can watch from there if you like."

He opens the door fully and I watch from the marble floor. The breeze is nice.

"It should be fine so long as I don't leave the gate, right?" I ask him.

THE LAST PRINCESS

"Strict orders, miss."

"Orders from Kyoya-sama?"

"Yes, miss."

Figures he'd tighten the leash.

"So where are you from?" I ask him. "Han?"

"Yes, miss."

"Do you like it here?"

"I do."

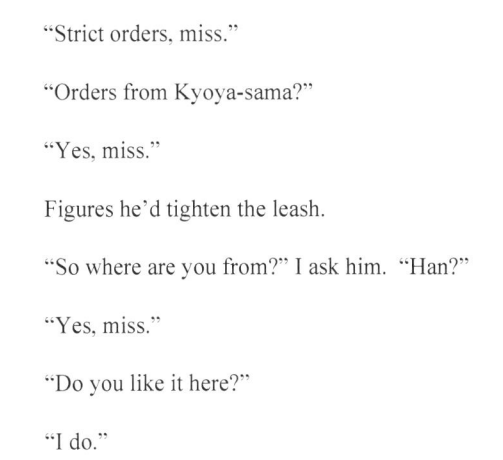

"Han people and Morinaga people look alike; you can't tell the difference until you discover their outlook. We share the same ancestors. We lived together as one people thousands of years ago. But there was a rift between brothers, Hanshu and Nagashu. One favored conquest and the other favored peace."

"They don't teach that story in Han," he tells me.

"There was so much hate at one point that the countries went to war. But when so many Morinaga citizens were killed, the Han leader called a truce. A young princess came to him and told him to stop and he did only to make her stop crying."

"They married," he jumps in.

"Yes, but he abused her greatly. Her father pulled her back and declared Han the enemy that would never be fought. And the countries kept their distance for hundreds of years. Then my father choose to close the gap. Probably cause I'm the last of the Asahina family. And marrying a Han royal would keep the bloodline strong."

I have to take the sheltered treatment again cause everyone is counting on me.

"What story do they tell in Han?" I ask him

"There were two brothers. One planned a conquest and the other tried to sabotage it. So the people siding with Hanshu created a language to keep their secrets. Rather than killing his brother, Hanshu gave him a piece of land and told him to keep out of the way. They kept interfering so they went to war."

I speak to Nagashu. He's my go to ancestor. I wonder that he would think of me. Maybe I should speak to Hanshu a bit to discover what he thinks about me too.

THE LAST PRINCESS

"It should be fine for you to come out a little bit," he tells me.

"Thank you. I won't go far."

I walk around the house and sit in a flower patch. I should have brought my sketchbook. This one is wilting; now's the time to capture it.

"You look so lonely sitting here."

I look beside me and see Captain Saki. He came back.

"I keep telling you flowers can't talk back-"

I hug him and he goes silent. I haven't seen him in so long. He's okay; I was afraid he wasn't. He's tough so he'll always be okay. He's back in uniform just like I remember him. Smells just like I remember him.

"Ayato-san," I say to him.

"D-don't call me that."

He pushes me away and hides his face. I felt so alone this morning; he came back at the perfect time.

"Did you just get back today?" I ask him. "How was your vacation?"

"I went back to Han."

"Oh….you miss it there?"

"Not really."

He turns back to me.

"I can live anywhere," he continues. "But…I wanted to visit my mother's grave."

He never talks about her; I don't want to pry. He lost his mom just like I did.

"Her name was Yuna. She died when she was thirty five; I can only picture her youthful face. She was nice…a bit of a slob but smiled often."

He's speaking without me asking.

"She was a secretary for some local real estate agent. Didn't make a lot of money. Wore the same clothes every day and the same hairstyle. She wasn't glamorous at all."

THE LAST PRINCESS

"I would have loved to meet her."

"I wish you could."

He seems sad talking about her.

"You've accomplished a lot. She would be really proud of you. Both your parents would be."

"My father died at the same time but I don't care about him so much. He's buried right next to her but I never pay him any mind. I see you talk to the dead so much so I wanted to try. Wanted to say I fell in love with a girl."

"Did she speak to you?" I ask him.

"No, don't think she wants to. I'm not like she remembers. Probably didn't know I was her son."

He lies back on the grass. I'm tempted to lay with him but don't want to get too comfortable.

"I never told anyone my mother's name. Just you. You're a good person. I just want her to know that I'm surrounded by good people, people she would like. Even if I'm no good, figured she would be happy with that at least."

"You're a good person."

"I'm not. But I'm done soul searching. Done searching for answers I already know."

He seems different after his time away. I can't put my finger on it but there's something different about him. Maybe a little more mature.

"How have you been?" he asks me. "I heard about your little scare yesterday."

"More than a little scare. I was terrified; thought I was gonna die."

"But you didn't."

"Only cause…"

I'm not supposed to mention that.

"You're a tough girl," he says to me. "Tougher than any of those normal girls you aspire to be. No one could have handled that situation better than you."

381

I smile. It's good to have him back. I lie back next to him and look into the sky.

"I missed you a lot," I tell him.

"I missed you too. Don't you think that means something?"

I take a deep breath. It definitely means something. Feeling uncomfortable just like I thought I would. I hold my ring to my heart and breathe out again.

"There aren't enough flowers here," he says. "Why didn't you ask for more?"

"There are bigger concerns than that. Like the upcoming wedding."

"I hear it's soon."

"Yeah."

"If you choose me-"

"Don't bring that up-"

"Just listen," he quiets me. "If you choose me I would buy us a small house with a big yard. You could get the dog you wanted to play with and the cat you wanted to watch over you. You'd be able to go to school if you wanted to and make friends. Wear whatever you want and go anywhere you want. One choice could lead you to infinite choices."

"There are bigger things at stake-"

"And you could come home to me every day. Greet me with a kiss."

I think he's talking to himself more than he's talking to me. He continues on smiling. It's making him happy just picturing it. It's making me smile too.

"You wouldn't be able to see Kyoya-sama again," he continues.

"B-but-"

"You should know why."

Having infinite choices sounds great but I can't imagine not seeing Kyoya-sama again.

"You can't see any of them ever again."

382

THE LAST PRINCESS

They're my family. Kira-kun, Kantarou-sama, Tomoko-sama….the Niwa family is my family. Yumi-chan is like my sister. I can't leave them all behind.

"I can't," I say to him.

"I know. Just knowing that you love me is enough."

I wipe my eyes clear. Thinking about leaving them was enough to make me cry.

"But you'll always have me and you'll always have the choice," he says. "I won't stop loving you and I won't leave your side."

He rolls on top of me and I immediately look to the house. There are people here. What's he doing? Before I speak he puts his finger to my lip.

"I want to give you this before it's too late."

He leans down and kisses me. He grips my face and doesn't let go. My heart's spinning. I feel so much from him. He needs me and he wants me. And I….feel so free with him. We part and I'm breathless.

"Ayato-san," I speak.

His face immediately blushes.

"I said don't call me that."

"I love you."

He leans down to kiss me and I turn my head away.

"I can't," I say to him. "Please don't."

"I have something else to give you."

"I said-"

"Most of your things belonged to someone else so….I wanted you to have something of your own."

He holds a hair pin out his pocket and puts it in my hair. He rolls off me and we both sit up. I wanna know what it looks like. I pull it from my hair.

"It's beautiful."

It's a pink flower; a cherry blossom. He actually got this for me.

"I can't give you a ring but I wanted you to have something to show that I love you."

I hold my lips thinking about our exchange.

"Your lipstick is fine," he says to me.

"It's not that. Thank you."

"You're not mad I kissed you?"

I shake my head.

"Does that mean I can do it again?"

I shake my head. I get to my feet and reach my hand out to him.

"Let's go plant some flowers. I'll have the guard pick up the stuff. And I'll make lunch for all of us."

He takes my hand and I help him up for a change.

"Really…knowing you love me is good enough for me."

"Same with you, Ayato-san."

"If you want to call me that, it's fine. I suppose you know me well enough."

Chapter 83: Kyoya

"Are you kidding me with this small house. Why can't I go to the hotel with mother and father?"

"It's Setsuna-san's idea. She wanted to entertain house guests. You'll be sharing a room with Kan-nii," I tell him.

I kind of like the idea. We're so use to living separately in a huge palace. Now it seems like we're a regular family. Kan-nii slaps Kira on the shoulder and he goes into his normal pout.

The wedding will take place tomorrow on the lawn of the old palace. The same place we had the funeral will be the venue for the wedding. That's the one thing Setsuna-san insisted on. Before that I get to spend a night with my brothers. I keep thinking about her so it's hard to be present.

THE LAST PRINCESS

She's at her family's crypt again. It's the only place I'll allow her to go. She wanted to take Ayato-san and I couldn't deny her. Wanted to show that I don't see him as a threat. Still…I hate how they look together. He puts his hand on her shoulder just like I do. She was beaming when I agreed to let them go; he was too.

"Kira, I heard you got yourself a girlfriend," I say to him.

"Huh?"

"It's about time," Kan-nii says slapping him again.

"How would you know about that?"

"There's very little I don't know."

"Anyway she's not my girlfriend," he says collapsing on the couch.

He hides his face in a pillow. First time Kan-nii heard of it; he'll give him a hard time.

"She's just my partner."

"Sounds a lot like a girlfriend," Kan-nii teases.

"She's not. We study together and eat together-"

"Does she make future plans for you?"

"She wants me to join the black ops with her and be in her unit."

"Hmph-"

"She's not my girlfriend! I don't like Naoko-san like that."

"Hmph-"

"Stop it!"

"What's the big deal if she is your girlfriend?" I ask him.

I don't think anyone has had "the talk" with him. We all assumed he was smart enough to figure things out on his own. We sit across from him and he tenses up. He grips the pillow harder at his chest.

"I saw her picture," I tell him. "She's pretty. She's from western Han, right?"

THE LAST PRINCESS

"She won't tell me where she's from."

"That's where you'll likely find blond hair. Her family runs a farm. She has two younger sisters that still live there."

"How do you know that?" he asks me.

"Why don't you know that? She's your woman after all," Kan-nii says.

Kira sighs and sits up to meet us. Finally he drops the pillow and stops hiding.

"If I did want to make her my woman," he starts. "How would I do it?"

"Women like a show of strength," Kan-nii tells him. "And they like to be bossed around a bit."

"Don't listen to him. Women are sensitive. You have to show you understand them. A good pat on the head helps-"

"You've been engaged since you were thirteen. What do you know about courting women?" Kan-nii asks me.

"A lot more than you. I know how to keep women happy."

"With your hard to reach approach?"

"Leave Setsuna-san out of this. Is your "you're worthless to me" approach still working?"

"Leave Yumiko-san out of it."

"At least my ways didn't make her sleep with someone else-"

"Don't speak just yet."

I look at him sharply. I'm not in the mood for comments like that. Especially not when those two are alone.

"What are you guys talking about?" Kira asks.

"Just don't mess things up," I say to him. "Be yourself and see what happens."

"Naoko-san's a bit scary. It's hard to get used to. She runs faster than me and throws knives for fun. She's stronger than me too."

THE LAST PRINCESS

"I like her already," Kan-nii says.

I need a drink. The two of them can entertain each other. In the dining room I sit with a bottle. Just what are they up to? It's just the two of them in a dark crypt; it's hardly romantic. Is she really going there to pray? Maybe it was some excuse so they could run away together.

I dial his number quickly then hang up. She loves me more. She wouldn't do anything stupid. And he knows I'll kill him if she does. Well….I guess that's an empty threat. I could never kill him. That's the problem with all this. He's my best friend. He's like a brother to me. There's nothing I can do to stop him. Not with my normal way of doing things. And Setsuna-san…I can't blame her at all.

He's calling me back. I pick up.

"Hey, you checking in?" he asks.

"Kira's asking for her. He just got in."

"Little brat can wait. It'll probably be another hour before we return."

"What are you two up to?"

I take a drink and wait. I can tell he's smiling. I want to know why.

"We went to the crypt but then she wanted to go into the palace. Said she wanted to see her parent's old wedding pictures."

"I see."

"She really likes it here. But I think she's anxious and trying to distract herself."

I wonder if she's having second thoughts. I pretty much blamed her for the incident at Highland Row. She accepted that and chose not to talk about it. She apologized to me for sneaking in there. And since Ayato-san returned she's been spending time with him. They do innocent stuff but I hate seeing it.

While I'm stuck inside reading papers the two of them frolic about the yard with giggles. I've never seen him look so happy. I always wanted him to find someone to make him happy but it's not going to be her.

"I think it's fine to let her stay a bit longer," he says.

"That's not for you to-"

THE LAST PRINCESS

"Is that Kyoya-sama?" I hear on the other line.

"Yeah, he said Kira just got in. He wants to see you."

"Why can't everyone just come here?"

"Just cause you're comfortable here doesn't mean others are. You and I can stay. You can show me your old room-"

"We're on our way," I say to them.

I'm not leaving them alone for the night. I hang up and go to the living room.

"We're going to the wedding site early," I tell them. "Pack a bag."

"I'm not staying in a haunted house," Kira says.

"You wanna stay here by yourself?"

"Maybe we can have Naoko-chan protect you," Kan-nii teases.

"Don't joke like that. She's not here is she?"

I better text Yumiko-san. She's out with Chiyo-san again. I want everyone in one place so I can keep an eye on things.

The late night ride makes me remember everything all over again. I'm recounting all our moments but I don't have a clear ending. I don't know what's going to happen tomorrow.

"Stop worrying so much," Kan-nii tells me.

"After we're married, what will happen? Her feelings for him won't instantly go away."

"Well, your wedding night will fix a lot of things."

"It'll be her first time. She'll probably hate me for it."

"Are you sure it will be her first time?" Kira chimes in. "We do have a past, you know."

He wishes.

"You don't think I'm serious?"

"No," I tell him.

THE LAST PRINCESS

"Setsuna-san and I have a thing. But I'm willing to let that go because you're my brother."

An attempt to seem important. I better humor him.

"Thank you, Kira. It'll be smooth sailing now."

"You're welcome."

We pull up to the old palace and I feel out of place. I haven't stepped inside this house since the funeral. I made sure it was left intact. Nothing has been removed or changed in there. Her parents are looking down at me saying I have no business going inside of their house.

I'm going to fulfill their wishes. I'm going to marry their daughter and restore the bloodline. Despite what I did to them I plan on honoring them in my own way. I was going to name the first son after her father.

"Kyoya!" Kan-nii calls.

It's a lot to take in. I look to the palace not realizing I'm standing in the middle of the guest chairs. I follow my brothers up the aisle and everything feels blurry.

Tomorrow she's going to walk out that house and walk this long runway. She'll see me at the other end and see Ayato-san standing next to me. I keep thinking she'll ask me to step aside. If she knew what he did, she wouldn't like him. I try to contemplate which one of us she'll forgive and which one she won't. It's risky to tell her the truth about that night when I don't know which one of us has wronged her more. And….it seems cowardly to rely on that. I could never turn my back on Ayato-san. He would never turn his back on me.

I continue walking and the heavy door closes behind me.

"Scared yet?" Kan-nii says to Kira.

"It seems a lot like the first time we were here. I can't believe it's a murder scene. Setsuna-san is so weird for coming back here."

"She's strong, not weird."

I stay quiet and watch them gaze upon the walls. The family portraits line the foyer; all their eyes are staring.

"This palace is all she knows. She was never allowed to leave. And I suppose with everyone gone, this is all she has to remember them."

THE LAST PRINCESS

"Seems weird."

"Remember she likes to talk to the dead," I step up. "That's how she keeps from feeling lonely. This house is just one big dead thing. She doesn't find that scary at all."

"I'll never understand her religion," Kira speaks. "Dead is dead. There's no talking to it."

I'm starting to get it. The two of them walk upstairs and I continue down the hall. My favorite room is down this hall; the room I met her in. I stop just before I reach it.

"It was the happiest day of my life. I never smiled so much," Setsuna-san says.

I peek in. She's sitting with Ayato-san on the ledge that overlooks the courtyard pond. That's where she once sat next to me.

"No matter what he's done and no matter what he might do in the future, I can never forget how he made me feel that day."

Ayato-san looks at her gently. He's sharp; I know he knows I'm listening. But maybe he's distracted sitting close to her.

"Sometimes I think he's a monster like those people said. He probably can be but tries hard not to be. If he would show more of himself to me, I would help him with his struggle."

I put my head down. She says what I want to hear. She's too perfect.

"We've always had that in common. We admire him too much," he tells her.

"You think he feels burdened by it? I mean, he's been alone out here trying to be a king in a place that's foreign to him. I'm sure he feels the pressure. Neither of us has been at his side to help."

"He's use to being alone-"

"I don't want him to be alone. I don't want any of us to be alone anymore."

She leans over to him and he puts his arm around her. I stay back. I want her to finish speaking.

"You know it's not gonna end like that. One of us will be alone. Depends on who you choose."

THE LAST PRINCESS

"You said you wouldn't leave-"

"I won't."

She has so much affection for him. I can't watch anymore. I follow after my brothers. I can hear their chatter upstairs.

It's like they've never been in a girl's room before. Kan-nii is looking through papers and Kira is opening drawers.

"Whoa, is this how big she is," Kira says pulling out a bra.

"Have a little respect," I say snatching it from him.

This must be Yumiko-san's room. She hasn't lived here in years. She's a different person than what this room reflects. I'm guilty of snooping too. I see a picture on her nightstand. It's Yumiko-san and her mother.

While I'm staring, Kan-nii leans over my shoulder.

"She looks about ten," he says. "She has the same smile."

He takes the photo from me.

"Kan-nii, you like Yumiko-san, right?" Kira asks.

He puts the picture down and sits on the bed. He's ruined it. She wants nothing to do with him anymore. It's all cause he pushed her aside and made her watch him take someone else.

"She's still young. She'll come around," I tell him.

"Yeah...I guess."

"She will. You know how she is. Just do something nice for her and she'll come back to you."

"Are all girls like that?" Kira asks.

"Just make them feel special, that's all they want," Kan-nii says to him. "Although Naoko-chan is stronger and tougher than you, she still wants to be treated like a girl. She still wants to feel like she's special to you."

"It's not like I like her like that," he says shyly.

THE LAST PRINCESS

    I leave them and go down the hall. Setsuna-san's room isn't too far. She told me lots of stories about how she would sit in her room and listen for the sound of her cousin's door. Then she would run down the hall before anyone could see.

    Setsuna-san's door is cracked. I step in and it's bare like I remember. She keeps all the things she likes hidden. It's all under the bed like before. Reaching down I feel the box she once pulled out for me.

    "The color she didn't know the name of….the movie actor she wanted to ask me about…."

    I continue going through the box.

    "Questions to ask Kyoya-sama," I read.

    There are so many. She just kept adding to it over time.

    "Do you know how to swim? Do you sleep with socks? Do you like clowns? Will you teach me more Hangese?"

    Pages and pages of questions. I was the most important person she had. I want to believe that hasn't changed.

    "No, you can't read that!"

    She runs in and dives over the box. I stand up and see Ayato-san waiting at the door. While she scrambles to collect everything I stare at him. What did they come up here for?

    "Setsuna-san, Kira wanted to see you. He's in Yumiko-san's room."

    "In Yumi-chan's room?"

    She stuffs the box away and goes to the door. She stares back at the two of us.

    "Go greet him," Ayato-san says to her. "Leave us alone for a bit."

    She hesitates and looks over at me. I nod to her but she stays hesitant. She walks back to me and I lean down to her.

    "What's wrong?" I whisper.

    "What are you gonna do?"

    "Nothing."

THE LAST PRINCESS

"Then why do I have to leave?"

Has she picked up on the tension? She looks down at my feet as she talks.

"I don't want you to stop being friends," she says to me.

"You don't have to worry about that."

She turns back at him then lays her head on my chest.

"You're nervous about tomorrow?" I guess.

She nods.

"Whatever happens will happen. I just want you to be happy."

She squeezes my shirt. She doesn't like it but it's all on her. Whatever happens tomorrow will be her choice.

"I've enjoyed falling in love with you," I say to her ear.

She pulls away from me and runs away. She pushes pass Ayato-san trying to hide her tears.

"You don't seem nervous about tomorrow," he says to me.

I wave him in.

"Should I be?"

"It's your wedding day. It's fitting that you should be."

He starts to walk around her room. I sit on her bed and reach for a cigarette. No, I disrespected this place enough.

"She hates that you smoke," he says to me. "Says you should try talking more."

"I know that."

I stuff it back in my pocket. I don't need him to tell me how she feels about me.

"You know what bothers me in all this is that….you still don't see me as your equal."

THE LAST PRINCESS

He's at her vanity looking at her trinkets. I wince when he picks up her things so casually.

"What do you mean? You've always been my equal."

"Don't lie. You always saw me below you. I was your little orphan from the street. Some community service-"

"You know that's not true! What's got in your head this time? You're my friend, you're like my brother. You've been subservient to me on your own. I never asked you to be that way."

He saved my life. I'll never forget that.

"I want you to be happy. That's why this is killing me," I tell him.

I stand up to meet him. He puts down her perfume and stares at me.

"I see how you are with her. I see how you happy you are. It's what I always wanted for you," I admit to him.

He turns his head away. Everyone is trying to ignore what we're going through.

"Look at me!"

I rush over to him and put his chin in my hand.

"Look!"

He tries to push away.

"You are my equal. Do you see how scared I am? Scared that she'll choose you. You're the only man on this earth that I see as my equal, the only one that could take all this away."

I release him. I breathe out and try to control myself.

"Any other man I would have killed. You would have killed them for me. But I'm competing with you. Whatever happens tomorrow…you'll still be my brother."

I turn from him and go back to the bed.

"Kyoya-sama, I'm sorry."

THE LAST PRINCESS

"Don't say "sorry." Don't be sorry for anything."

He comes over to me and sits next to me on the bed. We're quiet for a bit. I wish we could drink.

He takes something from his jacket. I look closer and snatch it from him.

"What are you doing with this?"

He snuck my journal out the palace. Everything is in here.

"Were you going to show her?"

"She should know the truth."

"No."

"She should."

"All this would be for nothing if she knew the truth. She would just run away. She wouldn't trust anyone."

"She should know what kind of people we are," he adds.

"No."

I've thought about telling her but I don't want to hurt her anymore. I just want to make her happy. Deep inside, I'm certain she knows what kind of people we are. She was in Highland Row long enough to learn a thing or two. Whatever she knows or is suspicious of, I'm sure she'll hide it so she can keep smiling.

"If you care about her happiness, you'll continue to stay quiet about that night. Staying quiet hurts me too but it's for her own good."

He nods.

"You're right," he says.

He keeps looking around the room. There's nothing here to find.

"Let's go find a place to sleep," I say to him.

"Why not here? I'd like to experience a little of what Setsuna-san had."

"You wanna sleep in her bed?"

"Yeah."

THE LAST PRINCESS

If he's staying then I'm staying. I can't have him one up me in experience. Setsuna-san will probably sleep with Yumiko-san anyway.

"Fine. Just keep your hands to yourself. I don't want a repeat of last time."

"That's was five years ago."

"I still remember it."

He lowers his head smiling. There's still one thing I wanted to ask him.

"Have you been upfront with me about everything?" I ask him.

"No, but I figured you already knew that. Whatever you're thinking, it's true."

So every terrible thing I have in my head is true. I'm really nervous about tomorrow.

Chapter 84: Yumiko

"Is this the right place? We're supposed to stay here?"

Chiyo-san stays at the entrance. This is my old house. Of course this is the right place. I pull her inside and close the door. I couldn't forget this place even if I wanted to. Especially not after what happened here.

"It's fine," I tell her. "Let's just go up to my room."

She shrieks looking at a picture. That's grandfather. I suppose it's a creepy picture but I've gotten used to it. He was a bug-eyed king.

"Are you in any of these portraits?" she asks me.

"Uh....I think so."

I haven't seen my family portrait in years. I walk down the hall and spot it. This is from when everything was all together. My mother and father were in love and there was no scandal. She was the most glamorous woman in Morinaga. I miss those times.

THE LAST PRINCESS

"Your mom is beautiful," she says to me.

"Yeah, she was known for her beauty. She was in a lot of magazines and stuff."

I have all her pictures and editorials in a box in my room. I thought she was the most beautiful woman in the world without all the headlines. Then when the scandal came out I saw her like all the others did. It was only cause I was so hurt.

"I should make up with her."

"Where is she?" she asks.

"Living in a condo on one of the outer islands. She's still in exile."

"I don't think what she did was too bad."

"She embarrassed the royal family. The king had no choice."

I turn away from the portrait. The past is the past. There's greater things about to happen. Setsuna-chan and Kyoya-sama's wedding is tomorrow. It'll be a world event.

"We have to get our beauty sleep."

I go upstairs to my room and see Kira-sama hugging my pillow.

"Where have you been?" he shouts at me.

"Were you expecting me?"

"He's scared. He thinks only a family member can protect him," Kantarou-sama says from my window.

I didn't notice him. My mind must be somewhere else; he's hard to miss. I turn my eyes away as he approaches me and Chiyo-san.

"Can I have a word with you?" he says.

I look up and see him watching me. What could we possibly talk about? It's finished between us. I'm trying to move on. I invited Hisoka-kun as my wedding guest. I have no business being with a man like Kantarou-sama. I should be with a boy my own age.

"I'll protect Kira-sama," Chiyo-san says stepping inside.

397

THE LAST PRINCESS

"I don't need protecting!"

"Now now, prince. Settle down."

I turn away from the room and he follows me back downstairs. His boots match my steps. It's so bothersome to have him so close. He probably wants to yell at me and put me back to work.

"What is it?" I ask turning around.

"I know what I did wrong."

He's admitting a fault. That's not like him at all.

"You're special to me. I understand why you don't know that. I never said it. Never tried to show it. Never bought you a gift or took you on a real date."

I push my hair behind my ears. I'm nervous looking at him. I take a step back and he follows me. There's something different about his eyes and his voice. He's not talking down to me or acting like he's so much better.

"Yumiko Yamamoto is the woman I love. I'll gladly say it to the world. You're the only one I think about before I go to sleep. The only one I can let my guard down with."

I take a step back. He's not supposed to do this. I'm supposed to move on.

"I care for you, there's no question about that-"

"Kantarou-"

"I know you're still young and exploring the world and yourself. But when you're ready…please consider me seriously. I'll be waiting."

He turns away from me and goes down the hall.

"You idiot," I say to myself. "You big idiot."

I hold my eyes and try to stop myself from running after him.

"Kantarou, you idiot."

I wipe my eyes and go the opposite way. My head's all messed up again. They're probably all wandering around the palace. I don't want to run into any of them. I step into the dining room and close the door behind me.

THE LAST PRINCESS

"Yumi-chan?"

"Uh?"

She's here.

"Why're you in here?" I ask her.

Setsuna-chan lifts her head from the table. Maybe she has stuff on her mind too. She only gets one wedding day; I'm sure she's nervous.

"Tomorrow's the day," she says.

"The day you always wished for."

I clear my tears and walk over to her. She should be happy but she looks scared.

"Don't tell me you're having second thoughts."

"I know what I have to do."

"But what do you want to do? Never mind what people expect from you. What is it that you want?"

I sit down next to her and try to look in her eyes.

"All this time I wanted choices and I realize it was easier not having them."

She's still thinking about the captain.

"Choices are hard," I tell her.

I have one to deal with.

"But it's a part of being free. Kyoya-sama helped you be free, right?"

"Ayato-san did," she says softly.

She touches her hair and pulls out an ornament. That one looks new. It's modern.

"Where'd you get that one?"

"Ayato-san gave it to me."

I want to help her. I know it's wrong of me to interfere but I have to.

THE LAST PRINCESS

"You will marry Kyoya-sama tomorrow. Do you understand?"

I grab the flower ornament from her. Things like this are just confusing her. It's just a pretty flower. She'll forget about him if I get rid of it. I leave out the dining room and she follows after me.

"Yumi!"

"You don't need things like this. You don't need to be confused. You have a perfectly good man-"

"He's not perfect!"

I stop and look back at her. She always said he was perfect.

"Give it back to me," she says.

"You better know what you're doing."

I drop it and she runs to pick it up. I don't know what to do for her. I don't know how she let the captain get in her head. She cradles it in her hand, the same hand that has her engagement ring.

"I know what I'm doing," she says. "You're the one who doesn't."

"Don't go thinking-"

"I know what I'm doing! I'm not lost like you. I know what I want and where I want to go."

"Setsuna-"

"I know who I want to be with."

"I was with the captain. He's-"

"You think you know him cause you slept with him. All you were was my replacement."

Something is definitely wrong with her. I feel like I'm talking to one of the girls from my school. Her eyes are like daggers. She's really jealous that I slept with him.

"He loves me. He saw nothing in you. And don't ask if I'm really getting what I want if you're gonna force me to do things your way."

THE LAST PRINCESS

"You're jeopardizing everything! You'll ruin this palace if you don't marry him tomorrow."

"Don't talk to me like you're my mother," she says deeply.

"You obviously need to cool down. I'll be in my room. You have the house to yourself."

I leave her and go towards the stairs. I wouldn't steer her wrong. Kyoya-sama is perfect. She doesn't know how easy she has it with him.

Chapter 85: Setsuna (Final)

My whole life I've been conditioned to be one man's wife. A man I only met about three years ago. He's wonderful in every way. Responsible, respectful, a good leader. He protects me without owning a weapon.

Today is my wedding day and my thoughts are so jumbled. So much has happened since I met him. I lost my parents; they created me and maintained my world. I didn't think I could make it without them but I prayed for guidance. I heard my parents tell me to hold on to Kyoya-sama and hold him tight, all the while the captain was loosening my grip.

I look out the front door window and shield myself from the light. The guests have already arrived. There are cameras, and microphones set up. It's gonna be a spectacle.

I convinced everyone that's it's a tradition for the bride to prepare herself. Really it's the exact opposite. I just wanted some time alone. I still don't have it all figured out.

I'm so used to this house. It's easy for me to avoid all the frantic people.

"Mother, can you stop. I'm capable of dressing myself," I hear Kira-kun say.

"Your hair's not laying right," she chases after him.

"Mother!"

When they pass I continue upstairs. I haven't been back to my room yet. I spent the night in father's office looking at his pictures. Didn't get much sleep. I wonder if Kyoya-sama was able to sleep.

401

THE LAST PRINCESS

I open my bedroom door. Something's amiss. Things were touched in here. The bed is unmade.

"Hello?"

Someone slept in my room. I step in and walk around. The bathroom's empty. Now I just gotta check the covers. Approaching slowly makes my heart race. I stand back as far as I can and tug on the blanket.

"Geez."

No people. The blanket falls completely and I see a book resting in the middle of the bed. My heart beats faster. I know what that is.

Kyoya-sama must have stayed here last night. Oh gosh. I know what that is and I'm so afraid of it.

"Kyoya-sama's journal."

All his intimate thoughts are in there. I've read his earlier years; it's extremely detailed with his feelings for people, his frustrations and joys.

I should return it to him. He can't be without it. But…somehow I can't bring myself to touch it. If I touch it, I'll open it. If I open it, I'll know what he really thinks about me, about this wedding, about Ayato-san's feelings for me and my feelings for him.

I'm just staring. Have to get out of here.

I run to the door and see Yumi-chan down the hall. She's already dressed. She's in her royal robes although she hates them. Last night I was mean to her. She was just trying to help and I yelled at her. It always bothered me that she had a causal relationship with the captain. So much was bothering me and I lashed out at her.

"I'm sorry," I say aloud.

I know she can't hear me but I want to say it. She spins in her clothes and locks eyes with me. Even though I said I wanted to be alone I figured she could push her way in like she always does. Chiyo-san emerges from the room and they walk away. She ignored me.

That's the first time she's ever ignored me. She's going her own way; she doesn't need to be affiliated with me anymore. I hear their giggling and run back to my room and slam the door.

THE LAST PRINCESS

I'm back staring at that book again. Maybe there are positive things in there. It could help my indecisiveness. I walk along the wall and approach it cautiously.

"Just one page. I'll read one page."

I hear someone in the hall and pull away. I don't have the guts to do it. He told me not to read his journals. He stayed here last night. Maybe he left it for me to find. Or maybe this is a test.

"I'll pass it."

I throw the blanket back on the bed and head towards the bathroom. I have a wedding to get to and I'm the last one ready. I bathe and wash my hair.

Sitting at my vanity I sort through my hair ornaments. Mother wore this one on her wedding day. I'll add it to the bun. And….the jeweled cherry blossom pin. Ayato-san gave this to me. I want to wear this one too.

Time to face everyone and be seen as queen. I put my hand on the door knob and look back towards the bed. I can't go through with this without knowing what's really on Kyoya-sama's mind.

I run to the bed and hide under the covers with the book at my chest. I have to read it. I have to know if we belong together. I have to know what kind of guy he is and what he has in common with Ayato-san. I have to choose one of them and I know this journal has all the answers.

Okay, page one. It's five years ago when Kyoya-sama was eighteen.

"I've been thinking about where I should go after graduating. I don't want to join the military and I don't want to run a department or bureau. I'm supposed to be king at some point. Whatever career I start will be interrupted. I'm hoping he won't dismiss my plans again. When Ayato-san comes back I have to run this by him seriously."

He's making plans but for what. I close the book briefly and take a breath. I have to read on. I keep turning pages and see notes about my parents and me. He added to it multiple times; I can tell by the different pens.

"Setsuna Asahina: twelve, black haired, brown eyed, speaks five languages…huh?"

He wrote down everything he knew about me. Things I said in letters or told him are all here. I guess that's sweet. I kept a similar chart on him. This isn't so bad. I keep flipping the pages and skimming the words. He admits how he wishes he was as

THE LAST PRINCESS

tall as his brother so he could command a room like him. I had no idea he was jealous of Kantarou-sama.

I stop after glancing over one word.

"Murder."

I take a breath and read on.

"Ayato-san agrees with the plan. After I meet the princess and Kantarou talks to the security guards, we'll make our move. We'll need to know how they move and when if this is to be successful. He'll...."

I hold my mouth. I can't believe this.

"He'll..."

I can't speak anymore. They couldn't have done this.

"He'll kill them all and leave the princess safe."

I cry into my blanket. My throat is hot. I scream into the blanket and hold it tightly. They've been responsible. I ran to Kyoya-sama for help and it was all his doing. And Ayato-san...he was the masked man the whole time.

"She'll cling to me," I read on. "She'll allow me to do anything. She'll give all her power to me cause I'll be the only one she trusts."

How could I love either of them when they're monsters. This whole time they've used me. Played with me and manipulated me. It's hard to move but I keep reading. He talks about how he fell in love with me and about his regrets. He talks about not going through with it but convinces himself it's for the best.

"Setsuna-san has the prettiest smile. Her cheeks get so big. And she's so sexy when she takes her hair down. I could go on and on describing all the things I love about her."

I read on and he talks of his jealousy for Ayato-san and his struggle with keeping his best friend as his rival.

"No!"

No matter what he feels today it can't fix what he did, what his true intentions were. He struggles with greed and love. That's why he stayed away so long. So today I'm suppose decide if he has more love than greed in his heart. I can't forgive him.

THE LAST PRINCESS

And Ayato-san…he became my friend and said he would protect me from my parent's killer. It was him the whole time. Scaring me to push me closer into his arms. What's his angle in all this?

I pull the blanket away and continue crying.

"What's wrong?"

I shriek seeing Kyoya-sama. I hold his journal on my lap under the blanket. He's in his suit with his hair slicked back. Just like I pictured him on our wedding day. He's supposed to be my hero. All I see now is a shady wolf.

"Why are you crying?" he asks.

He takes a step forward. Which words are lies? Which words are genuine?

"Don't come any closer!"

"Setsuna-"

"Don't…don't say my name."

"Everyone is waiting for you," he speaks quietly. "Will you be coming out?"

I can't look at him. This monster took my family away all so he could stand in my father's place. My father respected him. If Kyoya-sama wanted to take his place as king, my father would have stepped aside. He told me so!

"Setsuna-"

"Just go!"

He looks at me shocked. I can barely see him with my blurry eyes. He walks away and closes the door behind him. I keep wiping my eyes on my sleeves and they never dry. My wedding dress is all covered in tears.

I turn to the last page he wrote on. It's from last night.

"I sit in her room and I wonder if I should tell her. Tell her everything. I'm a coward so I don't think I can. I just want to make her happy. She'll never look at me the same again if she knew. He wants to tell her too. I told him we can't. We have to keep the secret. I bet she looks at him with those big eyes too. It's unbearable to have her smile and love a me that's one sided. Can't she just let me take care of her and make it up. I think that's what both of us are trying to do. I love her so much that it's killing me to keep lying."

THE LAST PRINCESS

Is there more love than greed in his heart?

"If she leaves me, I'll understand. I won't go after her. Ayato-san says the same. He admitted everything to me. He told me everything that went on between them. How he stayed at her bedside during the lightning storms; had no idea she was afraid of lightning. He told me about their time at the movies. Can't believe she kept that from me. He says I should give her choices cause she was raised with such a rigid path. Who do you want to be with, Setsuna? Are you willing to live the same life once the past has been cleared up for you? I want to give you at least one choice cause afterwards you won't have any."

I rub my eyes and hide under the covers. Which one of them left this for me to find? The music starts outside. What am I supposed to do? They're both murderers but do I want to live captured by one or living free with the other. Or should I abandon both of them. Abandon this name and this county.

"Would you be alright if it stayed like this?" Ayato-san once asked me.

I'd be living like a fool if I didn't know the truth.

"Then I'll work hard to make you fall in love with me all over again," Kyoya-sama once said.

I can't get in his grasp again. I'm too afraid.

"What am I supposed to do?"

I get up and go to the vanity. I straighten my hair and makeup. My hand pauses when I touch the jewel cherry blossom. It still belongs there. I gather his journal in my hand and my bouquet in the other.

The house is empty as I walk through it. I check in each room feeling for the people that use to occupy them. I'm a princess; I know what that means. It was instilled in me since I was born.

The guard at the front door looks over to me and I hide behind a corner. I can't go through with this. I hear his boots coming closer and I run away to the back door. Soon everyone will be looking for me. They'll stare at me like I'm a conspirator. I have been happier ever since they all disappeared.

With all the attention on the guests out front I dart across the back yard towards the crypt. I trip over my white robe and lay still in the dirt. I pound the bouquet on the ground until it crumbles.

THE LAST PRINCESS

How could he do this to me? How could he trick me? We're supposed to be in love.

I get to my feet and continue running. I make it to the crypt and collapse in front of my parent's statues.

"What do you want me to do now?" I scream at them. "Kyoya-sama is your murderer."

"They knew."

I get up and hide behind my stone father. Ayato-san emerges from the shadows. He's just as dangerous. The sword he protects me with is the same one he takes innocent lives with.

"I told them Kyoya-sama's plan before they died. They knew and accepted it."

"What?"

"A man that did what he did is ambitious. That's how your father saw it-"

"Don't speak for him. I won't believe a word that comes from you."

"Just wait-"

"Don't come any closer!"

He takes a step away and leans against the wall.

"I knew you would come here. You're always seeking answers from someone other than yourself."

I hate him. I hate both of them. Only webs and lies comes from their mouths; I'm tangled in all of it. I have to keep my eyes on him; he's incredibly fast. Eyes are getting blurry again. It's the dang mascara. I reach up and wipe my eye and he's gone.

"No."

I step out from behind the statues and there's nothing. So he's gone; does that really fix anything.

"It's easy for you to hate me but feelings of love don't easily change."

Where's that coming from?

THE LAST PRINCESS

"Ahh!"

He wraps his arms around me from behind.

"I'm sorry," he whispers.

The grip is so tight. I was right about him from the beginning and he made me like him so I would forget. I knew I was right when I looked in his eyes. He's a murderer.

"So much is wrong with you," I say to him.

"Just the other day you said I was "good." You gonna go back on your words now?"

"You cut me and hurt me. You took everything from me."

"You wouldn't listen."

"You almost killed me-"

"I also saved you."

When I was in Highland Row he did come for me. I refuse to weigh out the good and the bad. But....I said I loved him. As much as I hate him right now it's not going away.

"Let go of me," I say to him.

"You'll just run."

"Let go! I don't want to be anywhere near you."

"That's not true. When you saw me in mask you talked of forgiving me. We sat inches from each other and I know you wanted to kiss me."

I was confused. Right now I feel betrayed. He played with all my feelings. His arms slide away from me. What he says is true; I did want to forgive him. I wanted to let go of all my fear and hate. Refused to admit that…things have gotten better for me.

"I'm sorry you're hurt but I'm not sorry for anything I did," he says.

He walks away and slides his hand on my parent's coffins.

THE LAST PRINCESS

"I don't make excuses for my behavior anymore. I do what I do because I want to. I wanted to kill them; I wanted to see you cry about it. To run from me in the dark thinking you're getting away. To have you touch the scar on your face and think about where it came from."

I turn my eyes on him.

"I'm not sorry for any of it. I'm still in love with you and it's because of everything that's happened."

Looking at my hands I see how red they are. I'm still gripping the journal. I stumble back when he comes close to me. His hand graces the pin he gave me.

"My offer to you is still the same," he says. "Cause I know nothing has changed. In fact, I bet you're happy knowing the truth."

I'm still as he leans down to my face. Don't kiss me. Please don't. I don't have the strength to push him away.

"And if you think I'm bad, what does that say about the man that made me do it."

"Stop it."

"He maliciously planned everything. For years he wanted them dead and he didn't even know who you were. He wasn't doing it for you."

"Stop," I say to him. "Stop trying to control what I think. You're nothing but a monster. Of course your mother wouldn't want to speak to you."

He moves away. He looks hard at his fist and I move away from him slowly.

"You're right," he speaks. "You know, I thought you'd be disgusted with me but you haven't taken your eyes off me. You still love me, don't you?"

I've seen every side of Ayato-san now. Putting the masked man and him together I see the real him. He's a more outspoken version of Kyoya-sama. Does the things Kyoya-sama can only speak of. Soon I'll have to face him.

Kyoya-sama has shown his regret the whole time. He's begged me for forgiveness and I never realized. I see the side of him he was trying to hide. He's sweet, caring, and quiet but also deadly. I'm not….mad at him.

The door opens with a creak and he moves away.

"Why are you hiding?" Kyoya-sama says walking down the cement steps.

THE LAST PRINCESS

Now isn't the time to be embarrassed. I'm supposed to be angry. I try to hide my reddened face and he snatches the journal from me. He looks at it then looks down at me. No groveling. He looks at me with no shame in his face. Not a "sorry" or anything.

"So you know," he says coldly. "Does this change something? Is that why're you're late for our wedding?"

"Don't talk to her like that," Ayato-san speaks up. "Of course she's hurt."

"She's fine."

What kind of man is he? He lifts my chin to him and I quiver.

"You're fine, aren't you?" he asks.

"What's gotten into you?" I ask him. "Even if all the words in that book are true, you've shown me a different side. The Kyoya-sama I know-"

"You know nothing. Don't you get that?"

"Kyoya," Ayato-san says to stop him.

There's no need to interfere. If he wants to say cruel words to me I'll listen. I look into his eyes and see he's not as tough as he's pretending to be.

"You're shaking," I say to him. "You're more scared than I am."

He lets go of my chin and scoffs.

"Tell me why," I say to him. "Why did you go through with it? My parents loved you. They said you would be a light for our country. My father stood up for you when people said a Han man could never fit in. My family, the ones you killed, had unwavering support for you-"

"Enough-"

"You're here trying to manipulate the public to support you. To create this story that will make you lovable. You didn't have to."

"I said, enough-"

"If you would have opened up to me, you would have been given everything you ever wanted, without the bloodshed."

THE LAST PRINCESS

I stare at his back; he refuses to turn around. I take a step towards him and tug on his jacket. He still keeps his face hidden.

"I wanted it this way. I'm not sorry for anything," he says.

"Ayato-san said the same thing. I believe him; he's not a liar. But I don't believe you."

He shakes my hand away and goes back to the entrance. I run after him and pull on his hand. He's just going to avoid me again. Who knows how long he'll stay away this time.

"Don't go pushing me away cause you're scared. You left that for me to find so we could face this. I'm upset…I'm scared, and angry. But…finally….you're no longer a stranger to me."

I release him and he steps away. He drops his journal and hides his face. I'm not afraid of him. Right now he's the one afraid.

"Kyoya," I call after him.

"Leave him."

Ayato-san grabs my shoulder to keep me back. He steps up the stairs into Kyoya-sama's shadow.

I look back at my parent's statues.

"I don't care what you're thinking," I say to them. "I can't care anymore. You're not here. You're never gonna be here. So it's up to me to make my own choices…even if you don't like them."

I stay in the crypt a while longer. The sun goes down a bit and I peek out. Most people got fed up and left. Neither one of us showed up. What a waste of money. No one notices me as I take a seat in the back row.

So many people prepared the venue for this day. I owe it to them to see it.

"I really like the ribbons."

Someone sits next to me and I tense up.

"So both of you got cold feet," Kantarou-sama says.

I keep my head down.

THE LAST PRINCESS

"Leave her alone," Yumi-chan says.

She sits on my other side and pulls me into her chest.

"Are you okay?" she asks me.

"I'm fine."

"Talk to me. What happened?"

"We weren't ready to face each other," I admit to them.

"What a waste of time?" he says sighing.

"You're not helping. Go somewhere else," Yumi-chan snaps at him.

"I'm trying to console her."

"You're terrible at it. Go talk to your brother."

"He needs to be alone now. He had an expression on his face I'd never seen before."

I look over at him. He refused to show it to me. Whatever face he made, it's from the genuine Kyoya.

"I'm sorry for wasting your time," I say to him.

"Save it. If you're not ready that's fine. I'd rather you waste millions of dollars than be unhappy. Try to steer clear of my father."

Yumi-chan pulls me closer and rubs my shoulder. It's nice to know she's still my close friend. She came to me when I needed her.

"You wasted nobody's time," Yumi-chan says to me.

"Whatever happened between you two, everyone deserves a second chance. Right, Yumiko-san?"

She's hesitant. She pushes me back in my seat and stomps away.

"You're trying too hard," I say to him.

"Just go find him."

THE LAST PRINCESS

He shouldn't be hard to find. I go back to the place and follow the faint smell of cigarettes. He really should stop with that. I have to help him. He's not bad. Neither is Ayato-san. I can't turn my back on them.

I slide the door the room we first met in. He's alone sitting on the ledge. I'm sure he can feel my presence. Slowly I walk to him and sit beside him.

"I don't deserve you," he speaks.

"That's not for you to decide. It's my choice and I choose you."

"How can you-"

"Because I love you. And you love me too. You're not a monster-"

"Yes, I am-"

"You're not. You're my husband. You have been since the day we both sat here. Our hearts were beating like crazy. I heard yours very clearly."

I look up at him and he stares straight; a tear rolls down his face.

"I know you had regrets and guilt. That's why you stayed away for so long. I know you tried to rationalize it as best you could. So many times you offered to give me whatever I wanted. I kept saying....I only wanted you. And that's still true."

He puts out his cigarette and looks down at me.

"You're right. I am sorry. I regret everything."

"Regret is a hard thing to live with," I say.

"I've been trying. Masking it...distracting myself. I try really hard-"

"Just stop then. I smile when I think of the past. I remember when Yumi-chan opened up to me. Remember when mother hugged me after I passed my cooking test. And when father showed me pictures of his adolescence. I can only smile. "

I cried on their coffins and asked for help. I felt them hugging me. They said, "everything will be okay. We're not in pain, so why should you be."

"I promise I will always make you smile. I'll lead you out," he speaks.

He takes hold of my hand and ring.

413

"I'll hold you right next to me and I'll lead you out. We'll walk out of the darkness together."

I nod to him and he hugs me close. My heart is still beating like crazy. His hands cradle my face and I lean forward and kiss him.

"It's not too late," he says smiling. "You still want to marry me today?"

"Yeah."

"It's what you want? You really want this? Cause after today I'm never gonna let you go."

"I want you. So, yes, I want this. I'll be Setsuna Niwa, your queen."

My whole life I've been conditioned to be Kyoya-sama's wife. I'm ready for it.